Empty Streets

MICHAL AJVAZ

EMPTY STREETS

A NOVEL

TRANSLATED BY ANDREW OAKLAND

Originally published in Czech as Prázdné ulice in 2004.

First Dalkey Archive edition, 2016

Library of Congress Cataloging-in-Publication Data

Names: Ajvaz, Michal, 1949- author. | Oakland, Andrew, 1966- translator.
Title: Empty streets / by Michal Ajvaz ; translated by Andrew Oakland.
Other titles: Prâazdnâe ulice. English
Description: First edition. | Victoria, TX : Dalkey Archive Press, 2016.
Identifiers: LCCN 2015040707 | ISBN 9781564787002 (pbk. : acid-free paper)
Subjects: LCSH: Meaning (Philosophy)--Fiction. | Magic realism (Literature)
Classification: LCC PG5039.1.J83 P7313 2016 | DDC 891.8/635--dc23
LC record available at http://lccn.loc.gov/2015040707

Partially funded by a grant from the Illinois Arts Council, a state agency.
This translation was subsidized by the Ministry of Culture of the Czech Republic.

www.dalkeyarchive.com
Victoria, TX / McLean, IL / London / Dublin

Cover: Art by Nathan Parks

Printed on permanent/durable acid-free paper

CONTENTS

Part One
Double Trident

Part Two
Room by the Track

Part One
Double Trident

Chapter 1
Desk

It was ten in the morning and getting hot. I'd already been sitting at my desk for two hours, rummaging through the papers that covered its surface. Now and then the sheets shivered in a gust of hot air that entered the room through the window, which was open to the street. All these pages bore my handwriting, their irregular lines filled with crossed-out words and sentences. Quite often I failed to find on the desk the one I needed, even after a long search; so I would climb under the desk, where the paper was piled almost as high as it was on top. And there in agitation I would go through sheet after sheet, each of which bore the same crossings-out as those on the desk. A time later I would emerge from this confined space clutching the page that was the object of my search. Sometimes as I was working down there on the floor I would see that the draft had carried some sheets into the middle of the room, and I would crawl after them across the faded carpet.

Each time I succeeded in finding a lost page on the desk or under it, I was possessed by the excitement of a predator that has just sunk its teeth into its prey and is impatient to get it back to its den. What was gathered before me on the desk I gave a shove with the elbows to clear my path, in so doing knocking the pages on the edge off the desk and onto the floor. Then I would spend some time in the feverish inking out of words on the prized page that had so far escaped the cull, scribbling more words and sentences in the gaps between lines. When these insertions had proliferated to such an extent that there no longer remained a scrap of empty space, I pulled out from the half-open drawer by my left knee one blank sheet after another and flooded these with text. But the speed with which pen moved across paper gradually slowed, until in the end the pen came to a halt, often in the middle of a word. The river of words and images that had coursed through me transformed into a dried-up tributary. For a while I would sit at the desk motionless; then I would mount a search—on the desk and under it, sometimes about the whole room—for another handwritten sheet; once again I would shove out of the way all the sheets I'd been working on to that point (some of these would again end up on the floor), place in the freed-up space of the desktop the page I'd hunted out, and proceed to the crossing-out of sentences and the writing of insertions in gaps. In this way the papers would circulate between desktop and floor in an ever-greater torrent. This mass of restless, elusive, metamorphosing, barely legible pages was turning into a monstrosity. It had been going on like this for five days now.

A year and half earlier I'd broken up with my girlfriend. Sometime later I began to feel that the sorrow, resentment, embarrassment and comedy of our parting had borne an unexpected fruit—the experience was forming itself into the embryo of a novella. I hadn't written anything for several years and had come to accept that I'd written my last. So I was glad after all this time, when my thoughts and feelings were at a low ebb, to recognize those familiar movements that announce the germ of a new work pushing to be given life. At that time I was working as an editor for a publishing house and I had to go to the office every morning; in the evenings I'd be too tired to write; besides in the course of the day my language would have absorbed the style of the manuscript I was reading. I would sit in the kitchen and gulp down a cold dinner straight from the greasy paper I'd bought it in on my way home; then I would sit down at my desk and start to write. But before long I would realize with disgust that my sentences were steeped in the bad habits of the author whose text had been assigned to me. I would try to write on Saturdays and Sundays, but by the time I'd gained access to the game of words, images, and thoughts I'd started on a week earlier, it was Sunday midnight, time for me to switch off the light and sleep.

So in the end I told myself I'd put the writing off. I'd save enough money to last me for a few months of modest living, then I'd give notice at the publishing house and be able to devote myself to uninterrupted work on the novella. I bought a notebook to write my thoughts and ideas in and looked forward to the time when every morning I'd get up early, make myself a coffee, and sit down at my desk. Everywhere one turned they were talking about the forthcoming end of the millennium, so I promised myself I'd finish the novella before there was a "2" at the beginning of the year. I reckoned the writing would take me about six months, so I announced at the publisher's my intention to leave at the end of June. On my calendar for 1999 I circled July 1st as the day I'd start writing. How rapturous my thoughts through winter and spring of the days of concentrated work ahead! But now it was July 5th and I'd been sitting at home for five days, pushing paper from desk to floor and picking it up again—and I had no idea how to stop the turning of this devil's mill.

Today, as on the preceding days, I sat wrestling the unruly text until late afternoon; as on the preceding days it got hotter and hotter and the page was dotted with letters smudged by the sweat of my brow. I opened window after window and the draft would sometimes make the curtains billow and blow through every room, tossing the pages further and further away from me. Some of them ended up under the bed, on top of cupboards, in the hall . . . The bad mood wrought in me by all this fruitless work was mixed with the listlessness and tiredness induced in me by the heat. My *vita nuova* isn't getting off to a very good start, I thought.

And just as on the four preceding days I gave it up in the end, telling myself that tomorrow it would probably be cooler, that once I'd had a good night's sleep the writing would be easier, that once this mad carousel came to a stop and the pages lay still on the desk the words would present themselves slowly and calmly. I laid down my pen and looked up at the window, allowing my gaze—tired from a day of floundering among letters—to wander free over the facades of the buildings on the opposite side of the street, to jump from balcony to balcony, to slide down the soft lines of the dusty Art Nouveau adornments, to circle the stains on the flaking plasterwork. And as on the preceding days I told myself that my day-long tribulations gave me the right to go and sit in the local pub, termed by its landlord a "garden restaurant," although the garden part was nothing more than a few tables and benches scattered across a stretch of asphalt that plugged a gap in a row of buildings. I got up from my desk and trotted down the stairs into the street.

The row of facades trailed off into the distance left and right. Apart from two men in oil-stained shirts bent over the open hood of a battered car on the opposite side of the street, there seemed to be no one about. But the main thing was the joy in seeing no letters but those of a few shop signs, which told of innocent things and wanted nothing from me. It was still hot, although on the buildings opposite a purplish light was descending and adornments in the stucco, accentuated by the long shadows, scrolled up the walls like creepers. A dazzling orange fire was burning in a distant car. Like great sponges, the buildings on my side of the street were beginning to absorb the dark, into which all edges were dissolving. The street extended in both directions in the monotonous rhythm of blocks of equal lengths; some distance off to the right it ran into a modest-sized square with its sounds of cars and trams braking and accelerating. This sound mingled with a muffled hum that seemed to be coming from behind the wall of one of the single-story workshops that occupied the whole of one side of a short cross street that began across from where I was standing and ended in a bank of overgrown bushes.

The street where I lived was long, straight and wide, but it contained only a few stores—most of them repair shops and pawnbrokers—so it tended to lifelessness. To my left, too, the regular blocks of buildings scrupulously followed the lines their architect had drawn for them. Off in the distance where both rows of buildings ended, the gap between them was filled by a space that glowed pink. It took me a moment to figure out what

I was looking at before it came to me that it was the wall of a factory illuminated in the rays of the setting sun. This view of the empty street was beguiling. I decided I would take a walk; there would be plenty of time for me to sit about in pubs. I headed for the factory wall. It had been a long time since I'd walked this way—usually I would hurry off in the opposite direction, to the streetcar stop in the square.

I passed no one except a child with a dog, and in one of the windows I saw leaning on the sill a suntanned, bald-headed man in a white undershirt who was smoking and thinking hard about something he saw on the empty sidewalk. When I reached the end of the street the factory wall was submerged by the shadows of the buildings. I took a moment to consider whether I would walk right or left along the wall. I knew that if I followed the wall to the right I would reach a small market composed of just a few stalls; if I went left I would come to the bottom of a low, rounded hill covered with a drab spread of single-story houses, built by workers at the factory some time before the war. I turned right, but I'd not gone far when I changed my mind; I retraced my steps, then went the other way. The factory wall, which was topped with barbed wire, continued for a fair distance. On reaching its end I was in for a surprise: there was no settlement here. All that remained of it were the foundations of walls and holes in the earth. Looking down impatiently from the top of the hill were some new white villas born of a dreamlike fusion of Bavaria and California. Clearly they were intending to make their way down the hill. The yellow bulldozer that was now at rest halfway up the bank at a slight angle to a number of corrugated-iron huts, was leveling the ground to clear the way for their advance.

Chapter 2
At The Dump

I made my way up among the remnants, interior walls roller-painted with silvery patterns and sprouting bunches of chopped cables with frayed ends that looked like sorrowful black flowers. I wondered whether the new villas would stop at the bottom of the hill, or whether they would march on into the city. I found out that the corrugated-iron huts concealed a dump where the bulldozer had gathered everything that remained of the demolished homes. It was impossible to walk around this, as its upper edge was skirted by a barbed-wire fence, but I didn't want to return the way I had come. The dump looked fairly safe, so I decided to make my way across it.

A few steps in I realized my chosen path was more complicated than I'd imagined. This mass of laths, struts, spills, sheet metal and plywood cooperated in an elastic system of levers that carried across the whole expanse of the dump every application of pressure, wakening movement in the most unexpected places. After I stepped on the end of a plank, for example, a vision of rags hanging off a bird cage reared up menacingly five meters away; then I excited a phantom in the shape of a white cord caught on a bed's headboard. As figures of plastic and polythene rose out of the gloom, the gray city beneath me was like some great mass of mineral. I trod carefully, scrutinizing as I did so objects belonging to different periods of the life of the houses. I saw pots and pans of tin and aluminum folded in on themselves—these probably had their origins in the early days of the workers' colony and had lived on in attics; I saw aerodynamic food blenders and hair driers from the sixties, Nepalese fabrics with golden thread from the time some bohemian had set up house in the colony, and dirty sleeping bags, obviously a reminder of the months immediately prior to demolition, when the empty houses had been occupied by the homeless. It was apparent, too, that the dump had been discovered by people living nearby, who had dragged here whatever they wanted to be rid of.

Here lay appliances with exposed insides full of twisted wires and shards of glass, incomplete cupboards, books with their pages curling and sticking together, earthenware elephants with missing tusks, porcelain hunting dogs with no head or tail, bundles of letters whose characters had dissolved and colored the paper blue, pieces of car engines, mattresses with their now-brown foam prolapsed, not-quite-empty bottles of light-green and yellow liquids, crumpled cardboard boxes, crumbs of white polystyrene, pickle jars whose insides had developed mold, great bunches of decomposing clothes, ripped lampshades, Bakelite gondolas bearing the legend "Venezia," dozens of opened and crushed tin cans, flowerpots containing hard, dry, leafless stems, porn magazines showing pink and brown bodies dotted with mysterious green stains, bed frames with islands of white enamel, refrigerators with missing doors and patches of rust, used tires; and in the midst of all this, flapping in the evening breeze, were strips of plastic sheeting, tangled-up magnetic tape, and scraps of cloth.

Some of the things lay on their backs like dying animals, their wounded innards, once tightly guarded, now open to the world in resignation. There were many outcrawlings, spills, discharges, trickles. Here at the dump things from different worlds had forged new friendships: a quilted jacket, the height of fashion a few seasons ago, had placed a tender arm around a black-and-white Mánes television set from the fifties; a crumpled reproduction of Botticelli's *Birth of Venus* had attached itself to a radiator and assumed the shapes of its ribs. In some places two, three, even four things had grown into a single body: to the remnants of a snowboard was stuck the mottled torso of a plush animal of a species unknown, and this creature had grown a long tail in the form of an extension cable. The rain and the sun were gradually bonding everything into a single mass with many protuberances and cavities. In this mass I saw that between the laths and chunks of Formica, caves of all shapes and sizes opened up—shallow ones and deep ones, their wondrous walls composed of things rusty, crumpled, sodden and putrid. Suddenly I felt like a diver walking on an undersea coral reef; I half expected some great, sharp-toothed chops to appear from the darkness of one of the caves and snap at me.

Then I felt a sharp pain in the sole of my right foot. I cried out and lurched forward, and something reared up in front of me and drove itself into my belly. Then my assailant sank back to the ground. This was no predatory fish, just one of the thousands of things lying idle on the dump. Now it lay there calmly before me, and I was able to see what it was. It was made of wood and about a meter in length, and it was coated in a light-green varnish that was scaling in many places. It was an upright pole finished at both ends in some kind of trident; the outer curves of the larger trident were turned back on themselves and tapered to sharp points, while the ends of all three arms of the smaller trident rested against a wooden oval. In the middle, between the bases of the two tridents, the pole was intersected by a short, transverse wooden bar.

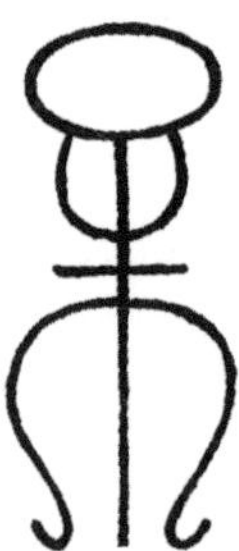

Judging by the size, position and shape of this object, it was a simple matter to reconstruct what had happened. It had been hidden beneath a pile of broken Formica panels. I had stepped on a protruding point of the large trident and this had pierced the sole of my shoe and stabbed me in the foot; the curved ends of one of the arms had worked to lever the whole thing up, and this had served to throw off the Formica panels and for the thing to catch me in the belly, fortunately only by the oval on its end. The pain in my foot wasn't that bad, although I could feel the blood soaking into my sock. About to walk on, I took another look at the object lying on the pile of Formica in front of me. I just couldn't figure out what it was. Was it a tool? Quite likely, but I didn't have the foggiest idea what it might be used for. At first I imagined it to be some kind of fork—the oval could be the handgrip. But the curved ends of the large trident would make the performing of most of a fork's tasks impossible. So perhaps the object was intended as a conveyance—but its load would have to be something pretty big if it weren't to fall between the prongs of the large trident. Then it occurred to me that the oval might be used to pull something—although my consideration of the object as an agent of traction led me to no meaningful conclusions. All I could see in the object was an image of a man gripping something in both hands; perhaps he was pulling an obstreperous beast by horns that were locked in the curved ends of the large trident (on the way to the slaughterhouse? to the arena? to a place of sacrifice?), with the trident's central prong affording the butcher/matador/sacrificer some protection from an unexpected attack by the beast. Of course, I was less than satisfied with an explanation that included a mysterious beast and a fantastical ceremony. And wouldn't the performing of such a ceremony require some enigmatic sect?

The object wouldn't remain in an upright position regardless of whether it was stood on its oval or the open trident; probably it was supposed to be hung, by either its oval or one of the bent ends of the side prongs. I kept coming back to the idea that the oval was an eye through which to pass a rope that would then be tied in a knot; by this means the object could be attached to other, probably much larger objects. By its shape, what the object resembled most of all was an anchor. Had it been made of metal, I would have said it was indeed an anchor, and maybe I would have been satisfied with my explanation and gone home quite happy. But an anchor made of wood was nonsense. If it really was the case that a rope should be tied to the object, it was perhaps used as a float or an extra-large kind of fish-hook. But a gigantic float would call for an enormous animal—the mysterious sacrificial bull was joined in my imagination by a phantom whale.

And why would a hook for use in the hunting of whales be lying about in a dump on the edge of the capital city of a country that had no sea? As it really didn't matter to me whether or not I discovered the true purpose of an object which had no bearing on my life and which I would probably never see again, there was no reason why I shouldn't allow my imagination to run free. More than likely there was no whale hunter living in this part of town, but surely I could invent something better than whale hunting? Let's imagine that a group of people who busy themselves with the investigating of various mysteries make an enormous fish-hook and take it with them to Scotland, where they try to catch the Loch Ness Monster. When they return from this unsuccessful quest, one member of the group dumps the thing here. Or better still, dozens or even hundreds of meters beneath the deepest tunnel of the city's metro there is a secret hollow leading to a subterranean lake where a mysterious Leviathan or Godzilla lives. In the cellar of a particular house, an inconspicuous locked door might conceal a long flight of steps down to the shore of the lake. In this case the wooden hook in front of me now could be a leftover from an expedition to catch the monster of the deep.

But I was not satisfied by these inventions of subterranean lakes and the monsters that lived in them. I couldn't stop myself contemplating the real purpose of the thing. Could it be a weapon, some kind of catapult? Or it might be the body of a musical instrument: in terms of its shape it was somewhat reminiscent of the lyre. But with a catapult or a lyre there would need to be grooves for the affixing of a string or strings. I ran my fingers over the surface of the object, in so doing dislodging a few flakes of the green varnish: I encountered no grooves or notches. But perhaps it was not an instrument or a tool at all. Could it be a work of art? When I held it so that the oval was at the top, it looked like a man with his hands behind his head. By its shape it reminded me of the symbolic way artists of primitive peoples represent the male form. It occurred to me that I was looking at the figure of a man who, in an attitude of deepest despair, was pressing his hands to his temples. But I didn't wish to continue this train of thought. I turned the object round so that the oval was at the bottom and considered it in this aspect.

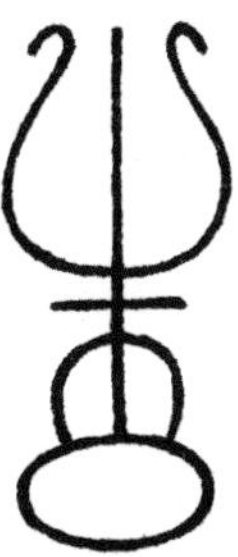

It was immediately clear to me that the object was now in its proper position. Now, too, it looked like a human figure: With the oval at the bottom it reminded me of a diagram of a female, the like of which I had seen in drawings by Native Brazilians or Australian aborigines. I had the impression I was looking at a woman who was lifting her arms in some kind of gesture of excitement—horror or disgust perhaps, or maybe someone was threatening her. The object might also be a simplified representation of a flower (the Blue Flower?), chalice (the Holy Grail?), or a bird (the phoenix?). Of course, in the event that I ever discovered the true significance of the strange object, I was quite prepared for it to be a garden tool or the emblem of some football club. But still I remained in the darkening dump among the scraps of polythene performing the ghostly dance of the elves of the forest, doing my best to figure out what this object could be.

I got to thinking that the object might be a hieroglyph or a character of an unknown, perhaps secret alphabet. It was highly likely that the cryptic character was connected with a secret brotherhood. In my mind's eye I saw its initiates, sitting stiffly in their ceremonial garb around a round, heavy table. But why was the character so big? It had to be part of an inscription that sat high on a wall. As the character was secret, it was likely the inscription would be on an inside rather than an outside wall;

judging by the size of the character this would be the wall of a very large hall. The suppositions were stacking up nicely, encouraging me to go on. The building containing the great hall would have to be pretty vast, yet if it belonged to a secret brotherhood it would have to remain hidden. It would be quite impossible to conceal a building of that size anywhere on the Earth's surface for a period of centuries (a proper secret brotherhood has to have been in existence for at least a thousand years), so probably the hall was to be found somewhere underground. Why, here we were again, back in the subterranean world! For that matter, the co-existence of a subterranean hall and subterranean lake was by no means out of the question: the room in which the council of the brotherhood met could quite easily be contained in a palace that lay on the shore of a subterranean lake. And if it were, the initiates might also be guardians of the monster . . .

Then I dropped all thoughts of subterranean palaces and monsters and told myself that to consider the object a character of some kind was far from fantastical. There were many people in the city today who had come from Asia, so the character could quite easily be Chinese or Thai. Perhaps it had been part of the sign of a shop patronized by the owner's countrymen . . . I looked about me in the hope of finding other characters from the sign, but I saw nothing that was in any way similar in shape or size. Besides, it was getting difficult to see anything at all; the deepening dusk had erased the last borders between objects, turning the dump into a single entity that looked like a great sponge grown onto the bank. So I stopped my search for other characters; I left the object—the instrument, tool, statue, character, emblem of a secret brotherhood, or whatever it was—where it lay. I stepped carefully to the edge of the dump, which did not attack me again. I came out on the other side by a path that twisted around the hillside. I could see the railway line down at the bottom; the steep path was scattered with gravel which slid beneath my feet. I clambered onto the embankment, where the curve of the tracks glinted red under green lights strewn in an intricate network of wires. Against a backdrop of red sky, the black silhouette of the railway station came into view, like a Chinese lantern made of thin paper.

Chapter 3
Luminous Snake

The wound in my foot healed overnight, and for the next two days I gave no thought to the object at the dump. First thing in the morning I sat down at my desk and tried to get on with my novella; sometimes I would scribble feverishly for an hour, at other times I would sit motionless for two hours with my pen poised over the blank page. The circular flow of paper between desk and floor continued and swelled. This work gave me no pleasure: its rhythms alternated between frenzy and languor and all I had to show for it was an outpour of floating piles of illegible pages. In those two days I came up with dozens of reasons not to go on with it. To prevent myself from succumbing to this temptation, I determined not to get up from my desk until the streetlamps came on. Unfortunately these were the longest days of the year; I waited for the lamplight with the desperation of a castaway watching the sea for the lights of a ship.

When at last the lamps came on, I practically ran from the apartment. I wandered about the city until late into the night, avoiding busy streets with streetcar traffic and storefronts. I imagined that the gloom and quiet of empty side streets would serve by morning to heal and invigorate the features of my face, which, I felt, were etched with the poisonous breath of the letters I'd been sitting over all day. So I walked past dilapidated front doors patched with sheet metal, wide gates giving onto damp, empty passageways, doors of aluminum and frosted glass set in Neo-Renaissance portals with battered Corinthian columns, long lines of parked cars momentarily aglint in the headlights of passing vehicles, high walls with the tops of metal structures or towers of stacked containers visible beyond, and walls on which a shadowy figure with my profile rose up, faded and unraveled as I made my way from one streetlamp to the next. I walked past barred iron gates giving onto yards whose asphalt was awash with the cold glow of fluorescent light and where great reels of black cable lay at rest, under viaducts riveted together from heavy pieces of metal and which boomed when a train passed over them, gatehouses that clung to dark factories and were lit up like aquaria, and bridges over shallow, smelly urban streams that gurgled in the dark.

This world too, had its islands of light, but unlike the lights on the main avenues these were non-violent and non-intrusive, like a handful of colored gemstones that a friendly god of the city's peripheries had scattered on smooth, dark velvet as a gift for lone late-night walkers. As it was still hot, lit interiors were opened to the street. I passed a bar whose figures were bathed in white fog as though a thick mosquito net had been stretched across the doorway, pawnshops where, like an Andy Warhol picture come to life, the same excited/weeping woman's face with its mute, moving lips appeared in various shades on the screens of many television sets, amusement arcades where from the depths of narrow rooms monotonous little lights whirled and flickered red, green, and blue, and hundreds of windows opened to first-floor apartments in which I saw hundreds of overhead light fittings, tops of cupboards, and fragments of dusky pictures of unknown landscapes.

On the third day after my trip to the dump, following more hours of fruitless labor, I again set out on an evening walk. This time I reached a part of the city I'd never been in before. There in a dark side street I saw a single sign shining over a building entrance: a white disc showing a stylized blue heron on water, stretching its wings. I knew that this was the symbol of a computer graphics studio—indeed, I knew one of its owners, a young graphic designer who sometimes came by the publishing house where I used to work. On one of his visits I'd handed my laptop over to him so that he could install some programs on it. I knew the picture of the heron in the circle from the business card he'd given me; at that time I hadn't recognized the name of the street the studio was on. All this was six months earlier. Since then I'd several times intended to take out my map, check where the studio was and fetch the computer, but something had always got in the way. I knew from what the graphic designer had told me that the studio exposed photographs for the morning editions of a number of magazines and so it was open all night. As chance had practically led me to his door, I decided that now was finally the right time to pick up the laptop.

As soon as I stepped into the small first-floor office I saw the man I knew—dark complexion, long black hair tied back in a tight knot—staring intently at something I couldn't see on his computer screen. In one hand he held chopsticks poised over a plastic bowl with Chinese characters printed on it, which was next to his keyboard. I said his name and startled him. He turned away from his screen and laid the sticks down next to the bowl. His long, thin frame rose from the narrow space between his desk and the wall. He returned my greeting and went immediately to a room at the back in order to look for my laptop. I sat down in a lightweight armchair and picked up and proceeded to flick through a magazine that I found on a glass table, but almost straightaway I put it down again and continued in my study of the lights of nighttime. Through the window I studied a brightly illuminated billboard showing the enormous face of a girl whose eyes were narrowed in an expression of bliss as a jet of mineral water issuing from the neck of a bedewed green bottle struck her parted lips. Below this billboard was an illuminated white rectangle with a red dragon and red Chinese lettering—the same as on the designer's bowl; next to this, above the door of an amusement arcade, was a neon clown in a checkered outfit and enormous shoes who was forever juggling three colored balls with jerky movements. The strangest of the lights was an illuminated green ribbon that proceeded up and down a facade in a circular movement, all the time wriggling and twisting in many different ways. I had no idea what this might be, but by now I was starting to feel sleepy and didn't want to think about it.

From the next room I heard shuffling feet, muffled bangs and dissatisfied mumbling: the designer was struggling to find my laptop. The restless green snake was still twisting about and still not digressing from its circular path. Its green changed gradually to blue, then to purple, then to red. Suddenly I realized that the luminous snake wasn't climbing the facade but gliding over a window—I'd been looking at a changing figure on the dark screen of the computer that the graphic designer had deserted: The gyrating snake was reflected in the glass. Quick as a flash, an enormous shiny anaconda shrank to become a nimble little grass snake. Clearly this was one of those changing ornaments that appear automatically on computer screens after a period of inactivity.

After a while the luminous snake split into two. These halves proceeded to chase each other and the distance between them shortened and lengthened, yet at no point did either of them depart from the circular path. Then each of the halves split into halves, so that now four snakes were wriggling and twisting, rippling, coiling and uncoiling, up and down in a circular motion. The snakes remained four, and after a while each of them assumed an unchanging form. One of the snakes froze into a straight line, the second became a circle, the third bent itself into a crescent, the fourth came to resemble a question mark without the dot:

I O U ?

All four figures then continued on their circular course and their speed did not diminish. Soon the fourth figure broke into a short arc and a straight line. The movement of these two parts slowed, and soon the figure behind them on the circular path drew level with them. The break-away parts then joined this figure, so that from this moment on there were only three figures moving around the screen:

Then the circle flattened and became an oval, which attached itself to the lower end of the first figure. As to the crescent, first its ends bent around and then it fused with the remaining figure. Now I was looking at something I knew well:

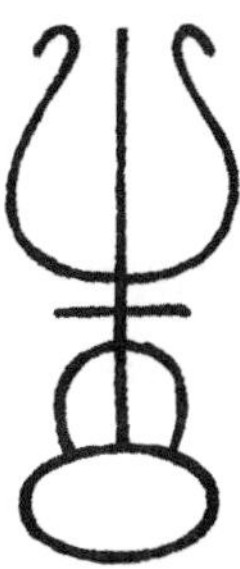

The circle around which the figure was moving became a spiral. Slowly the double trident made its way to the center of the screen. It rotated around its vertical and horizontal axes as it moved away from and then toward the center, all the time changing color. Then it became ever narrower until all that remained of it was a line, which began to follow a circular path along the edges of the screen, before dividing into two and then four parts, which came together . . . I watched the story of the endlessly repeated birth and breakup of the character that had stabbed me in the foot three days earlier at the dump.

The designer came back into the room, my dusty laptop in his hand. I asked him about the changing, luminous character. He turned the monitor towards me and then picked up his chopsticks. “It’s a screensaver,” he explained. “One of a series I made to order last year.”

I said that I’d be interested to know if he had designed the figure or if he’d seen it somewhere. I described my encounter with the double trident at the dump. Listening to me with great attention, he laid down his chopsticks, settled himself in the swivel chair next to the computer and wheeled himself in my direction. By the end of my explanation he and I were sitting right next to each other. “How strange that you, too, should have come across it!” he said. “My encounter with this character was very peculiar, and I’ve no idea what to think about it.”

Chapter 4
Apparition in a Villa

Then the graphic designer moved his chair back a little and embarked on the story of how the double trident came into his life. A year earlier he had answered a classified advertisement offering a room for rent in a villa. Upon meeting, he and the owner reached an agreement within a few minutes; a few days later the designer moved into one of the many rooms of the villa, which he described to me as a dilapidated Modernist building from the thirties with a tubular railing on the terrace and round windows above the staircase that hinted at the architect's inspiration in sealiners. But now the building was more reminiscent of a shipwreck. The villa was pretty vast, but no one lived in it except the designer and his landlord. As he walked its corridors—which were covered in black-and-white tiles like a chessboard—he would find himself treading on tiptoe so as not to violate the silence of the house. These corridors were lined with closed doors. Sometimes he would carefully push down one of the handles and look inside—he never saw anything except curtains filtering a cold light from the garden and sweeping in motionless folds to the dark carpet, and the rounded shapes of bulky furniture on whose highly-polished wood and glass lay a narcotic sheen. According to the designer, all this tired Modernism evoked a far deeper sense of the sadness of transience than the cabinets of any antique collector.

The owner of the villa was taciturn and unwell. The designer thought of him as "the old man," although he was unable to estimate his true age—he might have been sixty or seventy. It seemed to the designer that the old man had grown together with the villa to such a degree that at first he imagined him to have lived there all his life. The designer saw the same shadows on the old man's face as lay in the corners of the rooms; in the half-light of the corridors it was difficult to distinguish his skin from the patterns on the faded wallpaper. At rest on the top of the desk, the old man's hands were just as motionless, heavy and (probably) as cold as the bronze statuettes of horses and women that stood within easy reach. And his bulky, barely mobile body gave the impression it had been mimicking the villa's furniture for many years. The old man was always distracted; the designer had no idea what he might be thinking about, but he felt that the thoughts must bear some resemblance to the expirations of the damp linen he had seen lying folded in the depths of the cupboards when out of curiosity he had quietly opened their doors.

The graphic designer and his landlord hardly ever saw each other. In the beginning the designer would attempt conversation for politeness' sake when occasionally they met in the hall, but usually the old man did not even raise his eyes, answered in a monosyllable, and after a moment's silence disappeared behind one of the many doors. So the designer desisted in these attempts at conversation. After some time he became friendly with the neighbors and it was through them that he made the astonishing discovery that the old man had moved into the villa only seven years earlier. At first he had lived there with his daughter, but she had moved out two years prior; since then he'd had the whole vast villa to himself. The villa used to belong to an aged professor of entomology who had died in the early nineties. Apparently the old man had had some property returned to him after the political changes of 1989, sold it immediately, and with the money bought the villa from the professor's heirs. He had bought it complete with all fittings and furnishings, and it seemed that he hadn't changed the position of a single piece of furniture in the whole house; all the tables, chairs and cupboards stayed exactly where they had stood when the professor was alive.

The neighbors wondered why he had brought no furniture of his own. Apparently he and his daughter had arrived in a small van with nothing but a few banana boxes containing various small items and a number of plastic bags filled with clothes. Above all the neighbors thought it strange that he had brought no books with him, as it was said he had been a literary critic and had taught literature at the university. It was true that the designer saw plenty of books in the villa, but they were behind glass in bookcases in empty rooms, thick volumes with their spines arranged in careful lines. Some of the bookcases were locked, and the designer suspected the keys to them had been lost many years earlier. It appeared that the old man did not have any books of his own, nor did he read the books that had been left in the villa by the previous owner. He had no television or radio, and no newspapers or magazines were delivered to the mailbox; apart from advertising leaflets and occasional letters from the gas company, he received no mail at all. The designer often worked from home, sitting at the computer in his room. When the patter of fingertips across keyboard ceased, there was usually no sound at all; the villa was in complete silence. The only occasional sounds were made by the landlord's feet shuffling down the corridor and his labored breathing.

The neighbors had never seen the old man receive visitors. Plainly he had been forced to rent out one of the rooms because he was short of money and because of his worsening illness. The old man's shuffling gait relied on the use of a stick, and there were days when he couldn't manage even to walk to the store on the corner of the street. Then he would leave for his lodger, behind the frame of the mirror in the hall, a note with a list of the things he needed; they had an arrangement that the designer would leave the shopping on the chest under the mirror. Within a few hours the plastic bag with the shopping would have been removed; obviously the old man sneaked into the hall like a timid animal and carried it away.

In the beginning the designer saw the old man on the first day of every month, when he paid the rent. But perhaps this contact was too much of a disturbance for the old man. One day he left a note behind the mirror in which he announced that he had opened a bank account so that from now on the designer could make the payment by postal order. After this the designer might not see the old man for weeks at a time; nor would he hear a sound from him to prove that he was still alive. Just as he was beginning to wonder whether he should take a look in the old man's room, a note requesting shopping always appeared behind the mirror.

In the days when the old man still came in person to collect the rent, they would usually meet in a room that appeared to have served the professor of entomology as a study and library. If the designer was the first to arrive he would seat himself in one of two black-leather armchairs. This chair stood in the corner of the room beside a highly-polished, round-topped wooden table, in the center of which was a chessboard inlay. While he waited for the owner of the villa, the designer would always study a picture that hung on the wall opposite. It showed a young woman with a childlike face and short fair hair; she was sitting in front of a window through which part of the facade of the building opposite could be seen. It seemed to the designer that this picture was the only new thing the villa contained. He asked the neighbors about it; they were fairly certain the young woman was the daughter of the villa's owner.

"Once when I was waiting for the old man and studying the picture," the designer told me, "something happened that I still can't explain. The building in the picture at the girl's back had a lot of windows, and all of them were dark. Then suddenly a light went on in one of them."

"I don't understand."

"It's not something anyone would be able to understand. Quite simply, a light went on as if someone had entered the room and flicked the switch."

"Real light was emanating from the canvas?"

"Of course not. But in the place where the painting had shown an unlit room, there was now a lit one. I jumped out of the chair and went to take a closer look. In the lit apartment I could see part of a bookcase and hanging on the back wall a picture in a gold plaster frame. It showed a purple double trident on a pink background. As if in a daze I scrutinized the room—I was so confused I was expecting someone to enter or for the girl in the foreground to get up and walk out of the picture. But nothing else happened in it—the room with the mysterious symbol remained empty while my landlord's daughter remained just as she was, gazing through me into the distance. After a while the square of light on the canvas went out so that all that could be seen of the room were the vague outlines of the bookcase and a dark mark where the mysterious symbol had been. I ran my finger over the canvas, but I felt nothing unusual. I lifted the picture off the wall and looked at the back of it, then at the wall behind where it hung, thinking it might conceal some kind of electronic device. But I found nothing. I sat back down in the chair, asking myself what kind of place was this gloomy villa I had moved to, and what other surprises it might have in store for me. Perhaps I would be addressed by one of the statues in the hall or meet the ghost of the late entomologist in the corridor. Might my landlord reveal himself as a vampire who had moved to the villa from Transylvania? Admittedly the last of these wouldn't have come as much of a surprise.

"I was reluctant to tell my landlord about the light at the window, but when at last he shuffled in, I couldn't restrain myself, and I told him. I had the impression it quite spoiled his mood. He was not at all keen to talk about the mysterious room. All he said was that it was some kind of trick, that there was nothing much to it, that it was of no significance. He took my money and disappeared again. That day I worked into the night on a set of changing patterns for use as computer screensavers. I was getting short of ideas, and then I remembered the symbol I'd seen in the picture. And I thought I might use it as a starting point for one of the screensavers. Not long after this the old man set up the bank account and we never again met in the study of the entomologist. I sneaked in there a few times, but whenever I did, the window in the picture was always in darkness."

The graphic designer's story of the professor of literature who didn't read, the spooky Modernist villa and the window with the light had left me none the wiser. But the designer did not appear to be making fun of me. By this time it was after midnight, so I thanked him for the laptop and said my goodbyes. I had my hand on the door handle when it occurred to me that it might be useful to know the name of the owner of the villa. Could he really have been a critic and a professor of literature? So I asked the designer, who told me the old man's name was Jonáš.

I let go of the handle. "Surely you don't mean Jakub Jonáš?" I said in amazement.

The designer nodded. "That's right. Jakub Jonáš. Do you know him?" He had already propelled himself on his wheeled chair back to his computer.

I said that I didn't know him personally, but I'd heard about him and several times seen him. I left the building. At last it was somewhat cooler. I returned home along the chain of streetlamps that stretched off into the distance, all the time thinking of Jonáš. At the end of the seventies and throughout the eighties Jonáš had been a well-known figure. Nothing had been heard of him for a long time now, and I'd forgotten about him completely, just as I'd forgotten about a lot of people from that time. But as soon as the designer had said his name I had seen in my mind's eye the bulky frame thundering through the cloisters of the Faculty of Arts. I remembered the articles he had written, the content of which was always the same, a denunciation of any kind of art in which he glimpsed a flicker of imagination, playfulness or freedom. He inveighed against everything he termed "decadent": subjectivism, individualism, formalism, anti-realism, irrationalism. Everything that in that time of extinguished words and dummied-up images shone for me and my friends like a magical constellation. That this dark being from the swamps of the eighties was one and the same with the solitary owner of the spooky villa seemed to me so absurd that I told myself the matching names were a mere coincidence.

Chapter 5
The Portrait

I spent the whole of the next day putting my books in order. As it was still hot, I opened all the windows in my apartment. I heard the sounds of a grinding machine coming from a workshop in the next street and trains moving in and out of a distant station. The white curtains billowed over my quivering papers; it was as though a white phantom, some demon of the empty streets of summer, had come to visit and was now dancing tirelessly on my desk. Several times a draft lifted handwritten sheets from the desk, carried them across the room to where I was standing and lay them on the carpet at my feet. I left them where they fell: for one day at least I wanted a break from this unfortunate text. As I organized the volumes of my library, more than once I came across the spine of a book I hadn't reached for in ages. I would open it and read a passage or two, go back to ordering my library, start reading another book—and before I knew it, it was dark. I switched on the lights, gathered in my arms all the books that were still on the floor waiting to be ordered and shoved them into the empty spaces on the shelves any old way. Then I opened a can of tuna and took a half-finished bottle of wine from the fridge.

I turned on the TV and for a while watched elegantly-dressed people at a mansion in (probably) Scotland untangle problems in their love affairs. During a heart-rending scene with a mother and daughter who apparently loved the same tweed-suited man, the telephone rang. I lifted the handset and with a mouth full of tuna I hadn't succeeded in swallowing, mumbled my name.

"My name is Jonáš," said the voice on the telephone.

Before I was able to say anything, Jonáš began to explain that he had gotten my name from his lodger and that he needed to speak with me as a matter of urgency. His every utterance was accompanied by an apology for having disturbed me. For a long time I had no idea what all this was about, not least because Jonáš was whispering and his words were encroached upon by the dialogue of the weeping women on the TV. But I had no doubt that the voice on the phone belonged to the Jonáš whose articles I had read twenty years ago. With the clarity of a hallucination, I recognized, in a distant corner of my memory, the voice I used to hear on the radio; like a station you can't turn off, it kept coming through amid harsh, tremulous sounds that were reminiscent more of laboriously articulated sighs than of actual speech.

The voice was very much changed, but it was definitely that of Jonáš. It seemed to me that it reached into an empty space just as it used to, although today's emptiness and that of the past were different. I remembered how this voice, imbued with the menace of power, would cut into the dead silence that remained after it had dispelled all other voices. Over the years his harshness had given way to the tired, resigned huskiness of a man who no longer needs to spread the silence around as he remains trapped forever within it, as in a cell without a door. Eventually I understood that Jonáš's plaintive whisper was urging and pleading with me to come to him immediately. He would send a cab for me, wouldn't keep me long and would have me driven back home. He apologized for not coming to me: He was a sick man, and besides, there was something in the villa where he lived that he needed to show me.

The request put me in a bad mood: Jonáš was not a person I would ever wish to see, even if in the years since he'd dropped from view he had indeed changed from a crusader for the socialist regime to a Dracula-like resident of a spooky villa. It was likely that his invitation had something to do with the mysterious symbol, as this was the only thing that might connect us.

But whatever it was he wanted of me, I doubted I'd be able to help in any way. As he continued to press me, I considered how I could talk my way out of this. But Jonáš was not an easy man to put off, even though it seemed that at any moment his voice might fail once and for all. The humility of the humbled came together with an old man's obstinacy and perhaps also flashes of his former imperiousness. My curiosity was beginning to get the better of my aversion for Jonáš and my wish to finish my bottle of wine. In the end I promised I would come. After I rang off, I pulled back the curtains and looked out on the evening street. In almost every window the light gained and lost intensity to the same rhythm, as the residents of the Scottish mansion moved from the darkness of the drawing room to the terrace and back again. Before long a car with a white roof light pulled up in front of my building. I switched off the TV, put the bottle back in the fridge and went downstairs.

The car drove along the edge of the city and soon came to an area I didn't know. We waited at the barrier of a railroad crossing until a blurry strip of lights flashed through the darkness, passed a treeless hill that overlooked a street of low, rustic-looking houses and then some vast office buildings in which all the lights were out. Before long we found ourselves on a busy, well-lit street. Above us appeared the stern of a streetcar, its standing passengers motionless, as though in the gondola of a balloon that had lost height. Then the outdoor lights thinned out. Now the beam of our headlights picked out white picket fences; beyond these, I supposed, were deep gardens. The car pulled up at one such gate. As I prepared to pay, the cab driver informed me that his service had been ordered by a regular customer with the instruction that the fare should be charged to his account.

The cab drove away and I stood alone surrounded by fences. A warm, fragrance-imbued darkness reached me from the gardens. A light appeared amid the tall conifers beyond the gate, but nothing moved and there was no sound. I pressed the bronze bell button on the gate, which then creaked open. I followed a footpath strewn with sand toward the dim light. Supple branches of overgrown conifers brushed against my face and then flew away again into the darkness. From somewhere near came the smell of rotting leaves on the bottom of an emptied pool.

To the eight bronze arms of a chandelier were affixed eight frosted-glass globes; only one of these globes was lit, dimly illuminating a hall at the back of which a staircase covered with reddish-brown plush carpet rose to a gallery that was lost in the darkness. I took a few steps in; reflected globes of light flashed on and off in wall mirrors and glass cabinets.

"Hello, hello." The rasping voice came from above. Until then I hadn't noticed the motionless, indistinct figure leaning on the railing of the gallery. As I mounted the stairs, I heard the clicking of switches in the dim space above; lamps came on all the way along the gallery. These lamps were shaped like geometric lilies, their bronze stalks growing out of the pale-green wallpaper. Jonáš whispered a greeting and motioned for me to follow him. I watched him in the weak lamplight; he had difficulty walking, with one hand on a stick, the second holding on to the railing. Neither of us spoke. I recalled the man I used to see around the Faculty of Arts and the Academy of Sciences. Jonáš had once been famously hefty and robust—one of his students had told me how his conversation partners would instinctively back away from him because his body seemed to be in but brief repose before it proceeded to expand and crush everything around it. Jonáš hadn't lost much weight since then, yet the change in his bearing was even more remarkable than the change in his voice. I saw that his corpulence had become a burden that was constantly pulling him groundward, as though he dragged a large, bulky animal around with him.

He stopped at a door and opened it. We stepped into an oblong room containing so much heavy furniture that there was very little space to move. Running the whole length of the room was a dark table with tall chairs at regular intervals around it. These chairs had black-leather upholstery attached to the seat with mighty metal studs. Jonáš held on to the edge of the table and the backs of the chairs. He led me to a corner of the room where there stood a low round table with a chessboard inlay. On one side of this was a bottle of port and two glasses; next to the table was an ebony box with a Moorish pattern carved into it—this had to be the little table the graphic designer had mentioned yesterday. Leaning over the table, like a chess player engrossed in contemplation of his next move, was a lighted lamp on a stand of bent chrome. Along the room's shorter wall was a capacious desk on which stood a ceramic vase of dried flowers, an old black telephone and a number of metal figurines. Hanging on the wall opposite, bathed in the light of the lamp, was a painting about a meter high.

Jonáš's course through the room was a sorrowful downward arc that ended in a leather armchair by the round table. As I sat down in a second armchair, the picture gave off a gleaming veil, and I saw that it was a portrait of a girl with short, fair hair, wearing corduroy pants and a loose top.

"Is it a portrait of your daughter?" I asked straight out.

Jonáš nodded but didn't speak; obviously he wanted me to take a good look at the picture. But I was struggling to tear my eyes from his face, which was now lit by the lamp. It appeared to be composed only of a great many folds of loose skin, to have been hastily assembled from the lights and shadows of the villa just for me and it seemed that it would melt back into the gloom once I had left. At last I did succeed in turning my gaze from this pitiful face to the portrait on the wall. Its subject was about eighteen years old, I supposed. She had a round face whose childlike features were underscored by her expression—brows knitted, lips slightly pursed; the girl's face put me in mind of a little boy in a sulk. The girl was sitting in front of a window, probably on a low stool; it was possible to read in her posture something like vigilance.

Only part of the window was visible in the picture, but from the shape of the panes and perhaps also the fact that the room was bathed in the pinkish light of early evening, I had the impression that it was the edge of a great expanse of glass the like of which is found in an artist's studio. Behind the girl's back I saw the cracked facade of an apartment building, none of whose windows were lit. I noticed that among these windows were a great number of small, narrow ones belonging, I supposed, to bathrooms and pantries, suggesting that this was the building's back and that the window of the studio looked out on the yard rather than the street.

The painting was in a style reminiscent of New Objectivity: its objects and the girl's body were encircled by a distinct black line that also enclosed smooth expanses of paint in the pink tones of evening light. The black line created the impression of tranquility; at first I imagined the slow, unperturbed movement of the brush on the canvas, but as I continued to look at the picture it occurred to me that this was an illusion; suddenly it was obvious to me that the slow rhythm of the line was an expression not of real tranquility but of resignation, perhaps also of desperation. It was as though the artist had given up trying to understand the mystery of the face he was painting. And it seemed to me that at the bottom of the cool tranquility of the line encircling the face and body of the girl, I even glimpsed hate.

"A peculiar portrait," I said, more to myself than to Jonáš.

Then I turned back to him and asked how old his daughter was.

"She has just turned twenty-four," he replied.

"When was the portrait painted? Six, seven years ago?"

"Oh no, it's only two years old. Viola has always looked younger than she is."

"There's something childlike about her," I said. "Does she still look like this today?"

There was a moment of silence before Jonáš spoke. "In September it will be two years since Viola disappeared. I haven't seen her since then."

I asked if he had contacted the police.

"Of course, but they didn't find anything. They suspended the case long ago. I hired a number of private detective agencies, but they didn't come up with anything either."

"Did just the two of you live here?" I asked.

"Viola doesn't have any brothers or sisters. Her mother and I parted before she was born. At first she lived with her, but when Viola was four, her mother died, and after that she stayed with me."

"Have you no idea at all where she might be?"

"Viola confided nothing in me. She was silent and headstrong, although there were no real problems with her. I don't know what could have happened to her. I found out the names of several of her friends, but they don't know anything about her either . . ." He paused for a moment before adding: "I can't help thinking that someone is holding her prisoner and she's waiting for my help . . ."

Chapter 6
Photographs from New York

From the tone of Jonáš's voice I understood that he must have spent the past few months in his bleak mansion in a state of desperation. He spoke so quietly that his words were only slightly louder than the creaking of the furniture and the occasional gasp from the armchairs in which we were sitting. Then he fell silent for a long time. I felt sorry for him, but still it wasn't clear to me what he actually wanted from me. When the silence had gone on longer than I could bear, I asked him what his daughter did.

"Viola had a gift for languages. She studied English and French. After she finished school she made her living as a translator and interpreter."

"Before she disappeared, did you notice anything strange, or any changes in her behavior?" I liked to read detective stories, and this was the kind of question I imagined a detective asking.

Jonáš poured wine into two glasses. "As I said, Viola was always reserved. But in those few months before she disappeared I did indeed notice that there was something the matter with her. I'm sure that the change began in America—something important must have happened there. If I only I knew what it was . . . I can't sleep, and in all the nights that I've been living here alone, I've gone over thousands of possibilities and seen thousands of terrible images in the dark . . . The year before last, in May, Viola was on vacation in the United States. She spent two weeks in New York, staying in a cheap hotel in north Manhattan. She called me several times, the last time a week after her departure; everything was fine then. After that something must have happened—maybe she witnessed some strange incident or met someone, I don't know . . . When she got home she was restless and more reserved than ever—now she hardly spoke with me at all. She made several telephone calls and she whispered into the handset so that I couldn't hear what she was saying. A time later this portrait appeared in her room. When I asked Viola who the artist was, she told me it was this guy she knew, nothing more. I didn't question her further as I knew there was no point . . ."

"And later?"

"In mid-September, four months after she came back from America, she disappeared, and I never saw her again . . . I remember the last few days before her disappearance very well. She looked strange, as if she were feverish. She never answered when I spoke to her; I don't even know if she heard me. On the last evening but one she came home at ten o'clock. I could see that she was extremely agitated about something: She was all atremble. I saw her only for a moment. In the short time that she looked at me I saw something in her gaze that scared me even more than the fever: a terrible anger, perhaps directed at me, perhaps directed at all people . . . Then she darted into her room and locked herself in."

I was reminded of two figures I had seen at the dump, born of two positions of the double trident—a man holding his head in desperation and an angry woman making a threat; these became Jonáš and his daughter.

"Please don't be mad at me for asking, but did Viola have any reason to detest you? Could she have left because you did something bad to her?"

"Believe me, I'm sure I never did her any harm. After she disappeared, I pondered long and hard on whether I had hurt her in some way. I went back over everything that had happened between us, but I couldn't think of anything that could have upset her . . ."

I trusted that he would never have hurt Viola knowingly. I could imagine that Jonáš really loved his daughter and had always spoiled her.

"I understand," I said. "So—on the last but one evening she came home in a state of agitation and locked herself in her room. What happened after that?"

"I was very worried about her. Several times I stood in front of her room and listened at the door."

"And did you hear anything?"

"I thought I heard a faint sound, but through the door it was impossible to tell what it was. It may have been the bubbling of boiling water, but it could just as well have been the sound of an animal. After a while I was aware of a strange fragrance, one that is terribly difficult to describe. It had several components, including the scent of roses and the sharp smell of steel . . . I went away and came back half an hour later. By then there was no sound coming from the room. The fragrance was still there, but it wasn't as strong as before. I went to bed, but I woke up many times that night; I can see the window of her room from mine, so I know that her light was on all night. All the next day she was locked in her room, except for the few times she went to the kitchen or the bathroom. Each time she left her room she locked the door and took the key with her. That night Viola's light burned until half past twelve. Then she burst out of the room out as if in a great hurry, was away for half an hour, darted back into the room and again locked the door. Then I saw a bright flash in her window. Again the light in her room burned deep into the night. I fell asleep in the small hours. As soon as I awoke I rushed to her room. The door was wide open; the room was empty. That was the 17th of September the year before last. I haven't seen Viola since."

"Didn't you find any clues in her room?"

"I searched it thoroughly. The police and the detectives took a look, too. But they didn't find any notes, any address books, or any telephone numbers. They didn't find anything that would help me in any way."

"Did Viola ever hint at what had happened to her in New York?"

"Never. But there is one thing that bears witness to her stay in America. It's probably worthless, but it's all I have." Jonáš lifted the lid of the ebony box and pushed it towards me. It contained a pile of glossy color photographs and three rolls of negatives.

"Among her things I found two exposed but undeveloped strips of film. I also examined her cameras—Viola liked photography and had three of them. Two were empty, but the third still had film in it. This was the camera she'd taken on her American vacation. I had all three films developed: they had Viola's photos of New York on them. Take a look—from the negatives I've sorted them in the order in which they were taken."

Jonáš took the photos out of the box and handed them to me. I studied the pictures one by one, looking for some kind of clue, even though I didn't know what would represent one. But all I saw were the kind of photos tourists commonly take, of various places in Manhattan; they showed the Empire State Building, the Guggenheim Museum, the neon lights of Broadway, coffee shops in Greenwich Village, the lake in Central Park, the streets of Chinatown. As I finished examining them, I put the photos back in the box. I was expecting Jonáš to tell me something about them, but he had fallen silent again. Not until I reached the last few shots did I see something that was obviously not of Manhattan: low houses of unplastered brick, defaced by the doodles of graffiti artists and stores with writing in Spanish on their windows. The very last photo showed a small bar next to an overground railroad station, its name obscured by a traffic sign.

I laid the photo of the bar aside and directed a questioning look at Jonáš; I had absolutely no idea what I was supposed to read in Viola's pictures. Without speaking Jonáš took one of the three rolls from the box. It was three-quarters empty—the shot of the bar was the last Viola had taken. This may not have been significant—but it may have meant that in the area where the last roll was shot an incident had occurred that caused Viola to lose interest in photography. The last pictures appeared to be of the Bronx, Brooklyn or Queens—perhaps somewhere here even, by the overground railroad station, Viola had had a life-changing encounter that ultimately led to her disappearance. What could it have been? Jonáš had spoken of mysterious telephone calls. Maybe Viola had gotten to know someone in New York with whom she had stayed in touch after her return; maybe it had been necessary to keep this New York acquaintance a secret, not only from Jonáš. Could it be that drugs were at the bottom of the case?

I asked Jonáš if Viola used any drugs. At first he denied this indignantly; then he conceded that after her return from America she had drunk quite a lot and sometimes really had behaved as though she were under the influence of drugs. This had gone on for a month, he said. Then Viola was suddenly different; but she did not return to the person she had been before—she became even more distant, in fact, and spoke with Jonáš even less, but he never again saw her drunk, and if she had been using drugs before, she had obviously finished with them.

I took another look at the last photo, but I didn't find in it anything suspicious, or any clue. But perhaps it was otherwise: perhaps everything in it was suspicious and might be a clue; perhaps every object and every figure in it were elements of a vague, sinister plot. The Hispanic man turning into the street at the very moment Viola released the shutter, for instance—was he not wearing a suspicious, mischievous expression? And the indistinct outline behind the glass door of a produce market—was that someone lying in wait? And at the edge of the sidewalk there was an unidentifiable, suspicious object. And wasn't it possible to read that weirdly twisted graffiti as the word "Viola"? Yes, it was. At this last discovery I was overcome with excitement, until I realized that it was possible to read in it any word that came to mind. Then I wondered if the mysterious thing could be the bent frame of a bicycle someone had left there. And wasn't the expression on the face of the Puerto Rican after all a kindly one?

As he let me study the photographs, Jonáš said nothing. I suppose he had looked at them himself a thousand times and knew intimately all the figures and objects captured in them. He had surely tried more desperately than I to find connections between some of the objects or faces in the pictures and Viola's disappearance, and still he had come up with nothing. Not until I had returned the remaining photos to the box did Jonáš speak again. Now his voice was louder and more animated; it was as if his desire to find his daughter had stirred up all the strength left in his body.

Chapter 7
The Dreaming Hippo

"I couldn't keep out of Viola's room. In the early morning three days after her disappearance I was in there again. I happened to look at the portrait, which at that time still hung in that room, and to my amazement I noticed that something had changed in it overnight. In one of the windows in the background a light was burning; in the room beyond the window I saw a picture with some kind of symbol in it. My first thought was that someone had broken into the villa and painted over the picture. Even though I couldn't see the sense in that, there was so much about Viola's disappearance that was incomprehensible and strange that I was fast reaching the conclusion that anything was possible. So I just sat there staring at the mysterious symbol. After ten minutes the light in the painting went out and it was the same as before. After that I saw the light come on four more times, but as I wasn't sitting by the painting the whole time it's quite possible that it happened more times than that. When I first saw the mysterious window it occurred to me that the symbol might have something to do with Viola's disappearance; it might even lead me to her, if only I could find out what it was. Maybe it was the emblem of a secret organization or sect and Viola had become one of its members. Maybe the members of the sect had abducted her because she'd discovered an important secret in America. Maybe it was a map of the path that would lead me to Viola, or else the map of the catacomb where they were holding her . . ."

Jonáš's voice trailed off, as though he was burdened by the weight of the hundreds of possible interpretations of the symbol, each of which escaped and dissolved as soon as he tried to follow and grasp it. How strange it was that Jonáš had obviously spent many months occupied by what had occupied me a few days ago at the dump—the attempt to decipher the double trident symbol. It was stranger still that he had come to the same thoughts as I, albeit by a completely different route—of secret organizations and underground spaces.

"In those days I was still able to walk better," Jonáš continued. "So I went around asking people if they knew anything about the symbol. But all my investigations were in vain: no one recognized the symbol. I found many similar figures—there are various company logos and characters in exotic scripts that differ from the symbol in the painting only slightly, such as the emblem of a Latvian seafood-processing firm and that of a Spanish TV station. In all these cases the similarity was probably just a coincidence. After a while I started to find something that reminded me of the symbol in almost everything; it leapt out at me wherever I happened to look; everything appeared to be the symbol in an embryonic or disfigured form. In the end I gave up searching for the meaning of the symbol; the opportunities to do so became more limited as it got more difficult for me to leave the house."

Among the various feelings which the humble, ailing voice on the telephone had evoked had been a momentarily irresistible glee at Jonáš's humiliation. Now, as I looked at the figure slumped in the armchair, the last remnants of this feeling evaporated, to be replaced by pity, sorrow and compassion.

"I kept going to Viola's room even though my visits caused me great anguish. I'd sit for hours on her bed and weep . . . Then I told myself that I had to put an end to this; that I had to pull myself together. I still believe that I'll see Viola again, and I'd like to think I'll still be here when she comes back. So I started to take antidepressants, last fall I had her room cleared out and I started renting it, and I had the portrait brought in here. I'm no longer searching for my daughter—I don't have the strength, and I don't know where else to turn. All I do these days is sit here and wait for Viola to turn up or at least for some clue as to where I should look for her. But I'd had no such clue for months and months—until today, when my lodger told me there was someone who had encountered the very symbol that I knew from Viola's portrait. For the first time since Viola's disappearance something had at last appeared that might show me the way."

Jonáš was so agitated that I was worried he might faint. I wondered how to break it to him that what had happened to me at the dump contained no clue of the kind he was expecting. Perhaps he saw that I was about to refuse, because he waved a hand in a weak gesture of resistance and said, "I know that what happened to you is trifling. And yet it's not as insignificant as you may think. For many months I had the desperate feeling that everything to do with Viola's disappearance was contained in a closed circle; that it was all linked and everything referred to everything else, but that none of it had any relation to anything beyond the circle. What happened to you at the dump doesn't belong in the circle containing Viola's disappearance, yet somehow it is connected with it . . . Do you see what I mean? It's important that the closed circle has finally been broken—that at last some connection has emerged with something beyond it. A way out has opened up, even if we don't yet know where it will lead . . ."

But Jonáš had failed to convince me of the importance of the incident at the dump. It seemed, regrettably, that he had fastened onto me as a last hope. I felt bad because I didn't know how to help him and I knew that there was absolutely no point in my offering to help. An object shaped like the figure in Viola's portrait had stabbed me in the foot as I walked across a dump, and that was all; I couldn't take his thoughts on the breaking of an enchanted circle seriously. Now Jonáš wanted me to tell him in detail what had happened to me, even though I was pretty sure he had had the graphic designer describe it to him thoroughly and there was nothing for me to add to the story. I explained that I had found nothing at the dump that might have any connection with the object; that people from a wide area carried their junk to this place and there was probably no way of knowing what had belonged to whom. Although Jonáš continued to look at me from under his heavy eyelids as though as I was the only person in the world who could help him, he didn't venture to ask for my assistance. As we sat there in silence he was perhaps expecting that I would offer this help myself. The more his anxious, imploring gaze moved me, the more it irritated me. I heard the ticking of a clock in some dark corner. Embarrassed, I moved my half-empty glass about the squares of the chessboard.

The silence had been going on for some time when Jonáš said in an even quieter voice. "Very well. I accept your position—I wasn't expecting anything different, in fact. Thank you for coming here and hearing me out. And forgive me for having bothered you. I'll call you a cab."

He placed both hands on the tabletop and leaned into them. With effort he lifted his heavy body from the chair into which it had sunk; I looked on with a sense of shame. The impression he gave was even more pitiful than it had been in the gallery. Perhaps our conversation really had exhausted him, but perhaps he was exaggerating his impotence slightly in a last attempt to move me to compassion and extract a promise of help from me. I'd been feeling anguished throughout my time at the villa; the sight of him now served to heighten that anguish. I could hardly wait to be back in the fresh air outside, although I knew that the pitiful, broken figure would stay in my memory for a long time.

Jonáš moved to the desk, picked up the handset of the telephone and dialed a number. As he waited for the connection with the receiver against his ear, I stood up in order to inspect Viola's portrait one last time. I studied her frown before my gaze slid to the horizontal lines of the rooftops, which, thanks to the play of perspective, grew out of the outline of Viola's head. And suddenly—on the most distant plane of rooftops, in a thicket of television antennas—I saw something. The Dreaming Hippo.

Although the Dreaming Hippo had been with me throughout my childhood—I had seen this creature daily and known it intimately—it had been many years since I'd thought of it. Whenever I'd raised my head from my school book or the adventure story I'd been reading and looked out of the window, I'd seen the Dreaming Hippo wallowing peacefully on a distant rooftop, as though the haze of the distance was the warm mud of the Nile.

The Dreaming Hippo: thus had I named a group of chimneys that appeared from my window like a blissful hippo at rest. He may have been more angular than his African relatives, but there could be no doubt that they belonged to the same species. In actual fact the hippo's body was composed of chimneys that were quite far from each other. I discovered that the chimneys came together and formed the hippo only if looked at from a point in line with our apartment; seen from any other point, the chimneys were scattered about the distant roofs and there was no suggestion of any hippo.

The hippo in the picture was definitely the one I'd known as a child. Judging by its size relative to that of the girl, I knew that the largest of the chimneys that formed it was around the same distance from the studio as our apartment had been—about one kilometer. While the hippo of my childhood had looked left, the hippo in the picture was looking right. The sun used to rise above my hippo, so I figured that the room I imagined to be an artist's studio was about two kilometers east of the street on which I'd lived as a child. Might Jonáš have been right to speak of the breaking of a circle?

In the meantime Jonáš had finished his call and noticed that I had found something in the picture; he was waiting anxiously for what I had to tell him. I showed him the hippo and explained how I thought I might be able to find the studio in which the unknown painter had produced the portrait of his daughter. Jonáš hobbled to the picture and put his face close to the canvas at the place where the hippo was painted—so close that his nose was almost touching it. His lips moved soundlessly. Again he turned his dumb, pleading eyes on me. No, I can promise him nothing, I said to myself; it is complete nonsense that I should help a stranger with actions that are hopeless anyway, not least of all because this stranger was quite a rogue in his day and some might say deserving of his current misery. I can't get involved in the search for a lost girl that flummoxed the police; I'm not a detective and I have a great many other things to do.

Our silence was broken by the sound of a car drawing to a halt. "Your taxi's here," said Jonáš. "I suppose you can find your way to the gate. Once again, thanks very much for coming to see me."

I could resist no longer. "I'll try to find the studio," I said. "But I suggest that you don't get your hopes up."

An expression of such bliss washed over Jonáš's face that my sense of shame was intensified. He took a photograph from his breast pocket and handed it to me. It showed Viola leaning on the rail of a terrace. The photographer had caught her at the moment she noticed his presence; she was turning her head towards him and looked mildly surprised. I accepted the photo and hurried from the room down the aisle between the furniture and out of the dark villa. Jonáš trailed behind me—I heard his heavy breathing and shuffling steps at my back. Down in the entrance hall I turned to see that he had stayed at the top of the staircase—the very place he had been standing on my arrival. I called to him: "I'll be in touch if I find anything." Jonáš said something in a quiet voice that I didn't understand and then vanished into the dark.

As the taxi drove me through streets where most of the windows were dark, I was angry with myself. With irritation I imagined what was likely to happen: I would wander the streets for a day or two, then call Jonáš with the news that I'd found nothing; Jonáš would immerse himself even more deeply and quietly in the well of his despair and his world of shadows, and I would feel even more awkward than I felt now. But I knew, too, that I would be deceiving myself if I claimed I'd decided to search for Viola only out of pity for Jonáš. I knew my choice was influenced by the desire to avoid the birth pains of my novella, but there was something else besides. The three-quarters blank negative, the mysterious sounds behind the door, the unfamiliar smells and flashes, the nighttime disappearance of a young woman, the changing portrait and the two coincident shapes whose meaning nobody knew—all this together presented me with a puzzle that I wanted to solve so badly that I couldn't resist. And all these facts gathered around a hieroglyphic symbol which floated before my eyes and urged me to decipher it.

When I got home I went straight to bed. I switched off the

light and lay there with my eyes closed; questions swirled around in my head without my knowing who was asking them. Where was this place in which Viola found herself, a place which seemed to close all passages to our world? And what had lured her there? Had she been drawn by the brilliance of a magnificent treasure and descended in quest of it, or had she been abducted by evil powers that lived there? Maybe it was a cold place on the shore of an underground lake that was the home of an ancient monster. Was Viola the monster's slave? Or perhaps she was the queen of a subterranean empire? Was she waiting for someone to come and free her from captivity or would she lure them into a trap from which there was no escape? These thoughts mingled with images from the dream I was entering. Suddenly I was walking through a gloomy stone palace, wandering huge halls lined with tables heaped with precious stones. In the last of these halls, there was Viola, in the corduroy pants and T-shirt the unknown artist had painted her in, a tiara of large sparkling sapphires and rubies on her head, raising a hand in a gesture I didn't understand. Was she bidding me to come to her or warning me away?

Chapter 8
Courtyards

I got up early in the morning, found my map of the city and folded it out on top of the sheets of paper containing the fragments of my novella. I dug about in the drawers of my desk and found in one of them the scratched ruler made of transparent plastic I had used in elementary school. On the map I found the street where I had lived as a child, figured out the approximate location of the building we had lived in and marked this with a cross. I reminded myself that judging by what I'd seen in the painting, the mysterious studio ought to be about two kilometers east of that place. I laid the left-hand edge of the ruler against the cross so that it was parallel to the lower and upper edges of the map; as the map was in 1:10,000 scale, I made a second cross twenty centimeters to the right of the first. Then I pushed away the ruler and drew a circle about two centimeters in diameter around the second cross—thus marking the area where I would need to look for the studio. I looked out of the window; a strip of clear, cloud-free sky was visible above the roofs. At this moment neither Jonáš nor Viola were much on my mind. I was looking forward to walking the streets at a time which in the recent years I'd been used to spending at work. It occurred to me that the early-morning city was a world less familiar to me than many a foreign country.

The shadows of the roofs with their silhouettes of chimneys and antennas reached high above the facades of the buildings opposite, whose walls were awash with the pure light of early morning. After half an hour I came to a concrete bridge over a stream. According to my calculations, beyond this was the territory that contained the studio. It was a world of dreamy, dilapidated buildings hung with stucco ornaments like cheap jewels around an old woman's neck; a world of rickety wooden fences, sprawling warehouses and vacant lots. I was dazzled each time the low sun emerged suddenly from behind walls. I began my search for the window of the studio, walking the streets with my head back, looking up at the highest floors of the buildings. From the painting I was sure that the studio was situated in a courtyard, so I tried the handles of entrance doors; if these weren't locked, I went in and explored the hidden, blocked-in spaces.

But I told myself that I was about as likely to discover the studio in this neighborhood as I was to happen across a minaret on the corner of one of these streets. I reproached myself for trusting in the painter's attention to realism; after all, he might have seen the Dreaming Hippo elsewhere, at another time in his life, and brought this into Viola's portrait. Still I spent almost three hours creeping about courtyards. I saw dozens of carpet beaters and dozens of wrecked cars, but there was no sign of the studio. To tell the truth, I couldn't imagine an artist's studio in this district of workshops and warehouses. I got hungry—I hadn't eaten since yesterday evening. I decided to find a pleasant pub, where I could have a bite to eat and call Jonáš to tell him I was very sorry, I'd found nothing. In any case, I could hardly have expected anything else. At last, at the end of the block, I spotted the hanging sign of a pub. I hurried towards it past a long row of buildings. As I was passing a wide, open gateway I noticed beyond it a dark passage leading to a deep yard. I'll just take a quick look, I said to myself.

At the end of the passage I found myself at the edge of an area that formed a right-angled triangle; I was surprised to learn that it was more extensive than it looked from the street. The legs of the right angle were formed by two apartment buildings, while the hypotenuse was the high embankment of a railroad line overgrown with dark, impenetrable bushes. The area was divided into the yards of individual buildings, which were separated by low walls that were easy to step over. Some of the yards had been asphalted and had a variety of sheds and garages on them. The residents of other buildings had tried to turn their yards into gardens, in most cases with little success; this year, it appeared, no grass had sprouted from the dusty gray clay, although here and there were leafless bushes which were practically indistinguishable from the rusty, twisted skeletons of the appliances scattered among them. A similar transformation to a non-living thing had occurred on the embankment, where wads of black shrubbery resembled carelessly wound cable or wire.

As I was making these observations, I reached the middle of the triangle. There I stopped, looked up and let my gaze wander the walls like a great transparent spider, over dark windows and narrow balconies, where junk lay wrapped in plastic and rolled-up carpets stood against the wall. My gaze fell on the back of the building through whose passage I had reached the yard. There was a light near the top: at a point along the edge of the sloping roof the gray tiles had been replaced by broad panes of glass whose lower ends came up against other, vertical windowpanes. The glass construction I was looking at was surely either a greenhouse belonging to someone who cultivated exotic plants or the window of an artist's studio.

This glass wall shone with hope that was stronger still than the rays of the sun it reflected—the hope that the story I had entered at the dump several days ago was about to continue. Forgetting my hunger, I hurried back to the building on whose roof the studio shone like a celestial glass ship. I pushed my way through the metal and wood of the junk that lay everywhere, sharp protrusions catching against my pant legs; I hurried as though I feared that the glass ship was about to lift off and fly away.

The courtyard entry led to a well-lit flight of stairs lined by a smooth rail. The light came through the glass doors that gave onto a small balcony on each landing. The tops of the buildings emerged anew from each of these; each time more roof ridges were visible, as though a magician's hand were fanning out a pack of cards. I stepped onto the last landing to see the bluish hippo floating above the roofs in the distance. Apparently I had reached my destination. From this final landing a narrow flight of stairs led into the shadows and up to the attic. Looking to the skylight I estimated which door would lead to the studio. A weak strip of light lay across the nameplate by the door—I read the Christian name "Dominik" but couldn't make out the surname. In the darkness I felt for the bell and pressed it. It buzzed on the other side of the door right next to my head, giving me the impression that its sound penetrated the silent building like a sharp needle. On one of the floors below me, a dog barked.

For a long time there was no further sound; then at last I heard rustling beyond the door. When it opened I was blinded by a fierce white light and I saw only the dark silhouette of a figure standing there. When my eyes were again able to take in my surroundings, I saw that the door gave straight onto a large room with no divisions, that practically the whole of the facing wall and a large part of the sloping ceiling comprised sheets of glass, and that the light coming through these gleamed brightly on the parquet floor. Gradually the black figure before me acquired a human face. When the transformation was complete, I was pleasantly surprised: after what Jonáš had said about mysterious paintings and enigmatic encounters, I had been afraid that the door would be opened by some kind of magus, but this rather short man of about thirty in baggy work pants and an old, paint-smeared shirt looked more like a laborer. He had a serious face with a few deep wrinkles in his brow and at the sides of his mouth which reminded me immediately of the black line that divided the things in Viola's portrait.

As I hadn't prepared what I was going to say, I stood in the doorway wondering how to bring up the hippo, Viola's disappearance, the changing painting and my getting injured at the dump; none of these struck me as a good opening. In the end I threw them all in together. At first the painter looked surprised, but as soon as I mentioned Viola his expression changed. I told myself that this was perhaps because he knew her and that she had appeared to him, too, in a network of torn and improbable relationships, so he understood that she was a character that couldn't be remarked upon in coherent, ordered sentences. While I spoke, he indicated wordlessly that I take a seat in an armchair by the window. After I'd done so, he pulled up a stool, sat down and continued to listen.

So I told Dominik about my trip across the dump and my visits to the graphic designer's studio and Jonáš's villa, how Viola had vanished and her father's desperate attempts to find her. As I was talking, I looked about the room. The area we were sitting in contained, by the window, a painter's easel and an old wooden table whose top was stained with paint of all colors. A number of canvases in wooden frames were all turned to face the wall against which they stood. The distant parts of the room, cast in a quiet light, were inhabited by a white, made-up bed, a cream-colored dresser, a bulbous refrigerator, a dining table, and a closet. Obviously the room served simultaneously as studio, living room, bedroom and kitchen.

When I had finished my story the painter said thoughtfully, "So Viola disappeared. I was expecting something like that to happen. I knew her a little, and I did indeed paint the portrait that hangs in the villa. But I can't help her father, I'm afraid. I've no idea where she could be. It's been a long time since I last saw her, and to tell the truth, I'm not interested in seeing her again. I'd been hoping I'd seen the last of her."

"So Viola's disappearance is news to you?" I asked.

"Yes. Although it doesn't surprise me. At the time I knew her, it was clear she was on some kind of journey. Either she was looking for something or she was running from something, perhaps both. I don't know what it was, as she never said anything about it to me. Viola came to me because she needed something from me. Once she had it, she went away again."

"But you must know something about the symbol in the portrait? What does it mean?"

"I'm sorry to say that I've no idea."

"But aren't you the one who painted it?"

"Yes, I am. But I don't know what it means."

I could see that I had my work cut out for me with this painter.

"As the painter of the symbol, you can surely explain its strange coming and going," I insisted.

"Indeed I can, but there's no mystery to it, and I can't see how it could help in the search for Viola."

"Never mind, go ahead and tell me about it. Why not try telling me about it from the very beginning? Then we can decide what makes sense and what doesn't."

For a moment the painter looked pensively at the wall, as though trying to recall an old painting that had slipped from his memory. Then he began.

Chapter 9
Frankenstein's Mistress

"Three years ago I was going through a bad time. I was incapable of completing even one new painting. Before that I always longed for the moment I would start painting—the moment I looked at a blank canvas it would seem to me there were thousands of undulating lines on it, challenging me to choose among them, grab them and fix them there. Having taken the line I wanted, I would go hunting among its relations, which now began to flock around it. But suddenly everything was different: I would stand in front of a canvas all day, and it would still be blank by the end of it. None of these invisible lines would show themselves to me. I'd make a few strokes with my brush, in the hope that they would attract other lines, appearing out of curiosity—and then everything would be as it used to be. But the lines on the canvas remained isolated and meaningless; in fact the canvas made even less sense than when it was blank.

"When things had been going on like this for weeks on end, I did probably the best thing I could have done: I fled from the empty canvases and traveled around Europe for a few months. At that time I didn't have much money, so mostly I hitchhiked. Whenever my money ran out, I made more on the streets of the town I happened to be in by painting portraits of tourists. In early October I was planning to travel from Lausanne to Dijon. It was raining all over Europe, but I still wasn't ready to return to my studio and those empty, hostile canvases. On the French border I was picked up by a truck driver. It'd been a while since I'd had a good night's sleep, so the bumping motion of the truck and the monotony of its wipers sent me into a pleasant doze. I watched the blurry landscape through sleepy, half-closed eyes. Soon everything dissolved in the darkness, and all I saw was the highway unfolding in the headlights.

"The driver took me almost to my destination. He set me down on the square of a small town some thirty kilometers from Dijon, as he was about to turn off to the north. Although I didn't notice the town's name, this didn't really bother me. There I stood, alone in the dark and the rain in the middle of a great empty square. I looked at my watch—it was half past nine. I decided to find the station, have a nap on a bench there and resume my journey early in the morning. I looked around. The wet paving glistened in the lamplight. Not far from me in the middle of the square was a Romanesque church with a high bell tower whose outline merged with the overcast sky. The square was lined with low, narrow buildings with steep rooflines. On one of these buildings I saw the oval sign of a brewery above lighted first-floor windows. A bar, for sure, I said to myself. I realized I was longing for a glass of wine and a little ham or cheese. I threw on my rucksack and headed for the friendly lights.

"There were about twenty men in the bar. I sat down at an empty table in the corner of the room and ordered some Camembert and local red wine. After a while I noticed that the atmosphere in the room was rather strange. A peculiar tension was apparent in the behavior of all the customers. Although they were talking together about things people commonly talk about in bars, the conversation was quiet and the speakers distracted; it was as though they were waiting for something or someone. Then a new man, his coat gleaming with raindrops, came into the bar. Was he the one the others were waiting for? No—no one took much notice of him. The new man pulled down his hood and moved toward a portly, wrinkled man with thick white hair who was sitting at the head of one of the tables. Then a scene was played out that I couldn't make sense of. The man in the raincoat handed the white-haired man a banknote. Gently the latter pushed the hand of the former away and pointed to a clock that hung over the counter—it showed five minutes past ten. The man in the raincoat looked displeased and stuck his wristwatch in front of the other man's face. The other customers at the table rolled up their sleeves and watches were compared. After a brief conference the white-haired man nodded before accepting the banknote. The new man took one of the empty chairs at my table and draped his wet raincoat over the back of a neighboring chair.

"Only now did I notice the pile of banknotes on the table in front of the white-haired man. I was keen to figure out what was going on in the bar. I began to follow the eyes of the customers, and soon I realized that they kept returning to a single place—a point on the wall above my head. I had to turn all the way around in my chair to see what the other customers found so fascinating: a painting on the wall which was not particularly large and which I hadn't noticed before. I moved to an empty chair on the other side of the table so that I could get a good look at it.

"I liked the picture; although crudely painted, it had a naive charm. It showed a room at the center of which was a glass bell jar about a meter and a half high and a meter wide. Out of the transparent sides of the jar came many twisted, intertwined cables and tubes of different widths; the tubes led to cylindrical and conical metal containers at the back of the room, the cables in a wall on the right-hand side of the picture that resembled the control panel of a spaceship from a sixties science-fiction movie. The panel contained a prodigious amount of buttons, keys, lights of various colors and vertical slits with levers ending in black knobs coming out of them. But the man by the wall was not the hero of a sixties sci-fi movie—a spaceship captain in tights or a girl astronaut in a miniskirt—but a hunched figure in a white coat, with large round glasses on his nose, a bald crown enclosed in a wreath of wildly disheveled white hair and an uncommonly long beard sticking out rather menacingly from his face in two points. The painting showed this man—surely a brilliant but mad scientist—at the moment his right hand was pulling eagerly at one of the levers on the control panel; at the same time he was striking an anatomically impossible pose by turning to look at the bell jar behind him.

"The tension in the bar continued to grow. When the clock above the counter began to strike eleven, the talking stopped abruptly and all customers looked at the painting. After the last stroke the conversation came streaming back, all tension dissolved. Some of the customers got up and went over to the table where the white-haired man was sitting. He distributed the money on the table among them. Now no one was looking at the mad scientist in the laboratory. Although I didn't understand what was going on in the bar, I was reluctant to ask. I ordered another glass of wine, thought some more and then dismissed the painting on the wall from my thoughts. But when I looked up a little later and caught sight of the painting, I noticed that something had changed in it. A number of pink spots had appeared under the glass bell jar. As I stared at the painting in astonishment, I realized that the pink spots were increasing in number. These islands of pink came together until they fused into a human figure. Now a naked woman was sitting in the transparent bell jar in a somewhat immodest pose. The painter had taken a lot of care with her generous curves. She was looking at the scientist with a challenge in her eyes. Doctor Frankenstein had created his artificial mistress. Remarkably, the female apparition in the bell jar was of no interest to any of the customers, even though their eyes had been glued to the painting just a few minutes earlier.

"I could restrain myself no longer. I leaned across the chair with the raincoat on it and asked my neighbor, who since his conversation with the white-haired banker had been sipping his wine without speaking a word, about the mysterious painting. He came to life immediately—it was clear that he was glad of the opportunity to tell the story of the painting to someone who was new to it. He took his raincoat from the chair between us and moved into it to reduce the distance. He insisted on buying a new bottle of wine for the two of us."

Chapter 10
A Package at the Bottom of a Drawer

"My neighbor worked as a laborer for a company that had been based in the town for 170 years. It produced various cosmetics and toiletries. The leadership of this small family business had for several generations passed from father to son or son-in-law. The company fared surprisingly well considering that its competitors were multinational corporations and its name wasn't emblazoned across billboards or spoken by the seductive lips of models in TV commercials. Although large companies with hundreds of staff and research teams offered better, cheaper products, everyone in and around the town knew the owner's family, were accustomed since childhood to use soaps, colognes and anti-aphid sprays from the local factory and would have thought it an eccentricity to buy international brand-name products even if the possibility of doing so had crossed their minds.

"Old people who had spent their whole lives in the town and could still remember the grandfather and great-grandfather of the factory's current owner said that all owners were remarkably similar to one another in appearance and character. This similarity was so great that their memories tended to confuse the owners; it was a common occurrence in the bar that old men would argue about which incident was connected with which owner. Had, for instance, that vat of alcohol been stolen from Jacques during the Second World War or from Charles during the First?

"The one exception in the series of merging faces and figures was the last owner—an uncle of the current one. He had attended the bar and the church like his father and grandfather, but his neighbors had thought this was just a game to deceive others. Although they were convinced he was hiding something from them, no one had any idea what this might be. He managed the business well and seemed to understand his work, but it was apparent that he was little more interested in running the factory than he was in what went on in the town. This was no disaster for the company—production was unchanged in decades, so basically it ran itself and there was no need to attend to it much; indeed, it was actually preferable that the owner pay little attention to the factory than if he were to threaten the well-established order by overzealousness or ill-considered innovations that none of his customers wanted.

"Nor in this regard did his outward behavior differ much from that of previous owners—all of them had been easier to spot on the promenade or in a café on the square than in the office or workshops. Even so, the townspeople felt where the conduct of previous owners had been a manifestation of affectionate and proud trust in the reliable operation of a factory with which they were inseparably linked, that of the new owner was an expression of cold indifference. The factory had been under his leadership for ten years when his sister's son finished his studies in '91. Then the owner turned the factory over to the nephew, left the town and France altogether and settled on some Greek island. Three years later came news of his death. He had committed one last eccentricity before he died, in expressing a wish to be buried in the cemetery on the island. So his was the only name missing in the long gold-lettered roll call of the factory's owners on the marble obelisk of the family tomb.

"While the old boss was alive, the young boss kept his office in the state he had left it, perhaps because he couldn't believe that his uncle had exchanged the tranquillity of his hometown and its streets of familiar faces for a foreign island where, it was said, the heat of summer was unbearable and it rained all winter long. The maid was told to go to the former owner's room every Saturday, where she would dust the furniture and library and vacuum the carpet. The nephew had the room cleared only after his uncle died, and before he did so, he took a look at it himself. It wasn't actually the first time he'd peeped into it; late in the evening in the bar, with a bottle or two of wine inside him, he had several times spoken of how in his uncle's empty room he felt uneasy and afraid, and how he was afraid to turn the key of a single door or to pull out a single drawer. Like everyone else in the town he believed that his uncle had had a secret. He feared that he'd find a cavity in the room that would reveal something terrible about the former boss, such as his having committed a murder in a foreign country.

"So after his uncle's death, when the time came for him to inspect the room, he didn't feel very good about it. In the bar he also spoke more than once about this visit to the dead man's room. First he had pulled a few books from the bookcase and leafed through them. They were volumes of poetry and novels, mostly in languages he didn't know, some of them in alphabets he wasn't able to read. (The antiquarian who purchased his uncle's library complete told him they were in Russian and Greek.) Then he looked into the bureau and opened the closet. In the bureau he found twenty or so half-empty bottles containing a variety of liquors; in the closet were his uncle's suits, on hangers. Apparently the room was keeping no secrets. The new boss was relieved but also slightly disappointed. He plucked up the courage to pull out the three wide drawers in the lower part of the closet. The first two contained folded laundry, while the third and lowest was crammed with papers.

"He sat on the floor and started going through these, picking up the sheets in handfuls, scanning the contents and then setting them down neatly on the carpet. These papers were from his uncle's years as a student; they included notes taken at lectures and from various scientific books but also a great many love letters that in those years his uncle had received from a number of different women. The nephew was somewhat surprised—the townspeople had known the company's former boss as a loner and no one had ever seen him with a woman—but this scarcely amounted to a big secret. At the very bottom of the drawer was a package tied up with string. The nephew opened this up and found that it contained chemical formulae. He read through these and established that they concerned the manufacture of paints that were supposed to have an unusual property: the notes stated that in normal circumstances they were completely clear but in certain conditions they took on different shades of color. Evidently this was one of the inventions by his uncle of which the young boss had heard his mother and grandfather speak many years earlier.

"Different substances acted on different sets of paints. The documentation called substances that were able to color unseeable paints 'activators,' and it divided them into two groups, hard and soft. Hard activators were various solutions; clear paints took on certain colors when vapor produced by the boiling of these solutions acted on them. Soft activators were various substances dispersed in the atmosphere; although their effect on paints could be predicted to some degree, it always depended on chance. The formulae from the drawer showed the exact chemical composition of each group of paints and the hard activators that acted on them. The notes on the soft activators were more general; the new owner read, for instance, that one set of clear paints often took on a color when warm spring rain was falling and another tended to do so in dry weather. The effect of soft activators was impossible to predict, as the transformation of a clear paint to a colored one depended on a large number of various factors. How colors came and went depended on subtle changes in atmosphere; it depended on temperature and humidity and the presence of different gases and vapors in the air. Also, the appearance or disappearance of a color could bring about a subtle shift in the balance that held among factors.

"Although for decades none of the owners had made any changes to what was produced, perhaps all of them had been through a phase after taking over the company when they had dreamed of new products and technologies and the glory of the business extending far beyond the boundaries of the town. The period of entrepreneurial dreaming had in most cases not lasted longer than two or three years. During this time new or at least greatly improved products would appear regularly in the drugstores of the town and its neighborhood. Although their customers would sniff the unfamiliar fragrances of the soaps and colognes with sullenness and suspicion, they were forbearing and patient: they knew that things would soon be back to normal—and weren't the repeated bursts of innovator's enthusiasm part of the tradition, after all?

"Following his arrival at the factory the current owner, too, went through such a period, although it was limited to vague ideas—which was perhaps why it lasted a little longer than had been the case with earlier bosses; indeed, at the time of his uncle's death it hadn't yet ended. So it was that there on the carpet, amid the chemical formulae and declarations of passion from his uncle's old lovers, the new boss began to daydream. He noticed that the formulae in the package didn't match those on the list of contents—only about a third of the original total had been retained; still, it occurred to him that fantastic things could be achieved with the remainder. In his mind's eye he launched new products, and enormous production halls grew in the field beyond the factory's workshops. Then he realized that it wasn't really clear to him what his uncle's paints could be used for. He was slightly disturbed by this realization, but as he didn't wish to interfere with his mood of elation he told himself that he was bound to come up with something. And sure enough, a little while later he did: Could the paints not be used in advertising? He imagined a magazine with a color photograph of a landscape in which a new model of car would eventually appear, along with the advertiser's slogan. That very evening he enthused about this in the bar while his tablemates nodded in silence and wondered how long his enthusiasm would last.

"Immediately after this the new young owner had a series of trial paints and hard activators produced from the formulae. It turned out that everything really did work as described in his uncles's papers. But by now the dream period was coming to an end, and the owner took receipt of all the samples with the announcement that he was now working on something else. He gave the instruction for the phials containing the paints and hard activators to be put into storage; he would attend to them as soon as he had a little time to do so. The workers stored the samples in a distant corner of the warehouse and heaved a sigh of relief: they knew that no one would ever again lay a hand on the phials containing these paints and activators.

"So it was that the painting in the bar was the only work to which the last owner's invention had been applied. It had been produced by one of the workers, an amateur painter, when the paints were being sampled. First he had painted the mad scientist and his laboratory in ordinary oils, then he had added the man-made woman in a disappearing paint. He had given the painting to a cousin of his, who had hung it on a wall of his bar. It turned out that the soft activators which acted on the paints the painter had used were plentiful in the atmosphere of the bar and that the figure of the woman often appeared around eleven o'clock in the evening. Before long a new form of entertainment developed in the bar: its customers would bet on whether Frankenstein's mistress would appear before eleven o'clock. All bets had to be placed by ten o'clock.

"As I listened to my neighbor at the table and looked at Frankenstein and his artificial mistress, it dawned on me that the transformation in the picture might provide the solution to the agonizing problem that had driven me from home. I explained to my tablemate that I, too, was a painter and that I would like to use the changing paints in my own work. He was glad that the invention could be of use to someone without the need to change anything in how the factory was run. He told me that I could spend the night at his place; he would take me to the company first thing in the morning."

Chapter 11
Dominik's Pictures

"That night I couldn't sleep. The room I'd been put in was almost entirely taken up with a large bed, under whose cold, heavy quilt I tossed and turned. I was asking myself if the appearing and disappearing paints really could help me; perhaps I'd fallen into an industrial trap. There in the darkness I saw all my pictures in the sequence that I'd produced them. As they passed beneath my closed eyelids they became a single changing picture. Beginning with the first drawings I'd made as a child, the canvas gradually took on all my works, right through to the clueless rippling lines of my last attempts. At the very end I saw the entirely blank canvas I'd stood in front of, helpless, in the weeks before my departure . . . But forgive me for getting carried away—this has nothing to do with Viola's disappearance."

"Please go on. Tell me everything nice and slowly. I've got plenty of time." I said this not out of courtesy but because I sensed in the story's seemingly insignificant digressions a likelihood of encountering clues that would lead me to the lost girl.

"That night, in a strange room in a little French town, I thought about the history of my paintings," Dominik continued. "In my first period, which began while I was still at the academy, I painted lone objects and empty spaces. Critics laid into me, accusing me of coldness and a lack of interest in people, but that didn't bother me. I learned how things and spaces are shy; I knew that they would speak only if they were alone and

I also knew that part of what they communicated was a report on humanity, perhaps the only report on humanity that is truly important; things know far more about us than we do ourselves. For several years I painted deserted streets and squares, walls and fences stretching from one side of the picture to the other, factory chimneys towering over hillsides, rooms someone had just left, empty chairs in morning cafés. But after a while I started to feel dissatisfaction with my work . . ."

"So you accepted what the critics had been saying about you?"

"Oh no, the accusations of antihumanism seemed to me just as silly and nonsensical as they always had. It was about something else. Suddenly I had the feeling that my humility in the face of things was inadequate, even hypocritical. I told myself that if I thought I was listening to the language of things, I was deluding myself; it's only truly possible to listen to them if the listener tries to make sense of what he hears, and in my case that meant understanding the language in which things were speaking, trying to explain what they were communicating and translating it into my own language. And I wasn't doing this—all I was doing in my pictures was repeating the quiet murmur of things.

"Making sense of the language of things and interpreting what they were saying was possible only if I tried to picture images and scenes that were concealed in their whispering. So I began to paint shapes that emerged from the breath of deserted things and spaces. I was surprised by how many magical beings, trees and plants, palaces, rocks, lakes, and seas burst forth from the heart of the silence in which things are soaked and swim, and by how many terrifying, grotesque silhouettes merged with the outline of a thing. Now when critics spoke of a lack of interest in people, I was sure that the extraordinary beings, buildings and natural structures that were beginning to appear in my pictures spoke still more clearly of humanity than the whispering of things they had grown out of, and that they revealed the secret pattern of the map by which our lives are oriented as well as the true, invisible destinations of our travels . . .

"Thus began a new period in my painting. At the end of suburban streets I painted caves, seashores and jungles; beyond the wooden fences of the suburbs I painted oriental palaces of opal; I painted fantastic plants and animals behind windows and colorful, magical birds in the roofs of apartment buildings; houses and factories burst open like pupae to reveal temples of cruel gods and castles of mysterious queens. I trained my eyes so that whenever I walked along a street they rested in an almost physical gaze on all the palaces and magic mountains. These apparitions verged on hallucination; perhaps this was the beginning of madness, but if it was, it was funny how madness merged with a strict order of cognition; in the relationships between what is known as reality and the magical spaces there was no place for the random or arbitrary, and I knew that it would be possible to create an exact science that would address the laws of these relationships.

"In my magical period I experienced strong feelings of happiness. But then a new anguish arose that was worse than the old one. I realized that in trying to express what a thing communicated, I was making a thing of the communication—an unusual and fantastic thing perhaps, but just a thing nevertheless; and in so doing I was falsifying and damaging the communication, as things speak not of things but of what is not yet a thing, a matter from which things are formed. It seemed to me that my pictures were untruthful and that I had actually played down the importance of what things were saying. Now I had the feeling that things were angry with me for translating their communication into the banal language of shapes, which was foreign to them. To punish me they fell silent again for a long time. And that was the crisis that drove me to travel Europe.

"A solution occurred to me only when I saw the painting with the mad scientist in it. It came to me that I could paint the shapes I discovered in the dreams of things in paints that were true colors only at certain moments before they disappeared; thus I would leave their fate to changes in the weather. That way I would avoid simple repetition of an undeciphered message, and at the same time shapes originating from the expirations of things would have the character of volatile revelation—they would keep switching from defined shape to shapeless memory and uncertain idea, and in that way their objectness would never be able to stabilize and close. Yes, I said to myself, as I pondered all this in bed, this may be my way out of this blind alley.

"In the morning I accompanied my new acquaintance to the factory on the edge of town. It wasn't much more than a grouping of single-story workshops connected by paths beaten through beds of dusty tomato plants. He took me directly to the young owner of the business and told him of my wish to paint pictures with the disappearing paints. I was afraid that the owner would throw us out, but to my surprise he was as helpful and kind as my host. He said he was glad to be useful to an artist in some way. Immediately he placed one call to a workshop to order samples of the paints and hard activators and another to the office for the copying of the documentation. Now I understood that although the factory owner had ceased to crave new products, he still felt bad about hiding his uncle's discovery in the warehouse. He was truly glad of my interest in the paints; indeed, perhaps he was more grateful to me than I was to him—his conscience was relieved and he didn't need to start producing anything new.

"While the samples and formulae were being prepared for me, the owner led me around the workshops and with evident pride showed me the ancient production lines for soaps, shampoos, and perfumes. He insisted that I stay for lunch, which was served by his unassuming wife at the old-fashioned villa that adjoined the factory. When I left, he gave me a small case containing a set of phials with the paints and the copied documentation. His wife gave me a basket of tomatoes and kohlrabi from their garden."

Chapter 12
Spy

"I abandoned my plan to continue to Dijon and used what remained of my money to buy a train ticket home. Within half an hour of unlocking my studio I was painting my first picture. It was of a station concourse in which from time to time the ticket windows became overgrown with an impenetrable jungle. After that I produced urban landscapes where buildings, objects, and creatures painted in the French paints appeared and disappeared unexpectedly; a plant would grow up in the middle of an empty square, a statue of an unknown queen or a large crystal would dissolve, leaving only a quiet street with parked cars, a row of houses and a graffiti'd fence . . . I used the hard activators only when painting. The clear paints would color when I warmed them using a burner beneath the canvas; some time later, of course, they would again be transparent. After that I left their appearance to chance—to the unpredictable constellation of soft activators in the air.

"Apparently things and spaces had no objection to such a subtle unveiling of their thoughts; they began to speak to me again. And they spoke so much that I didn't have time to record everything they were telling me. In June I held an exhibition of my new work. It attracted a decent amount of interest, but ultimately it brought me only disappointment—visitors and critics alike saw the pictures as little more than technical trickery.

"About a week after the opening Viola called me on the

phone. She did a little painting, she said, and she was very interested in my method, which she would love to learn about and try for herself. At first I refused her request: I didn't feel like talking about my pictures, least of all with someone for whom they were probably little more than a curiosity. But Viola would not be put off—obviously she was determined to get into my studio at any cost. Such intransigence, it seemed to me, couldn't be the product of a mere whim; as she continued to insist, the feeling in me grew that there was a connection between the paints and something extremely important to her. I began to wonder what this might be, and in the end I invited her here.

"But instead of providing an explanation, her visit just deepened my confusion. The girl who appeared at my door in a T-shirt and tattered pants was skinny, short-haired and frowning. She looked about seventeen, although she claimed to be twenty-two, which may or may not have been true, like everything else she told me . . ."

The painter looked towards the door. Perhaps his mind's eye saw Viola entering the studio on her first visit.

"She asked me in great detail about the properties and manufacture of the paints and the hard and soft activators, and she examined the formulae. From the first moment it was plain to me that she'd never held a brush in her hand and that everything she'd said on the phone about her interest in painting was just an excuse to get to me. This achieved, she never mentioned her painting again—she made no attempt to behave in accordance with her original lie. Apparently she was sure I would let her stay and tell her everything she wanted to know—and regrettably she was right. She came to see me every day. When she wasn't looking at the documentation and taking notes, all we ever did was talk about the paints.

"It was obvious that she had known something about the paints before they appeared in my exhibition. But how could she have learned the contents of a package that had lain for years at the bottom of a drawer in an out-of-the-way French town, which even the closest family of the man who had hidden it there had known nothing about? There was little doubt that the package with the formulae had been stored away when Viola was a small child and that nobody had removed it since. On the other hand, judging by what she asked me about the properties of the paints, she seemed to have only the most superficial knowledge of the documents contained in the package. I was miles away from guessing what she needed to find out so urgently. I often watched her as she studied the formulae—the look of concentration on her face, the way her hands would shake when she turned a page—and it seemed to me that she was making a strenuous effort to find something that was more important than anything else in her life."

"Did you ever ask her what she was looking for?"

"Of course I did—in the early days I asked her all the time. But she always gave the same reply: 'I told you—I want to paint pictures like yours.' She never tried to make it sound even a little convincing, which I found mortifying as it seemed like she was ridiculing me, and it made me angry with her. I don't suppose you would understand why I didn't throw her out . . ."

"Oh, I would. It's not really that complicated. You'd simply fallen in love with her."

The painter sighed. "You're right, of course. It was a strange love, the most terrible I've ever known—worse than all the crises of my painting. I don't know what my love contained more of, love or anger. And it didn't stay at anger, it became hate. Whenever Viola left I found I was shaking with rage. I told myself over and over again that when she appeared the next day I wouldn't let her in, and I repeated the words I would say to her. But such ideas were the only delights of my wretched solitude. Deep in my soul I knew that when Viola turned up again, I would be happy to see her. Yet even now I don't understand what was feeding my obsession. It wasn't as if I knew anything at all about Viola. We'd never spoken about anything but the paints and their properties. If I asked her about her life, she always gave me an absentminded answer, a lie that she'd thought up on the spur of the moment—and then she went back to the paints and their chemistry."

"Perhaps there was some connection between your falling

in love with Viola and her mysteriousness. There's a thin line between the sense of mystery a woman evokes and love, and certain women are very well able to take advantage of this."

"I agree. But a skinny girl who looks altogether ordinary and talks the whole day about nothing but chemistry doesn't match most people's idea of a woman of mystery. I imagine that most men would have said that if there were any mystery about her, it wasn't worth finding out."

"Did you ever let her know that you were fond of her?"

"Not for a long time. At first I was waiting for the right moment, but then I realized that the right moment would never present itself. I'm not backward in coming forward, but in Viola's behavior I never read any indication of coquetry or the slightest interest in eroticism; there were no moments of closeness between us. All she was interested in was the chemistry of the paints and the activators. At the thought of the indifferent or irritated look with which she met my every declaration, I lost all courage to speak and continued to suffer in silence."

"Did she notice what you were going through?"

"I'm sure she did, and that made me even more embarrassed. Then one day when I asked again why she really came to see me and she repeated the stupid lie about her interest in painting, and I realized how she was using me without even bothering to think up a more plausible tale, I couldn't take it anymore. All the rage and hate I'd tried to suppress for so long came bubbling to the surface and I raised my hand as if to strike her . . ."

Dominik fell silent. I felt guilty for having woken bad memories that quite possibly he had succeeded in putting to rest only recently, and I asked myself if this man's pain was not too high a price to pay for a search that was probably pointless. But in any case it was now too late to put things right.

"I didn't strike her," the painter went on after a few moments. "But I did start yelling at her about how I couldn't stand her. I told her to leave and never come back. If she rang my doorbell again I wouldn't open up, I said. While all this was going on she just stood there calmly searching my face. My outburst gave me no relief; in fact I felt worse than I'd felt before. Viola could make up her own mind about whether to stay or go. I lay down on my bed and watched the clouds through the window. A little while later I heard her quiet steps on the parquet. She lay down beside me and embraced me without speaking.

"That was the beginning of our strange relationship, if I can even call it that. Viola never pretended to have any feelings for me. She gave herself to me without restraint but she never asked anything of me. As soon as it was over she would get dressed quickly, sit back down to the documentation and carry on with her note-taking. Sometimes she would ask me about some technical matter. I don't think she was repelled by our lovemaking but nor did she particularly desire it. Instead of feeling calmer, I felt more humiliated still: perhaps our lovemaking was first and foremost a reward for services rendered. But although I now felt an even bigger fool, I could no longer tell Viola not to come to me. In the end she left of her own accord, as soon as she found what she was looking for in my studio, I suppose."

Chapter 13
A Deadly Invention

"Have you ever wondered what she actually wanted to find out from you?"

"In the month after she left I did practically nothing else. I sat in the studio amid my unfinished paintings and went over all the possibilities. Naturally I couldn't shake the idea that there was some connection between Viola's secret and that of the former owner of the chemical factory. But to explain one mystery by another was a pretty hopeless undertaking. In any case, in the void between two fragmentary and incomprehensible life stories, different tales were born. For instance, might the odd uncle of the current owner have made some staggering discovery in the course of his experiments, taken fright at the possible consequences and destroyed the documentation that could have made it a reality, while hiding the formulae for the paints in the closet drawer? Viola might have found out about the discovery, perhaps from an erstwhile assistant of the former owner, who may have told her that the way to the discovery was through the formuale for the paints. But this owes more to imagination than deduction, of course."

The painter sighed.

"But maybe the key to Viola's secret really is to be found in fiction," I said. "If you were to write a novel, what would this terrible discovery be?"

"Something that would explain the solitary life of the former boss after his return to France and before his departure for Greece. Even as they were telling me about him in France, I had the feeling that he was running from something or atoning for something. Perhaps his discovery had spawned some great evil. I thought of the picture in the bar in the French town—when the artist painted the mad scientist and his dangerous research, was he not thinking of the factory's former owner, whom he must have known? Often I would sit here for hours on end, just thinking about it all, not even switching on the lights. And there in the darkness—formed from my childhood reading and the faces of Doctors Moreau and Frankenstein and also the professor in Verne's *Facing the Flag*, whose name I've forgotten—the vaguely defined face of the inventor would appear next to Viola's . . . And Viola and the inventor would look at each other conspiratorially as they guarded their common secret from me. I told myself that it might concern a weapon or a chemical substance that affected genetic structure."

"What if the mysterious inventor had created a monster by genetic manipulation and then taken fright at his invention?" I suggested.

"I, too, had ideas like that—and even crazier ones. All of them were fictions. But I confess that at one time I was so clueless that I almost began to take my own fantasies seriously. I had dozens of stories about secret weapons and artificial beings. Then it occurred to me that things might not be like that at all. I realized that the paints were capable of reacting to the presence of trace amounts of a substance in the air, provided that substance was a soft activator. I said to myself, What if there is no mysterious discovery? What if Viola needed a paint as a detector, and the whole time she was with me she was trying to determine which of them was suitable for this purpose?"

"A detector?" I said, surprised. "A detector of what?"

"I don't know that, of course. But it would have to be something that wasn't easy to detect by other means. Something concealed in a cavity that was difficult to penetrate, but which released at least a few molecules of its inner atmosphere through a super-thin gap or a tiny crack. Maybe something hidden in a deep cellar or an underground passage . . ."

"Or in an underground cave?"

"In an underground cave, if you so wish . . ."

"OK, so what then?"

"Luckily, I eventually succeeded in forgetting about Viola and the stories I'd built up around her. And I hoped that I would never hear her name again."

"I'm sorry for having reminded you. I won't bother you for much longer. Just one more thing—you still haven't said anything about the symbol that you painted in the portrait."

"Viola had it tattooed on the left side of her belly. When I asked her what it meant, she said it had no meaning, it was merely decorative."

"Did you believe her?"

"I didn't believe a word she said. But perhaps it really was as she said. Who knows? I painted her portrait at a time when I'd begun to feel she was getting close to what she was looking for and would soon be leaving me. Once, when the portrait was almost finished, I was alone in the studio when the idea came to me of adding something in the French paints that had brought us together. My eye was drawn to one of the windows in the background, so it was over the dark interior visible through that window that I painted the same space in the bright light of a chandelier. Let chance decide when the room should be lit, I told myself. The outline of a picture could be seen on the wall at the back of the dark room. At first I thought about painting a landscape in the frame, but then I remembered the symbol tattooed on Viola's body and opted for that. I told Viola nothing about the invisible part of the picture, so I don't know if she even discovered it before her disappearance."

The restless symbol had moved from the dump to a computer screen, on to a painting hanging in the creepy villa of an erstwhile theoretician in Socialist Realism, then on to the skin of the theoretician's daughter, along the way revealing nothing about its meaning. Where else might it appear? In what place would I finally catch up with it? Or would it run from me forever?

"Did Viola ever mention any people she associated with?" I asked the painter. "If she was looking for something, chances are she was searching in other places, too . . ."

"I've told you already that she confided nothing in me. I have to admit that in the days when she made me most jealous, I went through her bag several times while she was in the shower. But I never found anything—no address book, no phone numbers, no letters . . . Once I woke up early in the morning to find her in the hall, talking quietly on the phone. Although I held my breath, I didn't manage to catch a single word of what she was saying. But I was surprised by her tone: I had the impression that it contained something like tenderness, a feeling that she'd never shown me and I'd assumed was foreign to her. At that moment my insides were gripped by a burning jealousy. No sooner was Viola out of the apartment than I raced to the telephone and pressed redial . . ."

"Did anyone pick up?"

"Yes, Nereus."

"The sea god?"

"For all I know, he may have been. The voice was male and deep. It said 'Nereus' and I hung up."

I asked the artist if he still used the changing paints in his pictures.

"I didn't paint anything at all for a long time. Now, slowly, I'm getting back into it."

"Things are speaking to you again?"

"Most of the time they're silent, but occasionally they whisper something that I barely understand, and I'm grateful for even that; I paint their incomprehensible whisperings. I don't use the French paints anymore. I've realized there's no point: Shapes in pictures disappear anyway, lost in memory and forgotten more thoroughly than any chemistry can manage."

The painter went over to some canvases propped against the wall and turned them round for me to see. Each displayed a few simple lines that ran together; some were reminiscent of tangled threads, others of undulating cigarette smoke. It seemed to me that the painter was right: they expressed nothing more than a life of waving and bending, twisting and untwisting that was closed in on itself and had no desire to assume any shape. And if the lines in the pictures did actually say anything, their tongue was so old and so distant from our languages that there was no hope of our ever understanding it.

"I almost forgot," said the painter. "About a month after Viola left me, I had another encounter with the symbol tattooed on her body."

I looked up from the paintings and asked the painter where he had seen it.

"I didn't actually see it," he said. "I read a short story in a literary magazine in which it was described so accurately that it couldn't have been anything else. It was written by Jiří Zajíc. When I stopped by the magazine's office to ask who this Jiří Zajíc was, they told me that the story had arrived in the mail and that the author's name was probably a pseudonym. He didn't even claim his fee, I was told. I've still got the magazine here somewhere. If you're interested, you can have it. It's the last thing that connects me to Viola and I'd be glad to get rid of it."

For some moments the painter rummaged through the magazines piled high on the floor and leaning against the dresser. He found the one he was looking for and handed it to me.

We said our goodbyes. I went out into the dark corridor and ran down the steps.

Chapter 14
Paper Women

As soon as I reached the street I headed straight for a nearby bar, which was empty but for three men in overalls sitting together over flat beer, watching a soccer match on a TV on a high shelf, next to a figure of Mickey Mouse woven in black wire. The bartender sat down at their table and started to watch the match with them. I took a seat next to a broad window and laid the magazine down on the table in front of me. For a while I looked out at the unpopulated street that was by now bathed in the warm shadows of evening. Only the balconies on the upper floors of the buildings opposite were still in sunlight. I had the feeling I was looking up at a distant shore from the bottom of a deep lake whose waters were crystal-clear.

Scenes from the painter's story appeared to me like movie clips. In rapid succession I saw images of the French town, the exhibition hall and the painter's studio, all accompanied by the gabbling of the TV sports commentator. At the conclusion of a dramatic on-screen goalmouth incident the bartender got up and came over to me. I discovered that there was no cooked food, as the cook was on vacation, so I ordered a double portion of headcheese and a beer. Moments later the bartender set a plate and a glass in front of me; then he returned to his soccer match. When I had finished my meal, I reached for the magazine and found the short story the painter had told me about. I took a slug of beer and began to read.

Jiří Zajíc
Letters of the Night

It was a summer night and Tomáš couldn't sleep. Long after midnight he was still tossing and turning in his large double bed. His wife had gone on vacation with the children, and he wasn't used to being on his own at night. To top it all, it was unbearably hot. Tomáš threw off his duvet, sat up in bed and looked from the dark room through the open window at a city whose streets were lit only by streetlamps and bright-colored neon. He considered switching on the bedside lamp to read in order to drive away the thoughts that were troubling him and so at last fall asleep, but then he realized that if he did, he would soon hear the annoying whistle of mosquitoes and the confused buzzing of moths. So instead he reached for the shelf above the bed and his binoculars, which he put to his eyes. Slowly he moved the glasses back and forth across the colorful words of one neon sign after another.

Then he focused on two words, the first of six letters woven in glowing blue neon tubes and the second of eight—but what were these letters? Tomáš had never seen a script like it. Each word began with the same character. Its upper part looked something like a Greek psi and its lower reminded Tomáš of a fork; at the very bottom was a zero lying on its side or perhaps a potato, which the fork had stuck its tines in. Now Tomáš was angry with himself for picking the binoculars up. The mysterious sign had so engaged his attention that the last remnants of his sleepiness were dispelled; now he knew he wouldn't get to sleep before dawn. As far as he could tell, the sign wasn't far away, so he got dressed and went out into the nighttime streets to get a closer look at it.

Before long Tomáš found himself in front of the metal gate of some company or other. It was difficult to tell whether the low, light-colored building housed a workshop or an office. Above the gate rose a frame of metal tubing filled with wire mesh; to this mesh were attached the glowing blue letters he had seen in his binoculars. Although he was now looking at the sign up close, he couldn't make any more sense of it now than he had earlier. A small door was built into the large gate. As it was ajar, he peeped inside and saw that a light was still burning in one of the first-floor windows.

He told himself that maybe there was someone in there who would explain the meaning of the sign; after that he would be able to go back to bed and maybe he would manage to fall asleep. He crept up to the closed window and looked cautiously into the building. In the middle of a large room well lit by strip lighting in the ceiling was an oval-shaped mahogany table behind which were sitting seven young women in white blouses and gray, beige, and mauve skirt suits; in front of each woman was a pile of documents. Although one chair was empty, there was also a pile of papers in front of it. From the head of the table a fair-haired woman in black square-framed glasses was talking. Tomáš could see her lips moving, but through the closed window he couldn't hear a word she was saying. This woman looked like the boss even though she was younger than the others—nineteen at most. On the floor next to her a Great Dane with spiny gray hair was sleeping fitfully.

It seemed that the women were having an important meeting that had run on into the night. Although Tomáš was wary of disturbing them, he didn't wish to give up on the intention that had brought him here, so he stood at the window, irresolute. I'll wait a while and see if they have a break, he told himself. Maybe one of them will come outside for a smoke. But then the woman in the square glasses spotted Tomáš's face, stood up and came to open the window.

"Come on in, we've been waiting for you," she said. "You're late."

While Tomáš was deciding whether or not to run away, one of the women got up diligently from the table, opened the door and pushed him into the room. Another woman pulled out the empty chair and offered it to him with a smile. So Tomáš sat down, and he was surprised by the strange softness of the chair, as though he were sitting on a pile of old rags. The table, too, which had looked so solid, bent under the weight of his arms. He looked about, his face set in a puzzled smile. Having retaken her seat at the head of the table, the boss said to him, "Please be quick. We're waiting on the annual report." The women looked at him in silence. "There must be some mistake," said Tomáš. "You must be taking me for someone else." The women laughed. "We appreciate your sense of humor," said the boss impatiently, "but that's enough of it for now, we don't have time. The annual report is on the table in front of you, so please get on with it." Embarrassed, Tomáš rummaged through the papers, but all he saw on them were characters like the ones over the company's gate. The incomprehensible text contained illustrations in the form of graphs and black-and-white Xeroxed photographs, some of which were of complex machinery; others appeared to be illustrations from a treatise on unicellular organisms and others still seemed to have been taken from a pornographic magazine. Tomáš shuddered when he recognized in one of the latter the living room of his own apartment. On the couch, kneeling between two tattooed men with soft, sagging bellies, was a naked woman. The poor quality of the Xerox copy notwithstanding, he recognized this woman as his wife. On a shelf above the couch were framed photographs of their children.

"That's my wife!" Tomáš groaned, as he shot a look of reproach at the boss. He realized that he had been pursued all his life by a strange anxiety; he had never been able to determine what he was actually anxious about, but now, suddenly, he knew this was it, it was here at last. His terror was shot through with a feeling of happiness, which no doubt came from the knowledge that the worst was behind him and he was free of his anxiety once and for all . . . "Who else would it be if not your wife?" said the boss with impatience and irony. "So are you going to get down to your reading or not?" "I won't read anything," babbled Tomáš, as he pushed the papers as far across the table as he could. "I won't read. I don't know your script and the photographs in your records are disgusting."

The Great Dane was roused from its doze by the raising of its mistress's voice; perhaps it thought that someone was hurting her and she needed protection. It jumped onto all fours, bared its teeth and approached Tomáš. As its growling became ever more menacing, Tomáš got to his feet in panic without realizing that he was still gripping the annual report containing the photograph of his wife. At his back the chair fell to the floor. Tomáš retreated to the door, only to find that it was now locked. The dog came closer and closer, still growling darkly. Tomáš rested his back against the door and slid down it until he was sitting on the floor. Would he truly receive no help from any of the women? Would they allow him to be torn to pieces by a bloodthirsty beast simply for his refusal to read something to them? But the women remained seated at the table, motionless, just looking at him. "You're evil—all of you!" Tomáš shouted at them. By now the dog was almost touching him with its nose; Tomáš could feel its hot, quick breath on his face; he curled up into a ball, covering his head with his hands as he waited for the sharp fangs to sink into him.

But for a whole minute—maybe two—nothing happened, so he opened a small crack in the hands over his face and looked out. The dog was still standing in front of him, but it appeared to be unwell: it was struggling to stay on its feet, and, odder still, strange, horizontal stripes were breaking out all over its body—and for this Tomáš had no explanation. So captivated was he by these changes that he forgot his fear, placed his hands in his lap and took a long, close look at the dog, whose legs were more and more unstable and whose stripes were ever more distinct. Then Tomáš took a look at the women at the table. To his great surprise he saw that pronounced stripes had appeared on their bodies, too, and that the corrugation had even spread to the table the women were sitting at. No longer afraid of the dog, Tomáš looked into its eyes. But they were eyes no longer, just as the open mouth was not a mouth. There was still something of the animal in its outline, as if it were holding itself together with the last of its strength, but its transformation into a pile of old, torn, soggy newspaper was by now almost complete.

Tomáš was even more interested in what had happened to the women. They were in much the same state as the dog; though their outlines could still be made out, their bodies were piles of old newspaper rather than human figures. He stood up and went over to them to take a closer look. In the silhouette of one of the piles, the profile of the boss was still discernible and her soft skin remained in some places, but as Tomáš brushed her belly with his forefinger he felt its skin dry and crack to form the edges of sheets of paper. Her painted lips lasted longest; when he touched them he felt their heat, and they were still moving slightly but no longer making any sound. At that moment Tomáš didn't know whether the boss wished to berate him or to whisper words of conciliation; but then the lips, too, were transformed into old paper.

Tomáš took a step back to examine the boss. She had become a wobbly pile made up of bundles of old magazines and newspapers, school exercise books with their pages filled, forms, advertising leaflets and disintegrating books. When Tomáš prodded the pile, it wobbled some more and the bundle that made up the top half of the boss's head fell off; then the whole boss collapsed. Now scattered about the floor were bundles of paper that had obviously lain outside in the rain, as they were curled and stuck together and covered in brown stains.

Tomáš looked at the other women. They, too, had changed into bundles of soggy magazines and newspapers. The table they had been sitting at had also become a pile of scrap paper. Tomáš was dumbfounded by this universal transformation into paper. Fearfully he inspected the skin of his hands, which he then moved about his body; no, luckily it seemed that for now he was not changing into torn magazines. He looked out of the window. Day was breaking, and in the dim light Tomáš studied the plaster on the walls of the buildings outside: they showed no sign of the folding and splitting that was going on inside. He breathed a sigh of relief—for a moment he'd had the image of a city and its inhabitants transformed into piles of scrap paper. Nothing had changed outside but the neon characters over the entrance. From his standpoint he could see the mesh sign in mirrored, back-to-front form. But even so he recognized that each character had changed into another character of the same size; the mysterious legend had been replaced by the shining words "Scrap Salvage." The change was not yet quite complete—unabsorbed pieces of the nighttime characters were still visible in the letters of day. For instance, although the first letter of each word was clearly an "S," in their upper parts, like stunted outgrowths there remained short, thin remnants of the lateral arcs of the symbol. But as Tomáš watched, these outgrowths quickly shortened, and soon there was nothing about either "S" shape to distinguish it from any other "S."

Chapter 15
Concerns of a Collection Point Manager

I put the magazine down for a moment, finished my beer and ordered another. Now the sun was illuminating only the chimneys on the rooftops. No more customers had entered the bar. The soccer match was still going on; only now did I realize that the commentator's voice had been audible the whole time I'd been reading the story. It occurred to me that it would be possible to illustrate the story using the technique discovered by Dominik: the piles of paper would be painted in the French paints over the figures of the women, who would become paper at a certain moment (or it might be the other way round). I wondered if there was some connection between the object at the dump and the characters in blue neon; indeed, it had occurred to me at the dump that the object might be part of an inscription of some sort. But then I told myself that the paper collection point in the story was an invention and that neither the changing letters nor the paper women belonged to the real world. Viola's case had given rise to a great deal of conjecture and a great many fantastical fictions, I reasoned. I was worried that there would soon be so many insistent images connected with it that I would be unable to distinguish them from reality. But for the time being I was yet to believe in the realness of the paper women. I took a swig of beer and returned to my reading.

Only now did Tomáš realize that he still had the annual report in his hand. He saw that it had changed into a ragged copy of a car magazine. Carefully and anxiously he turned the yellow-spotted pages: There was no sign of the unknown script, nor of the horrible photograph. Still, he was less than calm—he couldn't rid himself of the anxious feeling that one night soon the photograph would reappear. He considered throwing the magazine away, but then he folded it and put it in his pocket.

Tomáš heard the rattle of keys in the lock of the door. He was startled: Was he about to come under attack again? He looked around for something he could use as a weapon, but all he saw were bundles of scrap paper. But the slight, bald man who stepped into the room looked harmless, even kindly. He betrayed no surprise at seeing Tomáš among the piles of paper. Smiling, the man called from the door, "Don't tell me—the paper women have been giving you a hard time, right? How about I make you a cup of coffee? When I see the women next, I'll tell them to exercise a little more restraint." Relieved, Tomáš asked what kind of creatures they were. "They're paper women," said the man with a shrug, as though there was nothing to add. "Do they appear here every night?" To this question the man, presumably the manager of the facility, nodded. "Is it always the same women?" Tomáš continued. "Yes," said the man. "I know them all by now, and they know me, too." Tomáš thought for a moment before saying: "Then there's one thing I don't understand. I suppose that people keep bringing paper to the collection point and that from time to time this paper is taken away. That would mean that the same women are produced from different paper." "I don't understand it too well either," conceded the manager. "But that's the way it is. Every night it really is the same women and the same dog, all produced from the paper that's here at the time. All that's required is that it's old and damp enough. A few times it's happened that the paper was too new—unused fliers and the like—and then all that appeared was a woman's head here and a few fingers there."

The manager settled comfortably on the bundles that a while earlier had been the nighttime boss. Apparently he was glad to have someone to complain to. "I don't know why it is that paper women have become so widespread recently. Ten years ago they appeared only at two or three places in the whole republic; now they're at almost every collection point. When I started working here, I tried to work out what to do with them. Everyone had his own reliable means of getting rid of them; I probably tried them all, but none of them worked for me. In the end I told myself it was best just to leave them be. They're harmless, so why not let them manage their own affairs at night, if it means so much to them? Sometimes they attract a nighttime walker and give him a proper fright, but they never truly hurt anyone. They couldn't even if they wanted to: they're made of paper, and their dog even has paper teeth. In winter, when the days are shortest, I meet them in the morning and they try it with me, too, but I ignore them; I just drink my coffee and see to my delivery notes. From time to time I look over to see if they've turned back into paper. The truck drivers don't bother about them at all—in the dark mornings when they're hurrying to take the paper away, they think nothing of throwing a woman onto the loading platform, and they're oblivious to their threats and yells. "What about the letters over the entrance?" asked Tomáš. "You're right—that's the only serious problem," the manager of the collection point conceded. "Most of the time that doesn't matter either—how many people would notice unintelligible lettering above a collection point? And if people do happen to notice it, it rarely occurs to them to go somewhere to complain about it. But people are strange, and it has happened a few times. Why should they care about the fact that for a few hours at night the letters above the collection point are different from the ones that are there during the day? And what am I supposed to do about it?"

By now Tomáš was no longer listening to the manager's prattling; he couldn't stop thinking about the photograph of his wife. "Last night," he said, keeping his voice low out of embarrassment and for fear that the women might still be able to hear him, even though they had returned to paper, "I saw a photograph that upset me very much. I know that it was just a part of their freak show, but still . . . do you think there might be something in it?" "My goodness, you can't let a thing like that worry you! That whole world's nothing but scrap paper," said the manager. But Tomáš was less than convinced by these words; he had the feeling that the man was trying to calm him down and was not telling him all he knew. It was suspicious that he had been so chatty a while ago and now he was standing there in silence. Had the paper women shown him something like that, too? Tomáš knew that as soon as he got home he would hide the car magazine at the bottom of a drawer and in many nights thereafter go to it in secret to check if it had changed back into the nighttime women's document. Realizing that he would get nothing more out of the manager, he said goodbye and went home. After his experiences of that night he felt wretched, and he knew that he would struggle to shake the feeling. Out on the street he told himself that next time he saw some unintelligible lettering, he would do well to ignore it.

Although I wasn't sure whether the last sentence contained the moral of the story, perhaps I should take its wisdom to heart. I pondered a possible connection between the mysterious figures of Viola, Zajíc and the former owner of the factory in France, in addition to the double-trident connection between Viola and Zajíc and the disappearing-paints connection between Viola and the French chemist. Although my search for Viola had only just begun, I was assailed by a sense of futility; it seemed to me that I would never discover a connection between the figures that had emerged. And even if I did, more than likely it would turn out that the symbol on Viola's body was the emblem of some rock band she'd had made into a tattoo when she was sixteen, and that the object at the dump—the same emblem—had hung from the stage when the band had played live. Maybe Viola really had inquired about the paints because she was interested in painting and it was Dominik's jealousy that had kept finding hidden motives in her behavior and eventually dreamed up a deadly invention and a mysterious detector.

I wondered, too, if the motif of young women who lived in a strange nighttime space beyond our world was some kind of symbol that held a clue to where Viola was hiding or being held. I realized that the nighttime office in the short story I'd just read had induced in me similar feelings to those I'd had when I'd tried to imagine the place where Viola now lived, although it was difficult to imagine an appearance less like those of the elegant nighttime women managers than Viola's as I'd seen it in the portrait and photos.

The nighttime lettering and Viola's tattoo remained the only real connection between the short story and Viola, but even that connection was questionable. The author described the character in broad terms, and it was understandable that both the painter and I had seen in it the symbol that was so much on our minds. When I reread the words the short-story writer used to describe the character, I realized that it might look quite different. Zajíc made no mention of the horizontal line that separated the upper part of the character from its lower part. And even if he really did have in mind the same character, that didn't mean that he knew anything about its meaning. Perhaps he was in the same boat as the painter and I: He had encountered the mysterious figure somewhere or other, wondered what it meant, failed to come up with anything, and so had written a story about it in order to deal with it somehow.

So on the whole I was none the wiser. Maybe the author was talking about the character I knew, maybe he wasn't. If he was, then maybe the story had something to do with Viola, but maybe it didn't. If there was a connection, it might be of some help in my search for Viola, but this was unlikely. So I decided to put Zajíc and his writing out of my mind. Again I heard the voice of the TV commentator and the murmur of customers in the bar; I could smell cigarette smoke and I was aware of odors wafting from the kitchen. I looked around: there were more customers in the bar now, although most seats were still empty. The buildings on the other side of the street were now entirely immersed in shadow, and all that remained of the sunshine were stripes of orange and violet on the bottom of a cloud. I paid up and went home.

As I lay in bed I couldn't stop myself from thinking about the painter's narrative and the short story I'd read in the bar. I went over all that I'd heard and read. Was there really nothing in all those words that might turn up some kind of clue to lead me to Viola? When I came to the part where the painter talked about Viola's phone call, I sat up. What if Viola had been searching for a deadly invention or a treasure in an underground cave? But I refused to believe that a god of the sea had a telephone. I got out of bed, switched on the light, picked up the non-commercial telephone directory and went to the letter "N." Nerad, Neradil, Nergl, Neruda . . . Then I picked up the commercial one. Neos Computer Ltd., Neoset, Nepa Ltd., Nepal round-the-clock locksmith service, Neptune Plus Ltd. (so gods really were listed); Nera Ltd., Neret Ltd., Nereus Ltd. On a slip of paper I wrote down the telephone number and address of the latter. Then I went back to bed. This time I managed to get to sleep quite readily.

Chapter 16
Nereus

When I woke up it was after ten. I made myself a cup of coffee and sat down with it by the telephone. I dialed the number I'd written down in the night. The call was picked up and a male voice named the deity of the sea. I asked about the business that Nereus Ltd. was engaged in. After a moment of astonished silence, the voice replied in an almost offended tone, "Pump manufacture, of course." I finished my coffee and set out to find the company's offices.

It was the first overcast day in a long time, although it was still hot. The humidity that trickled from everything transformed into dense odors. I suffered through a few stops on the streetcar, which I alighted at the beginning of the street whose name I'd found in the phone directory. There was rather a lot of traffic here. I passed the Neo-Renaissance and Art Nouveau facades of banks and government offices, buildings not much lower than those downtown. Overhead, lounging across doorways and oblivious to my progress, floated half-naked stucco women with dusty bosoms; higher still, edging towards the invisible land that extends behind us, the heads of National Revivalists grew from the facades like great polypores. Behind most of the windows I passed stood designer-clothed mannequins, rigid in mysterious gestures. If Nereus was housed in the vicinity of these splendid caves of luxury, it was surely a big international company.

But then the street underwent a quiet transformation that

was first reflected in the storefront windows. The mannequins disappeared and the displays came to contain more and more objects and ever more clutter; before long I had the feeling that the accumulated pressure of things would cause the windows to shatter and the goods to spill onto the sidewalk. I met ever fewer pedestrians and the cars gradually disappeared into the side streets; after a while the streetcar rails swerved away and were lost. On my face I felt a warm drizzle whose drops seemed to be coming not from above but out of the supersaturated odors.

Although the street continued under the same name, it had changed as if by magic. I still passed windows of stores, but now their tired, resigned expressions told a sorrowful tale: their proprietors didn't have enough money to rent in the elegant part of the street and had settled here in the hope that something of its liveliness would spill over. This hope had proved to be a vain one. The window displays of some stores still comprised chaotic piles, but others had been emptied and offered a view of dusty shelves on which the only exhibits were dead flies lying on their backs. No car had passed for some time.

Then I saw it above the treetops on the other side of the street: the word "NEREUS" in big letters which sailed on three regular waves representing water. The angular, glass-encased two-story building had probably been built in the sixties, and it appeared that the glass of its facade hadn't been washed since then. Through the open windows of the second floor I spotted drawing boards and glowing computer screens. This building was adjacent to a lower one with a saw-tooth roof. I supposed that the glass building housed the designers' studios and offices and the low one was the assembly shop. The glass building had its own entrance. When I walked in nobody stopped me, so I proceeded up the stairs to the second floor. I found myself in a well-lit corridor with a green felt carpet, along one side of which ran a glass wall showing the roofs of workshops and the wilted treetops beyond; the other side of the corridor was lined with closed doors. After walking indecisively from one end of the corridor to the other several times, I gathered up my courage and opened a door at random.

I found myself in a large room full of people bent over desks covered with papers, standing at drawing boards or staring at computer screens. I realized that I could have entered by any of the doors—all opened onto this room. No one took any notice of me. I stepped up to the man seated nearest to the door, took out the photograph of Viola, placed it on the desk in front of him and asked if he knew her. He looked at the photo absently and said, "Yes, I remember her, she's one of our customers. I think Julie dealt with her order." He pointed out a young woman seated several desks away with her back to me and returned immediately to his papers. Julie was wearing a simple summer dress and had wavy black hair that reached down her suntanned back. Apparently her eyes were glued to her computer, and as she gently moved the mouse a luminous cobweb turned about on the screen. It was probably a spatial diagram of some kind of instrument.

I walked down the aisle between desks and drawing boards to where Julie was sitting, leaned towards her and asked if she knew Viola Jonášová. She flinched and turned her face to me; from out of the wavy black hair appeared a dark complexion with heavy eyebrows and full lips. Before answering she looked me up and down. "Yes, I worked on her order a while ago," she said at last. "But I haven't seen her since then."

The indifference with which she said this was not very convincing. I heard in her words a disquiet that I knew from the painter's voice; apparently Viola left this in everyone she knew. Even now I didn't believe that Viola had been just another of the customers who ordered a pump from the company, and for me this was a good sign. Wanting to test her, I said, "Forgive me for interrupting your work. I was hoping you might be able to tell me something about Viola." And with that I made as if I was about to leave.

"Why are you asking about Viola? Has something happened to her?" Julie looked at me with an expression of anxiety that she didn't try to hide. I told her that Viola had been missing for two years and I was trying to find her, and that I was right at the beginning of my search and things weren't looking too promising so far.

"Do you think she's suffered some kind of misfortune?" Julie asked. It was obvious that she was really worried about Viola.

"I don't know, but I don't think so," I said reassuringly. "There's something strange about her disappearance and I don't understand it much, but I'd say that for some reason Viola is hiding somewhere."

"I'd like to help you," said Julie. "And I'd like to help Viola. Maybe you're wrong, maybe she really is in danger and waiting for help. When I was working for her we became friends and she came to mean a lot to me, maybe she still does . . . But I haven't seen her for a long time, and I've no idea where she might be."

"Did she disappear from one day to the next without saying goodbye?" I asked, as it occurred to me that this was Viola's usual way of breaking with people.

"Yes," said Julie. "But I wasn't angry with her. I'd suspected it was going to happen. The whole time Viola was trying to get through to somebody or something, and probably the moment came when she couldn't stay with me any longer, even though we were good together." She gave this some thought and then said, "Yes, I think she felt good with me." Again she paused briefly, before asking: "How did you know that she left me without saying anything? Did she do something like that with you? And is that why you're looking for her?"

An image came to me of Viola and Julie as little girls holding hands, one frowning and rebellious, the other anxious.

"Oh no," I said quickly, again to reassure her. "Viola and I have never met. And to be honest, I don't even know why I'm looking for her. One reason is that I feel sorry for her sick father. Did you know him?"

"No, Viola never introduced us, and I wasn't interested anyway. Do you have any clues yet?"

"Nothing to speak of. So far I've only spoken to one person who knew Viola and read a short story that might have some connection with her disappearance. And what I've heard and read hasn't helped me much, in fact if anything it's made things more muddled and obscure. I was hoping to learn more from you."

"I'm afraid I have to disappoint you," said Julie with a sigh. "Viola confided nothing in me, and I think there were certain things she never spoke about with anyone—or perhaps only with those mysterious associates she sometimes called on the phone and never told me anything about. From the very beginning I had the feeling she was keeping a secret, but even now I've no idea what it might have been."

In this matter, it seemed, the testimonies of everyone who knew Viola would coincide.

"How about we sit down together somewhere and you tell me about Viola?" I asked. "Maybe some small thing that you consider unimportant will connect with something I've found out and reveal at least a little of Viola's secret."

"OK, let's give it a try. I've got something to finish up here, but it's my lunch break in half an hour. Across the street you'll find the Blue Parrot café. Wait there and I'll come and join you."

Chapter 17
The Blue Parrot

Outside it was still drizzling. The cafe's sign showed a brightly colored parrot whose feathers were predominantly blue; its head was cocked to one side to take a good look at the customers who entered. In the window's reflection I could see the trees on the other side of the street, the building of the Nereus company and the hieroglyph that the reflection made of the letters above its entrance. I pressed my forehead and nose against the glass and the reflection cleared. What I saw now was a small room with too many tables and chairs. There appeared to be no one inside. I stepped into a café with no customers and no staff in sight. The scent of burning sandalwood sticks hung in the air; on the walls were copies of African masks and Tibetan mandalas. I couldn't imagine that many people who lived in this area would go to a café, and I was moved by the defiance the proprietor must be showing in refusing to turn his unvisited café into a taproom or a penny arcade.

I supposed that this room had served originally as a small store, perhaps selling dairy products or vegetables. In order to reach the window where I was certain the store's display had been, I had to create an aisle for myself between the chairs and tables; it was this shuffling of furniture that summoned the waiter from the back. I presumed that this thin young man with dreadlocks reaching halfway down his back was also the proprietor. He was wearing a Nepalese or Andean tunic and had colorful wooden beads around his neck. After ordering a coffee, I went to the coat rack and took down a wooden frame containing a newspaper. On discovering that the newspaper was a month old, I hung it back up again. I sat there listening to the buzz of the ceiling fan and looking at the street beyond the window, of which little was visible. An old woman went past slowly, dragging in her wake a bag on wheels that made regular creaking sounds. A fat dog hobbled on crooked legs along the sidewalk behind her. Then a delivery van drove down the street. After that, all was still beyond the window. I hadn't finished my coffee when I saw Julie crossing the street.

All she ordered was a large bottle of water. Once the waiter had brought this she began on her story.

"Viola turned up at Nereus in the middle of August two years ago. She came to my desk and spoke to me. I don't know why she chose me—women customers always go to one of my male colleagues. She told me that she needed a special pump made. I started to ask her about where this pump would be put, what purpose it should serve and the type of water it was intended for. Viola answered none of these questions; instead she took from her pocket a folded sheet of paper that she spread out in front of me. It was a Xerox copy of a diagram of a pump. Actually it was a set of twelve small pumps attached to the ends of twelve hoses of different lengths, the longest was five meters thirty centimeters long, the shortest two meters, ten centimeters. At the top the hoses fed into a cylinder-shaped chamber, in which water from all the pumps was mixed.

"I noticed one strange thing immediately: When the page was copied, someone had covered the top and right-hand side of the drawing with two sheets of paper. It was clear that the pump was to be placed at the front of a set of machines that might have been quite extensive. It occurred to me that the copy was probably just the front page of a long series of pages concertinaed together that showed the whole unit of which the pump was a part. Apparently Viola didn't want anyone to find out about the other parts of the unit. Later I often wondered about the series of machines the pump was connected to, what was at the end of this series, what the water that fed the machine turned into, and what was the point of the unit as a whole. I also tried to figure out what the twelve pumps were immersed in, of course; I imagined all kinds of wells and springs. Then it occurred to me that the pumps might be placed in vessels containing some kind of liquid processed by another machine unit, meaning that the unit with the pump in it might be just a small component in a much larger set of machines."

"I suppose that you're still none the wiser about all this," I said.

Julie replied with a sigh.

"What did you say to Viola when she showed you her drawing?"

"If anyone else had brought me a tatty piece of paper and asked me to design a pump from it, without even telling me what that pump was for, I wouldn't have given them the time of day. But with Viola it was different . . ."

"It was impossible to refuse Viola anything," I said. I was thinking of the painter.

"That's exactly right: It was impossible to refuse Viola anything." Julie sighed again.

"Didn't it seem to you that Viola took advantage of people?"

"Oh no. You shouldn't think that Viola wanted to manipulate people. I'm sure she was unhappy about the need to enlist the help of others in order to achieve her aims and sorry that she couldn't treat them as helpers ought to be treated. When I first saw her drawing, I was taken aback by her audacity; I folded it up again, intending to give it straight back to her. But one look at her stayed my hand: I saw the desperate plea in her eyes. I understood that the pump was enormously important for her and that she had a serious reason for keeping its purpose and intended location from me. Viola offered me no explanation or apology, nor did she try to persuade me, but suddenly I knew that I was her last hope and that she'd be desperate if I turned her down. So we looked at each other for a moment in silence before I opened the page out again and began to study the diagram. In the end I told her that I'd try to do something with it. Viola just mumbled in reply—neither then nor later did she show her feelings much—but I saw the gratitude and relief in her face . . ."

"You never asked her again what the pump was for?"

"Not that day, although later I inquired about it many times."

"And you truly learned nothing at all?"

"In the beginning Viola always somehow glossed over it. When we knew each other better, she'd usually make some kind of jokey reply; she'd think up various fantastical and absurd uses for the pump. Once she told me that the machine drew nectar from the cups of twelve giant flowers discovered by an expedition in a clearing in the Amazon rainforest. Another time she claimed that the pump was intended to draw water from a subterranean lake in a cave far beneath the city; the lake was reached by a long, winding staircase that began beyond a door at the back of a closet in an apartment on the edge of town. At first when she told me such things I got angry, but soon I was joining in. Together we made up stories about the pump. Sometimes we'd talk about it for hours, into the early hours of the morning. At that time Viola often came to my parents' villa, where I live. We'd sit on the terrace or in the garden and have great fun with our stories about the pump."

"Don't be angry, but there's something I really must ask you. Did you really never have the feeling that Viola was just pretending to be your friend because she needed you?"

Julie smiled and said, "It wasn't like that at all. Viola was after something she was willing to sacrifice everything for, if it came to that. There was no reason for her to pretend to be my friend, because she knew I'd do what she wanted, no matter how she behaved towards me. She never pretended anything with me, and she never sucked up to me. She never tricked me out of anything, and she owes me nothing. Although we never spoke of it, we understood each other perfectly in everything that really mattered. She needed something important from me and was grateful for my help. She was grateful for my friendship, too, and it gave her pleasure. I believe it was important for her at that time; the fact that she was able to relax in my company was perhaps no small thing. Sometimes it seemed to me that Viola was terribly tired. When she left, it was clear to me that she could stay with me no longer. I took her leaving pretty hard, but I never blamed her for it. In the few weeks when we saw a lot of each other, it was lovely how she tried to please me. When she came to see me she always brought me a gift. Once it was an old book about beetles, with yellowed pages and beautiful colorized engravings; we spent ages looking at it together. Another time it was a Chinese puzzle; we sat on the terrace composing its pieces into different flowers and animals. Then there was a little box containing beautiful colored butterflies made of silk paper; our breath as we spoke was enough to send them floating about the room. I've come to believe that she brought me presents as an advance apology for her disappearance from my life without saying goodbye."

"You said that you would sit in the garden making up stories about the pump. Tell me some."

Julie smiled. "I can't remember them all. We had the idea that nectar of the Amazonian flowers was a special drug. Whoever drank it would hear beautiful music instead of human words. We kept returning to the story of the subterranean lake, making it into an adventure novel in which we were the main characters. We got into the apartment with the secret door and descended the winding staircase to an underground kingdom, where there were towns made of metal on the shore of the lake. The people of these towns worshiped as a deity a monster that lived in the lake, bringing it human sacrifices. I forget the details. I think we were captured by priests of a subterranean cult who wanted to sacrifice us to the monster but we managed to escape in the nick of time and we ran up the never-ending winding staircase with the thud of our pursuers' footsteps and the rattle of their weapons in our ears . . ."

I'd been wondering where the subterranean monster had gotten to.

"Would it be possible to use the pump you designed for Viola to draw water from an underground lake?" I asked.

"Certainly not," Julie laughed. "The pump was quite a weak one with barely enough capacity to pump out an ordinary well. But it's true that if all that was needed was to clear an overflow blocking access to the lake, even a weak pump might unblock it. Like the siphon under the kitchen sink."

"So you believe that Viola's stories about the pump were all fictitious and had nothing to do with reality?"

"I wouldn't like to say that. It was impossible to believe anything of what Viola said. You couldn't even believe that her lies were really lies."

"Didn't that offend you?"

"I know that Viola was worried that her lying would offend me. And since she couldn't tell me the truth, she handled her discomfort by answering my questions with jokes. Jokes don't tell the truth, but they don't tell lies either. Of course I never took the talk of an underground monster seriously. But even then it occurred to me that Viola's fictions might be a distant echo of what she was trying so desperately to conceal and that maybe they pointed towards the truth. Besides . . ." Here Julie paused for a moment. "Besides, twice I experienced something with Viola that I can't explain; it was like a strange confirmation of her most fantastic stories."

She paused again, as if she were recalling memories buried deep.

"It sometimes happened," Julie went on, "that someone would call Viola on her cell when she was with me. I always pricked up my ears—I didn't want to miss a word. But all Viola's answers were curt, most of them nothing more than 'yes,' 'no,' and 'maybe.' There was no way of knowing who she was speaking with and what about. Just once the subject apparently couldn't be dealt with in words of one or two syllables, so Viola went off with her cell into the next room so that I wouldn't hear. I confess that I stole out of the room on tiptoe and stood in the hallway listening at the door. The snatches of utterances I heard didn't make much sense. First I heard Viola pronounce quite clearly the name 'Tannhäuser,' then for a long time I couldn't make out a single word. Then I heard her say: 'The bird catcher should be OK now. We should turn our attention to the puppeteer.' She saved the weirdest words till last. 'We'll need to check the water level in the cave,' she said."

"Maybe she was joking with the person on the other end of the line, just as she joked with you."

"I'm sure she wasn't. I could hear the concern in her voice."

"So how do you explain Viola's words?"

"I don't have any explanation for them. When Viola mentioned the cave, it sent shivers down my spine. I realized that something of what she'd told me about the underground lake and the monster might be true."

"And what about Tannhäuser, the bird catcher and the puppeteer?"

"I don't know anything about any bird catcher or puppeteer in connection with the pump. Viola never mentioned any such thing to me. As for Tannhäuser, if I remember well, part of the opera is set in a cave in the mountain of Venus, on the shores of an underground lake . . ."

Julie paused. I pondered on a possible connection between Tannhäuser, a bird catcher and a puppeteer on the one hand and what I'd heard from Jonáš and the painter on the other, but I didn't come up with anything. I turned back to Julie with a reminder: "You mentioned two experiences . . ."

"The second experience was even more disturbing . . ." she said. "Sometimes Viola slept over at my place. Once I woke up in the night and saw, in the weak light of the streetlamp beyond the window, Viola sitting bolt upright in bed. I looked at the lighted hands of the alarm clock on the nightstand: it was ten past three. When I asked why she wasn't asleep, she told me to be quiet—in an unfriendly voice that might have belonged to a completely different person. At that moment I realized that she was listening intently to something. So I tried to hear something in the stillness, too . . ."

"What did you hear?"

"I don't know—maybe nothing. It was the quietest time of night, when those who stay up late are already asleep and those who get up early are not yet awake. A blend of the softest nighttime sounds, muted by immense distance or many thick walls, washed in and out of the fizz of blood in my ears. These sounds were on the very edge of silence. Maybe it would be better to describe them as sounds from which silence itself is spun. It was barely possible to separate one from another and to classify them. It was difficult to tell if the sounds were even real; if they were, their reality was so weak that it was practically indistinguishable from the ideas produced by sleep, which I was nearing again. It was a strange feeling; that mass of formless silence lay on me more heavily than the most dreadful din would have done."

"Truly, you were unable to identify a single sound?"

"Some of the rustling may have been the sound of a train a long, long way away, or a streetcar, or a radio someone had switched on in another building in another street . . . Interwoven with these sounds was one that I couldn't place at all—the softest rhythmical rattle, something like this . . ."

Julie took the plastic bottle from the table and ran a fingernail over the fine indentations of its narrow part. This sound was no louder than the quiet hum of the ceiling fan; I had to bow my head to hear it.

"It may have been the sound of a tiny insect that had flown into the room through the window," Julie continued. "It may have been the growl of a machine at a great distance, or the sound of an unknown animal coming from the bowels of the earth . . ."

"Was that the sound Viola was listening to?"

"I think so, yes."

"Did you ask her about it in the morning?"

"When I woke up in the morning, Viola wasn't in the room. She never came to see me again. That sight of her in the night was the last I ever had of her."

Chapter 18
Sea Anemone

"Tell me more about the pump," I said. I had the idea that if Julie spoke of the instrument, she would be released from her sad reminiscences about Viola.

"I said that I had no idea what followed on from the pump's mixing chamber, but that's not entirely true. In the sketch that Viola gave me the top of the chamber ended in a standard closure; beneath this there was an empty space. But the sheet of paper covering the upper part of the original drawing had seemingly shifted slightly as the lid of the Xerox machine had come down on it. This was enough to allow a glimpse of the bottom of the component that sat on top of the chamber. Even when Viola was still coming to see me, I'd wondered what was on that part of the sketch, but at that time we were living in our stories of fantastical flowers and subterranean monsters and I couldn't be bothered to follow up such a tiny lead. But after Viola left me, I spent long hours looking at a strip less than a millimeter in height, wondering what it was a fragment of. It was tiny, yes, but it was the only piece of the rest of the unit I had any kind of view of. Now it was extremely important for me to find out what was closest to the pump. I was hoping that I would then find another link that would take me a little further forward, and that in the end I would get all the way to Viola. I was missing her terribly."

Julie was daydreaming, so I brought her back to the topic.

"You spent long hours looking at a thin strip of something above the chamber of the pump . . ."

"I struggled to get even a vague idea of what the construction above the pump was like. I was struck by three things: Its bottom was hatched in the same way as the tube below the chambers, so I assumed that the whole of the design was hatched; secondly, on both sides of the construction the contour lines were not perpendicular to the chamber's closure but instead formed a slightly obtuse angle, of about a hundred degrees; and thirdly, the hatching became more and then less dense at regular intervals. That was all I had to go on."

"I must confess that I probably wouldn't know what to make of such observations."

"I figured that the hatching meant the construction above the chamber was of the same or a similar flexible material as the tube at the bottom; the obtuse angles revealed that at least the lower part of the construction was in the shape of a truncated cone standing on a small base; the dense hatching suggested shading and indicated regularly-occurring depressions or grooves in the casing. All this gave me the idea of some kind of grooved pipe of a soft material—rubber or plastic—that broadened out as it went upward. Then I asked myself why the piping broadened out. It may have been because somewhere higher up it fed into a wider opening. But the flexible material and the regular grooves gave me a different idea—of a bendy tube whose grooves got deeper and deeper as you went up it, until the whole thing sort of exploded into many small, proboscis-like tubes that climbed upward and seemed to narrow while their weight caused them to open out, which was what created the approximate shape of an inverted, truncated cone. I say 'approximate' because in its upper part the body's circumference must have been at least slightly concave. I didn't know how long the pipes were, of course. If shorter, they would have headed up, like flowers in a vase, and the water would have jetted upwards; but had their length and weight exceeded a certain limit, the pipes would have bent back at a certain point, so that the whole thing would have looked like a sea anemone. I inclined more to the second possibility:

water jetting upward would fall back onto the machine and be difficult to re-capture for further processing, whereas in the case that the ends of the pipes turned downward, it would be easy to put a circular trough beneath them for the water to fall into. If I'm not mistaken in my hypothesis, the whole construction with the pump might look something like this."

From a nickel silver stand on the table Julie took an unprinted paper napkin. On this she drew in pencil a vertical rectangle and to the bottom side she added twelve lines of various lengths which bent in different ways (obviously this was the mixing chamber and the tubes that fed the pump); on its top side she drew the anemone-like shape with its many twisting proboscises. The drawing put me in mind of a mythological beast.

Probably Julie had similar thoughts about it. "Right from the beginning I had the feeling that if I resolved the mystery of the machine, I would expose Viola's secret," she said. "But you tell me—what am I supposed to make of this phantasm?"

Looking at the drawing on the napkin I wondered how many more phantasms I would turn up in the course of my investigation. Then I asked, "Did Viola ever mention changing paints?"

"No. What are they?"

I didn't want to tell Julie about the painter, so I just said: "Viola was interested in paints that reacted to minute amounts of various substances in the atmosphere. One possible use for them is as detectors of hidden things."

Julie gave this some thought, then said, "Do you think she wanted to use them to reveal the origin of the sounds that we heard in the quiet of the night?"

I shrugged. Suddenly I'd had my fill of mysteries and again regretted my promise to Jonáš. What greater happiness could there be than to sit at home working on my novella? Now I reproached myself for having thrown it aside so carelessly. But since I was sitting here with Julie, there was one more question I needed to ask. The pencil was still lying on the table, so I picked it up and on the napkin drew something next to Julie's picture of the pump: the double trident.

"Ever seen this before?" I asked her.

Julie answered immediately. "It's what was tattooed on Viola's belly."

"Did you ask her what it meant?"

"Well, yes, but she answered with one of her jokes. It was a sign of a secret society of alchemists, she said. But it occurred to me that it could quite easily be a schematic illustration of a pump with an attachment on top of it."

I looked at the napkin again. Julie was right, there were similarities between the two pictures on it. The arms of the lower trident might represent the tubes at the bottom of the pump, the middle part the mixing chamber, and the upper trident the anemone-like cluster of tubes above the chamber. But what about the horizontal oval?

"And the oval?" I said, looking from the napkin to Julie.

"If the symbol is a diagram of the pump, the oval must be a representation of a mysterious tank the machine draws water from."

Again she was right. Looking at the oval, I imagined the surface of an underground lake with Godzilla living beneath it. Dear God, would I ever discover the strange place Viola was hiding in?

There was another long silence as we both explored our thoughts.

Then Julie said: "When the pump was ready, Viola came to the workshops to pick it up. I remember she came in a taxi—a white van with a big picture on its bodywork of a kingfisher with a fish in its bill. She'd told me she was coming at four in the afternoon but she arrived at two, claiming she'd had to change the time of the appointment because something important had gotten in the way. But I knew she'd done it on purpose because she didn't want me to see who she was coming with. As it happened, I'd had to go down to the workshops on another errand, and so we met there. I could see that this was uncomfortable for her. I was unhappy too. I'd had the feeling that the pump was our common child—Viola its father, I its mother— and that we'd both been looking forward to the birth. It was the pump that held us together, made something like a family out of us . . ."

"Mom, Dad and a big metal baby . . ."

"Exactly. And here was Viola with a stranger, taking our child away and not even telling me where."

"So who was this stranger?"

"Two men got out of the van. The first must have been the taxi driver; he was short and curly-haired. The second man, who looked about fifty, had a grizzly, close-cropped beard. We loaded the pump together, even though Viola didn't want my help. I noticed that Viola's friend had fine hands; I'd say they were the hands of a pianist or a violinist."

"Did she introduce you?"

"I wouldn't have expected her to. But anyway, we'd only just gotten the pump into the van when her cell rang."

The cellphone again! I thought. Without treacherous phones, there wouldn't be a single clue for me to follow up in this case.

"Again Viola's answers were mostly 'yes' and 'no.' But maybe because her unexpected encounter with me had put her off her stride, at one point she said, 'Yes, Chuh-yuh is here with me.' Then she handed the phone to the man with the gray beard. Her face wore a startled expression: She'd realized she'd said something in front of me that she shouldn't have."

"What did she say again?"

"Something that sounded like 'Chuh-yuh'—and she meant the man she'd come with. As to whether it was a name, a nickname, an occupation, or a rank . . ."

"And after that?"

"The man with the beard took the phone, said 'yes' and 'no' into it several times, handed it back to Viola, and then the three of them got into the taxi and drove away. I lost Viola a week later."

"Do you remember the date?"

"Yes, I do. I last saw Viola on September 15th at 3:00 a.m."

"Her father told me that she left him in the night of September 16th to 17th."

Julie looked at her watch, then jumped out of her chair. "I'm running terribly late, I have to dash. In any case, I've told you all I can. If you find Viola or learn anything about her, will you let me know? Please don't forget me."

Then I watched her run across the street. I ordered myself a glass of wine and tried to put what I'd heard into some kind of order. The cast of the freak show had grown by five—the mysterious Chuh-yuh, the bird catcher, the puppeteer, Tannhäuser and the mysterious machine. It was time for me to pay and go. The young man took my money but continued to stand over me, as though he wanted to tell me something but lacked the courage. Then he made up his mind, leaned down to me so that the ends of his dreadlocks were touching my arm and said: "Excuse me for listening to you. But I know the man whose name is Chuh-yuh. Not that I know him personally, but I know who he is. Chuh-yuh is a pseudonym, not his real name."

"Who would choose such an awful pseudonym!"

The waiter seemed to take offense. "As it happens, I rather like it. His first name is Vuhulum."

"This guy has taken the pseudonym Vuhulum Chuh-yuh? What kind of artist is he? I've never heard of any such person."

"That's your fault, not his. Vuhulum Chuh-yuh is the best contemporary composer of music I know."

"You're right, the fault really is mine. I don't know much about music. The pseudonym is unusual, but actually it is rather nice."

Taking this as the apology I intended it to be, the young man said affably: "Don't worry that you've never heard of him. Unfortunately not even the music critics know Vuhulum Chuh-yuh, but that doesn't mean that his compositions aren't the most interesting new music of recent years."

"I'll make sure I listen to some of them. I don't suppose you know where I could find him?"

"I don't, I'm afraid. But you can buy one of his CDs at Tam-Tam."

He explained that Tam-Tam was a store that sold cassettes and CDs of various kinds of alternative music. He also told me that the store was located at a railroad station on the outskirts of the city.

That evening I sat at my desk for a while and rummaged among my papers, but soon it was plain to me that I would be unable to concentrate on the writing of a novella. Having moved to the armchair, so that I wouldn't have to think about the double trident and Viola, I picked up the book I'd started to read a week ago and had no time for since. It was Lovecraft's *Call of Cthulhu*. I opened it at the page I'd marked with a streetcar ticket and read: "It seemed to be a sort of monster, or symbol representing a monster, of a form which only a diseased fancy could conceive. If I say that my somewhat extravagant imagination yielded simultaneous pictures of an octopus, a dragon, and a human caricature, I shall not be unfaithful to the spirit of the thing. A pulpy, tentacled head surmounted a grotesque and scaly body with rudimentary wings . . ."

As I imagined the terrible Cthulhu, suddenly I saw in it the figure that had been pursuing me these past few days. Might the double trident be a primitive representation of Lovecraft's horrific creature from the stars? The upper, octopus-like part of the monster was in place of a head, the horizontal lines were vestigial wings, the lower trident represented legs and a tail. And the oval? I didn't doubt that that was the aperture leading to the citadel in the ancient city of R'lyeh in which Cthulhu slept, the aperture through which the monster would one day crawl, out into our world . . .

I thought of the subterranean monster that kept meddling in my search for Viola. Now it had taken on the form of the creature in Lovecraft's story. What if this story wasn't pure fantasy? What if the writer had had access to some secret knowledge? Had Viola wanted to track down Cthulhu? Had she fallen into his clutches? Was she in R'lyeh, somewhere deep under this city? Although I knew that these were confused thoughts brought on by the onset of sleep, I couldn't rid myself of a sense of anxiety . . .

Chapter 19
Tam-Tam

I awoke in the night and heard that it was raining, but in the morning I looked out of the window at a clear sky above the rooftops. I reached the railroad station at about ten. Although it was hot, in the empty station hall a moist coolness breathed from the white walls with their large brownish stains, and the smooth stone floor gleamed in a cold light. I took a look around. Squeezed between a snack counter and a popcorn vendor's was a dark storefront window; above this window was a painted sign on which "TAM-TAM" was almost lost in a tangle of vines and palm leaves. The artist had made the letters out of stylized bamboo stalks. Two monkeys—one on top of each "A"—were playing catch with a coconut shown in flight above the hyphen between the two parts of the word. I was pretty sure that this sign was the work of the artist who had painted the parrot at the café where I'd been yesterday with Julie.

It was no great surprise to me that a store selling cassettes and CDs should be at a railroad station. I assumed that its proprietor had settled here in the nineties, when the city was reshaping itself in chaotic fashion and businesses often ended up in unlikely places. Unexpected and sometimes rather poetic neighborhoods had formed out of this, I remembered. Since that time businesses had either moved to environments more appropriate to their needs or created such environments where they were. But I knew a few stores whose proprietors refused to leave the landscape to which they had been transported by accident in a time of confusion, for the simple reason that they had come to love it there. I was always delighted to happen across a little store selling semiprecious stones in the lobby of an austere administrative building, for instance, or a purveyor of esoteric literature by the main gate of a factory that produced nails.

Before I stepped into the store I took a look at its window. I hadn't seen most of these cassettes and CDs on display in any other store. They were recordings of ethnic and experimental music, many of whose cases showed strange musical instruments that I didn't recognize. I opened the heavy glass door and went inside. It was even colder in the store than it was in the hall. A muted wind instrument was playing softly. Wrapped in a plaid blanket and sitting in a rocking chair behind the counter was a man of about fifty. He had long, thin hair and a musketeer's moustache, and he was reading a book. Looking over the top of little round glasses, he returned my greeting with a nod and then went back to his book.

It didn't take me long to find a CD whose cover bore the following text in mauve lettering:

Vuhulum Chuh-yuh
TWO COMPOSITIONS

The lettering was backed with irregular black and white spots, which I studied for a while; it occurred to me that this could be a small square segment from a Chinese ink-wash painting, magnified many times. I turned the case over and froze: I was looking at a black double trident. Above this I read: "The Manifestation and Extinction of the Orange Book: a sonata played behind walls at 3:00 a.m." The double trident was the same size as the capital letters these words were printed in. Apparently the words were the title of the first composition and the double trident the title of the second.

I handed the CD to the storekeeper and asked him what the second composition was called. He pointed at the double trident and said, "That's the title of the composition." Then he returned to his book.

"I don't understand. Is it a pictograph? How should I read it?"

The storekeeper was obviously annoyed at the interruption in his reading. "I don't know how you should read it," he said. "As far as I know, it's neither a letter nor a hieroglyph, and you don't read it at all."

Then he was back in his book again. His lack of courtesy was starting to get on my nerves. Day after day spent alone in this glass cave rocking in that chair of his had perhaps made him uncivil. I couldn't imagine that he got many customers; the music he sold was probably of interest to just a few people in this city, and no doubt they would have difficulty finding a store tucked away in a railroad station.

"So you're not able to tell me what the composition is really called?" I insisted.

The storekeeper wasn't going to let me disturb his peace. "I told you, didn't I? Why does the title of a piece of music always have to be in words? Is there some kind of law about it? Why can't it be a picture or an ornament or simply a mark? The composer told me that was the name of the piece, so that's what I put on the cover. I didn't ask any questions."

"You're the publisher of Chuh-yuh's CD?" I asked, surprised.

"Sure. Tam-Tam is primarily a record label," said the storekeeper.

Before he could get back into his reading, I said: "I need Vuhulum Chuh-yuh's real name and his address urgently."

The storekeeper frowned and looked at me with suspicion. "Did Bernet send you here?"

"You mean the multimillionaire? Christ, no! Whatever gave you that idea? I've never seen Bernet except on TV," I said defensively. Bernet was one of the richest men in the country. Many suspected him of acquiring his vast wealth by illegal means, but no one had ever pinned a crime on him. I remembered the thirty-year-old face I'd seen a few times on TV; it was so devoid of expression that its owner's thoughts were impossible to read. What could a young parvenu have in common with Vuhulum Chuh-yuh and the double trident?

Noting my alarm at the thought of being connected in any way with this man, the storekeeper calmed down. "Bernet came here not long ago," he said. "He, too, inquired about Vuhulum Chuh-yuh."

"Do you have any idea why he was interested in Vuhulum Chuh-yuh?"

"No. Ours was a brief conversation. He started on about money right away, promising me an enormous sum if I introduced him to Chuh-yuh. He said I'd be able to move my store to the city center. So I threw him out," the storekeeper said with satisfaction. "But why do you need Chuh-yuh's address? Are you an admirer of his?"

"No. I heard of Chuh-yuh for the first time yesterday, and still I haven't heard any of his work. I'm looking forward to it, though. I need to find him because I'm looking for a girl who disappeared two years ago and apparently knew him. And there's some connection between the symbol you say is the title of Chuh-yuh's composition and the girl's disappearance. Do you know Vumuluh . . . Vuhulum . . ."

"Vuhulum Chuh-yuh. Yes, I do, a little. I've known his name—I mean his pseudonym—for almost twenty years, but I didn't meet him in person until two years ago. Although I published that CD you have, I spoke with him only twice. So I don't suppose I can help you much. I don't know Chuh-yuh's real name and I don't even know where he lives . . . But that girl you mentioned . . . Was she a skinny blonde with short hair?"

I whipped out the photo of Viola and showed it to him.

"That's her," he said. "I was there when she and Chuh-yuh first met . . . although they may have known each other already. Their encounter was a strange one, and I didn't really understand what passed between them. I had the impression that Chuh-yuh had either known her before and forgotten about her or that he'd mistaken her for someone else . . ."

I was glad that the storekeeper was now more communicative. He even closed his book and laid it down on the counter. Seeking to take advantage, I said, "Do tell me about your meeting with Chuh-yuh and Viola."

"What are you? A cop or a private detective or something?" he asked, suspicious again.

"Do I look like a cop or a detective to you? All I've done is promise Viola's sick father that I'll try to find her or at least get news of her. And since I started my investigations, the case has begun to interest me in itself. I'd be really grateful to you if you could tell me all you know, from the beginning."

The publisher-cum-storekeeper gave this some thought before saying, "If you want it from the beginning, we'll have to go right back to the early eighties."

"That's no problem for me. I don't have to go to work these days, so I've got plenty of time on my hands. You can go as far back as the First Republic if you need to. I wouldn't like to keep you from your work, of course, but maybe you could find some time this evening."

The publisher laughed. "Keep me from my work? What a ridiculous thought! Usually I don't get a single customer in a day. Behind those ticket offices is a coffee vending machine. Bring me an espresso with sugar, and something for yourself if you like. Then I'll talk till midnight about Chuh-yuh, Oo and Num, the White Triangle, and the Orange Book."

I could hardly wait, I said. I jogged along to the machine, which stood at the other end of the hall against a white wall, agleam in the slanting rays of the sun. I made the return trip more slowly: In each hand I held a plastic cup filled to the brim with steaming coffee. I heard the echo of my footsteps on the stone floor of the station's large empty space. I opened the glass door of the store with a shoulder, put both cups down next to the cash register and sat down on a crate next to the storekeeper.

He sipped the foam from the cup, then wiped his beard and began. "I first heard of Vuhulum Chuh-yuh sometime in the early eighties. I've always been interested in music. For several years I played various instruments in all kinds of illegal and semi-legal bands. Then I decided to go into the distribution of recordings. After the revolution I founded a record label and set up this store. Although hardly anyone ever comes here, I'm not complaining: The nine years I've spent at this station have been the happiest of my life. I read, listen to CDs and think. Believe me, a desolate station is a better place for contemplation than a log cabin in the mountains of China. Occasionally someone comes along who is interested in the same music as I am, and he buys something. I don't need much money: the rent here is low and as a record label I don't have to pay anyone's wages because I'm the only employee."

The storekeeper rocked in his chair contentedly. I could well imagine that this store at the station was the asylum he had dreamed of for twenty years, and that he reveled in the happiness of sitting here undisturbed among his cassettes and CDs, listening now to the quiet of the station hall, now to the music he loved. Through his solitude, maybe he really had gotten out of the habit of making contact with people, but now that he was over his mistrust and shyness, his voice had taken on a tone that was amiable and reassuring, and I felt that I could happily listen to him until nightfall.

"In the seventies and eighties, my life revolved around secret concerts that were mostly held in halls attached to pubs in the provinces," he continued. "When I look back, I can't tell all those smoked-filled rooms with their stale beer smell apart—all I see is a single hall lit up in the night."

He paused, took another sip of the hot coffee and looked through the glass door at the ever-empty station. "In those days I spent much of my life in pubs and bars, where my friends and I talked incessantly about music and literature. As far as the regime was concerned, we were the lowest of the low. It was a strange world where news was spread by word of mouth and in whispers, so some things got twisted or turned upside down, and sometimes speculation became certified news overnight and vice versa. Even so, our world was much more real than the bland dream they called reality in those days. When the regime fell, I realized I would regret it if all of that was forgotten, so I decided to try and write a memoir of that time."

From a shelf under the counter he took out a thick sheaf of papers covered in ballpoint ink. "I still work on my memoir occasionally, but I don't make much progress. It's such a difficult task. The main problem is, all the faces and stories, all the characters and events became shrouded and steeped in a mythology that was constantly renewed, that clutched at every minor incident and that fed on the flimsiest of facts. So by the early nineties it was practically impossible to tell what had arisen out of real events and what had been pure fantasy born out of desire. There were characters whose realness no one doubted even though apparently no one had ever met them. There were also implausible characters, considered phantoms born out of the dreams of the time, who suddenly turned out to be real people."

Chapter 20
The White Triangle

From outside in the station hall came a man's voice in the unintelligible, barbarian tongue of the railroad loudspeaker. The storekeeper stopped speaking and waited patiently for the silence to resume.

"In those days the White Triangle artists' group was a popular topic of conversation in bars," he went on. "It was said that its membership included three artists with strange pseudonyms. These pseudonyms occurred in many various forms; as words, they were as unusual as they were difficult to pronounce and remember, so they often changed as they passed from one table to the next. Now I know that although all the forms I knew back then were distortions, it all revolved around the correct pronunciations. Those members of the White Triangle called themselves Vuhulum Chuh-yuh, Iui Num, and Vuh-gah Oo."

I had the impression that it was a pleasure for the storekeeper to pronounce these weird names. He took care to enunciate each individual sound, which he separated in the manner of a gourmet rolling a tasty oyster around his mouth. Finally he paused to savor the "Oo" sound as it faded into the quiet of the station hall. This was an infectious delight; involuntarily I repeated all three names with my lips and tongue but not my voice.

"It was said that Chuh-yuh was a composer, Oo a sculptor, and Num a writer. As far as I know, no one ever thought that they were real, but this didn't stop us from talking about them.

It was rather like people inventing stories about war heroes. I remember the joy we felt as we listened to someone describing how Oo's abstract sculptures had appeared overnight at an exhibition of officially-approved art held to celebrate some anniversary, or that the White Triangle had cracked into the wavelength of the state radio service and broadcast the oratorio 'Cold Clefts of Despair'—even though all of us knew that these were just fantasies, part of the mythology of a sad time. I, too, thought that Chuh-yuh, Oo, and Num were mere phantoms. I assumed that they belonged to the folklore of the day, and that they had remarkably long endurance, rather like that secret society who used the crush in the Metro to push people from the platform in front of an oncoming train. Remember them? No one actually knew anything at all about the White Triangle, making it an empty notion into which everyone could project their own dreams. During our endless discussions about it, I don't remember anyone minding much that we kept contradicting each other and that we'd said one thing two days ago, another yesterday and yet another today.

"Two winters ago I had a visit from the editor of a music magazine who'd heard that I was putting together a memoir on the seventies and eighties. He asked me if I'd write an article for his magazine about the lives of the musicians I'd known. So I did. It seemed to me that if I failed to mention the legends of the barfly mythology of the time, I'd be excluding something important, so I referred to the White Triangle and its members with the weird, changing names. About a week after the article was published, a gentleman with a grizzly beard appeared in the store. What I'd written had interested him, he said, so he'd gone to the magazine's office for Tam-Tam's address and come to me in order to point out a small inaccuracy in the article. Naturally I was keen to know what this was. 'You were in error,' he said, 'when you wrote that the White Triangle was just a figment of the collective imagination of the time. Most of what was reported about it was fabrication and dreaming, of course, but the group really did exist.' I asked him how he could be so sure of this when apparently no one had ever met a White Trianglist. 'I know because I was a member,' he replied. In amazement I asked what his name was. He bowed and introduced himself as Vuhulum Chuh-yuh.

"At first I thought he was pulling my leg, but when I looked into his serious, honest face I understood that he was telling the truth. It was a miracle: suddenly the old dream had transformed into reality. My visitor added that 'Vuhulum Chuh-yuh' was of course a pseudonym, and he apologized for not revealing his real name to me. I argued that these days there was no sense in concealing one's name, to which he laughed and said, 'It's a game I've been playing for years, and I'd be sorry to ruin it. Besides, I'm bound to it by a promise that hasn't been dissolved.' All the time he stood there talking to me I felt as though Batman had just appeared in my store."

"Could you tell me exactly when this was?"

The storekeeper considered my question and then said: "It must have been two years ago, at the beginning of June of '97. I told Chuh-yuh that I'd heard stories about fantastical symphonies, epic poems and sculptures created by the White Triangle. 'I heard all those legends, too,' said Chuh-yuh, laughing. He was aware that many stories had been told about the White Triangle, he said, but it had never been its aim to encourage the legends, and in the beginning it hadn't occurred to any of the three members that by taking mysterious-sounding pseudonyms and leading lives even more secluded than was common at the time, they would stimulate the myth. It seems they wanted to remain anonymous—partly because it was safer, partly because anonymity or the weird pseudonymity of changing, unreal-sounding, disappearing names was an expression of the aesthetic they had formed in the late seventies and early eighties. In the course of their debates, Chuh-yuh explained, they had developed a kind of minimalism that demanded of its art fragmentary forms that stimulated the imagination of its listeners, viewers and readers. The artists' names—stumps of words that everyone misheard and that couldn't be held in the memory for more than a few minutes, that kept changing and indicated not a particular person with a recognizable face but indistinct, confused gestures in the gloom—were well suited to the originators of works that were not finished wholes but birth processes that were never completed."

Although I still didn't understand what all this had to do with Viola, I neither minded this nor asked the storekeeper to get to the point. Anyway, this case was so mixed-up that I didn't know what "the point" was.

"Chuh-yuh said that the White Triangle's program of that time boiled down to two requirements: to say as little as possible and not to finish the whole. This was born of a reaction against the garrulousness of officially-approved art and probably also out of a desire to use the secrecy and concealment demanded by the times as a part of its aesthetic. In those days the Trianglists called this 'homeopathic art,' claiming that a work is most effective when served in extremely small doses. Iui Num wrote some kind of manifesto in which he tried to express the main thoughts of Trianglist minimalism as it was at the time. Although the manuscript of the manifesto was lost long ago, Chuh-yuh still remembered its central principles. In it, Num even rendered the aesthetics of the White Triangle as an exact formula."

The storekeeper wrote this formula down in the empty margin of one of his sheets of paper.

$$0<EF<0.1C$$

"What in Heaven's name is it?" I asked.

"It was supposed to mean the following: 'The subject acquires aesthetic functions when the quantum of relations provided within the framework of contemporary society of the subject as a whole is reduced to less than one tenth of its total.' Chuh-yuh told me with a smile that neither he nor Oo knew how Num had come up with this figure, but that both of them would have argued for hours on end in defense of its accuracy, had there been anyone to argue against; Chuh-yuh, Num and Oo associated with hardly anyone else, and their debates were conducted among the three of them."

The loudspeaker gave another wheeze. The storekeeper paused in his telling until the announcement was over.

"The manifesto also challenged the opinion that the foundation of a work of art is an organic unity of all its parts; for Num, Aristotle's *Poetics* in particular was an untidy mixture of the worst kind of delusions. Num maintained that a work should be fragmentary and disjointed, a claim he justified by a theory tinged with mysticism, in which the person we are used to calling 'I,' who yearns instinctively for unity, is surprised and confused by the fragmentariness of the work; in his confusion he scurries about the whole expanse of consciousness, looking for something by which some unity might be established; in the process he opens dozens of doors along the corridors of consciousness, including some that usually remain closed—and at a moment of luck it may happen that he releases the latch of a chamber where the secrets of the birth of 'I' and the birth of the world and the births of all possible 'I's' and all possible worlds are hidden. It happens rarely that this latch is lifted, but aesthetic pleasure is actually a presentiment of the possibility.

"But rather than programs and manifestos, I was interested in the individual works the members of the White Triangle had produced, so I asked Chuh-yuh to tell me about them. First, Chuh-yuh spoke of Vuh-gah Oo, who in the beginning made sculptures that looked like fragments of mysterious machine units. Later his sculptures began to change: The fragments grew, but rather than coming together in the shape of an entire machine, they assumed submarine, organic shapes; it was as though the sculptures captured the shape of a machine just as a cogwheel was transforming into the umbrella of a jellyfish or a castellated shaft was changing into an eel. I was told that Oo and Num had had many arguments about fins and tentacles; at a time when Oo had already abandoned orthodox fragmentism, Num continued to insist on the original principles of the White Triangle, although not even he remained true to the program of minimalism forever. Chuh-yuh told me, too, that the disputes over theory that often erupted in the White Triangle's latter period were probably no more than an expression of personal disagreement, but when I asked him what these were about, he led the conversation away without having answered my question."

The mention of machine fragments that transformed into

sea creatures reminded me of Julie's napkin drawing of the day before. "Did Oo also make a sculpture of a pump with a sea anemone growing out of the top?" I asked.

"I don't know," said the storekeeper. "Chuh-yuh didn't mention it. Anyway, apparently the period of Oo's producing sculptures that combined machinelike and organic shapes didn't last very long either. In his next phase, Oo produced sculptures by the mere direction of his gaze, by viewing different everyday objects—fire hydrants, streetlamps, various machines and domestic appliances—as sculptor's creations that expressed certain feelings and thoughts and a certain world; he attributed these to imaginary artists, about whom he wrote extensive studies. One of these fictitious artists was a depressive sculptor whose works were a crumpled decorative blanket in Oo's living room, a light fitting belonging to Chuh-yuh, a parking meter on a sidewalk, a wrecked wall he saw from a bus and a wastebasket; another of his imaginary sculptors had produced a cushion, a gas compressor, a radiator and a corrugated-iron fence—he was a pompous type who got on Oo's nerves by the sweeping gestures with which he took in the whole universe, although Oo tried to understand and appraise his work without prejudice. Before long this way of producing sculptures transformed Oo's whole world into an enormous gallery. He felt extremely tired; it was as though he spent all day, every day walking through the halls of a giant museum whose exit he couldn't find. A time later Oo emigrated. According to Chuh-yuh, by then they were no longer in touch. I had the feeling that the members of the White Triangle hadn't parted on good terms. But one reason for Oo's departure may have been the hope that in a different environment he would at last escape his giant museum.

"The second member of the White Triangle was Iui Num. He was a foreigner who had learned to speak Czech well and had been living here for several years. I asked Chuh-yuh about Num's nationality, but Chuh-yuh pretended not to hear my question; it seemed that for some reason Num's origin was one of the things Chuh-yuh refused to talk about. In the days of the White Triangle, Iui Num wrote four novels. He produced these on a typewriter; in each instance Oo then carefully bound three copies of the typescript in bookbinder's cloth. It's true to say that the typing of his novels was not a particularly laborious task for Num. Although each was about three hundred pages long, most pages were entirely blank and across the rest were scattered just a few words, sentence fragments, a truncated paragraph at most. According to Num's minimalist theories, the reader was supposed to create something like a story out of these fragments. There were problems with this: Num strictly guarded the orthodoxy he himself had established, and it was difficult to adhere exactly to the spirit of his intentions. The principal difficulty lay not in the inferring of relations between the fragments—according to Chuh-yuh, it required little effort on the part of the reader to find whole clusters of connections among the words separated by the white pages, and stories grew easily across the blank spaces between the words and sentence fragments; the problem was, Num wasn't interested in these stories, because in his opinion, all they did was replicate, in a different form, the collectiveness he'd striven to expel from his work."

"So what did he actually want if there should be neither empty space nor story between the fragments of text?"

"Something in between—a brittle emptiness whose cracks produced a story that was still in the process of hatching from the egg of the void. Num wanted the reader/creator to allow the nascent story to develop only up to a certain point; the story should be soft-boiled, remaining at a stage where it had the form of a rhythmical rippling and pulsing, out of which objects, bodies, spaces, actions and thoughts were yet to emerge in full. Num hated finished shapes; he asserted that he wasn't writing a fragmentaristic work in order for someone to make it whole again.

"Num was forever dissatisfied with his work: It seemed to him too verbose. So in his third novel, which was called *Rebirth* and had three hundred and sixty pages, there was text only on page 24 (the words 'green glass'), page 76 (the word 'star'), page 173 (the words 'fringes of the shade') and page 248 (the words 'listened to a quiet lapping'). In his final novel, *The Centaur*, the white pages bore only isolated letters and unidentifiable word fragments; it seemed to Chuh-yuh that Num was heading for the equation EF=0—the empty page on which everything would be present, albeit in wrapped-up form. But Chuh-yuh didn't know how Num's work developed after that, because following the break-up of the White Triangle Num went back to his native land."

Chapter 21
The Orange Book

The storekeeper was silent while he finished his cold coffee.

"You haven't yet spoken of what Chuh-yuh did," I reminded him. This was the figure in the White Triangle that interested me most.

"I'm getting to that. But it's not so important to talk about Chuh-yuh because unlike the work of his two friends, at least some of his has survived—you can listen to two of his musical compositions on the CD you have in your hand. Chuh-yuh claimed that each of the three members of the White Triangle came to homeopathic art by his own path, and he told me of an incident that provided the impulse for his own version of minimalism. Although it was an entirely banal experience, it seems it released something in Chuh-yuh that had been germinating for a long time. Sometime in the early eighties he and his then girlfriend went to a classical music concert. Sitting in front of them in the concert hall was a man who kept making a rustling sound with a bag of candies. That's actually all there is to tell. While his girlfriend was angered by this, the combination of rustling and music transported Chuh-yuh into a strange state. At that time he was going through a creative crisis; he couldn't bear his old work but he didn't know where to go next. There at the concert he felt his disquietude recede and a strange joy flow into him, and he realized that these states of his were somehow related to the conjunction of the musical composition and the inappropriate rustling. Telling himself that he had to get to the bottom of this, he began to think about his feelings while he was still in the concert hall.

"I'm sure that the fact of the inappropriate sounds spoiling the musical composition gave him no pleasure—this was a piece by a composer he liked. So where did his unceasing joy come from? And then he realized what had happened: Suddenly the notes of the music had recalled an affinity with the rustling sounds, a common origin, and the miraculous world of this origin; the rustling of the bag rubbed against a fine film that coated the musical notes. For the first time Chuh-yuh touched notes in the state in which they lived beneath the film. Suddenly it occurred to him that we always perceive music only through this film, which is why we don't really understand music, as we are unable to hear something essential that it is telling us. Although notes carry their origin with them, the hygienic film we coat them in doesn't let out the unclean juices produced in their birth, and thus a note comes to us as a finished thing."

"I don't really get it. Do you?"

"Oh yes. But maybe I wouldn't if I knew the plot Chuh-yuh spoke of only as theory. But I realized immediately that I'd had the same experience as Chuh-yuh several times. So, yes, I knew what he was talking about."

"You, too, had sat at a concert next to someone rustling candy wrappers?"

"Well, no, but several times I've been surprised that indistinct music coming from, let's say, the windows of the hall has mingled with the sounds of traffic in the street to produce a strange, unprecedented, moving message. Chuh-yuh explained it as follows: We know the pure notes of the concert hall well; the classifications into which we place them are seamless, which means that they succumb immediately and without resistance to the languages we have prepared for them and don't have time to convey what they want to tell us—about why they have broken the surface and what they can pronounce only in their own language. Always and immediately we convert their messages into our own language, and in translation they lose what is interesting about what notes communicate, namely what they utter in their own language, the language of their birth. Only when they are too quiet, on the very frontier of audibility, or when they mingle with other sounds—only at moments of impurity such as these are they able to resist our languages and retain their own, ancient language, with all its peculiar, ages-old cases and grammatical categories that link them with other sounds and also with colors, tastes, smells and touch sensations."

"I see. But how are we to understand them when they don't speak in our language? Did the bliss felt by Chuh-yuh originate in absolute unintelligibility?"

"Chuh-yuh said that we know the language of notes from somewhere—perhaps a previous life or a strange dream—and can call it to mind. He was still at that concert when he sensed that the way to music had at last re-opened for him, and he couldn't wait to get started on a new work. He had the feeling that a whole program of new work would grow out of this experience, yet this program would also bring back old memories; this new knowledge suddenly encapsulated and clarified many scattered and vague experiences in his life. All at once it came to him that he knew this composition in impure notes well; he'd been listening to it all his life, but he'd never paid enough attention to it. It seemed to him now that all the musical compositions he had heard were mere parts of this continuous composition and that their notes and melodies were just one of the forms of original sound matter that gush from an impure source; they weren't in any way especially distinctive from other sounds and they took on meaning only if they didn't renounce this affinity. Deep in his consciousness he understood the message of the unceasing composition and its idea, which was the death and birth of all ideas. And for several months after that he really did compose music that was an expression of the new place he'd found in the world of sounds."

"What did such music sound like?"

"Chuh-yuh's work from that period is on the CD. It would be best if you listened to it yourself."

"I'm terribly curious. But there's one thing that puzzles me: Was the rustling of the candy wrappers truly the only thing that impelled him to take up his new style and develop his metaphysical theories? I find that difficult to believe."

For a moment or two the storekeeper rocked pensively in his chair. Then he said: "This brings us to something strange. From what Chuh-yuh told me, I, too, had the feeling that there existed some source of major influence on him and the other members of the White Triangle. I still believe that there was some kind of shared experience; Chuh-yuh came at this subject several times from different angles, but he always pulled away from it at the last moment and guided the topic elsewhere. It was as though the mysterious incident had an irresistible attraction for his story yet still he was afraid to speak of it, or as though to speak of it were forbidden to him.

"Yes, there was a kind of blind spot in Chuh-yuh's story that he kept avoiding but around which everything revolved. It even seems to me that the incident lost in the blind spot meant much more to the White Triangle than the common source of their work. I've said already that Chuh-yuh kept certain details of his story secret, including how the members of the White Triangle met and why they parted company, what their real names were, what Num's nationality was and which country Oo left for. It's my belief that he didn't want to talk about these things because they were somehow connected with the mysterious incident and might give something away about it. But without them the whole history of the White Triangle remains nothing more than an incomprehensible fragment."

"Which in the spirit of homeopathic art and fragmentism is just as it should be."

"But as all three of them had abandoned the aesthetics of minimalism many years before, according to Chuh-yuh, why would he have adapted his story to suit it?"

I wondered, of course, whether the mysterious incident Chuh-yuh had refused to speak about might have something to do with Viola, although Viola was still a small child when it was said to have occurred.

"You really have no idea what it might be?" I asked.

"When I thought about it later, something did occur to me.

But I suppose it's a red herring . . . After Chuh-yuh had told me the story of the White Triangle, I offered to publish some of his music on CD. He hesitated over this for a long time, before at last giving his agreement. He promised to choose some pieces and bring me recordings of them he'd made himself. None of Chuh-yuh's compositions had ever been performed live, and as far as I could tell he had no interest in such a thing. The music of his minimalist period was totally unsuited to the concert stage. He kept it on magnetic tape, perhaps believing that such a form of existence was the most suitable for it. His later music, too, was recorded on magnetic tape. If someone had offered him a concert performance, probably he'd have declined. We agreed that he would stop by to see me at the same time the following week—at 5:00 p.m. on a Monday, I remember. He brought me two recordings, the first from his minimalist period and the second, named by a symbol, composed ten years later, long after the break-up of the White Triangle. While you were surprised by the title of the second piece, I was more struck by the name Chuh-yuh had given the older one. I don't know if you've ever heard of the Orange Book . . ."

"No. I read the name for the first time on the back of the CD."

"People talked of the Orange Book fifteen, twenty years ago. In those days, like the White Triangle, the Orange Book was a common topic of discussion in bars; it, too, took on a great variety of forms because everyone projected their own ideas onto it. Its existence in reality was even more dubious than that of the White Triangle. So as soon as I saw that Chuh-yuh had named one of his compositions after it, I asked him what he knew about it. He was quick to tell me that the Orange Book was just a myth and had never existed. Till that moment I'd never believed in the existence of the Orange Book, but my question had so unsettled Chuh-yuh, and he had denied its existence with such vigor, that immediately I suspected that the Orange Book was not a fiction after all and that Chuh-yuh knew something about it. The first thing that occurred to me was that the blind spot in his story concealed something related to the Orange Book. After Chuh-yuh left, I told myself that I was surely in error and my explanation of his conduct had to be flawed. But when I listened to Chuh-yuh's composition, my suspicion returned. In it, I heard a despair that sounded too real for its subject to be a mere fiction or myth."

I sighed: Here was another mystery to add to all the others. What could possibly connect the mysterious Orange Book, homeopathic art, Viola's disappearance, the changing paints, the pump, and the double trident? And what did the bird catcher, the puppeteer, and Tannhäuser have in common with all this? I felt like a reader of one of Num's novels, in which these words appeared in isolation, spread out over hundreds of blank pages.

"You said that years ago various legends about the Orange Book were in circulation. Can you still remember any of them?" I asked.

"I forgot most of them long ago. All I know now is that it was said to be some kind of Hermetic tract written by a high-placed initiate, an alchemistic guide or an ancient prophecy concerning the present. All nonsense, apparently."

Chapter 22
Meeting

Still the storekeeper hadn't answered my burning question. "So how *did* you meet Viola?"

"I was just getting around to that. The girl you call Viola turned up at Tam-Tam three days after Chuh-yuh first came here. She was looking for Vuhulum Chuh-yuh, she told me. I remember being struck by how fluently she pronounced that strange mix of consonants, as though for her it was the most common name in the world. She'd gotten the address of the store from the magazine that had published my article. While she was there she'd also found out that Chuh-yuh had been in touch with them and was planning to visit me. I told her that she'd missed him and regrettably I didn't know where he lived or even what his real name was, but if she wanted to speak with him, she'd find him here at five on Monday.

"Chuh-yuh arrived at the store with his recordings at the appointed time. We talked over some details and I tried in vain to press him for information on the Orange Book. At a quarter after five the door opened and Viola appeared. Her arrival had a strange effect on Chuh-yuh. He stopped talking and stared at her for a moment; then he recovered himself, as if coming out of a dream."

"And Viola?"

"Her behavior was perfectly calm. All she said to Chuh-yuh was, 'I've come to see you.' Finally Chuh-yuh smiled and said,

'Of course, that's fine.' He and I then quickly went through the remaining matters concerning the publishing of the CD. When I mentioned his fee, he just waved a hand dismissively. The whole time this was going on, the girl stood there silent and motionless. When our discussion was at an end, Chuh-yuh said goodbye to me and left. The girl went with him. As soon as I was alone, I put the tape on. I felt like I was dreaming: I was listening to music by Chuh-yuh which I'd thought for years was a fairy story."

"Weren't you disappointed?"

"Oh no. I liked both pieces very much and was moved by them. The first was just a jumble of quiet sounds. Most people wouldn't have made any sense of it or even have managed to listen to it, but I knew very well what Chuh-yuh's intentions were—to breach two musical boundaries, the one that separated music from other sounds and the one that separated it from silence. I listened with excitement to sounds from a territory that belonged neither to the realm of music nor to the realm of silence—a territory that belonged nowhere; I heard them in a void, as they recalled some kind of ancient order. The second piece was more similar to what is commonly known as music; its dominant notes of despair alternated with notes of resigned sorrow."

"Did you ever see Viola again?"

"No. Nor Chuh-yuh. I was hoping he'd show up when the CD of his music was released, but he never did."

Obviously the storekeeper had told me all he knew about Chuh-yuh and the double trident. I thanked him for his story, paid for the CD and prepared to hurry home to listen to it. The storekeeper settled more comfortably in his rocking chair, took up his book from the counter and gave me a wave. I saw from the round clock on the wall above the ticket offices that it was already three o'clock. I had reached the middle of the station hall when I heard someone calling me. I turned to see the storekeeper running across the shiny floor.

"There's something I forgot." His voice reverberated through the empty space. "I don't know if it's any help to you, but I've seen the symbol Chuh-yuh named his work by, from the train, on the wall of a building not far from here. The train circles the edge of the city. If you take the westbound, you'll see the building after a few minutes, midway between stops."

Then he returned to his store. For a few moments I stood irresolute in the middle of the station. I could hardly wait to listen to Chuh-yuh's music, but at the same time I was terribly curious about the building with the double trident. Above the coffee vending machine was a schedule composed of large black letters and numerals. From this I learned that the next train left two hours from now. Lacking the patience necessary for such a long wait at the station, I decided to go home.

Chapter 23
Two Compositions

As I left the station, the heat of the afternoon entered my lungs like a hot paste in which I distinguished the smells of asphalt, crumbling plaster and rotting fruit from the market nearby. The bus terminal stood on the other side of the street, the driver on a break with the engine switched off. Then the bus drove up and I took a seat right at the back. As the walls beyond the windows changed, I thought over my visit to the station. I still had no idea whether my chat with the storekeeper would be of any use to me in my search for Viola, but whatever it meant, it had left me feeling pleased.

I'd met people like the owner of Tam-Tam before. The life of one was very much like that of another. They had no real need to tell their stories; it was plain by the way they moved their hands as if directed by a light, invisible current that the rest of their bodies were too heavy for them. Thirty years ago, when the realities of life in this country were transformed into a kind of weird dream and hope retreated from the world, in silence these types of people went away into the void, a void which took various forms. There was nowhere in the now emerging world they were able to live, so they found themselves a no-place and settled there, for years. When ten years ago the dream dissolved, they were used to this void in which they had lived for so long; they loved their no-place, its magic was well known to them, they were at home with the miracle of its fauna and flora. What the world was now offering them, so it seemed, was precious little. All those years partaking of the wonderful nectar of nothingness had made them hard to please; they had no appetite for food of another kind, nor could the splendors of any other building compare to those of the palace of emptiness. So they stayed there. This does not mean that they all lived in abandoned station halls; often they walked among us. But wherever they were, still they were nowhere, carrying with them their emptiness as if it were a lightweight tent. Other people would feel rather sorry for them and were sometimes contemptuous of them: "He's not capable of coming back to the real world," they would say. Even so, perhaps those who said these things had some kind of awareness of how much our world needed the perspective of those who never came back. It was a point of view which protected the sick things in our world by spreading a healing emptiness over them, a balmy nothingness which took long years to mature and as such was a fruit of the past, bringing sense, conciliation, hope, and joy.

At home I put the CD into the player and lay down on the couch. The first composition I would hear had a strange title: "The Manifestation and Extinction of the Orange Book: a sonata played behind walls at 3:00 a.m." Though the Tam-Tam storekeeper had prepared me for it, at first I was quite confused by the music I heard. For a long time there was no sound at all, then after five minutes or so there was a sound that might have been that of a train in the distance. I had to quiet my breathing and strain my ears for the sounds that pierced the silence. There was another long silence before I made out the faint hum of distant conversation. This was submerged in another wave of silence, after which I unpicked from the blocks of silence various rustlings, creakings, something somewhere knocking into something, something rolling around something and then stopping, something pointed that was scratching, something crumbling . . . These might have been tiny sounds on the outer wall of a house, or a din softened by a great distance.

Try as I might to hold my breath, I was half an hour into the piece and still I hadn't been able to make out a single note from a piano. Perhaps the pianist was sitting behind so many walls that I wasn't going to hear anything of his composition. Then again, why should I be disappointed by a sonata which was swallowed up by walls? I was beginning to understand the man at Tam-Tam: These sounds that bordered on silence were changing my apprehension of sound and silence. No longer did it seem that there was any great difference between them. While silence was full of nascent sounds, sounds were drenched in the silence out of which they were born. And so it was enough for me to listen calmly to the silence of a night in the early eighties, the subject of Chuh-yuh's narrative, and to know that it contained a piano sonata.

But then the sonata really did make itself heard. The notes of a piano softened by distance and many walls insinuated themselves among the other sounds, where they were received in friendship. The piano music didn't rise above the other sounds. At that moment its notes were the children of silence just as the other sounds were. And likewise the main purpose of the piano was to protect and preserve the fabric of the silence, the breath of silence which continued to give life to all sounds without distinguishing between them. The pianist was surely playing far away, behind many walls; several times the sonata was lost for a while in the silence or else stifled by rustlings of the city at night, sounds which were barely louder than the sound of the piano keys.

I tried to make out the moods and sensations this distant composition was conveying. The problem was that everything seemed to be based in the mother, silence; their separation from her was incomplete, and each played their part in ensuring her peace. Yet the small step they took from the mother was enough to reveal a dark despair, which was then lost in the pacifying silence. At moments when the piece was heard somewhat more clearly, it was possible to make out a recurring melody that was playing variations on a basic motif of four notes—D, A-flat, B-flat, C—as they rode the mournful arc from initial rise to the resignation of decline, and back again. A short time later the sonata was lost again in the silence. The silence lasted some ten minutes, after which came a scraping and scratching before the piece ended.

I might compare the piece to a blank, white screen, upon which nothing but a few grayish lines appear, at first sight practically indiscernible. It lasted almost an hour, and for most of that time, all that was heard was silence. My thoughts returned to the man at Tam-Tam; I could understand why he liked music like this. His whole life long he must have cultivated an appreciation of nothingness and learned to savor the nuances of emptiness. I thought, too, of Viola listening to the sounds of the night, and I wondered if there was some kind of connection between the nighttime silence Julie had spoken of and this composition made twenty years ago. Indeed, Chuh-yuh's composition was a testimony to his having at that time sat at night in an unlit room, listening for something. Among the sounds of the night, had he been searching for the same voice as Viola? And, of course, I still didn't know what the Orange Book of the piece's title was. Perhaps it held the key to the Viola mystery and that of the double trident. All I could discern from the composition was that the book was closely connected with an immense sadness.

What followed was the piece that had the double trident as its title. If you weren't listening with great concentration, you probably would have noticed very little to set it apart from traditional forms of music. But it wasn't my impression that Chuh-yuh was humbly returning to tradition after his experimental period; apparently, silence was engaged here in an aggressive campaign on tradition's territory. It seemed that since the composer had spent some time in sound's borderlands and had explored the role of silence there, he now heard the rhythms of silence in every sound and every note. And now he wished to deploy the power of silence in the realm most distant to it and which put up the greatest resistance. This was the realm of notes, rhythms and keys, musical motifs and pure melodies.

The piece began with a babble of different motifs, dozens of them perhaps, invading each other's territory and then blending one into another, as if caught up in a dreamlike whirl. The world this music was opening up was one of chaos, but also one replete with hope and expectation. At the same time it seemed to me that it was shot through with the melancholia of reminiscence: Perhaps the composer was recalling a joyful beginning of long ago. Out of this whirl, three different motifs came to the fore and then fought themselves free; each of these took on echoes of the others, more and more they came to resemble one another, without, however, surrendering their uniqueness. In the piece's next part they became entwined to form a single melody, though not even then was the fusion complete, as each motif retained a semblance of independence. I had an image of a rope woven from three sources. And who was to say that these sources were only three in number? Out of the three-in-one melody I was able to distinguish with ever greater certainty a fourth strand, one that was light in both color and weight and that differed from the original three. It was as if the composer had wished to suppress it, as if he hadn't wished or wasn't supposed to refer to it but at the same time had been unable to prevent himself from thinking of it. I had the feeling that a darker and heavier strand would succeed the one that was denied, as if this were a thin, light, practically imperceptible thread from a coil of rope really immensely strong and able to bear the entire load alone.

While I was listening, I fiddled with the case of the CD. At one point my eye was caught by the double trident symbol that gave the piece its title; it suddenly came to me that it could be some kind of diagram of musical composition, where the lower oval represented the whirl of the beginning and the three arms of the lower trident the three strands of melody that would work themselves free. That the arms drew closer to each other meant a growing similarity between the individual motifs, while the vertical line that the arms of the lower trident led into denoted the weaving of the motifs into a single melody. Then I had another idea: Maybe the content of this piece provided a history of the White Triangle in music. Perhaps Chuh-yuh's music described how Chuh-yuh, Oo, and Num drew closer together, to the point where a fellowship was formed, which at that time may or may not have been the White Triangle. Let's see, I told myself, whether the shape of things will continue to correspond to the development of the music.

But what was I to make of this fourth, more luminous strand? There was something in it that reminded me of the melody in the last piece played by the nighttime, wall-muffled piano. And this it indeed became: The notes D, A-flat, B-flat, C sounded again. After this, the Orange Book motif melted back into the luminous strand out of which it had broken. What was the meaning of this? I had the feeling that the Orange Book had somehow closed, that it had retreated from the world. Might someone have stolen or destroyed it? If this composition really was referring to a time twenty years before, it was of course highly likely that the Orange Book—whatever it was—had existed in a single typescript, and that this had been lost. I recalled similar instances of disappearing manuscripts from my own experience.

Shortly afterward, the luminous strand, too, died away. The notes I was hearing now displayed the starkness of despair. With the death of the luminous strand, some kind of break occurred in the composition: I was convinced that this moment represented the horizontal line in the diagram that was the intersection with the vertical, thus dividing the symbol into two halves. As the piece went on, a dissonance built among the three remaining strands, and three melodies again extricated themselves from the whole; the vertical line opened itself up into the three arms of the upper trident—the paths of Chuh-yuh, Oo, and Num had parted. The whole thing drew to a close in notes that expressed conciliation and sadness, as in the first piece. Each of the strands held echoes of the magically transformed notes of the luminous strand and the motif from the Orange Book.

I had the impression that Chuh-yuh was letting me in on the secret I'd been struggling to untangle, that he was keeping nothing from me—but he was telling me all this in the language of music, which I was incapable of transferring into words and pictures. The least penetrable of the events the music described came in the middle of the piece and represented the line at the center of the symbol. This was the blind spot the man at Tam-Tam had spoken of; it referred to the time when the mysterious Orange Book had appeared or been discovered, soon after which—apparently—it had somehow vanished. It was my bet that during this time the double trident symbol had first appeared, meaning that the double trident was a diagram that represented its own creation.

For a little while yet I mused on the events Chuh-yuh's music was telling of, until the effort of doing so gave me a headache. I was feeling restless. Unable to stay in the flat, I determined to seek out the building with the double trident that the man at Tam-Tam had mentioned. I hurried out to make sure that I got to the station while it was still light.

Chapter 24
At the Porter's Lodge

The man at Tam-Tam had said that the building was not far from the railway line, and I would spot it midway between stations if I took the train which skirted around the city. It was my first intention to return to the railway station, but then I realized that there was another, closer stop and that it would be easier to start my journey from there. When I arrived at the platform, the passengers were just boarding the train.

No sooner had I found an empty compartment and sat down, the train pulled out. The tracks curved gently around a belt of low-rise factory buildings scattered around the city's edge. The area where the shadow met the reddish light (as reflected through the train's dirty windows) gradually pulled the gray leatherette of the seats opposite into darkness. Through the window of the corridor I saw rolling hills covered in yellowed grass, with geometric concrete shapes dotted mysteriously here and there. That side of the tracks, I thought, wasn't worth bothering with: I would concentrate my efforts on the window. It was far from easy to see much through it, with its layers of dirt made to look like gold dust, causing shapes to dissolve in the light of the evening sun. And the flame of the sun was now so low that it burned into the structures passing immediately alongside the train, then vanished behind dark blocks of concrete, reappeared in the gaps between buildings, flashed between the pillars of a construction site, rode the metal of electricity pylons, was lost for a time behind a high wooden fence, and when the fence flew away like a scrap of paper, painfully plunged itself into my eyes.

In this interplay of harsh light and gloom, it was difficult to make out shapes against shadows, sensation from perception. In the jumble of shapes flooding the window, I extrapolated rather than recognized things—an abandoned warehouse where some concrete arches had been stacked up and tangles of grooved, white plastic piping were lying about; transformer stations with ceramic insulation, their wires like great corals; low- and high-rise plasterboard hostels with bars on their windows.

After a while, the sun moved over to the other side of the train, but even so my view of what lay along the track wasn't made much easier. In the gloom I followed the restless interplay of the changing vistas; flitting past my eyes were houses and workshops, cranes, square towers made out of shipping containers (where one side caught the rays of the sun and shone pink), lines of parked trucks, machines. All these things rested motionless on the asphalt, but still they moved about madly, as if this inflexible world of ours was in the giant hands of some suburban demon who was playing a crazy game of dice with it.

I saw a great many letters and symbols. I caught brief, fragmented glimpses of the signs and logos of businesses; one unintelligible snippet of word followed another, as the aperture closed before I could make out the whole thing. As the shapes and signs came and went and the words expanded and contracted, I tried desperately to make out a double trident—but I was getting used to the idea that I would have to go over the route again in the brighter light of day. And I told myself that the storekeeper might have been mistaken; I myself had seen plenty of signs, letters, and designs in metal that my impatient imagination had tried to turn into the shape I was looking for.

There was a moment when I thought I glimpsed, darting across the edge of my vision between two stacks of wooden pallets, a rounded sign which opened out at the top. But it disappeared before I could redirect my gaze, popped up on the other side of the window for a fraction of a second, then was lost again.

It might have been playing hide-and-seek with me. I'd given up hope of seeing it again that day when the roofs suddenly dropped towards the ground; above them, right in front of my eyes, with nothing to conceal it, a double trident glided into view like a condor. It was painted on the wall of a white building submerged in the thickening shadows.

Passing the familiar ticket counters, I saw that the lights were out in the CD store. I bought a coffee from the machine and stood drinking it in the middle of the empty, ill-lit station. By the time I emerged from the station building, it was almost completely dark. I set off for the place where I reckoned the double-trident building might be, along lit-up wire fences and walls bordered by dusty clumps of grass. In the sky, the belt of red light above the long, low buildings got thinner and thinner. I passed the porter's lodges of warehouses and garages, their lights burning; I caught the sound of a TV thriller: muffled gunshots, screams and cars speeding off and braking.

It didn't take me long to find the building with the double trident. Its front wall was painted black and lit by a flickering fluorescent tube. The building's floor plan was shaped like the Greek pi; it opened onto the street and embraced an asphalt yard. I stopped in front of a wide, closed iron gate and inspected the building's silhouette in a twilight whose fading reds were reflected in the asphalt yard as if this were an expanse of dark water. Just beyond the gate was a porter's lodge with glass walls, reached by several concrete steps. To my surprise, there was no television blaring inside, just the sharp light of a desk lamp. All the other windows of the building were in darkness. Only then did it occur to me how foolish I was being; in seeking out a hieroglyph on a wall at so late an hour, I should have expected to find nothing more than a porter, and he was hardly likely to know much about the symbol. I'll come back tomorrow morning, I told myself. I'll ask one of the firm's office staff for all the details he can give me.

The door of the porter's lodge opened, and the porter appeared on the steps in an unbuttoned shirt and gray trousers that seemed to be part of a uniform. Perhaps he'd noticed that there was someone hanging about in front of the gate. A large, shaggy German shepherd darted out of the open door and into the yard, then sat down on the asphalt and started growling at me.

"Looking for someone?" the porter called out to me.

I put my face between two of the gate's vertical bars. "I was just taking a breather. I'll be moving on," I said, my tone apologetic, even though standing on the street was hardly a criminal offense. But the porter certainly didn't seem unfriendly; I thought perhaps he was bored and pleased to be able to speak to someone. So I asked him about the business of the firm whose premises he watched over. He told me they made office equipment. No mystery in that; I should have expected something of the sort, but still I was disappointed by the banality.

"I'm interested in the firm's emblem," I went on. "I need to know where it came from, and if it means anything. I'll come back tomorrow in working hours. I don't suppose you could tell me who I could ask about it?"

The porter came down the steps into the yard. In the lamplight, the perspiration on the top of his bald head gleamed and the thin skin of his eagle-like nose was taut. The play of shadows across his face accentuated prominent cheekbones and an elongated face that could have belonged to a hermit or an ascetic monk. He came right up to the bars.

"I couldn't, really," came his reply. "You won't find anything out about that emblem from the staff. None of them knows anything about the symbol's history."

"Well, I think I might try tomorrow anyway."

"As you wish, but it'll be just as I say," said the porter. He stayed where he was. Now that the German shepherd had seen that the porter was having a friendly conversation with me, it had stopped its growling. It stuck its nose through the bars and had a good sniff at me. I petted the dog and prepared to take my leave of its master.

Then the porter said, "There is one person who knows quite a lot about the firm's emblem."

"Would you mind telling me who? It's really quite important to me."

"I'm the only one here who knows anything about it," he

told me calmly. "If you've got time, I could tell you the story. It's pretty long, but it's no company secret. There's nothing for me to do here anyway. My eyes are bad, so I can't read, and there's only some stupid film on TV."

I told him I had all night. The porter rattled a padlock on a heavy chain for a few moments, then eased one wing of the gate open for me to slip through. The dog threw itself at me with joy and proceeded to lick my hand.

The porter's lodge was rather a small space crammed with an old desk and chair and a threadbare corduroy-covered armchair. On the floor next to the armchair was a folded blanket. The windows to the street and the yard were wide open. The porter motioned me to the armchair, himself taking the chair next to the desk. The dog lay down on the blanket, stuck its head under my chair's wobbly armrest and onto my lap, and closed its eyes. I sat and waited for what the porter had to tell me.

"Will it bother you if I start my story in the very distant past?" he asked. I had to laugh; I was taking it for granted now that everything to do with Viola's disappearance and the double trident had its roots in a time twenty or thirty years earlier.

"You can start with Franz Joseph, if you like," I said. I was still a bit puzzled that he hadn't asked after the reason for my interest in the firm's logo.

It was the porter's turn to smile. "If it's all the same to you, I'll start somewhat earlier—during the reign of the emperor Anastasius, 1,500 years ago."

Now that did surprise me, but I told myself that the key to Viola's secret might indeed be hidden in events of such a distant time.

Chapter 25
The Decline of the Athenian Academy

"Ever heard of a Neoplatonic philosopher called Dionysius of Gaza?" the porter asked.

"Can't say that I have."

"Dionysius of Gaza was born sometime between 503 and 506—we don't know when exactly. His father was a Greek and his mother a Syrian. We know little about Dionysius's childhood, though it's highly likely that the odder, darker sides of his nature—out of which was to evolve the story of his life—had their origins in the anxieties and dreams of Dionysius the child. He might have been illegitimate; it seems his mother was of far lower social status than his father, who made no official claim to paternity. But this is really just speculation: We don't actually have any firm evidence of the early years of his life. Perhaps we are swayed by the ambiguous and twisted attitude toward authority of the older Dionysius, his yearning to be accepted and revered while seeking to belittle those who loved him; to hurt them, even. I think that everything written about Dionysius's early years was a result of the projection of features of the adult Dionysius onto an unknown child in Gaza. As far as we know, in none of his tracts or letters did Dionysius refer to his childhood. So we get this hazy figure of a forbidding father, at once loved and hated; many historians have treated him as real. And of course, beginnings such as these would not have passed the psychoanalysts by. As the case may be, the shadow of the father comes to the surface in the deepest analysis of Dionysius's works, even though this father has no more foundation in proven fact than the deity of Asian legend which followers of his later teachings claim to have been his father.

"It seems that Dionysius was extraordinarily bright from his earliest youth. He grew up in Gaza, where he learned the basics of rhetoric and philosophy. Even then his teachers were investing great hopes in him and even then he was causing them upset by his indiscipline and spitefulness. At nineteen he left for Alexandria, where he attended lectures given by the pagan Platonists. There, too, he was spoken of as a future star of the school, while his teachers long tried to overlook the scorn and ironizing which accompanied his every expression—hoping that one day he would grow out of them. Some time later, Dionysius got on the boat to Athens; he was restless his whole life, roaming from place to place, until at last he reached somewhere he didn't wish to leave. But here I'm getting ahead of myself.

"At the Academy in Athens, they knew his name already. Though Dionysius's early fame as a philosopher had crossed the sea, news of his obnoxious character had not; so he was welcomed at the Academy eagerly and with open arms. The teachings professed here were nine hundred years old. Three hundred years earlier they had been rejuvenated by the beautiful writings of Plotinus, but since that time the signs of the old had returned. What Plotinus had built, once clear as crystal, was now shrouded in darkness, having fallen prey in the minds of his successors to overelaboration; the Athenian Platonists felt a sadness that their devoted efforts were failing to keep Plotinus's school of thought from becoming a maze of barbarism. So it is understandable they should dream that the teachings of the young philosopher from Gaza would bring revival, a return to the purity and simple fervor of the beginnings.

"From the very first day Dionysius appeared at the Academy and took part in a disputation in the round pavilion—through whose columns the high trees of the garden were visible—the academicians had a high regard for his intellect. And on that first day, too, he caused them exasperation with his diatribes and the vicious comments he would direct at one or other of them. While at the Academy, his intellect evolved still further and his behavior became more and more difficult to tolerate. What upset the others most of all was how he would sit leaning against a column, listening in sneering silence to what they had to say. They complained about him to the scholarch Damascius, but Damascius stood up for Dionysius, claiming that youth and homesickness excused his behavior, and that he would soon grow out of it; he asked the others to show him forbearance. But, of course, Damascius suffered more than any of them by Dionysius's impossible behavior. He had a genuine affection for him and dreamed that, by succeeding him as head of the school, Dionysius would revive the Academy's glory. Poor Damascius had no idea that he himself would be the school's last scholarch, that philosophy would soon fall into a deep sleep from which it wouldn't begin to wake for many years, and even then in the palaces of Baghdad. Do you mind if I smoke?"

I shook my head, and the porter lit a cigarette before continuing.

"But Dionysius's behavior didn't get any better. Quite the opposite, in fact, as his thoughts became darker. In addition to his insolent sneering and irony, he now provoked the others by the eccentricity of his views. It seemed almost as if he wished to cause Damascius pain; if so, his intentions were brilliantly successful . . ."

I had the impression that the porter felt real sadness for how Dionysius had behaved towards the scholarch of the Academy, as if the man so mistreated were one of his own friends. As I listened to his tale, I watched the twisting of the white smoke, a moving picture against the giant screen of the night sky, spattered by the colored lights of the railway track. I remembered the restless shape on the screen in the graphic artist's studio, the thing that had led me to Jonáš's villa. Would I have been surprised if the cigarette smoke had taken the shape of the mysterious double trident? After all, I no longer found it so amazing that the symbol Viola had tattooed on her body should have something in common with a long-dead Greek philosopher, who in turn was linked with a company that produced office equipment. But the tildes of smoke didn't settle in any particular form.

"Dionysius's theories became influenced by the ideas and beliefs of the Gnostics, which had originated in the cults of the Orient. The faltering Platonism of other schools of philosophy wasn't immune to this dark influence from Asia: The light of the teachings of Athens had grown dim. But the Platonists still believed the world to be a divine creation endowed with a dazzling beauty; they were terrified by the Gnostics' hatred of the world and would never be reconciled to the idea of an evil creator. Dionysius played a wicked game with them. He would articulate ideas that gave every appearance of having originated with the Gnostics, and when one member of his audience could bear this no longer, leaping to his feet to accuse Dionysius of betraying Plato's teachings, Dionysius, sarcastically, would set about demonstrating his critic's failure to understand the thesis, thus making a fool of him. The philosopher, his face burning with shame and rage, would then sit down again.

"Whether Dionysius really believed these ideas is unclear; it's quite probable he uttered them only to irritate his peers and the scholarch. I believe that over time Dionysius himself lost sight of why he was doing this. Damascius came to the painful realization that he could no longer justify Dionysius's position at the Academy, and that it would be necessary to dismiss him. It was 529, and Dionysius was between twenty-three and twenty-six years old. But in the early morning of the day Damascius had chosen for the vote on whether Dionysius should be excluded, a messenger appeared on the path between the trees. The news he brought was that the emperor Justinian had ordered the prohibition of schools of philosophy. After nine hundred years, the Academy was to close.

"The news shook them all, and the pain it brought served to unite them. The neurotic Dionysius burst into tears and fell to the ground—this time, it seemed, he wasn't pretending. Damascius put his arms around him and soothed him as if he were a small child. And in this way Dionysius gave them all some comfort, and they forgave him everything. The fragment of a letter has survived in which an unknown Platonist gives an emotional description of how the members of the Academy—led by Damascius and among them Dionysius—walked in the Academy's gardens for the last time. No one spoke; in silence they listened to the murmur of the leaves in the evening breeze and watched the dusk fall on the white buildings between the trees. When Damascius, Simplicius and a number of other Platonists took a boat from Piraeus, bound for Persia and the court of Chosrau Anosharvan at Ctesiphon, in the hope that their philosophy would live on there, Dionysius was with them."

As he spoke, the porter looked through the window into the darkness, where the stars twinkled and the lights burned above the railway track. He was silent for a while, then he turned to me and asked, "Don't you think it's odd that you should learn about things like this from a porter?"

"Not really," I said truthfully. The moment the porter had appeared in the yard, I had seen he was one of those people I'd been thinking about that afternoon—like the owner of the CD store. Many of them were about the porter's age.

"You're about fifty, right?"

The porter nodded. "Fifty-two."

"So I reckon you started studying philosophy, history or the classics at the end of the sixties, and you finished your studies in the mid-seventies. Then you either couldn't or didn't want to work in the field you were qualified for, so you lived in caravans, warehouses and porter's lodges and studied the things that interested you—let's say Greek philosophy or Byzantine history. When the changes came, you were over forty, and you saw those older than you return to the places they'd been kicked out off at the beginning of the seventies, while the younger ones still had the feeling they could make a start somewhere, if a little late. You were too young to have anywhere to go back to, but at the same time you felt yourself to be too old to start out somewhere—so you just stayed in the porter's lodge. Maybe at the beginning you told yourself that in time you would find yourself a decent job, but as the years went by, you thought about it less and less. When you're on the night shift you read, study and think; I should think you've always got a book open during the day, too, hidden behind the visitors' log, about the fall of the Roman Empire or Neoplatonism. Am I right?"

As I was speaking, the porter nodded his head and wore an expression of amused approval.

"Not much to add to that," he said. "There's only one thing you got wrong. Sadly my eyes have become so bad recently that I can hardly read at all any more. But let's get back to Dionysius. Now where were we?"

"On the boat, bound for Asia Minor."

Chapter 26
Dionysius in Persia

"Dionysius's peace with the school didn't last long. In Ctesiphon he soon started again with his gibes and bizarre theories. And now everything was worse than it had been in Athens. I can well imagine how impossible it would be among the white columns of Athens to give oneself up completely to the theology of whimsy or demonology. Once in Asia, Dionysius's thinking began to absorb like a sponge all the cults peculiar to the continent, while his Gnosticism became yet more eccentric and hostile to the world. And behind the backs of the Greeks he was meeting with the Persian bigwigs; it was not long before Damascius learned to his amazement that the Persians and even Chosrau himself spoke of Dionysius as the most venerable of the Greeks.

"Perhaps Damascius told himself he shouldn't be upset by such behavior, and he wouldn't allow the meanness of his former protégé to distract him from his spiritual labors; nevertheless, his heart was racked with bitterness, and not for a moment did he forgive Dionysius these actions. For hour upon hour he would sit on the terrace of his house and watch in silence the slow course of the murky Tigris. Who's to say he didn't see on its surface the white columns among the leaves of the Academy's gardens? What else was left to him but to watch images drifting over the river's surface? He knew he would never see Athens again, and his dream of reestablishing the Academy in Asia had proven to be nothing but a childish fancy. The person he'd once seen as a son wasn't only denigrating his work—which Damascius loved more than ever in the twilight of his life; he was conspiring against his teacher at the court of a foreign lord. Dionysius gathered around himself a group of followers made up of Greeks, Persians and Syrians. It was always very important to him that he had the acclaim and love of others . . ."

"Wait a moment, I don't get this. If what he desired was acclaim and love, why did he behave so terribly at the Academy?"

"Because it irritated him that he had to appear as one among equals and argue his ideas. Dionysius yearned to be heard as a great teacher and scholar, for others to acclaim his ideas purely because it was he who had uttered them. In Ctesiphon he had at last found the followers he had longed for, who received his words as if they contained revelations, never raising the slightest objection, in thought or in deed. And his mysterious, enraptured teaching performances—he would address his pupils in a low voice, with long pauses for dramatic effect—came to resemble philosophy less and less. The academicians felt uncomfortable in his presence. Whenever he appeared at their meetings, he spoiled everybody's mood; fortunately this had become a rare occurrence. And it seems he really was pretty unbearable—during philosophical debates he would usually say nothing, preferring to sit in the corner and pull all manner of faces. Once he went to a philosophers' banquet at which the academicians talked of the nature of the process by which the incipient, undifferentiated One flows out of itself. Dionysius remained silent and drank a lot of wine, but then he interrupted what Simplicius was saying. Once standing, he swayed slightly from side to side and started to babble some nonsense about the evil Demiurge and the blind archons . . ."

"Am I right to understand from your story that Dionysius really did have an excellent mind and understood perfectly well the solemnity of ideas? People don't usually forget such things for the sake of befuddled fables. How do you explain such a loss of concentration?"

"Dionysius hadn't lost his concentration—of course he hadn't. I very much doubt that during his time at Ctesiphon he genuinely believed the teachings he propounded; he just found them an excellent means of attracting admirers and simultaneously provoking his teachers. Later, possibly, he really did believe what he was saying—and became, like the last of his followers, a late neophyte in his own teachings. As the case may be, Dionysius's inebriated performance at the symposium seems to have exhausted Damascius's patience. As Damascius stood, his hands were visibly shaking. In a tremulous voice he said he refused to listen to such obscenities. Then he ordered Dionysius to leave the hall and never again attend a meeting of the Greeks. His face distorted in a sneer, Dionysius staggered out."

I asked myself how it was that the porter knew such details. Had they survived in letters the Athenian academicians had written in Persia? But those few days of searching for Viola, listening to strange stories of all kinds and getting hints of stories stranger still, were slowly depriving me of the ability to reason objectively. In the porter's long face with its dark, deep-set eyes which put me in mind of a figure from a Byzantine mosaic, I had the fantastic impression of a man looking back on a past life—in which Damascius, maybe Dionysius himself had played a part.

"This scene marked the end of Dionysius's dealings with the philosophers of Athens. He lived at the center of his small group of students, and they continued to listen with zeal and terror to his lectures, in which the ideas of Plato's *Timaeus* mixed with talk of a deranged Demiurge, the creator of the world. After three years, Justinian moderated his edict, with the result that the philosophers decided to move on to Haran in Mesopotamia. This was in the territory of the Byzantine Empire, though it was distant from Constantinople and even further from Athens. By messenger, Damascius sent a note to Dionysius asking if he wished to leave with them, but Dionysius did not deign to reply . . ."

The porter fell silent. He looked through the window at the black sky, which bore a thin, red, crack-like stripe. The smell of hot asphalt still reached us from the yard.

"And how did everything turn out?" I probed.

"Damascius and Simplicius lived out their days in Haran. There, pagan Platonism was still breathing. In fact it lived on comatose until it came into contact with the Arabs, after which it shook itself awake and embarked on the long journey back to

Europe—via the north coast of Africa and Moorish Spain. For a while Dionysius was Chosrau's favorite, but then there was some kind of scandal. They said he had violated the daughter of a king's counselor. Dionysius and his faithful followers had to flee Ctesiphon by night. Their path took them further from Damascius and Simplicius; they headed east, and their trail was soon lost. No one who had known Dionysius in Gaza, Athens and Ctesiphon ever heard of him again. We don't know his main reason for heading to the very edge of the known world. Did he go east because it was easier in the wilderness to escape Chosrau's soldiers, who had set off in pursuit of him? Had his old hatred of anything he could call home returned, and did he wish for this reason to get as far away from Athens as he could? Or did he catch the scent of a dark wind blowing from the heart of Asia? As the case may be, Dionysius was lost to his contemporaries for good."

"The Greeks must have been amazingly patient to stick it out with him for so long. Surely they had enough to worry about without having to listen to his insolent nonsense."

"Indeed. But there's something else. Perhaps they really needed Dionysius, without ever clearly understanding why . . . A scholar in Cambridge—I can't remember his name, unfortunately—reckons Dionysius and the Academy were joined by a fine and intricate web of sympathy and hatred. And so to view the relationship in terms of prodigal son and indulgent father would be a gross simplification . . ."

"I really don't understand what it was that bound the philosophers to him."

"The roles Dionysius played at the Academy were manifold. Apart from his being a philosopher of great promise, an ungrateful son, a star pupil—albeit a dreadful one—and a traitor to the teachings, Dionysius had another important function; although the philosophers might never have admitted it, they kept him for show, like an animal in a cage. It was a role they needed him to play, hence their willingness to pamper him to such masochistic ends. Dionysius's shameless, public utterings caused them great offense, but his words reached them as if from a completely different world; in them they heard words that found a resonance somewhere within, an echo in their own thoughts—though diluted, suppressed and disguised in all kinds of ways. The philosophers needed a visual representation of a sickness that terrified them to the core, and from which they were unable to recover. By putting evil in such a visible and concentrated form, they made it easier to confront; also, this manifestation served to convince them that they were still fighting it. They needed to hate Dionysius in order not to hate themselves . . ."

"Curious, to keep an animal that plays host to our demon, just to give it a body we can beat . . . Is that the end of Dionysius's story? Haven't you forgotten to mention the connection between these ancient tales and the company emblem?"

"No, we haven't reached the end yet. But now we have to jump forward 1300 years. Let's take a break, and in the meantime I'll pop down to the cellar for some wine."

This was an excellent idea; after the day's events I was tired and parched, and I'd long been thinking I could do with a drink. The porter went out, to return a few minutes later with a bottle, which he put down on the desk. I saw from its label that it was a very expensive French wine. I was taken aback that the porter should offer such a rare wine to someone he barely knew, but when I brought this up, he said that the pleasure was all his—and that he had reasons of his own for wanting to open the bottle. He filled our glasses and went on with his story.

Chapter 27
In the Wilds of Afghanistan

"In 1807 in London, a senior civil servant called Samuel Archer became a father for the first time. His son was named Archibald. Archer went on to have three daughters and another son, called Edward—you should remember him, because he appears later in the story, but all we need to say about him for now is that he became a designer of steam engines. Archibald went up to Cambridge to study Classics and Archaeology; he translated Sophocles, tried to write some poems of his own, and gave lectures in Archaeology. And he engaged in wild drinking parties that ended more than once in his arrest for disturbing the peace, he was something of an eccentric in his dress, and he counted Wordsworth and Thomas de Quincey among his friends. But he slandered the family name most by his expeditions of adventure to various sites in Central Asia, where he performed archaeological research. We might think of him as the Indiana Jones of his time.

"At the end of the 1830s, he found himself in the wilds of northern Afghanistan. He was traveling alone, by mule. Few of the natives saw a foreigner in the swarthy bearded rider who was dressed much as they were. Archibald spoke fluent Persian and Pashto, and he was able to communicate in several other, local languages. After two weeks on the road he reached a vast plain with a cold, wide river twisting through it; at its edge in the distant north rose a bluish belt of tall mountains. This intangible expanse of mountain range fused with the white light of the sky, providing a focus for Archibald's monotonous path over the plain. But as he approached the base of the mountains and the blues became beiges and ochres, he observed that the villagers saw a dark threat in the mountains. The windows of their dwellings were turned away from their slopes; only rarely would they lift their faces in that direction. For the villagers, the mountains were the home of demons, and they emitted a silent, indeterminate, but omnipresent sense of peril. The villagers still had something of the nomad in their blood, even though they'd settled here centuries back. They would embark on great journeys by horseback, but none of the expeditions would ever pass through the mountains a mere half-day's distance from their home. Men of great bravery who went around with daggers in their belts and regarded a skirmish with bandits as part of the life of the road, were afraid of the mountains, and nobody thought to mock them for it.

"When Archibald reached the base of the mountains, he happened upon the camp of a Royal Geographical Society expedition. Though its leader was no believer in demons, he tried to dissuade Archibald from entering the great unknown that the mountains represented. At dusk Archibald sat with his countrymen around the fire, paying scant attention to their tales of adventure and reminiscences of life in London; he was watching the darkening rocky inclines, a hugely oppressive presence that rose to astonishing heights out of the grassy plain. He asked himself who—if none of the natives—could have marked the faint path winding its way up the slope. As the last of the light faded, he wondered whether this might indeed be the path by which the demons entered the world of man, to steal into his dwellings and invade his dreams with thoughts of evil. Then the mountains were swallowed up by the darkness, out of which came nothing but the occasional screech of a bird and the barely audible rattle of stones released by the foot of some animal. Archibald helped his countrymen drain a bottle of whiskey, and then he made his bed on the ground between the tents. The next morning he awoke to a heavy fog, said his goodbyes to the leader, and headed off to where the mist concealed the nearest slope. He later described his wanderings in the mountains in a letter to one of his sisters . . ."

The porter checked himself. "I shouldn't have said that. Now I've given it away that all ended well, thus robbing my story of suspense. Oh well, it's too late to do anything about that now . . ."

To compensate for his clumsiness, he poured me more wine.

"Though he could see no more than a few steps ahead, Archibald, leading the mule behind, made quick progress up the narrow path of the demons. The mist receded and he saw a twinkling river meandering through the landscape. But then, at a sharp bend in the path, the mule plunged into the abyss, and with it his entire supply of food and water; it almost pulled him in, too. But Archibald refused to turn back. And at last he came to the summit, where an arid plateau opened itself up to his gaze. The path having vanished, he stumbled over rocks that were burning hot in the midday sun. From time to time he would pass the withered, oddly contorted trunk of a tree. He looked up to see an eagle wheeling slowly through the clear blue sky. Sometimes his ears caught the rustling of a small creature among the rocks; otherwise everything was still.

"Without food and water, in the relentless heat of the sun, Archibald spent two days on the plateau. For two nights he shook with cold, listening in the dark to the screeches of beasts. At midday on the third day, he came upon a ravine which led to a narrow valley enclosed by steep mountain slopes. The descent dipped gently to the bottom of the ravine. The slopes above him were covered with small bushes, on which black goats with long, thick hair were feeding.

"Then a village appeared to him almost as he was entering it. It was like the moment the outline of a thing becomes suddenly visible from among the tangle of lines of a picture puzzle: in this case primitive dwellings standing on the expansive bottom of a valley. The village had been practically invisible because it was built from the same stones as lay everywhere about; at first sight the small houses looked more like simple piles of rocks than human homes. Out of the low, shadowy openings that served these dwellings as doors, figures emerged on all fours—dour-looking men with shriveled, bearded faces and strips of black fabric bound around their heads. Women, at once curious and fearful, peered out from the dark insides of the hovels, withdrawing quickly when their eyes met Archibald's. The men surrounded him, their gestures indicating their excitement; then, in unison, they shouted something at him. Archibald understood very little of their prattle. He had good knowledge of the dialects spoken in the foothills, but the language these people spoke was only distantly related to them: It seemed that it had evolved over centuries in this mountain valley in complete isolation. From among the restless, stamping feet of the men, a little girl of about eight wriggled her way through to him; she handed him a drinking skin filled with water. Then she gave him a timid smile, said 'Idur,' and quickly hid herself behind the other villagers. Archibald drank deeply, after which the men led him off to one of the shacks and set a bowl of gruel before him. He gulped this down and immediately fell asleep.

"When Archibald awoke the next day, the sun was already high in the sky. He left the house and for the first time took a proper look at the village. Crumbling buildings climbed up to where the rocky slopes began. In the narrow strips of shade mangy dogs slept, while above the village, goats chewed on the dry thistles that grew among the rocks. High above the village's last house Archibald noticed a building which stood alone, a building that was different from the others. Its door was a simple black hole and it had no windows; but in front of the entrance was a stack of stones that looked a little like steps. To either side of the entrance stood two crooked columns of flat stones, laid one on top of the other like pancakes. Across the columns lay a kind of beam, and on this someone had placed a stone in such a way as to create a triangular gable. Next to the temple stood something that Archibald at first took for a tree; on closer inspection he saw that it was a structure about three meters in height, made of metal. Fastened to the large flat stone was something in the shape of an ellipse, out of which rose three arms, which eventually joined. In the center of these three arms something round and disc-shaped was fastened . . ."

I was fidgeting with impatience now, as it was clear to me

what was coming next. The dog opened one eye, looked me over, and then closed the eye again. I had the impression the porter had been playing hide-and-seek with me right from the beginning of his story. Each time the story moved on, I asked myself if in one of the streets of the new place described, in one of its squares or yards, the double trident would make its appearance. The porter had conjured up Gaza, Alexandria, Athens, Ctesiphon and London before shifting his story elsewhere—and all the time there was no sign of the mysterious shape. But now at last it did appear, at the world's end. I needed an explanation for the disc, which had not been present in any other version of the double trident.

"Above the point where the arms joined, there was a cross." The porter was continuing his tale as I had hoped. "And from the top of this three more arms opened out, longer than those below. And in the center of the upper arms there was a dark disc. Within moments of coming upon the temple, Archibald found himself again surrounded by villagers. When they saw where he was looking, they began to point in that direction and shout. In the hubbub he couldn't make out what they were saying, though he fancied he heard the words 'nauz' and 'piruma.' 'Nauz' reminded him of the Greek 'naos,' meaning 'temple.' And looking at the crumbling building above the village, he could indeed imagine this to be the product of Stone Age man's dream of a Greek temple.

"The villagers had been forming themselves into a human wall, from which a man with leather straps on his forehead now separated himself. He stood in front of Archibald and started to explain something to him in an excited voice. The others fell silent immediately; Archibald took this man for the village mayor. Now that he was confronted with a single voice, Archibald began to piece together some of the words. He realized, for example, that where the people of the foothills said 'o,' natives of this place said 'u'; their 'e' was closer to 'i,' and their words contained complex, strikingly archaic consonant clusters, which the language of the foothills had merged to form a single sound. But some of their utterances plainly had little in common with the languages of their neighbors. The words he was unable to classify made Archibald feel slightly queasy, and for a while he couldn't understand why this was. Then a fantastical thought flashed through his mind; though he dismissed this, it forced its way back in, until at last Archibald had to admit—in astonishment—that his bizarre idea had revealed a truth. In this confused tongue, which brought to mind rocks rumbling down crags, the bleating of goats, and the screeching of birds wheeling above the valley in search of their prey; in this tongue which gave constant expression to anxiety and rage, words kept surfacing which were corruptions of Greek. The preposterous temple above the village its inhabitants called 'nauz'; 'idur'—meaning 'water'—plainly had its origins in the Greek 'hydór.'

"Now he was getting to grips with the language of the natives, he began to pay attention to what the mayor was telling him. The man repeated again and again that someone called Dum Isi was waiting for a foreigner in the *nauz*. Archibald interrupted the mayor's insistent tones; he made an attempt to speak in the native tongue. 'Very well,' he said. 'Let us go for a visit.' On hearing this, the villagers started up their shouting and embraced one another in joy."

Chapter 28
Discoveries in the Temple

"They set off for the stone temple. The mayor took the lead, climbing the rocks as nimbly as a goat so that Archibald struggled to keep up; behind them, at a respectful distance, the men of the village clambered up the rocky path. As they were approaching the *nauz*, an old man stepped out of the building. He was strikingly tall, had long white hair and was even skinnier than the other men of the village. Standing motionless in front of the metal statue, he waited for the expedition to arrive. The villagers were now waving their arms wildly and crying, 'Dum Isi! Dum Isi!' At last Archibald reached the platform on which the peculiar temple stood. The old man subjected him to an appraising gaze that was stern but respectful. Looking into the old man's deeply lined face, with its toothless mouth and sunken eyes, Archibald thought that he saw hope but also fear there. Then he inspected the structure that stood next to the temple. He noticed that the upper and lower discs were bound together by three lengths of rope, the first joining the lower left-hand disc with the upper left-hand, the second holding together the central discs and the third connecting the lower right-hand disc with the upper right-hand. He supposed that this was some kind of idol that the villagers worshiped. He wasn't particularly surprised to see a pile of animal bones and blackened blood on the flat stone on which the structure stood. Most of the skulls were goats' and dogs', but two skulls stood out from the pile that were certainly human.

Archibald again had cause to regret that his rifle and pistol had ended up in the abyss.

"The villagers and the mayor quietly disappeared, leaving Archibald alone with the elder on the platform high above the village. The elder sat down on the steps in front of the temple and motioned for Archibald to sit next to him. As Archibald was about to ask him about the strange idol, the elder himself began to talk of it. This statue, he explained, was a true image of a demon of the mountains called Piruma. At night this demon would come down from the mountaintops and terrorize the villagers. Archibald wanted to know how many villagers had seen him. Almost all of them, the elder said. This didn't surprise Archibald: These mountains were full of bizarre rock formations that seemed to change shape with every shift of the light; after three days of wandering the mountain plateau, he himself had seen all kinds of things in the light and shadow of the rocks. He asked about the meaning of the six discs. They were the demon's 'kifali,' the elder told him; it occurred to Archibald that this could mean 'kefaloi,' heads. 'He leaps from one rock to another,' the terrified elder whispered in his ear. Archibald imagined a monster jumping about the stones in the ravine—a monster with three legs, three arms and six heads. He realized that the elder was a kind of priest whose task it was to pacify the demon with animal sacrifices. Apparently the elder shared the belief of the villagers that the demon was responsible for every death in the village, whether natural or unnatural. Someone fell into a rocky chasm and the demon had thrown him there; someone died of old age and she had been strangled by the demon, who had made himself invisible and stolen into her hut. Archibald preferred not to ask about the human skulls on the flat stone.

"The elder explained to him that the demon was basically good, but that he was angry at the villagers for their failure to fulfill his only wish, in the form of a task he had given them centuries earlier. Once they had done this, he would leave them in peace; and not only would he stop killing them, he would give them all the help they needed. The villagers would no longer die—they would become immortal. Piruma would teach the goats to milk each other and take the milk to the villagers.

Archibald said that the demon wanted something from the villagers that they would likely never be able to accomplish if they hadn't done so by now, although the reward for its accomplishment was so attractive. An expression of dejection appeared on the priest's face. 'Not at all—it is the easiest thing in the world,' he sighed. 'So why don't you do it and claim your peace?' Archibald asked. The priest looked more dejected still. 'Because we do not know what it is,' he whispered. Archibald learned that the demon's wish was recorded in books written by the demon many centuries ago; in these books the demon told of his life before he came to the valley in the mountains. The books were written in magical characters that none of the villagers were able to read. Archibald asked the elder where the demon's writings were kept. The old man stood up, took him by the hand and led him into the building.

"Archibald found himself in a dark, windowless room. A little light passed through the narrow door at his back, while in front of him was a ghostly column of light, which was coming through a hole in the roof. He had the uncomfortable feeling that these crooked walls, made of piled-up stones with nothing holding them together, could collapse at any moment. In the darkness by the back wall was a casket placed on some kind of stone altar. Archibald bent down to this and ran his fingers over its smooth surface, shallow depressions and projections; it was made of metal, perhaps bronze; Archibald struggled to make out its shapes in the gloom. As his eyes adjusted to the lack of light, he was gradually able to make out bas-reliefs depicting Achilles fighting Hector, the Laestrygonians throwing rocks at Odysseus's ships and Odysseus homesick on the shore of the island of the nymph Calypso; the more he looked, the more images he saw from *The Iliad* and *The Odyssey* . . . Straightaway the interest of the archaeologist was aroused; he reckoned that the cabinet was the work of a Byzantine artist of the fifth or sixth century.

"Archibald felt the elder's beard tickle his forehead as the old man leaned down to the casket, whose lid he lifted with dirty, bony fingers. Archibald saw that the casket was filled to the top with scrolls and books. He spread out one of the scrolls and in the dim light he could see that the text it bore was Greek. 'So these are the books the demon wrote,' he said to himself. The elder looked back toward the doorway; seeing that no three-legged, three-armed, six-headed demon was standing there, he said to Archibald in a hushed voice: 'According to the old prophecy, in the village there shall one day appear a foreigner who is able to read Piruma's books. He will reveal to us the demon's wish and we shall at last achieve immortality.' After a pause he added: 'The old tale also states that any foreigner who is unable to read the book shall be sacrificed to Piruma.' Archibald was unnerved by the recollection of human skulls in front of the temple, but then he told himself that if all the text on the scrolls and in the books was in Greek, he would have no trouble reading it. With the first scroll in his hand, he went to the steps and began to read. Before long he forgot about the danger he was in; he forgot about the priest, the village, London, Europe and Asia. He eagerly entered the world of the text and went deeper and deeper into it, with a sense of amazement.

"After that he spent days on his stone seat in front of the shrine, reading the tiny characters of the scrolls and the books. Although the priest went away, three villagers remained in front of the building, day and night, like a silent guard of honor. Archibald soon realized that they were standing there principally not as a homage to a man able to read the script of the demons, but in order to watch him and prevent him from fleeing. Theirs was an unnecessary concern: Archibald would never have abandoned the shrine with its scrolls. Here he had discovered a treasure that was beyond an archaeologist's wildest dreams. Later he said often that he had spent the greatest week of his life on the steps in front of the stone temple. The little girl who on the first day had given him water, brought him something to eat and drink from the village every day. Gradually she lost her shyness of him; often she would sit silent and motionless on the steps long after he finished eating, watching him at his work. It gave Archibald pleasure to lift his eyes from the ancient text to her smiling face; it was so different from the frowning faces of the other villagers, which had been set that way by some ancient bitterness."

We heard voices from beyond the gate. Immediately the

German shepherd opened its eyes and lifted its head from my lap, its hackles up. The porter looked through the window: It was just a couple of security guards, passing by on their way home after the end of their shift. Having quieted the dog, he poured out the last of the wine.

"I suppose you've worked it out that there in the villagers' temple Archibald Archer discovered the written remains of the sect that followed Dionysius of Gaza," the porter went on. "This was something like the sect's archive. The texts collected here originated over a period of two hundred years; the oldest of them were from Ctesiphon, seat of the Persian king, and some of these were in Dionysius's own hand. In other scrolls, Archibald read the history of the sect after it left that city. In the earliest scrolls, painful memories emerged of the years in Athens and that city's colonnades and gardens. Athens was a place Dionysius spent his whole life running from, but he never stopped dreaming of it.

"I've mentioned that Dionysius's thinking was infiltrated by the eccentricities of Gnosis and cults of darkness only after he reached Ctesiphon. The writings in the stone temple testified to what happened after his flight from the wrath of Chosrau; how Dionysius and his acolytes went ever farther east, and how his thoughts and visions became ever darker, more complex, and sicker, taking on voices from India and China and from the shamanism of the continent's interior."

"But did such voices necessarily mean decline? Mightn't encounters with them have brought enrichment? Is Athens really the center of the world?"

The porter smiled. "Of course not. I don't believe that the world has a center. And for thought that was pure, an encounter with Asia would certainly have been a great adventure and a source of new meaning. But wherever he went, Dionysius found only a mirror for the shadows of his own soul and echoes of the anxious moans at the bottom of his thoughts. And so from the ancient chants of India he didn't take courage to contemplate the great forces of the world; instead he found in them an oppressive, muddy absolute. He found in them not the Buddha's teaching of quiet kindness and compassion but a stolid catatonia that was intended as an escape from the horror of being but in the end proved to be just as terrifying as the world it was supposed to provide refuge from. In shamanism he saw not an imagination that grew out of understanding of natural rhythms but a strategy of retreat in the hopeless human struggle against the wild world of demons.

"As Dionysius ventured ever further into Asia, the ideas of Plato and Aristotle took on the names of evil deities, and the propositions of Plotinus's *Enneads* became magical incantations. Archibald asked himself whether Dionysius could have forgotten so completely the teachings he had heard in Gaza, the schools of Alexandria, and the Academy at Athens. The sources found here in the temple were equivocal; it seemed to Archibald that many characters bearing the name Dionysius could have been created from them. Now he saw a vain, cruel seducer, desirous of power, now a tragic philosopher looking on in agonized delight as sickness and decay ate away at a mental world he loved still.

"Archibald kept asking himself why Dionysius and his pupils had come to a halt in a wilderness on the very edge of the known world. Had they lacked the strength to go on? If so, was their exhaustion due more to the demands of the journey, or to doctrinal discord that had arisen among the pupils and resulted in groups of heretics separating themselves from the main group at several places along the way? Reading a treatise Dionysius had written in old age, Archibald was horrified by the avidity with which he twisted the propositions of Greece into a labyrinth of barbarous syntax. Sitting on the steps of the village's temple and looking at the rocky peaks, Archibald wondered what Dionysius had thought about as he lay dying in a distant, inhospitable foreign land. Had he returned to the shady pavilions of the Academy in Athens, or had he looked horrified into the faces of barbarian deities dreamed up by his terror and hatred?

"After Dionysius's death the process of disintegration accelerated. At this time, the Dionysians were living in a number of settlements in the foothills. Still active missionaries, they went among the local people and gained more and more followers. In their villages a mixture of the Greek and the local language came to be spoken, although over time Greek was used ever less and the few words that remained were changed beyond recognition.

The philosophy became ever closer to theology or demonology, and arguments proliferated concerning the correct interpretation of the teachings of the late Master, culminating in skirmishes between different groups, nighttime raids, and the cutting of throats. The leader of one of the sects, who began to call himself Dionysius the Restorer, denounced as unclean any relations with those Dionysians who didn't accept his version of the teachings. He and his followers left for the mountains, taking with them the sect's archive, which they had grabbed in a raid. These were ancestors of the villagers Archibald had just met. Only here, in this mountain village, had any memory of the original teachings, albeit a confused one, been preserved, and the language of these villagers had retained traces of Greek. The term 'Dum Isi,' by which the villagers knew their priest, was a corruption of 'Dionysius'; the demon's name 'Piruma' was likely derived from the Greek 'pléróma.' In the foothills, Dionysianism had been swept away by Islam, which arrived soon after the departure of the Restorer and his followers; there, no trace of the teachings of the prophet of Gaza remained.

"The later writings probably originated in the eighth century. The alphabet used was a strangely contorted one, and the writings were composed in an antiquated form of the local language with the occasional word of corrupted Greek. These were nothing more than prayers to evil gods and exorcisms against demons; they expressed a single idea—perpetual dread of a hostile natural world and a cruel, incomprehensible supernatural one. On the very last pages there was nothing but letters painted in crude, labyrinthine tangles of lines—by then there was no one left able to write or understand the written word. For a while longer the priests drew around the characters, which, apparently, were taken for magical symbols, adding to them the intricate ornamentation of their own fear. After that, the teachings were passed on by word of mouth only, transforming over the centuries into the demonology that Archibald encountered in the village.

"Although as an archaeologist Archibald took pleasure from his reading of even the late scrolls, by now other feelings were coming to the fore. He couldn't help being repelled by a language born out of a dark, malformed mishmash of Greek and local languages infused with sounds of mumbled exorcisms that were less an expression of fascination with mystery than of a cowardly, omnipresent fear bound up with servility and baseness. He realized, however, that this degradation was not caused by the tarnishing of the language of Plato by that of uncivilized, uncultured tribes. He had a good knowledge of the proud, hospitable natives of the foothills, whose sense of honor had been noted by travelers of olden times, too. Their pride and clear view of the world, which might have been born out of the wide, omnipresent horizon, were also present in their language. The bleakness of the language of the late Dionysians was the fruit of a sickness they had brought from Ctesiphon and that progressively worsened on their travels. Unable to keep their Greek alive, they succumbed to the local languages with an awareness of their own weakness and an aversion for foreigners; and as the indigenous languages were but mirrors of their own hatred, they adopted their words and syntax in a distorted, grotesque, monstrous form."

Chapter 29
Fever Gives Birth to the Universe

"On the very first day, Archibald saw in one of the books a figure that looked just like the idol in front of the temple; he then found it in many more scrolls and books. The figure was a kind of secret sign of a school of thought, and it had probably originated at Chosrau's court. According to one of the writings, Dionysius had drawn the figure for the first time in the sand of a path in the garden of the royal palace, with a stick. The figure was some sort of diagram illustrating the birth of the Universe. The ellipse represented the all-encompassing undifferentiated One. The traditional circle of the original figure became an ellipse at some point on the journey east; Dionysius came to prefer the ellipse, as it represented the constant conflict within the One and its constant parting into two centers. Nevertheless, at first this unrest was no more than the restlessness we feel in dreams, and it did as little harm as wounds inflicted on our bodies by the figures of our nightly dreams.

"But out of this initial restlessness Fever was born. Her hot breath ate into what had come apart in dreams while continuing to hold together in a two-way embrace. Then the two centers of the ellipse set themselves in opposition to each other, and the duality that thus originated led to division within the two poles, producing Multiplicity. When the One saw that it held Multiplicity within itself, it quivered with horror at the thought of the unknown that moved in its bowels: At first it didn't realize that Multiplicity was just a feverish nightmare that was not separate from itself. Multiplicity exploited this moment of fright, this brief hesitation, this weakening of the centripetal force, and with the help of the forces of Fever, which had taken a liking to it, forced openings through the boundaries of the ellipse, and thus escaped from the One.

"The escape of Multiplicity is shown by three lines coming out of the ellipse. Beyond the One, Multiplicity lacked the energy for further proliferation; the multiple remained of the same number, their shapes producing Ideas, or Archetypes. When Ideas escaped from the One, they were terrified by their isolation and wished to reconnect. Although they searched for something in common, among the multiple they found no such thing; they longed for the One, yet they were afraid to return to it, as Fever had led them to believe that they had an autonomous existence which would be extinguished if they rejoined the One. Meanwhile Fever had intercourse with figures from the heavy dreams that it produced, and it was of this union that Will was born. Cunning Fever saw how the Ideas/Archetypes yearned for the One, so she dressed her daughter Will in a robe she had sewn from rays emitted by the One and paraded her before the Ideas; these rejoiced that the One had come to them and embraced them without their having to surrender their independent existence, and they came together with Will in the union of marriage. As the Archetypes slept after the wedding party, at the behest of her mother Fever, Will swallowed her husbands. On the main feast day of Dionysians, a representation of the wedding of Will and the Archetypes was performed as a ritual drama; judging by allusions made at a number of places in the writings, in later years the performance was accompanied by orgies.

"Thus the Archetypes were subsumed by the uneasy unity of the One. Having devoured her husbands, Will felt lonely; a vision appeared in a dream of a distant land in which her future spouse, Eternity, was waiting for her. Thus Will embarked on a quest for Eternity. Fever accompanied Will, telling her that she would protect her on her journey, although she had quite different intentions. This period of Will's wanderings is represented by the vertical line that joins the lower arms. A time later, Will came to the murky lake Matter; the moment of encounter with Matter is marked by the point of intersection with the horizontal line at the center of the figure. Will and Fever reached the shore and Fever began to wail that she was dying of thirst; she asked Will to bring her water from the lake. Will was reluctant to oblige: She was afraid that she would slip from the muddy shore into the lake and drown there. Three times Fever pleaded with Will to bring her water, her plea gaining in urgency with each bidding. After the third plea, Will started at last for the water. Her mother tiptoed silently in her wake. As soon as Will reached the water's edge, Fever gave her a shove and she fell into the murky water.

"Will called for her mother's help, but Fever didn't respond. As she was drowning, Will heard the dark thrum of Matter and found it familiar: It was similar to her mother's voice and her own. She realized that Matter was Fever's other daughter—an unknown, lost sister her mother had once told her about. Fever had always preferred her other, lost daughter and longed desperately to see her again. She had accompanied Will in the hope of being reunited with Matter. When this came to pass, Fever and Matter embraced and agreed that together they would kill Will. Fever had never much cared for Will, and after the daughter had devoured the Archetypes at the mother's behest, the mother had begun to feel hatred for her, as it seemed to Fever that Will was too like the One . . . These passages are probably of more interest to a psychoanalyst than a scholar of the history of philosophy or religion. Note, too, the motif of the loved and the unloved daughter, which is so common in fairy tales.

"Will was suffocating in the mud, near death, when she recalled what her mother had told her about the One; she remembered, too, the Archetypes inside her, which had once dwelled in the One and might be of help to her against Matter. With the last of her strength, she ripped open her belly. The Archetypes jumped out into the mud, and using the power of unification that remained from their time in the One, they set about arranging Matter into beings. Air penetrated the gaps between these beings and Will was able to breathe again. But now the Archetypes turned against her: They wished to punish her for what she had done to them on their wedding night. They tore Will to pieces and then feasted on her, ingesting her power. Will came together within them by the power of unification that they had brought from the One. Both the Archetypes and Will used this power to defend themselves against Matter and her mother Fever.

"But the forming of Matter into beings was not a perfect victory over Fever. Fever rushed to Matter's aid and again merged with her in a single body. Thus Fever, together with Matter, went to the heart of things, where they changed shape. Their toxic breath was exuded through their pores, scaring the Archetypes and producing in them bouts of melancholy. The moment that the Archetypes emerged from Will is represented by the point at which the figure's upper branching begins, while the arms of the upper trident show the path taken by the unloosed Archetypes through the mud of Matter—a path that is also the origin of all things. As Matter was unified, some of the Archetypes realized that this bore a vague resemblance to the unification that they had known in the One; thus they desired to return to the One, their home, taking Matter along with them. The beginning of this reversal is shown in the bends in the two outer arms of the upper trident. Thus the path of the Archetypes within Matter is a constant crossing between emergent memory of the ancient light of the One and bouts of insanity evoked by the diseased breath of Fever, at the heart of things.

"In the manuscripts, Archibald came across this figure again and again. In some of the representations, the relation of other elements to the Archetypes was shown by the assigning of large letters of the Greek alphabet—alpha, beta, and gamma—to the arms of the lower trident; the same letters, now small, were assigned to the corresponding upper arms. On examining the blackened discs on the idol in front of the temple, Archibald discovered in them traces of the first letters of the alphabet, both large and small, which had once been engraved there. He imagined how in ancient times, before the discs became the heads of a demon, in the enactment of Dionysian rituals the priest would tug at the lower discs; this motion, which conveyed the ropes to the upper discs, represented objects' dependence on ideas.

"On the seventh day, by the pink light of early morning,

Archibald sat on temple steps studying a drawing that represented cosmogonic Fever. It occurred to him that in his childhood he had imagined the witch in the gingerbread cottage of the fairy tale to look something like this. He was thinking of how Dionysius connected Fever so closely with humanity because she represented the restlessness and revulsion he felt in his heart and which blew on him from all things and all shapes he encountered. Suddenly he saw Dionysius's face clearly and felt infinite pity for this man who had spent his whole life wandering from place to place, never finding a home. Lifting his eyes from the book, he saw a crowd of villagers climbing to the temple along the winding path. The crowd was unusually quiet. He recognized, at the head of the group, the tall figure of the priest. On reaching the platform in front of the temple, the villagers remained standing at a respectful distance. The priest stepped forward and requested that Archibald reveal to them the message conveyed by the demon in his books.

"Archibald had always managed to see into the souls of the indigenous peoples he encountered on his travels; on several occasions, this gift of understanding had saved his life. But as the priest stood there before him, he somehow failed to comprehend the man. Maybe he was still absorbed by his thoughts of the fate of Dionysius, or maybe his desire to speak of his discoveries was too strong to resist. When later he spoke of these moments, in the drawing rooms of London, he never failed to mention how he had acted like an idiot. Obviously what the villagers needed was to hear some invented episodes from the life of the demon. He should have used wild gestures of the kind the villagers liked, and told them that the demon wished them to wear a wooden ring in the right ear or a ribbon on the left wrist. The villagers would have been satisfied; they would have stopped seeing figures that terrified them in the rock formations and delighted in the belief that the demon had quit their valley at last. Although their goats wouldn't have begun to milk each other, Archibald would surely have been able to explain to them that it would take a while for the animals to learn how to do this. Then he would have departed, seen off by the tributes of the villagers.

"Instead, Archibald began to speak of what he had read in

the manuscripts. He told the villagers of Dionysius and of the Dionysians, their ancestors, and he told them of the journey from Tigris to the mountains of Afghanistan. As he was speaking, the crowd muttered angrily. Although the villagers understood little or nothing of what Archibald was telling them, it was clear to them that the stories they were hearing couldn't possibly be the true content of the sacred scripture, and that the stranger was making them up. Everyone knew that the scrolls described the history of the fierce, heroic battles of the demons of the rocks and above all the great unfulfilled wish of the terrible Piruma, the final fulfillment of which would bring them immortality. In short, when the villagers compared historical fact with the myths they believed, history seemed to them as fantastical and improbable as it tends to seem to us when compared with our myths. Soon they reached the conclusion that the stranger was talking such nonsense because he didn't wish them to obtain the immortality that was within their reach; instead, he wished them harm.

"Archibald realized his mistake too late. The villagers descended on him. After having punched the first two, he was seized by many hands, dragged to the bronze idol and bound by the wrists to the outer arms of the upper trident. In the din of voices, he identified the hysterical cries of the priest, who was encouraging the villagers to lynch him. By the time the arms and bodies surrounding Archibald disentangled themselves and moved away from him, poor Archibald was hanging from the idol. Having lost interest in him, the men walked slowly down the path, back to their huts. The women shouted a few more terrible curses and spat at him, then they, too, departed. Archibald was left alone.

"The sun rose above the tops of the mountains, and its rays dug into his eyes. The villagers had left his legs free, so the whole weight of his body hung from the ropes that cut into his wrists. He put his feet on the discs attached to the arms of the lower trident, thus easing the pain a little. But the upper disc, which was connected by the rope to the lower ones, now cut into his shoulders. He shifted his weight from disc to disc and looked down on the village, where the villagers were going about their ordinary day's work; by now, none of them even bothered to look up at him. As the sun got higher in the clear sky, he closed his eyes against it, but the glare was unbearable even through closed lids. He had the feeling that the terrible heat had lit his face like a torch. The chill of the evening refreshed him a little, but this was but a brief respite before the dreadful frost of the night. As night set in, he heard steps in the darkness, then a soft voice. It was the little girl who had brought him food and drink. She climbed onto the stone next to the idol and held a bowl of water to his lips. Archibald drank greedily. The next day he moved back and forth between wakefulness and the confused visions of feverish dreams. Again the face of the little girl emerged from the darkness, and again he was at least able to drink some water.

"Then delirium claimed him entirely. In one of his dreams he had a vision that probably originated in the shifting of his weight from one disc to another, interspersed with what he remembered of Dionysian cosmogony. In the vision he was standing on a soft white surface which stretched to the horizon, hundreds of thousands of miles away. Above was a black, starless void. Beyond the horizon stood a gigantic mechanism made of a strange, crystal-like material. This mechanism was similar to the idol to which Archibald was bound, but unlike the idol, its upper and lower ends branched off into a huge number of arms. On each of the lower arms was a disc on which was written a letter of an unknown alphabet. Each lower arm was connected by a crystal cable to an upper arm to which was attached a disc with the same letter drawn in negative relief. In the space beyond the horizon a large translucent hand was raised, and its fingers came to touch the lower discs; whenever an enormous finger pushed down on one of the lower discs, the crystal cable to which it was attached pulled down the upper disc that bore a disc with the same letter. It turned out that the bottom ends of the upper arms were fitted with joints; the crystal cable bent the upper arm at the joint and it fell in a dizzying arc to the white plain; the upper disc landed on it at enormous speed. When the translucent finger released the pressure on the lower disc, the disc with the letter in negative relief rose; an impression of the letter was left in the sand." The porter turned to me. "I suppose you can imagine what I'm talking about?"

"Yes, it does remind me of something. It looks like . . ."

"We'll get to what it looks like in a while. Anyway, in his feverish state Archibald imagined himself to be standing on a white plain on which the arms of a gigantic mechanism were falling; some of them hit the surface hundreds of miles away, others landed very close to where he was. He realized that he was watching the birth of a universe from archetypes, or ideas. Archibald walked about the plain, examining the various shapes that appeared on it. Suddenly the sound of the blows intensified and its rhythm became irregular, quickening and then slowing; the arms and their casts landed on the plain with destructive force, and with each impact a torrent of white matter jumped to a height of many miles. These heavy blows deformed the shapes remaining on the plain or caused them to disintegrate altogether. Raising his eyes to the cosmic mechanism, Archibald saw to his horror that Fever was dancing a demented dance on the lower discs. Like a madwoman, she was leaping from disc to disc. He could see her face, now contracted in anger, now wearing the stupid smile of an imbecile. Then the arms from the cosmic heights began to land in his immediate vicinity, every impact causing the whole plain to shake. Archibald ran from these awful hammers that were pounding the plain, screaming in terror . . .

"He was woken by his own screams. His eyes opened to the sight of green cloth above him. Then he turned his head and saw the face of the little girl who had brought him water. Still ignorant of what had happened, he stroked the girl's hair. He heard voices speaking in English. It was then that Archibald realized he was lying in a tent. A moment later, a man stepped inside—the commander of the expedition he had met ten days earlier."

Chapter 30
Return to London

"As a long time passed and still Archibald did not return, the commander sent a five-man, armed search party into the mountains, and these men found him hanging from the idol, unconscious. Men from the village tried to prevent the party from taking Archibald down, but a few gunshots into the air were enough to scatter them in flight. The little girl was fastened to a dry tree trunk next to the idol; having realized that she had been helping Archibald, the villagers had sentenced her to death alongside him. The Englishmen took the girl with them, back to their camp. They also took the bronze casket with Dionysius's writings—back in England, these would gradually be published in a meticulous bilingual edition. So there was a happy ending of the kind popular in British colonial literature.

"It was a few days before the weakened Archibald was even able to get up from his sickbed. During those days, he thought about the Dionysius manuscripts and everything he'd been through in the valley in the mountains. As he remembered his dreamed vision of the cosmogonic machine, it occurred to him that its principle might be put to use. First he vaguely imagined keys labeled with letters, connected by some kind of gearing with arms similar to those he'd seen in his dream. Unlike these keys, however, the letters would have a high relief. When the keys were pressed, the arms would bend and the letters on their ends strike paper and make an imprint. But how to apply ink to an embossed letter? On its way to the paper it would have to be immersed in a vessel containing some kind of dye . . . No, that was too complicated, and the ink would spatter the page, Archibald thought. It would be better if the relief was swept with a small brush. And would it be possible to place a ribbon impregnated with ink between the type and the paper? But in that case the ink would soon be used up, meaning that the ribbon would have to be changed frequently . . . At that moment the expedition's physician came in and began to unwind the strips of gauze from the bloody wounds cut into Archibald's feet by the sharp edges of the discs, prior to re-bandaging them—and it came to Archibald in a flash: Yes, that's how it should be! If rolled into a spool, the ribbon could be very long, it could move along slowly and join up with another spool. And maybe the ribbon could be moved along not by an independent movement of the hand but a special mechanism that used the power of the striking of the key . . ."

"In short, Archibald Archer invented the typewriter in Afghanistan."

"There at the camp, Archibald drew up the first plans for the instrument. On his return to London, he showed them to his engineer brother, who was very enthusiastic about the idea and spent a whole year improving the Afghan drafts and thinking through every detail. On the first anniversary of the day the soldiers took Archibald down from the idol, his brother showed him a finished prototype of the typewriter. Then the two brothers founded a company for the manufacturing of typewriters. When they were debating the emblem of the Archer & Archer Company, Edward suggested it should contain an arrow, due to their surname and also the speed and accuracy of the typing. But Archibald insisted it should be in the shape of the idol on which he had almost died but without which the idea of a typewriter would never have come to him.

"That's basically the end of the story. The Archer & Archer company was a success. After the emergence of other typewriter-producing firms, it concentrated its own production on luxury, mechanically-sophisticated models that were pretty expensive, which is why it never became as famous as Underwood or

Remington; among connoisseurs, however, it has always had a good name and is something like the Rolls-Royce of typewriters. Only last year, for instance, it produced for the Sultan of Bahrain a typewriter made of gold with jewel-studded arms. The Archer family still holds the majority of shares in the company. Archer's descendants had the foresight to anticipate the expansion of the personal computer, and since the seventies they have gradually refocused on other office technology, such as photocopiers and fax machines, with the result that the company has survived the fall in demand for typewriters without too much difficulty."

For a while I sat on in the porter's lodge, stroking the head of the German shepherd and wondering if there was anything in the porter's story that could help in my search for Viola. Was there a connection between the tattooed symbol on Viola's body and Dionysius or the Dionysians, or was the similarity merely accidental? It occurred to me that in the latter half of the nineteenth century, a time of great interest in eastern teachings, it was perfectly possible that on the basis of writings published in England, Dionysius's teachings might have been revisited—in the quest for the Absolute, various mystagogues had pursued teachings more foolish than Dionysian cosmogony, and they had never wanted for listeners. So a secret society of Neo-Dionysians could very well have sprung up.

Viola, however, did not give the impression of a person who would easily be taken in by the teachings of some dubious sect. Still, I was able to imagine that an occult society bathed in secrecy could become a hotbed of crime and provide an alibi for illegal activity. The sect might easily transform into a conspiratorial society of the mafia type, which wouldn't be entirely out of keeping with a teaching with such unclean roots as Dionysianism. I was afraid that Viola had encountered such a criminal organization (in New York?) and somehow gotten tied up in it. And what might be the connection with the pump and the underground cave Viola had talked about on the phone? Although the subterranean monster continued to surface in my mind with unusual persistence, my reason refused to accept that Viola's disappearance could be explained by a search for a Godzilla sleeping somewhere beneath the city. It was far more likely that it was related to treasure lying at the bottom of some underground lake. Maybe Viola had learned something in New York, let's say in the form of a map on which the location of a hidden treasure was marked and the criminal organization had found this out and gone after her; Viola was now either in hiding somewhere or they had tracked her down and abducted or killed her.

Then I remembered Viola's tattoo: That would suggest that she had joined the secret criminal organization voluntarily. Yet this assumption didn't convince me much. Although I knew Viola only from what I'd been told about her, she didn't strike me as the type to be attracted by crime. And, of course, the body tattoo didn't have to be either the sign of the Dionysians or the logo of the company in whose porter's lodge I was now sitting. Hadn't Julie told me that the pump was obviously a part of a unit? It wasn't out of the question that the main component in the mechanism was produced by Archer & Archer. So why did it have to be surrounded by so much secrecy? Was it a matter of the export of banned goods? Had Viola become involved in arms trading? Had she had to disappear because she knew too much about a firm's illegal transactions? This explanation didn't satisfy me much either. I'd given enough thought to Viola, the Dionysians and Archer & Archer for today, I decided. I thanked the porter for his story and the wine and prepared to leave.

Once I reached the street, the porter wound the chain around the iron bars. As the German shepherd whined, we shook hands through the gate. I gave the dog a final pat. As the porter was returning to his lodge, I realized that there was one thing we had forgotten about. "You didn't tell me what happened to the little native girl," I called.

The porter turned and came back to the gate. "Archibald took her with him back to England. He found her a foster mother and bought her a good education. He gave her the first name Mildred and allowed her to use his surname. Mildred grew up to be one of the best-educated and wittiest women in Victorian England . . ."

"And Archibald fell in love with her and married her."

"Not exactly. Mildred married a major in the British army, who was killed in the Punjab a few years later, leaving Mildred alone. Her salon became a renowned center of London literary life, whose habitués included Tennyson and Browning. As an old lady, she enchanted Henry James on his arrival in England from Boston. It is a little-known fact that thanks to him she made her mark on English literature. Mildred was an amazing storyteller. She never talked about herself, however, which is hardly surprising, as life in Victorian London seemed to her too boring to talk about, and she never wanted to talk about her childhood in Afghanistan, as her memories of it were too painful. But Mildred had an extraordinary gift for listening and was able to tell stories she had heard in such a way that all her listeners found her retellings far more interesting than the original story.

"An anecdote that she told Oscar Wilde in the 1890s is a case in point. A certain traveler had just returned to London from a dangerous expedition in unexplored regions of equatorial Africa. This man was well known for his unfortunate, dull, long-winded manner of speaking. Once, when Oscar Wilde was a guest at a certain London salon, the hostess caught him preparing to flee the scene when the traveler was in the process of describing how his camp had been attacked by lions. 'You don't want to hear the story to the end?' she asked Wilde, who replied: 'No, thank you. I shall wait for good old Mildred to make a real story out of this dull fiction.' Henry James, too, delighted in listening to Mildred's tellings of other people's stories; he was fascinated by how she was able to identify with their feelings and thoughts and see the whole story as if through their eyes. He referred in a letter to 'that magnificent and masterly indirectness' of hers; he went on to advocate the theory of indirectness and to use the same principle of indirect speech in his novels."

What I was supposed to make of all this, I had no idea, so I said goodbye to the porter and his dog once again and walked past the workshops and warehouses to the bus stop. I would need to look into the Dionysians and the Archer & Archer Company, I told myself, but tomorrow I would try to find out something about Bernet.

Chapter 31
Cameras Above a Gate

Some time ago the architecture of Bernet's house had attracted quite a lot of attention. While the general public disliked it, the opinions of experts were divided on the matter: Some praised the house's formal purity, others described it as cold and unwelcoming. Many thought the house was uninhabitable. From the tone in which certain journalists wrote of it, I sensed their sneers at the snobbery of the rich man who sacrifices comfort and homeliness for a geometric beauty that is splendid but austere. As it wasn't envisaged that a rich person could have an artistic bent, it was concluded that Bernet had had such a house built only to satisfy his need to impress those around him and to attract admiration. One journalist was particularly derisive, claiming that by his vain desire to own the most modern architecture, Bernet had closed himself up in an ascetic's cloister ruled over by geometry, metal, and empty space. No one had managed to discover what Bernet thought of all this. It seemed that Bernet was impossible to get hold of. He didn't go to tennis tournaments, nor did he attend banquets in the company of pop stars, or charitable events; whenever a reporter did succeed in tracking him down, he refused to answer questions.

From photographs I hadn't been able to form a very clear idea of what the house was like, and I was curious about it. I knew more or less where to look for it: It was said to be among villas that had been built at various times on the top of one of the hills on the edge of the city. Now I was walking past neglected buildings with peeling plaster and high piles of crumpled, broken objects, and parts of unknown machines leaning against the outside walls. These little houses stood at the center of gardens; between the tomato beds, enamel bathtubs waited in vain for rain, their bottoms stained with a thick, dark solution and their sides furred with a gray-green coating. The smells of dry grass and stagnant water mingled with the less pleasant odors of gasoline, oil and fried meat; music played from radios, children's voices called, and from a distant garden—like the snarl of an angry beast—came the monotonous bass of a gasoline-powered lawnmower.

By now I could see the roof of Bernet's house, where the road ended abruptly at the top of the hillside. I crossed the street, feeling its asphalt pull stickily at my shoes, and looked down. At the foot of the hill, which was covered with grass and low shrubs, the loop of the streetcar terminus glistened in the sun, and a miniature car was gliding along it. I saw the backs of apartment buildings and the glowing concrete of yards squeezed between the buildings and the steep slope. Beyond this, the solid verticals and horizontals of the city were blissfully dissolved in a bluish haze with a single fiery point, where, I imagined, a distant tilted window was catching and reflecting the sunlight. From I knew not where came a lulling, hissing sound with periodic interruptions; added to this, like tiny beads falling onto velvet, were quiet voices that rose from the city and rolled languidly down the hill. The road separating the last row of villas from the hillside curved into an arc around Bernet's mansion. At the center of this, immediately opposite the wide gateway, was a high, solid-looking rail that was obviously there to protect inattentive drivers from falling into the abyss. I sat down on this rail, which was hot, in order to study Bernet's mansion.

Beyond the high bars of its fence, which ended in menacing spikes that gleamed silver, I saw a carefully tended lawn. The bright house stood on a slight elevation and extended across almost the entire width of the plot; apparently the garden continued beyond the house. Sunlight was dancing on the front wall of the house, reflected from the surface of a swimming pool. Halfway between the house and the gate, a sprinkler was in action; the regular swing of arms dispersing the water flow created a rhythmical swishing that reached my ears. The slow rotation of the metal nozzle from which the water spurted and the flicker of lights on the white facade were the only movements I detected in the garden.

On both sides of the gate, cameras were mounted on the tips of the bars. Less than a quarter of a minute after I sat down on the rail, one of the cameras began to turn slowly toward me; it was soon followed by the other. These remained staring at me like the heads of a large, aggressive insect in a science-fiction movie. The fixed gaze of the two dark, Cyclopean eyes made me feel distinctly uneasy.

I tore my own gaze from the hypnotic camera eyes and began to study the house. It gave the impression that it was made of some incredibly light material. As it comprised many cubes that appeared to have been borne here and assembled at random by the wind, I wondered idly if a new gust might change its composition. The sense of lightness was evoked partly by the seemingly careless piling of the cubes—which must actually have been thought through ingeniously—and partly by the fact that the cubes of the front side were made entirely of glass. In an article about Bernet's house, I'd read that the transparent walls were composed of glass panels that could either be rotated around the y-axis or all pulled sideways in order to open up the front wall. And then I really did see that in some of the cubes the glass walls disappeared, making the whole room into a kind of covered terrace. Some of the rooms thus laid bare were protected from the sun and the gaze of onlookers by white drapes that reached from ceiling to floor. Although a gust of wind didn't disturb the cubes, it caused the drapes in the glassless rooms to lift and flap into the garden like snow-white flags.

I'd been looking at the house for about half an hour and still I wasn't able to say whether I liked it or not. In all this time no one appeared on the other side of the gate. The sprinkler continued its regular rotations, but the cameras were no longer moving. Remembering that I hadn't come here in order to study Bernet's mansion, I jumped down from the rail and walked toward the gate. Immediately the two cameras changed position so as to attend closely to my progress across the street—apparently their eyes had been trained on me the whole time I'd been sitting on the rail. I pressed a button on a metal panel that was punctured with small holes arranged in several concentric circles; there was no name on the panel. After a moment I heard a loud hum and then an unpleasant male voice, which asked me what I wanted. I said I needed to speak with Mr. Bernet.

"Mr. Bernet is not at home," the voice told me. I managed to ask when Mr. Bernet might receive me; the voice answered that he wouldn't. Then the hum cut out. For some time after that, I stood where I was, angrily pressing the bell, but no further sound came from the panel.

Slowly I walked away, looking through the tall railings at the inaccessible white building. A second before the house disappeared behind an ornamental shrub in the corner of the garden, I saw a tall man in light-colored summer clothing and a white hat emerge from the main entrance and set off toward the gate. Could this be Bernet? As this white figure approached the bars, the two wings of the gate parted noiselessly; once he reached the sidewalk, the gates closed with a soft click. I walked deliberately slow, and as the man passed I stole a look at his face, which was shaded by his wide-brimmed hat. The man wasn't Bernet, although his suntanned, clean-shaven face and lively eyes were familiar to me. I stopped walking as I pondered where I'd seen him before. Yes, I knew where: I'd seen a photo of him in a magazine with a piece about Bernet's house. The man walking briskly down the street toward the streetcar terminus, his white clothing radiant in the sun, was the architect who had designed the house. I ran after him, now thinking neither of Bernet nor of Viola: I wanted to exploit this encounter with the architect in order to ask him about his creation.

"I'm very glad to meet you," I said, panting, as I caught up and fell into step with him. "I've spent the past half-hour looking at your house."

The architect looked at me and smiled. "That makes you a brave man," he said. "I'm afraid it causes most people great suffering to look at it for so long as a minute. I still get anonymous letters from residents of this neighborhood threatening to seek me out and beat me up. So you're interested in architecture, are you?"

"A little, yes, although I didn't come here because of your work. I wanted to talk with Bernet, but they refused to receive me."

The architect frowned and quickened his pace. "If you think I can help you get inside, you're mistaken," he said coldly. Apparently he was used to such importunate requests.

"Oh no, it really hadn't crossed my mind to take advantage of you in that way. And I became so interested in the house that I almost forgot why I'd come up here." I was trying hard to get back into his good books.

But this was going to be difficult: The architect remained mistrustful, and his tone was stern. "Why do you want to get to Bernet? To offer him some amazing deal? Then I suggest you go elsewhere. Every day dozens of such people turn up at the fence and try and find a way of worming their way inside; at the very least they gawk through the bars at the garden, hoping that Bernet will appear and they'll be able to shout their great offers to him."

Now it was my turn to be annoyed. "I've no interest in business, and I couldn't care less about Bernet," I said. "I needed to talk to him on a private matter."

The architect didn't seem convinced. I was tempted to tell him about the trident and Viola's disappearance, but I realized that this story was so implausible that it would make me appear less, not more credible. The architect continued to make it plain that he didn't want to talk to me, keeping a stubborn silence and taking such enormously long strides that I could barely keep up with him. As we descended the narrow street, the villas with gardens gave way to gray walls of apartment buildings covered in graffiti'd scrawl. I stumbled on after the architect, determined not to be rebuffed, but I kept falling behind. I was getting pretty angry at him, and I decided that he should hear my story as a punishment; it would be up to him what he made of it.

So I called after him: "Hey, Mr. Huffy, slow down, will you? Don't you want to know why I wanted to speak with Bernet? I have a wonderful story to tell. I was walking across a dump when I was stabbed in the foot by the sharp point of some object—maybe it was a tool, maybe it was a sculpture, maybe it was a large letter. Who knows? A few days later, I saw a computer screensaver with a design that kept changing shape; at one point the design had the same shape as the object at the dump. Then I discovered that at certain hours of the day the very same character appears in a portrait of a certain Viola, daughter of an erstwhile theoretician in Socialist Realism whose property was restored to him and who today lives in and owns a villa. He told me that his daughter disappeared without a trace two years ago. I found the artist who painted the portrait by first finding a dreaming hippo on a rooftop; the artist told me about a picture of a mad scientist that hangs in a bar on the square of a little French town, and about a chemist whose legacy included an unusual formula. How do you like it, then? And that's not all. I met a woman Viola employed to design a pump whose top sprouted dozens of tubes like the tentacles of a sea anemone. I also spoke with the owner of a record label who released a CD with a composition by someone called Vuhulum Chuh-yuh—that's right, Vuhulum Chuh-yuh—that was so quiet as to be practically inaudible. That same evening at the porter's lodge of a company that produces office equipment, the porter told me a story about a sixth-century Neoplatonist philosopher and a nineteenth-century English explorer. I wanted to speak with Bernet because it seems to me he may know something about Viola's disappearance."

As I was speaking, the architect had lessened his pace; as I came to the end of what I had to say, we were again walking side by side. I saw that the smile was back on his face. Obviously he had realized that someone who wanted to get to Bernet on some matter of business wouldn't have invented the story he had just heard.

"Please don't be angry with me," he said, "and tell me what the hippo on the rooftop is dreaming about."

"Of his home on the Nile, for all I know."

"Naturally—I should have thought of that myself. There's something else I'd like to ask you. You talked of a shape you've encountered several times. Could you describe to me what it looks like?"

I stopped and began to draw with my finger—on the wall of a house, over the red scribble of an unknown graffitist—the imaginary double trident. First I drew the ellipse, then the lower trident, then the horizontal line in middle. When I came to the transverse line at the middle of the figure, the architect laid his index finger next to mine and completed the upper half of the figure himself. For a moment we stood there looking at the defaced wall, on which we both saw the same shape.

"I should have expected that," the architect muttered to himself. Then he went on his way. I walked alongside him, saying nothing, waiting for him to speak. We were almost at the streetcar terminus. There was a car by the platform with its doors open, empty and waiting. Beyond the pedestrian island was a wooden hut with the signboard declaring "Refreshments" and next to this a bench where a sweaty streetcar driver sat drinking coffee from a plastic cup.

Chapter 32
At The Streetcar Terminus

"Shall we sit for a while?" the architect suggested. We went to the kiosk, each bought a bottle of beer, and sat down on the bench next to the driver, who soon threw his empty cup in a trash can around which several wasps were circling, prior to climbing into the empty streetcar with a heavy sigh, ringing the bell and driving away. I sipped my cold beer slowly. I looked at where the rails were set into the asphalt and at the cracks in it, through which grass and thistles grew, and I looked at the other side of the loop and the green, corrugated-iron fence, beyond which the roof of a workshop was visible. This workshop leaned against the yellow side-wall of an apartment building; the wall was spattered with white rain spots and divided by a diagonal shadow into a dark and a light half. I heard a clock strike noon. I waited for the architect to speak.

He drank half his beer, set the bottle down on the bench and said: "I don't know what all you've spoken of has to do with Bernet. But it seems to me that the story of the lost daughter you mentioned has something in common with the story of Bernet's life, as though they were two novellas by the same author, written in the same style . . . I first met Bernet nineteen years ago, when he and I attended the same school. We were both twelve years old. But back then I scarcely knew him, even though for a whole year we sat together at the same desk. In those days no one knew Bernet: He was a taciturn, solitary boy who never made a friend in class. He wasn't a particularly good student; he even seemed a bit slow-witted to us. From what we could tell, nothing amused him. When, in the early nineties, newspapers began to carry reports about a successful financier called Bernet who had quickly risen up this country's wealth ladder, it took me a while to realize that he might be my shy former classmate."

The architect paused for thought. "Stranger still, he's that shy child to this day. Even stranger than that, he acquired his fortune for that very reason."

He took a sip of beer before continuing. "Bernet did that simply by sitting at home at his computer. Soon there were wild rumors about who he was. Bernet was able to anticipate the movements of the financial market with such brilliance that it seemed he surely knew the concealed pasts and presents of many companies and banks—and this gave rise to rumors of spies who walked the rooftops at night like Batman and broke into locked offices, psychics who read bankers' minds, and genius hackers who opened the most tightly protected files on the World Wide Web. I've heard bedroom tales of exotic beauties pumping managers of large companies for trade secrets, and how at such moments Bernet sits in his office listening to the conversations via a transmitter built into a ruby earring, a cigar in his mouth and a glass of cognac in his hand. This went so far that the moment an unknown beauty appeared in the corridor of a bank or the vestibule of a large company's boardroom, people immediately began to speculate in whispers about whether she was working for Bernet. Bernet has always lived a pretty solitary life, and his aloofness only added fuel to the fire of the legend in which he was the protagonist. The fewer people were to be seen around him, the greater the number of fantastical beings that stocked the imagination of the world of finance he moved in. As it seemed certain that Bernet was acting on the basis of information acquired by illegal means, many times his business engaged the interest of the police—but they never found the slightest evidence of illegal activity, so there were never any grounds for his arrest."

It was strange that the architect was telling all this to a man he had known for less than half an hour: He didn't strike me as a particularly garrulous type. But he, too, knew the double trident, and maybe the figure was a mystery that tormented him too. Perhaps he was hoping that if the two of us were to go over everything we knew about it, we would succeed in revealing its secret. But there might be a simpler explanation for his effusiveness: Perhaps he was bothered by the rumors that circulated about his former classmate and welcomed any opportunity to set things right.

"One day at my studio, I received a telephone call from Bernet's secretary, who informed me that Bernet wished to speak with me about a commission. I would have thought that Bernet had forgotten all about me, so I was greatly surprised that he knew about my being an architect. And I was pretty confused as I traveled to see Bernet in the car he had sent for me. Should I believe my childhood memories or the current myths? Should I be expecting someone who was slow-witted and anti-social, or a boorish mafioso who would want me to build him a smaller-scale replica of the Taj Mahal with Moravian folk ornamentation?

"The person who received me had nothing of the mafioso about him, nor did he remind me of my taciturn classmate of old. And he certainly didn't look like a celebrated figure from the world of finance. His behavior was relaxed and uncomplicated. Although he remembered me well, it turned out that he hadn't chosen me only because we'd gone to school together. He knew my work and was able to talk about it knowledgeably. After a few minutes of conversation I was entirely reassured that what he had in mind was not a Hollywood mansion with Baroque towers. He didn't know exactly what kind of house he wanted, but he was hoping that the two of us could figure it out. To my great surprise, he laid out on the desk photographs of all the houses I'd designed, pointing out the ones he liked. We spent three hours standing over these photographs, at the end of which we both had a rough idea of the kind of house he wanted. One week later, I took my first designs to him. Bernet looked at these for a long time, made a few objections, and I redrafted the designs as he'd suggested. This process was repeated many times. Only slowly did my drawings allow Bernet to understand the space he wanted to inhabit, and I took his ideas on board as I continued to search for new shapes and materials. I don't think I've ever had a better working relationship with anyone. And it was nice that he wrote me a large check at the very beginning and offered me a fee for completion of the work, ridding me of the need to worry about making my living for a long time.

"Bernet was different from all other customers in that his vision of his house became ever less material. He couldn't shake the idea that the building had too many opaque materials, and he wanted to open it up to the garden more and more. Although I was an advocate of glass walls, it seemed to me that Bernet was overdoing things; I warned him that it was impossible to live in a space completely open to the eye. But it was as though Bernet had no need of the thing my other clients emphasized above all else: the intimacy of closed space. I suggested concealing the glass walls behind blinds, but Bernet insisted on drapes. He was enthralled by the idea of a house where there would be only right angles and indescribable, ever-changing shapes made by undulating drapes—geometry and chaos. Also, he was fascinated by the fusion of smooth, shining metal and tall, soft carpets. Later I realized that all his peculiarities were probably related to what he had learned at a particular moment in his life, when he was working at his father's company—to empty his mind, and to love emptiness, track its movements and listen to its voices. But we'll get to that later.

"But Bernet's vision of architecture wasn't the strangest thing about him. I enjoyed seeing him even though he remained a mystery to me. He was no longer the taciturn, antisocial kid who would answer his classmates' questions with a monosyllable or not at all, although he was still repelled by social life. I never saw any of the hackers, psychics, or beautiful lady spies with whom he was popularly considered to surround himself. He never spoke of his financial transactions.

"The mystery of his life was revealed to me on the evening I brought my final draft of the house to him. For a long time he studied it with satisfaction; then he asked me to explain a few details, and then he signed the drawings to confirm his acceptance of them. Then he went to his liquor cabinet for a bottle of twenty-year-old Scotch and two glasses. We were halfway down the bottle when he said he would like to tell me a story from his childhood . . . and as soon as he started talking, I understood that this was the tale of the most important thing that had ever happened to him."

The architect took a long swig of beer and set the empty bottle on the ground. "There wasn't even anything particularly special about the story. It had a hint of mystery, yes, but anyone who explores his memory in greater depth will find in his childhood at least one such mysterious incident. In most cases the person with such a memory has no problem living a normal life. With the passing years, such mysteries acquire some simple explanation, or if they remain unexplained, we tell ourselves that it is only because we don't know all the circumstances. What Bernet experienced was truly no great mystery: He didn't meet an elf or a ghost. I'd even say that I myself had stranger experiences as a child. It would be possible to find dozens of normal explanations for the story that has stuck in his mind, but Bernet the child rejected all normal explanations, and to this day he remains faithful to the child's defiance . . ."

The architect must have seen how there on the bench I was practically trembling with impatience to know the secret from Bernet's childhood. I wondered if he was spinning the story out in order to torment me.

"Please stop torturing me and tell me what happened to him," I begged.

But the architect stood up and said: "Finish your beer and I'll fetch two more. Surely you can hold on a little longer! For now I'll tell you that at its center was treasure from a wrecked pirate ship."

Turning to the kiosk, I saw another streetcar driver leaning at the window and wiping the sweat from his red face with a handkerchief. Then I looked at the shadow that had climbed a little further up the blank wall of the house. What was the architect about to tell me? Could Bernet's fortune really have come from treasure at the bottom of the sea? If someone had told me such a thing a week ago, I would have laughed at him, but now such an explanation didn't seem at all unlikely. Nor was this the first suggestion of lost treasure in connection with Viola's disappearance. Could Viola have found out something about it? If so, in the search for the treasure, had she been Bernet's ally or rival? I heard the slamming door of a refrigerator, followed by two hisses. The architect returned to the bench, handed me a steaming-cold bottle and resumed his seat.

Chapter 33
The Lost Treasure of Captain Boustrophedon

"Bernet's parents divorced soon after he was born, and all his childhood Bernet lived alone with his mother," the architect began. "When he was ten years old, a distant cousin of his mother's came to stay with them for several days. Before this, Bernet had seen this auntie only two or three times, as she lived in a town far away. Bernet's mother was confined to bed with flu, so the auntie took little Bernet for walks in the city. Once she took him with her on a visit to a friend of hers in a dark apartment filled with old furniture and lots of books. The friend was at home alone with her little daughter. As the women chatted, Bernet found himself getting bored; the little girl, who was about three, sat on the sofa and frowned at him. His auntie's friend gave him a picture book to look at, but he soon lost interest in this. As he was still just as bored by the grown-ups' talk and the little girl was no more pleasant to him than before, he decided to explore the apartment.

"The next room was empty but for a large round table at its center. On this table was a thick book written in a foreign language. He picked the book up because he was attracted by the dusty space between its leather spine and its binding. Once he tired of inspecting this mysterious corridor, from which wafted a smell of glue, he was about to return the book to its place when he noticed a small slip of paper tucked underneath it. On this slip were some notes scribbled in pencil. All those years later, Bernet still remembered exactly what was written on it. Later, he and I spoke of this mysterious text so many times that now I, too, know it by heart. It read: 'S. Clara, pir., Ven. shipwr. Fol. 1572. Gem, diam. — seahorse, oct. (eye — w.'s 2nd lrg. st.). Pearls, b. & w. Nal. 1954. Liv. r., bookc., lever bh. 11th vol. Ott. enc. Add.: woman & dragon, sword, grn. embl. orng. shield. Obj. 3 shelves — 1st lett. Boustrophedon.' "

"I don't understand that at all," I said.

"At first Bernet didn't understand it much either. But from the beginning there was one thing he was in no doubt about: It was a message about treasure. On their way home, he asked his auntie who her friend was, but for some reason she didn't want to talk about her. Then his auntie went home, and Bernet never saw her again because not long after the visit, she and his mother fell out and broke off contact. Two years after that, a death notice arrived in the mail—Bernet and his mother were informed that his auntie had been killed in a car accident. Some years after that, when he set out to look for the house she had taken him to that time, he discovered that the whole block had been demolished for the construction of a Metro station. Since the moment he'd read the mysterious message, Bernet had never stopped wondering about what it was communicating. This was when he and I were sitting together at the same school desk, and I hadn't had the vaguest notion about what was constantly on his mind . . ."

"Did Bernet succeed in deciphering the message?"

"After some time, he came to the conclusion that it meant the following: The Venetian pirate ship the *Santa Clara* was wrecked in 1572. A large treasure was hidden in her hold. This treasure was composed of white and black pearls and jewels containing diamonds and precious stones shaped like creatures of the sea. (The eye of a diamond figure representing an octopus was made of a gem that was the second-largest of its kind in the world.) In 1954 someone pulled the treasure from the sea and hid it in a place that is reached through a secret door in the back of a bookcase that stands in the living room of an apartment; this small door can be opened by pushing a lever located behind the eleventh volume of *Otto's Encyclopedia*. The address of the apartment is encrypted in something that may be a drawing, painting or sculpture; this work shows a woman who is holding a sword in one hand and a shield in the other and is fighting a dragon; the shield sports a green emblem on an orange background. The drawing, painting or sculpture also shows a cabinet or display case with a variety of objects on its three shelves. The address of the apartment where the treasure from the *Santa Clara* is hidden can be discovered by reading the initial letters of the designations of the objects.

"Of course, some things were not entirely clear to Bernet. What, for instance, did 'Fol.' mean? (He still hasn't figured that out.) Nor at that time did he know the meaning of the word 'boustrophedon.' Over that bottle of scotch, Bernet told me with a smile that he had imagined Boustrophedon to be the name of the captain of the pirate ship that had gone down with its treasure. From the sounds of the individual syllables of the captain's name, Bernet had dreamed up a character and a life story for this tough pirate; in the 'bou' he heard the stamping of his feet on the deck, in the 'stro' his thunderous voice whose every utterance was laced with curses, in the 'phe' the swish of his rapier, and in the 'don' the opening of bottles as the pirates celebrated success in battle. Each of these images gradually gave rise to dozens more, until little Bernet saw in his mind's eye, down to the finest detail, the figures and faces of all members of the crew and all places on the ship—from the crow's nest at the top of the mast to the very bottom deck, which was infested with rats.

"Every night, Bernet told me, in the dark bedroom he shared with his mother, and to the sound of her breathing in the next bed, he would make long tours of the ship, peering into the cabins below deck and exchanging greetings with pirates. Then he would go up on deck, lean on the rail, feel the pleasantly cool wind as it came off the sea and ruffled his hair, stare at clouds still lit by a sun that had drifted beyond the horizon, and study his reflection in the shiny, metallic surface of the sea. After a while he would hear at his back a thudding tread, and soon Captain Boustrophedon would be standing beside him. The captain would join Bernet in his silent contemplation of the sea before telling him what had happened on board ship that day. In conversation with Bernet, the captain's rough voice was softer. When Bernet spoke, to describe small discoveries in his child's world or complain about his dense, spiteful classmates, the captain would give him his full attention. The captain always told Bernet that there was no point in getting upset because of such insignificant people.

"Bernet knew Captain Boustrophedon better than he knew his relatives and classmates; he knew all about his life, and he knew in detail every room of the house in Venice in which Boustrophedon had spent his childhood and youth. Boustrophedon had spent many years at sea in the service of the Venetian Republic, but an intrigue conducted by a dastardly marquis who was unable to cope with the fact that the beautiful daughter of the Florentine ambassador had chosen Boustrophedon over himself, resulted in his being unjustly indicted for treason. Boustrophedon had broken out of the Venetian jail in swashbuckling fashion and then become the redoubtable captain of a pirate ship.

"Once Bernet and his mother were watching a travel program on television about archeological excavations on Crete. When the narrator mentioned a code of law carved into the rock of the ancient city of Gortyn, Bernet, who was thirteen years old at the time, learned that the word 'boustrophedon' meant a text in which each line should be read from the side on which the preceding one ended. Bernet told me that at the moment he discovered no Captain Boustrophedon had ever existed, he felt a searing pain the like of which he'd never known before. He ran to his bedroom, buried his head in his pillow and sobbed for a long time.

"Later, he tried to persuade himself that the name wasn't so important. The pirate ship must have had a captain, he told himself, as he tried to keep his beloved Captain Boustrophedon alive under a different name. The name he gave him was Giuseppe Nero, that of an AC Milan soccer player he'd seen in the newspaper. But poor Boustrophedon had become so closely associated with the sounds of his name, having developed out of these along with the whole pirate ship and its crew, that the change of name slowly changed the captain's appearance, character and life story. Although Bernet became friends with Giuseppe Nero, the new captain was no match for the great Boustrophedon, nor did he and Bernet get on so well together. Bernet missed Boustrophedon a great deal—and I believe he still misses him today."

While the architect was talking, we had both finished our beer. Now it was my turn to fetch two fresh bottles. I saw no one at the window, but from inside the kiosk I could hear shuffling and the clinking of glass. I leaned on the wooden shelf and thought about the treasure. It seemed to me that the idea of pirates' treasure hidden in a living room in a nondescript city apartment block fitted in pretty well with Viola's story. I had the impression that a luster of diamonds and pearls shone in every word I'd heard since the beginning of my search for Viola. Again a picture emerged of a subterranean monster. I imagined myself in a stranger's apartment, removing a thick volume of Otto's Encyclopedia from a bookcase, then pushing a lever in its back wall; I imagined the creak of a gate opening to reveal a passage that led to an underground lake, where the monster was guarding the treasure from the pirate ship. At last I heard the voice of the kiosk vendor at the window, and I ordered two more beers.

"For many years Bernet was in no doubt that there was hidden treasure in a room somewhere in the city," the architect went on, as soon as I returned. "As he walked along the street, he would study the facades of the buildings. (His mother always said to him: 'Watch where you're going, or you'll fall over!') The windows in which he saw pieces of ceiling and fragments of furniture were so mysterious that surely there was hidden treasure beyond one of them . . . Many children live more in worlds of fantasy than in the world we call reality, although widespread opinion tells us has that the latter has earned a position of privilege among all the worlds. Some of these children grow up to enter the real world with a sense of repentance; others remain stranded in wonderful unreality forever, growing into men and women who live alone, practice some boring occupation their whole lives long and every day look forward to the end of working hours, when they'll close themselves up in their gloomy, empty apartment with a bottle of wine and return from the foreign world to their native land.

"Surprisingly, Bernet avoided both these fates. Unlike other dreamy children, he had proof of the existence of another world, and that this world was connected with our own. In childhood this had lent him strength—although we'd laughed at him in class, we'd all been a little afraid of him, too. As he grew up, the world pounced on him in order to defeat and recruit him, to convince him to accept its system and venerate its manifestation of truth, as it does with every child; Bernet resisted this pressure for longer and more bravely than other children. As his worried mother took this loner son who hardly ever spoke from one child psychiatrist to the next, he repeated in his thoughts over and over: 'They'll never get me—not ever. My own eyes have seen that what everyone tries to make me believe, is not true.'"

The architect paused. A streetcar drew in, and an old lady climbed out of it with difficulty. The angled shadow on the wall of the house was becoming a large stain in the shape of an octopus.

"But it was an unequal struggle, and in the end the child in him succumbed. Bernet conceded that the world was the victor, but unlike other vanquished parties he refused to take this lying down. It was as though he were telling the world: 'Very well, perhaps I was wrong—apparently there are no hidden treasures in city apartments and laws other than yours. Although it seems you were right, that doesn't mean your truth is worth anything or that I have to admire it.'"

Chapter 34
Birth of a Multimillionaire

"When Bernet's mother asked him what he wanted to be, he just shrugged. Bernet's mother despaired of him: He knew nothing about life and was unable to make the simplest arrangement. At first she hoped in secret that he would grow up to be an artist, but it soon became clear that he had no artistic or scientific interests. After the *Santa Clara* sailed out of his life, there was nothing in which Bernet found amusement.

"He was in the last year at high school when his mother started singing the praises of the son of someone she knew, who was a business graduate. Although he didn't care what she had to say on the matter, he placed an application with a business school to make her happy. He completed his studies there in the early to mid-nineties, still as indifferent, withdrawn and reclusive as he'd been before he started. Immediately after the changes of '89, his father had thrown himself into the world of business, and following the voucher privatization scheme, he had founded a company that was active with shares in the new market. Although he had no illusions about his son's abilities as a businessman, he had a bad conscience about leaving his family and paying little attention to the boy, so he offered Bernet a job with his company. Bernet accepted the job with a shrug; he was glad not to have to hunt for a position . . .

"When later I thought about Bernet's choice of profession, I came to the conclusion that it was about more than just indolence and indifference. His decision to occupy himself with securities might at first have been an expression of desperation that was using indifference as a mask. At the time, I imagine Bernet saying something like this: 'If the world I believed in for so long doesn't exist, and so everything has the same value, this means that everything is similarly worthless; so I may as well occupy myself with activities that always seemed to me the most useless, hopeless and boring of all—making money out of other money.' Sometimes a desperate person experiences a strange delight in doing the thing that he was once most repelled by; it intensifies his suffering to such a degree that it becomes a weird kind of thrill. In this way a poet writes a socially-engaged novel and a woman marries a man she once couldn't stand.

"It was Bernet's job at his father's company to gather and process information that would help in assessing movements in share prices. He didn't enjoy the work, and he wasn't good at it; he found it infinitely laborious and at the same time pointless, as tremors on the market had hundreds of possible causes, each of these was dependent on hundreds of other causes, and these too . . . He would stare into the screen of his computer at names of companies from all over the world, which would seem to him like the names of demons; he would watch the changing numbers that accompanied the names, and these would seem to him like vile little animals with bodies made of digits.

"He was in a permanent state of anxiety that he wouldn't be able to perform his duties. He overtaxed himself by working late into the night and then felt completely exhausted. Even so, the results of his work were poor; had the owner of the company been anyone but his father, he would have been given notice long before. The father soon came to expect nothing from the son. He didn't complain or blame him, nor did he expect Bernet to become a successful stockbroker, but it pained him to think that his son was too weak to handle any of the tasks most people have to deal with in life, he would never be a success in any line of work, he would never rid himself of enough of his anxiety and woodenness to be able to relax and have fun, he would never have enough energy for foreign travel, and no woman would ever be enchanted by him.

"The father allocated the son a small closet with a computer, and from time to time he would give him something unimportant to do. In his cubbyhole, Bernet lived a little like Gregor Samsa, and his father felt sad and quickened his pace whenever he passed its door. Bernet would usually spend all night on a single task. Then, exhausted and sleep-deprived, he would take the folder with the results to his father. As soon as Bernet was out of the room, his father would put the folder in his filing cabinet without first having opened it. He considered the salary he paid Bernet to be a private matter—an appanage. At this time, it seemed that Bernet's journey into society would end as it had begun. His only bond with the world of others was tedious, grueling work that exhausted him, and as this bond was not tight, again and again he would gradually shake that world off and quietly withdraw into himself. His colleagues gave up addressing him and then even stopped noticing his hunched figure as it crept along the corridors; he had turned into a harmless, invisible ghost. He was glad that everyone left him alone. Only occasionally did his heart feel a sharp pain—when a beautiful young woman walked by . . ."

Again the architect paused. The rays of the sun passed through the tops of the trees on the verge of the hillside, making them into a mosaic of green lights and dark shadows. The sounds of the city had quieted; all I heard was the soporific buzzing of wasps.

"Two events in Bernet's life have served to change it. The first, and easily the most important, was his discovery of the message about the treasure. The second took place in the cubbyhole at his father's company, about a year after he'd begun his ghostly existence there. One evening he was sitting at his computer as music, conversation and laughter came from the next room—the other employees were celebrating someone's birthday. He was feeling extremely tired, far more so than usual. Maybe the change in his perception was brought about by his tiredness. The screen he was looking at had luminous, changing numbers sailing across it. Although he was concentrating as hard as he could, he still wasn't able to see any sense in the movements of the figures, and he failed to establish any connection between the moving points of light and any other reality. The luminous shapes on the screen wanted nothing to do with share prices, let alone with the nature of goods produced by individual businesses, in-house relations, people's industriousness and morale, the political situation, technological innovations, happy events, various setbacks, or mining disasters in distant lands. Although the digits still maintained some kind of connection with the world of size, sums and accounting, this world itself transformed; now mathematical processes seemed to Bernet not so different from the growth and withering of trees or the movement of waves in the sea. Letters and numbers tore themselves away from the endless root system of causes and moved about in the void in a dance of liberation, just as in fall leaves separate themselves from the stem and let themselves be borne along by the wind.

"Bernet watched the dance of the digits with fascination. As he was doing this, he felt that the silent breath of the void had its own special rhythm, and that the process he was witnessing wasn't entirely without meaning and pattern. But this pattern was not at all like the ever-elusive one he'd been trying in vain to track down. It was more like the rhythmic pattern of a dance. To be in touch with this new unity was much more difficult and much easier at the same time. Its extreme difficulty lay in the impossibility of finding a point of contact in the void that spread out everywhere, making it necessary to forget everything and cast aside all knowledge and all memories. It was easy because at the moment Bernet determined to cast off his chains and jump headfirst into the swirling void—maybe because he had less to lose than other people—it was enough for him to abandon himself to the rhythm of the new dance and allow himself to be led by it.

"The world of lights on the screen was suddenly overflowing with meaning. Having felt his way into the rhythm, Bernet made the realization that he knew which movement was about to come; it was whispered to him by the present rhythm, in which past and future were already concealed. And Bernet knew the future just as a woman dancer knows the figure her male partner is about to develop; indeed, her body knows it before the first tiny movement of this figure; it knows it from the tensions that begin to rise in her partner's body before he even knows what he's about to do. Like the woman dancer, Bernet was suddenly able to respond to the movements of the dancing digits even before they were born and developed.

"So in the blink of an eye, the work that he'd found so laborious was transformed into an effortless dance—a game that began to amuse him. Realizing that his father's company hadn't provided him with the right dance floor, Bernet gave notice. His father tried to persuade him to stay but was forced to accept Bernet's resignation; now he worried that he was about to witness his son's ultimate failure. Bernet sat down to his home computer and began to play his game with the financial markets. He felt like a diver engaged in a dance with a stingray so supple that it could move every part of its soft, tensile body while its every movement produced a unified rhythm. Success came to him almost instantly. It was then that people started to be convinced that Bernet had some kind of access to secret information. Probably no one would have believed that Bernet actually knew far less than all the others, and that not only did he have no information, he wasn't even interested in acquiring any . . ."

The architect looked at me with a smile before adding, "No one, that is, except perhaps someone who walks about the city listening to stories about apparitions in paintings, Neoplatonist philosophers and inaudible musical compositions, with the hope of discovering the meaning of a mysterious symbol and finding a girl he doesn't know. So now you know the origins of the legends of Bernet's financial power and his private legions of hackers, lady spies and ninjas. And the mythology around Bernet was given an extra flourish when he took in two young women and started to share his house with them. After that it was crystal-clear to everyone that Bernet was an unscrupulous mafia boss with no sense of morality who would stoop to the lowest crimes to achieve his business aims. Anyway, although money was pouring into Bernet's accounts, he paid little attention to it; what interested him most was the on-screen game of lights he'd invented in the cubbyhole at his father's company . . ."

I felt the need to interrupt. "Wait a moment! This is a bit much even for me! I can just about imagine that Bernet had no thoughts for the outputs, products, and markets represented by the changing figures, but please don't expect me to believe that he didn't realize that the figures on his bank statements represented money! Surely he thought of it at least occasionally? And if he really was so indifferent to money, why didn't he hand it out to the poor instead of leaving it in the bank to no purpose? And what about his mansion? I can't imagine that came cheap . . ."

"I didn't say that money meant nothing to him," the architect said defensively, "just that his financial dance was certainly more interesting and important to him than what came out of it. Bernet knows how much money he has in his accounts, and he is able to enjoy his money. After a time, the ease he discovered in his game spilled over into his life, and he has largely rid himself of his woodenness and stress. He likes good food and drink and he likes to buy beautiful things. Interestingly, these things often remind him of his childhood dream of treasure: He likes diamonds, pearls, jewels set with precious stones or made of gold . . ."

"You say that Bernet acquired his fortune owing to the fact that he didn't lose his childishness. How am I to understand this?"

"I've thought long and hard about what happened in his cubbyhole on that fateful evening. I think Bernet must have remembered something that caused him to start viewing the world of finance with the eyes of Bernet the child, a way of seeing that he'd forgotten as he grew up. Maybe it was like this: At the moment little Bernet discovered the message about the pirates' treasure, all things slipped off the moorings that attach them to the world. To us it seemed at that time that Bernet was unaware of what went on around him, but in actual fact, the opposite was true: He believed that all things might tell him something about the treasure, and so he watched their behavior with an extremely attentive eye and learned to perceive processes that no one else sees, even though they take place on the surface—the unnoticed life of things, and their movements, hidden courses, stresses and releases, internal strifes, vibrations, pulsations, friendships and enmities, withdrawals into self and bursts outward. As a child Bernet was a dreamer, and I've often noticed that dreamers make good observers who see more than other people do."

"How can this be?" I asked. I was aware of a strange conspiracy between dreams and faithfulness to facts in many people including myself, and I was at a loss to explain it.

"I'd say it's because the unnoticed life of facts has much in common with dreams; not only do the two worlds resemble each other, each finds in the other nourishment for its own growth. In his childhood, Bernet has told me, on the basis of his secret life, facts began to compose themselves into wholly new species, genera and classes, so that a completely new classification of the world originated; in one species in this world you might find a cracked conker, a certain kind of apartment house (that is difficult to define by our terms), a tin box with colored threads, and a thin strip of land on the edge of a village. Had Bernet's knowledge of the existence of treasure not resulted in a state of despair in which he destroyed the world he'd lived in to that point, he might have cultivated his view of things patiently and become an artist."

"Instead of which the poor man became a mere multimillionaire. Please don't take this amiss, but it seems to me that you're too easy on Bernet. I can see that you like him, but I wouldn't want to be a friend of his myself. I know others who have played lone games, but unlike his, their games were clean. They didn't make any money out of them, and if by some miracle this had happened, I believe they would have either stopped playing the game or taken the money without creating some flimsy alibi for it or trying to convince people that their earnings were just some side effect of the game that mattered little to them. It bothers me that Bernet thinks himself a member of their club; he's not the same as they are. Doubtless it's impressive that Bernet discovered in his cubbyhole the Tao of the stock exchange or some such thing, but this does nothing to change the fact that he's a moneyman. My greatest sympathy is for the small treasure-hunting boy he betrayed. Now I come to think about it, maybe I would like Bernet more if he really was the mysterious, scheming boss they all take him for."

"There's a lot of truth in what you say," the architect replied with a sigh. "I don't actually understand my own relationship with him very well. If someone were to tell me the story of his life as I've just told it to you, probably my feelings would be similar to yours now. Yet I still feel the need to defend Bernet. How do you think you or I would behave if all of a sudden enormous wealth were to rain down on us? Would we not do far worse things? Maybe I haven't told you the most important thing that binds me to Bernet—I haven't spelled it out because I don't know what it is. Perhaps it's the child's helplessness that occasionally shines through his smile or wanders into his gestures; perhaps it's the wonder I sometimes see in his eyes as he looks at his mansion, as if he were saying: 'My God, how did I get here?' Maybe what binds me to him most is the expression that sometimes appears on his face in the middle of a conversation, as though he were begging me not to leave him. Since he met Andrea and Barbora, he's no longer so alone, but I'm still the only friend he has."

On hearing his sheepish apologies for his friendship with Bernet, I felt sorry for the architect and didn't wish to torment him further. I asked him to tell me Bernet's story to the end.

Chapter 35
A Trip to Garmisch-Partenkirchen

"As I was saying, Bernet bought precious stones and jewelry. He hired an expert to go around the stores of antique dealers in the city and photograph necklaces, brooches and bracelets that might interest him. Last March this man showed Bernet a photograph of a cut-diamond bracelet. This glittering object was lying in a jewel box lined with red velvet; to the left of the box stood a cut-glass tumbler, to the right a mirror in a pseudo-Rococo gilded frame. As Bernet was studying the bracelet, his gaze slipped to the mirror, whose scratched, half-blinded surface reflected indistinctly an object that stood next to it but was outside of the photo. This appeared to be a figurine, or perhaps a sculptural group in miniature, only part of which was visible in the mirror. It took Bernet a while to separate from the scratches on the mirror the patches of color that made up the object; these eventually came together to form a hurrying man in a hat and a beige raincoat, who was holding a briefcase in his hand.

"After a while he realized that the small sculpture was probably made of two materials. The figure of the gentleman in the hat appeared to be of porcelain, as was the sidewalk he was striding along and the wall of a building he was passing. In the wall was the door of a store and part of its front window, which were probably small sheets of glass embedded in the porcelain. It looked as though another figure or other figures stood beyond the glass door. These were even less clear than the man in the raincoat, because in addition to the mirror's scratches and reflections, there was a glare on the glass they were behind.

"Bernet was reminded of the movie *Blow-Up*; perhaps, he thought, there was more to be taken from this photograph than was clear at first sight. He didn't have an enlarger, so he ran about the house in search of a magnifying glass. At that point he couldn't have known what kind of discovery to expect; he was gripped by an excitement he himself didn't understand. The telephone was ringing, but he left it unanswered as he pulled out drawers and rummaged about in them until at last he found a powerful magnifying glass.

"With the aid of the magnifying glass, he discovered behind the glass door of the store the figure of a naked woman fighting a dragon. The dragon was angrily rearing up in front of the woman, its jaws open to show off sharp teeth. The woman was pointing at the dragon's maw with a sword held in her right hand and protecting herself with a shield gripped in her left. She had fair skin and wavy red hair that fell to the middle of her thighs; the monster was covered in emerald-green scales. These two colors appeared again on the front side of the shield, in the form of a dark-green emblem on an orange background. I imagine you can guess what this emblem looked like. This was the first time Bernet had seen it; he was to encounter it on two further occasions, but we'll get to that later.

"Bernet was reminded immediately of the message about the treasure. Although he hadn't thought of it for years, he found he still knew it by heart. He pointed the magnifying glass at the storefront window next to the door; unfortunately only a small part of this was visible in the mirror. Bernet saw the ends of three shelves. He studied these with concentration until the patch of gray on the top shelf transformed into a stoneware ashtray with a design of two polar bears, and the light shape on the middle shelf became the cylinder of a kerosene lamp; clearly visible on the bottom shelf was a figurine of a woman sitting on the back of a white bull, which she was holding nervously by the horns. The instructions from Bernet's childhood told him to read the initial letters of the designations of the objects. For the determining of the address of the apartment where the treasure was, however, three letters were very few.

"All the dreams of treasure Bernet had long ago dismissed, returned to him at a stroke. He went through moments of joy mingled with despair. The joy that washed over him grew out of the realization that he'd just been given proof that the world he'd surrendered did in fact exist; the despair stemmed from the knowledge that he'd once betrayed that world and so abandoned it for a long time. His earnings of recent years seemed to him dirty money; now he felt that the only property to which he had a right were the diamonds and pearls of the pirate treasure, and he told himself that these were surely still waiting for him in an apartment somewhere in the city, in a hidey-hole behind the broad spines of an encyclopedia. He also felt terrible regret for the time he'd lost—time he could have devoted to searching for the treasure.

"He set out immediately for the antique dealer's store, where the sales clerk told him that the statuette had been sold to a German tourist. As the sale was being processed, they'd exchanged a few words, and the sales clerk had discovered that the tourist lived in Garmisch-Partenkirchen, a mountain resort in the Bavarian Alps, had driven here in his own car, and that he would be returning home that same day. Bernet sent his man to Garmisch to see what he could find out there, and in the meantime he himself tried to find out something about the statuette here. From the store's acquisitions book he copied down the address of the man who had sold the statuette to the antique dealer, but this turned out to be false: The statuette had probably been stolen. Then someone told him that they'd seen the symbol that was on the porcelain shield on a compact disc of compositions by Vuhulum Chuh-yuh. Bernet went to the Tam-Tam store to ask about the composer, but the proprietor, who probably took him for the suspicious mafioso he was presented as on TV, was not inclined to speak with him. And that was when—thanks to the symbol—he met Barbora and Andrea."

"At last—Barbora and Andrea. Tell me about them."

"Barbora and Andrea are schoolmates and friends—both are

studying to be opera singers. As it happens, I was there when Bernet saw them for the first time. It was in a café. He and I were looking at a drawing of the symbol, discussing for the thousandth time what it could mean. The girls happened to spot what we were looking at, and they told us that they'd seen a similar drawing in a French book they'd read a long time before. We took this as no more than an interesting coincidence. Anyway, since that time they've been with Bernet . . ."

While the architect was speaking these last sentences, there was a dark, muffled, roaring sound. Hearing it, too, the architect stopped what he was saying. After he'd gotten the wasp out of his bottle, he went on with the story.

"Bernet's relationship with the women astonished many people . . . When he was a student and when he lived closed up in the cubbyhole at his father's company, women had a strangely ambivalent effect on him: They were the only thing that attracted him to the world of other people—it was thanks to them that he didn't break all bonds with it—but at the same time they filled his reclusive mind with such a heavy load of fantasy that he consigned them to the depths of his dreams, which not a single ray of light from the real world ever reached. It wasn't until he read Baudelaire's poem 'Le Beau Navire' that Bernet understood that remnants of dreams he'd had as a child were reincarnated in this dreamy eroticism: It contained the same waves and reflections, the same encounters and dangers, the same unknown shores . . .

"He later learned to turn his ignorance of the world into a strategic advantage in the world of eroticism, just as he'd done with the money markets. Even at the time of his rise as a financier, Bernet had little understanding of the everyday world. This was no great concern for him: He could hire people to do whatever he chose. But since the days when the purchasing of a few bread rolls caused him untold suffering, many things had undergone substantial change; although he'd never learned the world's rules, he would manage to outfox it by playing by possible rules—rules that he improvised on the spot based on a current situation. Usually this caught everyone out, as few people had the strength of imagination required to grasp that the rules of the game might be completely different; Bernet would use the element of surprise and confusion to secure an elegant victory. In a manner that was effortless and even slightly cavalier, Bernet managed a situation that might have led others to neurosis and suicide attempts, or at the very least to agonizing decision-making.

"Perhaps the most remarkable manifestation of this approach was in his relationship with women. In the days before Andrea and Barbora, he knew many women, who even today are trying to figure out what their relationship with Bernet was actually about—well, it didn't fit into any category of eroticism. Barbora and Andrea fell in love with him and Bernet grew to like them both at the same time. When the girls wanted a complex solution for their situation, Bernet suggested that all three of them should live together. At first the girls were shocked and offended by this, but then they decided to try it, and now the three of them have been living together for over a year in what to all intents and purposes is a very happy marriage.

"But if you'll allow me, I'd like to return to the Alps. When Bernet's emissary had been living in Garmisch-Partenkirchen for half a year and still hadn't discovered anything, Bernet brought him back and went to Bavaria himself. When he arrived in the Alps at the end of October, there was a strange numbness in the streets of Garmisch; the town was holding its breath in anticipation of the ski season, which was about to begin. Bernet questioned all those he came into contact with about the statuette—everyone just shrugged. After a month he was prepared to give up and go home. Snow had begun to fall in mid-November; by now the sidewalks were lined with dirty banks of ice, although Bernet barely noticed these. On the evening before his planned departure from Garmisch he lay on the bed in his hotel room, looking at the snowcapped peaks that were visible in the lower part of the window. The thought that he would have to return to his games of on-screen lights whose constellations transformed into money by some strange magic, made him feel terribly empty. As he was capable of no further thought, he just looked at the white hillsides bathed in a sad violet light. Suddenly he was sorry that in his whole month there he hadn't been out of the town. He decided to postpone his departure and take a trip to at least one of the mountains that were a constant, mirage-like presence above the roofs. At breakfast the waiter advised him to walk through the mountains to Mittenwald, which he would reach by evening and from which he could return to Garmisch by train.

"Above the town he met no one besides a few lumberjacks, and the mountain chalets and hotels he passed were closed. He'd been walking for an hour when the sun came out; before long the glittering snow was making his eyes smart, and he had to squint. He'd been on the mountain plateau for several hours when he chanced upon a small hotel made from logs, where a small taproom was open. When he entered the dark, warm space he was snow-blind—for a while, indeed, he could see very little. He bumped into a table and sat down. Patches of color gradually sailed out of the darkness. He heard a deferential male voice and ordered a grog. As his eyes got used to the gloom, he looked about the room, his gaze wandering along the walls from one set of antlers to another, from a painting of a chamois standing atop a pointed rock to an advertisement for a herbal liqueur in which a red-cheeked huntsman stood in the arbor of some mountain dwelling, raising a glass of brownish liquid—when suddenly he saw, on a shelf between two painted beer glasses—the object he longed for more than anything in the world; the object that in his childhood dreams had taken on thousands of different forms; the object whose vague image he'd seen in the mirror in the photograph . . . The bartender told him that he'd received the statuette as a gift from his brother, who lived in the town below. Bernet offered the bartender such a large sum for it that the man made no attempt to bargain."

Chapter 36
The Redhead and the Dragon

"Immediately Bernet rented a room so that he could inspect the statuette alone and in peace. He placed it on a table where the crisp, clean light of the snow-covered mountains fell. At last he saw the whole scene depicted by the porcelain and glass statue. The figurine was about twenty centimeters high and peculiar in that it showed an indoor and an outdoor space, divided by a wall. Bernet had never seen anything quite like it before. The lower part of the statuette was of a regular oval shape, its longitudinal axis formed by the porcelain wall with its glass door and shopfront. On the inner side of the wall was the interior of the store, at the back of which was a counter with a cash register standing on it. The contest between the redhead and the dragon was being played out between the counter and the storefront window; the dragon was so small that it reached only to the woman's waist, even though it was rearing up. Now Bernet saw that this wasn't a real fight, but a game, in which the woman was teasing her pet by giving its scaly neck a playful tickle with the point of her sword; certainly she wouldn't have hurt it. The dragon, too, was only pretending to be angry; it was swinging a paw at its mistress like a cat at play. Bernet was able to read the words LUNCH BREAK on the sign that hung from the door handle. On the other side of the wall, outside on the sidewalk, the man in the hat and raincoat was hurrying to work. Although it was possible to see through the glass door into the closed store, the man noticed nothing of the remarkable contest just a few steps away from him.

"Understandably, Bernet was most curious about the objects on display on the three shelves in the window. The beautiful saleswoman had placed six things on each of them. Obviously the store sold a pretty miscellaneous range of goods—probably it was some sort of bazaar. (Bernet imagined that during the day the emerald-green dragon snoozed in a back room amid heaps of old junk; during the lunch break his mistress would lock the door, take off her clothes and they would play together.) On the top shelf was a small bronze Roman eagle next to the kind of lamp that hangs at night in dug-up streets so that no one falls into them, one volume of an encyclopedia, a fountain pen with a marble casing, a plaster figurine of Osiris (presumably a souvenir someone had brought back from Egypt), and a stoneware ashtray with a design of two polar bears (which Bernet had seen in the photograph). On the middle shelf was an aerodynamic, Expo-58-type white vase with a crack in its neck, a small porcelain replica of the Apollo Belvedere, an extensible telescope, a paper fan with a picture of a hazy Chinese landscape, a milk-glass angel, and the fire-scarred cylinder of a kerosene lamp. On the bottom shelf was a glass paperweight with a bright-colored butterfly on its bottom, the shade of a table lamp with a stylized gladioli design, a reproduction of a painting of a small, winged elf in a metal frame, a chipped plaster figurine of Fortuna pouring a stream of fruit from the horn of plenty, some old military field-glasses, and a figurine of Europa on the back of a bull. According to the ages-old message, a text should be composed from the initial letters of the designations of the objects: thus on the top shelf from 'orel' (the Czech for 'eagle'), 'lamp,' 'encyclopedia,' 'pen,' 'Osiris,' and 'popelník' (ashtray); on the middle shelf 'vase,' 'Apollo,' 'dalekohled' (telescope), 'vějíř' (fan), 'angel,' and cylinder; on the bottom shelf 'triedr' (field glasses), 'shade,' 'elf,' 'Štěstěna' (Fortuna), 'těžítko' (paperweight), and Europa. Bernet picked up an advertising brochure from the table and wrote on it these letters in three sets.

OLEPOP
VADVAC
TSEŠTE

"Obviously this didn't make much sense. But then Bernet remembered that it was supposed to be a boustrophedon—this gave him POPELOVADVACETŠEST. Immediately he used his cell phone to call his secretary, who confirmed that there was indeed a Popelová Street, on the outskirts of the city.

"The very next day Bernet took himself off to number 26 Popelová Street. It turned out that the streets in this part of the city comprised nothing but rows of makeshift, single-story houses that the authorities had probably forgotten to demolish. The house with the number twenty-six nailed above its door was especially run-down; through gaps in the dense bushes that grew right around it, Bernet saw that its windows were boarded up. Obviously no one had lived here for many years. Bernet pushed at the rusted lock of the front door; it gave way and he went inside.

"Beyond this door was a single room. The roof had holes in it and all the things in the room gave off a smell of mustiness and mold. In the middle of the room was an office desk whose top was rippled with damp. Propped up against the desk were three canvases nailed into frames made of wooden slats. These were so large that they reached almost to the ceiling. Bernet assumed that they were parts of a stage set—each represented one wall of an ordinary room in the city. The canvases, too, had been badly damaged by rain and snow; doubtless they had been in the room for many years. There was no bookcase, no volume of *Otto's Encyclopedia* lying about, no lever in the wall.

"Bernet inspected every inch of the little house, finding nothing that might relate in any way to the treasure. The rotten drawers of the desk were empty but for the spiders running around in them. He picked up the magazines from the seventies that littered the floor and examined them carefully, page by page. Among them he found the torn half of a notebook that contained part of the score of an unknown opera. On the first page of this was the title of the work, *Medusae of the Past*, rendered in calligraphy. Neither the name of the composer nor that of the librettist were given.

"There at the house, Bernet read through the libretto carefully, but he found no mention of treasure in it. He engaged a detective from a private agency, who went over the walls and floor inch by inch but found no cavity or other clue that might lead to the treasure; nor did this man find the other half of the exercise book with the score of the opera. Bernet had the ink of the pages analyzed, and so he learned that the score had been written about twenty years earlier.

"Again the road to the treasure had closed. On top of this, Bernet's success in his games of finance had dried up; it dawned on him that he no longer understood the supple stingray of the market. The lightness of his financial dance had grown out of an indifference that itself had grown out of a resigned truce with the world. On the discovery that his dream of treasure might be true after all, his longstanding peace with the world had gone up in smoke, to be replaced by uneasy memories of his past defiance and feelings of despair at a defeat that needn't have happened. The lightness of his step disappeared along with his resignation, and the movements he made were now groping and clumsy. He didn't have long to wait for the results—the sums in his bank accounts began to diminish. Bernet is still a rich man, but in a few months or even weeks he may have nothing. The lost world of treasure revealed itself to him and then proved to be just as unattainable as ever; on top of this, the world he has built up around himself in recent years, and which he has learned to live in a little, has begun to crumble."

This, it seemed, was the end of the story of Bernet and the pirate treasure. For a while neither of us spoke. The light of the sun had yet to change color, although now it illuminated only the very top of the blank wall beyond the track. Bernet's financial mysticism had made no great impression on me, nor was I moved by his descent from great heights. But in saying that Bernet's story was not unlike my own and Viola's, the architect was right. Bernet, too, encountered in the course of his search clues that promised much but delivered nothing. And it was odd that our stories intersected at one point—both included the double trident. It occurred to me that some clues that were entirely useless to Bernet might be bearers of important information for the search for Viola. Maybe there was one such clue in the score of the opera. I asked the architect if I might get at least a copy of this.

"That may be possible," he said. "When he decided to study the opera, Bernet had the score rewritten and copies of it made."

"So the opera has been performed somewhere?" I said in amazement.

"Not yet," said the architect. "It's being premiered tomorrow. *Medusae of the Past*—at least the part of it that survives—is for two voices, and it occurred to Bernet that these roles could be filled by Andrea and Barbora. Although one is a male role, Bernet thought that by casting a young woman in it, he would only add to the work's charm."

"Please tell me the name of theatre. I'll like to try and get a ticket."

"That won't be easy, I'm afraid. The performance is part of a summer masquerade to be held in the garden of Bernet's home. The party is for invited guests only, and I doubt that I'd manage to get you in."

"You told me that Bernet leads a solitary life and doesn't have any friends. Now you're telling me he's about to hold a garden party!"

"Barbora and Andrea had the idea of having a garden masquerade last year, and they came up with the themes for last year's and this year's party. Last year it was 'Waves of the Sea'; this year it's 'Lights at Night.' The girls invite their friends and schoolmates. Bernet truly doesn't have any friends besides me, so last year he sent invitations to people with whom he has occasional, necessary dealings in the world of finance. These appeared in their fancy-dress costumes only because they would never refuse an invitation from a multimillionaire, even if it meant standing in an oubliette. Having seen how they suffered through the party in their uncomfortable costumes, he's invited the same people this year out of malice."

"I'm struggling to imagine what costumes representing waves of the sea and lights at night look like. Do the guests really disguise themselves as waves and lanterns?"

"Why wouldn't they? When Barbora and Andrea declared it a sign of unoriginal thinking to go to a fancy-dress party as a robber, musketeer or Columbine, Bernet was quick to agree with them. I happen to think they were right. The Waves of the Sea party was a success—guests walked about the garden in costumes showing gentle waves illuminated by the sun, menacing, dark waves, waves with crests of foam, and waves crashing on coastal rocks; I remember that one lady came as Aivazovsky's *Ninth Wave*. This year's guests will come as streetlamps, houses and stations at night, cars at rest, moonlit roofs . . ."

"How can you know that?" I asked suspiciously. "And anyway, where do the guests get their costumes? I doubt you can find waves-of-the-sea and lights-at-night in a costume-rental store. Nor can I imagine that people busy with matters of finance all year will make their own costumes."

"Some of them do, you know. For the chance of getting into Bernet's mansion, a chance that otherwise would be denied to them, some of them would probably be prepared to do more than make a frothy-wave costume and then suffer in it for several hours." The architect was laughing now. "But many of the costumes are made by my wife. She studied clothing design, and inventing crazy fancy dress is right up her alley."

"Could you somehow arrange for me to get into party?" I asked.

"I'm afraid not. Besides, it would be useless. You'd find no clue in your search for Viola in the opera: It was composed twenty years ago."

"That doesn't make any difference. Another strange thing about this case I've gotten caught up in is how all its stories are somehow connected with the past. I don't know yet which past this is: Most often my investigations have taken me back into the seventies and eighties, but that may just be the first flight of a staircase that descends much deeper. Just yesterday I encountered evidence suggesting that events of two years ago have their roots in the sixth century. I'm apprehensive at the thought of what tomorrow or the next day will bring. Some reference to the court of an Egyptian pharaoh, perhaps?"

"Just imagine someone finding the symbol you keep meeting on a wall of the cave in Altamira!"

"I wouldn't be exactly surprised," I said with a sigh.

The architect thought for a moment before saying, "Maybe I do know of a way I could get you into the party. My wife has one costume left over—yesterday one of the guests called her to say that he wouldn't be able to attend. You could wear that. The guests will arrive around eight, most of them already in their costumes. You can mingle in with the throng. You'll need to give Zachary—that's Bernet's bodyguard—a password at the gate. This year that password is 'Giuseppe Nero,' so make a mental note of it. Once you're in the garden, never remove your mask. Although it would be best if you spoke with no one, there's no need to worry that you'll be found out if someone addresses you: Most of the guests are strangers to one another, so your voice won't stand out."

Suddenly I recalled the arrogant voice of Jonáš as I had heard it on the radio twenty years earlier. Then, the idea of dressing myself up as a clown and embarrassing myself at the garden party of a multimillionaire for the sake of this man would have been totally crazy to me.

The architect told me that he would not be at the party himself: He was flying the next morning to the Hague, where he would be giving a lecture.

He lived not far from the terminus; we rode the streetcar for three stops before he got out, disappeared into a house, reappeared almost immediately and handed me a plastic bag containing some folded fabric in dark colors.

Back home, I put the costume on a hanger and hooked it onto the bookcase so that I could take a proper look at it. Shaped like a burnoose, it represented the flaking facade of an old factory, its windows fashioned with cutouts in the fabric and backed with cellophane. The insides of the windows were attached to small bulbs, which were connected by thin wires to a concealed device. This device turned the lights in the windows on and off, one by one. After a moment's thought, I realized what was happening: The night porter was on one of his regular patrols of the factory.

Chapter 37
On the Way to the Party

The next evening I stood waiting on the pedestrian island, my costume in a cloth bag thrown over my shoulder. Although the buildings were submerged in shadow, still their walls gave off the smell of the day's heat. The lit-up streetcar arrived. The car I got into contained two passengers, one at each end; its empty laminated seats gleamed in the light of the bulbs. The journey along the edge of the city was a long one, and the streetcar seemed to drag itself from stop to stop. Occasionally someone would get in, only to get off again one or two stops later; as far as I could tell, no one in these parts embarked on a journey of more than five streets. As darkness fell, the moving facades in the panes of the windows were replaced by reflected images of the illuminated inside of the streetcar. A few minutes from the terminus I was the only passenger left in my car, but at the penultimate stop a group of laughing masquers got on. They were wearing long black gowns with pieces of tinfoil and glittering sequins sewn onto them, obviously on their way to Bernet's party. The streetcar turned jerkily into the loop and stopped. The masquers hurried off and set off up the street toward the villas, where they were passed by an open-top car whose masked driver honked his horn at them, overlaying the sound of their laughter.

I stood irresolute between the tracks of the loop, the silent streetcar at my back. In front of me was the kiosk which had provided the architect and me with beer the day before; a bright light spilled from its window across the asphalt. Although the slope beyond the kiosk was in darkness, it made its presence felt by a light breeze that carried the scent of dried grass. For a while I studied the contours of the trees in the gardens and the roofs of the villas at the top of the hill, which formed a trail like the script of some dreamlike Arabia. In the sky, constellations were appearing amid the last remnants of the daylight.

The thought of what lay ahead was not pleasant to me: I would be among strangers on hostile territory guarded by stern, inquiring camera lenses in a garden surrounded by tall metal bars, with no prospect of escape, should I be exposed. What would they do to me? From what the architect had told me, Bernet was not the gangster of the popular imagination; but the architect had also spoken of anxiety and nervousness that had recently been apparent in his behavior, either from a lack of success in business or the ruin of Bernet's childhood—or childish—dream of treasure. I could easily imagine that in such a situation he might take an intruder on his private land for a scout sent by enemies in the world of finance who were seeking to bring him down, and so resort to the lowest moral behavior of his social class; I was reminded of pictures I'd seen on the news, from purple bruises on the faces of unfortunates who had fallen foul of the bodyguards of a rich man with an ax to grind, to divers retrieving from a lake bottom a metal barrel containing the remains of someone who had made the mistake of choosing the wrong business partners. Was it really worth taking such a risk for Viola, whom I'd never seen and who may even have found Bernet's pirate ship and now be sipping an apéritif in a bar on some far-away coast? Or for her father, who apparently had never done anyone a good turn in his life?

Yet I knew that the journey I had embarked on so unthinkingly a few days earlier had intoxicated me and deprived me of my free will. It was almost comical: As I stood irresolute in the middle of the loop at the streetcar terminus, it seemed to me that I wasn't sure even in my own mind what I was looking for. Was it the missing Viola, the secret of the double trident, Bernet's pirates' treasure, maybe even the Orange Book? I had the feeling that the true aim of my journey was none of these individually, but something lying at the center of a shimmering, silvery net that connected all these apparent aims and red-herring mysteries. I thought, too, of the incomprehensibility and deceptiveness of all the clues I'd found, realizing with sadness that the center of the net, where all the threads came together, would probably remain forever out of my reach. But still I was so obsessed by the search for it that I was about to trespass on a stranger's land and this misdemeanor, the unpleasantness that might ensue from it, and my fear of Bernet's bodyguards were not enough to discourage me.

I walked to the kiosk and leaned down to its lighted window. Although I didn't see anyone behind it, I spoke into the void, ordering a glass of a menthol liqueur from a bottle I'd spotted on the shelf. Like a scene from a puppet-theater play, there emerged from the opening a plump lady's hand that was carefully maneuvering toward me a glass filled to the brim with a bright-green beverage. As I leaned against the wooden counter mounted on the side of the kiosk, I sipped at the sweet, sticky liqueur in the hope that it would quiet my anxiety. The illuminated streetcar gave a jerk and moved in a slow arc to the empty platform where it waited patiently for all invisible ghosts to get on; then it rang its bell, closed its doors with a gentle sigh and moved away. I held my little glass, in which green liquid reflected lights which danced about. I looked at the facades of houses stripped by darkness of the moldings and ornaments that weighed them down during the day. An arc of lamps marked the road that led up to the villas. It occurred to me that I might go to the Lights at Night party dressed as a darkened kiosk with bottles of colorful alcoholic beverages or as my own reflection in the window of late-night streetcar, but for such poetic changes of costume it was, of course, too late.

I finished my liqueur and handed my glass back through the window. I reached into my bag for the costume the architect had given me, retreated into the darkness behind the kiosk, took off my pants and shirt, folded these up and slipped them into the bag, and put on over my underwear the factory-at-night costume. Then I pulled on a face mask that represented the night sky with the Cygnus and Aquila constellations. As I was already standing at the bottom of the steep, dark hillside, I decided to make my way straight up it. I clambered quickly through the tall, dry grass that snagged on the bottom edge of my long costume. Above me shone the first lights of the Garden District; an occasional car took the bend, its headlights slicing into the darkness like a beacon. When I was almost at the top, I looked down: The lights above the terminus and the lighted window of the kiosk had become a couple more points of luminosity in the swarm of city lights that hovered in the darkness. Lights at Night was a strange choice of theme for a masked ball, I thought again. By now I was getting curious about what I was about to see in Bernet's garden.

Before I reached the top of the hill, from above I heard voices, laughter and the slamming of car doors. I climbed over the rail where yesterday I had sat and watched Bernet's mansion, approached the guests gathered at the gate and mingled in with them. In the throng, dark fabrics rippled and bulbs sewn onto them to represent various lights at night flashed. Through the bars I saw the house on its elevation in the middle of the dark garden, illuminated by floodlights from below. I glanced furtively at the cameras above the gate—their alert gaze was passing slowly over the masked faces of the guests. As I got closer to them, one of the cameras gave me a searching look, before moving on indifferently to other guests. The gate was open only a few inches. Between its two barred wings stood a muscular young man with a shaven head, who looked like a member of the US Marine Corps. A stern expression on his face, he leaned down to each of the mask-wearers and let them through the gate only after they had whispered to him two words—the first and last names of a man who twenty years earlier had played on an Italian soccer team; the name given by Bernet the child to a celebrated pirate.

Admission to the garden was a slow process, so the mask-wearers were squeezed together at the gate. As I got closer to the bars, again I was seized by fear. Maybe the architect had lied to me; maybe he and Bernet had arranged to lure me here in order to learn what I knew about the treasure. Or perhaps the architect had been speaking the truth, but today the password had been changed, meaning that I was about to be exposed. To make matters worse, I couldn't seem to remember whether the soccer player's name was Giuseppe or Giovanni. Maybe I should leave while I still had the chance. But by now it was impossible to leave, whether I wanted to or not: Impatient, flashing masks were pushing at me from behind, and so I allowed myself to be driven forward until my nose was almost touching the arm of the massive bodyguard, which was barring entry through the gate. This custodian of Bernet's mansion lowered his head, and I said the name of the soccer player in a half-strangled voice. "Say again?" the bodyguard demanded ominously, as he stooped a little lower. I gave the Italian name somewhat more distinctly, cowering involuntarily as I did so. The bodyguard nodded and released his grip on the gate. The way to the garden—and the house—was open to me.

Chapter 38
Lights and Voices

Once beyond the gate, fabrics that had been squeezed into clumps rippled free again, appearing throughout the garden like dark streams in whose currents white and colored lights flashed on and off. No sooner was I past the bodyguard than a white-gloved waiter appeared bearing glasses of champagne on a tray, which he shoved in front of me. I took a glass before proceeding across the manicured lawn and paths coated with fine sand, sipping the wine slowly. All around me, in the folds of dark fabrics, pictures furled and unfurled. The murmur of voices rose and fell like waves of the sea, and I sailed currents and lakes of perfumes sweet and bitter. All these folds, lights and scents were making my head spin, so I moved off to the side—to the dark bushes that lined the garden; from a distance, I wanted to examine in detail the costumes that found themselves on the edges of the swirling crowd.

I saw them as ingenious, unsettled live statues of the nighttime city, and many of them inspired in me admiration for the imagination and technical ability of the architect's wife. Many of the costumes were of buildings at night, yet each building was completely different. A woman disentangled herself from the crowd, a cellphone ringing in her pocket; as she came to stand not far from me, I was able to study her costume in detail as she spoke into the phone. It represented an apartment house by a railroad track, the windows of which—like those of the factory of my own costume—were cut from cellophane, although none of her windows were lit, as though it were the middle of the night and all the tenants were fast asleep; but then a light did appear (the costume had to comply with the party's theme)—the windows of the first floor, which were at the height of the woman's calves, reflected the lights of an express train as it passed along the track on the opposite side of the street.

Moments later a small man came to stand a few yards from me. He, too, was dressed as a house at night. He had separated himself from the crowd in order to eat his battered crab claws in peace; he dipped the claws into a kind of pink mayonnaise before inserting them into a small hole between a stiff collar representing a roof with chimneys, lightning rod and TV antennas, and a face mask representing a night sky in which the edges of ragged clouds were lit by the moon. Two of the antennas were right in front of the man's mouth and so interfered with his eating; in order to pass them, he had to turn each claw to a certain angle, causing the mayonnaise to spill down the roof, facade, and windows.

This building was not as calm as the building on the costume of the woman with the cell. Inside it, lights, represented by tiny bulbs controlled by a device concealed somewhere in the fabric, kept going on and off. On the fifth floor someone switched on a bedside lamp with a green shade, plunging the room into underwater light; seconds later, the room was again dark—maybe the occupant was sick, had just taken his nighttime medicine and then lain down again. For a while all windows were dark. Then in one of the attic rooms a phone rang (thanks to a buzzer sewn into the costume); it was some time before the person living in the room woke up and turned on the light. As the light remained on for a long time, I began to ponder on who would wake a sleeper at night and what the subject of their long conversation might be. Had the occupant just learned of the death of a relative or a friend? Was it the hospital calling, to tell him that a loved one had had a serious accident? At last the light did go out, but shortly afterward the window was lit again, now by the changing colors of a television screen; the person woken by the phone call couldn't get back to sleep—I told myself that he couldn't stop thinking about the bad news he'd been given, so had turned on a satellite TV station (mounted on the wall right next to the window was a satellite dish represented by a slightly concave plastic button, with a trembling drop of mayonnaise hanging from it).

But not all the costumes were of buildings. One girl was wearing a costume representing a creek running through a city at night; clinging to its banks were plastic bottles and pieces of crumbling white polystyrene on which dirty foam had accumulated; the surface of the stream reflected the glow of a streetlamp. Another costume showed a streetcar at night, empty but illuminated, yet another an open garbage can in which a cigarette butt discarded by a late-night walker had ignited some old papers (the orange and gold face mask represented the blaze). Several guests were dressed as nightlights and fluorescent tubes. One woman had come as an empty factory yard, lit by a single lamp over a locked entrance gate.

Again I mingled with the guests and let myself be borne along on the current. I reached the terrace at the front of the house, where the tables were filled with glasses of wine and large, round trays on which fish and seafood were set out skillfully in a symmetrical design. I took another glass and returned to the dark garden. On my way, I passed costumes representing a lit-up night porter's lodge (I thought of my porter-cum-historian), graffiti-covered walls illuminated by a lamp swinging in the wind, the lights of gas stations and all-night bars, a lit-up railroad station, colored traffic lights whose monotonous play was reflected in the rails, floodlit hospital driveways, and night trains traveling the city's outskirts. One woman had come as a main highway with several rows of red and white lights.

In the general hum, individual voices surfaced and then dissolved.

I caught words in a high, unpleasant female voice. ". . . .o he holds this party to demonstrate that all's fine with him, but no one's buying that." I looked around for the speaker—I suspected she was wearing a costume representing a steamboat festooned with colored bulbs that was afloat on a river at night, but I couldn't be entirely sure. As the voice went on, I could hear the irritation in it.

"Everyone knows that he's on the way down. I'm pretty sure Barbora and Andrea are looking around for a new patron . . ."

"Is it any wonder?" answered a woman's voice which was thick was drink. This could have belonged to the wearer of a costume representing the entrance to a bar, above which was a neon sign that flashed on and off at a regular tempo; the bar's name was "Carioca." "Bernet's assets have shrunk by half in the past year."

"If he becomes the nineteenth richest person in the country rather than the eighth," growled a male voice, "I wouldn't call it a tragedy. If I were—"

"You should keep your mouth shut if you don't know what you're talking about," snapped the voice I'd heard first. "For the moment Bernet is still up there, but when he comes down, it'll be in an avalanche, and then you'll see where he ends up."

Then those voices were lost in the general hum. I wandered on until I picked up the voice of another woman. "Poor man. He shows that he's vulnerable, then they all fall on him and tear him to pieces."

A man's voice answered. "You believe those stories about him going bust? Don't be so naive. He spreads those himself—it's an old trick. I know very well that . . ."

A wave of interference washed over the end of his sentence. Apparently the range of conversation topics wasn't very wide.

A moment later, a quiet, male voice spoke practically into my ear. ". . . .e found treasure in a cave under the city, that's why he's lost interest in his affairs . . ." By the tone of his voice, the speaker was making it clear that he was privy to many things that he couldn't speak about.

"How come no one knows anything about it?" asked a girl's voice whose edge of naivety was flirtatious.

"He's hardly likely to broadcast it wherever he . . ." replied the voice of the initiate. These words, too, were lost in the overall hum.

The grating female voice behind me returned to the topic of money. "When you get to speak with Bernet, make sure you don't mention the loan straight away. You have to bring it up carefully, you should . . ."

The angry male voice didn't let her finish. "Quit giving me advice, will you? When I get to speak with him? Have you any idea how I'll recognize him among all these idiot costumes? I don't know why we even came here, I feel like a real clown . . ."

Another male voice was also complaining about the masks. "Only Barbora and Andrea could have thought up something as foolish as a masked ball with the theme of lights at night."

A woman's voice responded. "They wanted to be original at all costs, of course. They say next year's theme will be the desert."

"I wouldn't worry about that. There won't be any party next year. Bernet will be in jail, and his floozies will get kicked out of school and have to earn an honest living like anyone else."

Then I heard the voice of a girl. "Apparently it's an early Wagner that was found just recently . . ."

It seemed that these costume-wearers were talking about the forthcoming premiere of the opera.

The voice of a second girl contradicted the first. "I heard that it's the work of an unknown composer who committed suicide because Barbora didn't return his love . . ."

Then these utterances, too, were lost to me in the hum. Was the party getting louder, or was I getting more tired and drunker and less inclined to fish for fragments of speech? Now I was happy to listen to the clinking of glasses and isolated words that broke the surface of the hum like flying fish before sinking back into it; the names of Bernet and his girls and "money," "bankrupt," "immoral," and "jail" accounted for many of these words. At the beginning of the party I'd been hoping to overhear some reference to Viola, thinking that lapping waves, sparkling colored lights and whirls of words escaping their sentences created the right environment for a discovery about a woman who had become a character lost in the entangled world of a fantasy story.

But what the costume-wearers were saying disappointed and enraged me. In most voices I heard gloating over the financial problems of a man whose hospitality these guests were happily helping themselves to, and indignation at the morals of his girlfriends. Approximately half of the guests were convinced that Andrea and Barbora were calculating, cynical women who had brought Bernet to the brink of ruin, and that they were now in the process of choosing another victim to cling to once Bernet's bankruptcy was complete. The other half inclined to the view that a debauched Bernet had corrupted the girls, fate was now giving him his rightful punishment, and that probably he would drag the poor girls into the abyss with him. What, I asked myself, were the jealous cameras at the entrance for since admission to the garden was granted to such a callous, cruel, ungrateful band? Although I knew Bernet only from what the architect had told me about him, I found his guests' mean talk so distasteful that I'd begun to feel something like friendship for a character I could barely even imagine, who was spoken of in obscene, hate-filled words, of whom I myself had spoken with contempt only yesterday, who since childhood had been searching for treasure from a pirate ship, and who had the courage to live with the women he loved without regard for the morals of his honored guests.

I decided to take a look at the place where the opera would be held. I walked around the house and found another terrace on the other side. This terrace was illuminated by a round lamp above the rear entrance to the villa; it opened onto the dark garden at the back of the house. On the terrace, two cigarette-smoking men in overalls were working in silence, fixing a spotlight to a tall stand on metal poles. In the dark part of the garden, I made out two or three embracing couples, but I saw no one else there. The set of Popelová Street was being constructed on the terrace; it comprised three squares of canvas—each about two and a half meters square—hammered onto wooden frames. On the grass below the terrace were three lightweight, unsteady-looking music stands, each with a small lamp affixed to its top; in the light of these lamps, night flies were performing a jerky dance. The lamp above the entrance illuminated the front rows of the wickerwork chairs arranged on the lawn; the rest of the garden auditorium was lost to the darkness. At the very back I could see, under the stars, the silhouettes of tall trees at the garden's edge.

I inspected the set from all sides but didn't see anything of interest in it. Its three pieces represented three walls of an ordinary city apartment, as ordinary city apartments had looked twenty or twenty-five years earlier. On the lower part of the left-hand panel, the artist had depicted a radiator with such realism that there was a deposit of dust between its ribs; the upper part of the same panel showed a window with its drapes drawn—behind the pattern on the drapes it was possible to make out a city park, with the gray facades beyond it. The middle panel showed an angular sofa—I remembered seeing such sofas in prefabricated apartment blocks in the seventies—and, above it, a shelf filled with figurines and small vases against which were propped several postcards (with scenes of cities, lakes and coasts). There was a dark patch of damp in a shape reminiscent of South America, which began next to a jade Buddha on the shelf and touched gently against a color picture of Cape Horn that adorned the cover of a magazine which lay on the sofa. The right-hand panel showed a cabinet whose lower half comprised two rows of drawers and whose upper part was a small bookcase. I studied the spines of the books; although some of them bore short brushstrokes to indicate lettering, it wasn't possible to read the name of the author or the title on any of them. Nowhere did I see anything that even remotely resembled the double trident.

I looked at my watch: It was a quarter to eleven. I didn't wish to return to the front part of the garden, where all the costumes were, because I didn't want to listen to their wearers' foolish conversations, and besides, my head was aching from the flashing of all those lights. So I sat down in a wickerwork armchair in the middle of the empty auditorium and watched the lighting technicians at their silent work. On some of the chairs I noticed sheets of paper; I picked one of these up. It was a program for the performance.

Medusae of the Past
Fragment of an opera by an unknown composer

Cast:

Scientist in exile, c. 55 years old . . .arbora Bernetová
His wife, c. 35 years old . . .ndrea Bernetová

Music:
flute, lyre, bells

Obviously Barbora and Andrea had no problem in taking Bernet's name, even though neither one of them was married to him. The men on the stage soon completed the assembly of the spotlights, after which they placed a laminate-top table and two padded armchairs in front of the sets. Then they concealed the stage with a curtain—which looked rather like a large sheet drying on a clothesline—and walked away. Voices from the front part of the garden—excepting the occasional blast of woman's laughter—were barely audible here, so for some time I was able to enjoy quiet and solitude. But before long the first masquers appeared in anticipation of the performance and began to take up the chairs around me. The humming wave of voices had caught up with me; the fragments of utterances that emerged were on the same topics as before. Musicians sat down at the music stands. At precisely eleven o'clock the lamp over the entrance was extinguished and the spotlights came on, casting a dim light over the curtain. The hum in the auditorium died down.

Chapter 39
Exiles

The silence was broken by the first notes. Since hearing Chuh-yuh's minimalist composition, I'd come to think that no music could surprise me, but the strangeness of the overture went beyond even the bizarreness of Chuh-yuh's silent sonata. Although the latter might dumbfound the listener, it wasn't so difficult to find meaning in, not least as Chuh-yuh had given such a thorough explanation of the principle by which he had composed his work. The music I heard in Bernet's garden made a far less chaotic impression than the night time sonata, but its notes breathed out a distress the like of which I'd never before encountered when listening to music. My own anxiety grew out of the fact that it was altogether impossible to ascertain an order or intent in this music, or to see the sense in it. Nor could I find a world it might belong in—not because it referred to a distant, hard-to-understand world, but because it excluded the possibility of any world at all.

I heard a monotonous series of notes played on individual instruments; to my ear, these series defied any kind of classification. I couldn't catch in them any kind of fixed motif. Several times I had the feeling that a group of notes was about to be repeated or a variation played, but on each such occasion the connection was lost before it could be established. Like a slithery snake, the note sequences slipped away from the listener, who was beginning to believe he had a grip on them, twisting into a shape that made no reference to anything he had heard already.

The unknown composer's aversion to any kind of articulation expressed itself in another way, too: All notes sounded with the same strength, with the result that not only was the overture devoid of any motif or theme, it was impossible to tell where one bar ended and the next began and what the rhythm was. After a while, however, I got used to the vagaries of the overture and even began to take some pleasure in it. My enjoyment came from the sense that I didn't have to trouble myself to look for something I would never find, thereby allowing me to follow calmly the unexpected course of three writhing, snakelike melodies and their spellbinding dance.

Relationships between the melodies played by individual instruments were strange, too. They neither combined nor offered mutual support, cooperating only in the creation of a common musical fabric, and never interfering with each other. Although there was no dissonance, the overture gave rise to a feeling that this undisturbed concord did not come about intentionally; each of the melodies weaved dreamlike through its own labyrinth, never colliding in dissonance with another melody. I had a vivid image of ritual dancers intoxicated by a sacred drug, dancing in a trance, each of them, so it seemed, deeply immersed in his inner world and oblivious of his surroundings; and yet the ritual performance developed assuredly, without collision, and even produced a strange kind of harmony.

I kept asking myself if the composer of this music was Chuh-yuh—not just because he was the most eccentric composer I knew, nor just because he was linked with the opera by the double trident. At first it seemed unthinkable that I would be able to find any similarity between the overture and Chuh-yuh's compositions. Here, there was no fascination with the seeping of sounds into the folds of the soft fabric of silence, as was present in his early work, nor was there the tragedy of his second, later work, which referred to unknown stories woven from pain and conciliation, memory and forgetting, self-reproach and revenge. Yet, as I listened to the overture, the feeling grew in me that there was some kind of kinship between the mechanical indifference of this music and the agonized, ecstatic world of the composition labeled by the double trident. Maybe, I told myself, it was because the indifference heard in the notes of the overture was something that occurred either at the beginning or the end of a world of despair; where, surprisingly, it blended fulfillment of longing with utter resignation; where a calm, unexpected rhythm seeped into the roots of violent emotion, and that this was perhaps their secret binder, although I couldn't tell if it would bring the joy of conciliation in a unity of meaning or an incurable dread out of the monotony of everything that it was. I wondered about the story that could follow such an overture.

I had only just gotten used to this music without bars and motifs when I was torn from my repose by three notes—D, A-flat, B-flat—played on bells; the motif of the Orange Book. But after these three familiar notes, the melody didn't drop to C, as I'd been expecting. The Orange Book motif was closed up only in the silent composition, and it sounded in my mind along with the work now being played by the musicians on the lawn beyond the terrace. At that moment the melody of the true overture detached itself from the composition formed by memory and expectation; as it rose, instead of C, I heard middle E-flat, after which all traces of the Orange Book motif were lost. The music gave the impression that nothing had happened—that those three notes had never sounded; but I couldn't shake the feeling that the music was mocking me, and it didn't help at all that I told myself the opera had been composed some twenty years ago, when Viola was still a child and I knew nothing of her. Probably anyone would have told me that it was just a coincidence that those three notes had sounded in sequence, but from that moment on, I was sure of the identity of the composer of the opera. In that overture, the wily Chuh-yuh had opened the Orange Book and then snapped it shut again without giving me a chance to peek inside. I made him a promise: Just you wait, you phantom! One day I'll catch you in that thicket of notes you're hiding in.

The music reached no kind of finale. The instruments stopped one by one—first the flute, then the lyre, then, after a few more tinkles, the bells. The silence was broken by a brief, embarrassed round of applause. By ending as it had, the overture had given the impression that the musicians were leaving one by one, because they were tired of playing or because their feet were numb. (It wouldn't have surprised me to read an instruction in the manuscript in words to the effect of: "Play continues only for as long as the musicians are amused by it.") But when I looked beyond the terrace, I saw that the three musicians had remained in their places and were studying their sheet music by the light of the little lamps on their stands.

One of the men who had installed the lights stepped up and pulled aside the curtain, revealing the set of the room. The monotonous music of bells, lyre and flute set up again. Sitting at the table, leafing through a magazine with pictures in it, was a fair-haired girl in a simple dress—Andrea, I supposed. Standing by the painted window, looking pensively at the facade of the building opposite was a girl with short, black hair combed smoothly back and coated in a glossy brilliantine; this girl, who was a little shorter and thinner than Andrea, was surely Barbora. In my view, the visagiste hadn't tried very hard to turn Barbora into a man; all he'd done was put her in a man's business suit—the top she was wearing under the jacket did nothing to conceal her femininity.

After a while Andrea put down her magazine and turned to Barbora at the window. She sang:

Yesterday they introduced me to
a young scientist working on a doctorate
about your book *The City and the Ocean.*
For years a photograph of you has hung
above the desk at which he spends
his days hard at work,
next to a snapshot of his fiancée.
He thought that you died long ago.
When recently he learned
that you live still,
in the same town as he,
he could scarcely believe it.

I liked Andrea's voice. Although her singing was quiet and seemed to me at first as monotonous as the musical accompaniment, gradually I began to hear in it light tones of sorrow, as though at the bottom of the calm of conciliation, the muffled groan of some old pain hadn't quite faded.

"He didn't even dare," Andrea went on, "to ask for an interview with you, although I saw that there was nothing he desired more."

While Andrea was singing, Barbora turned away from the window, rested against its painted sill—although the canvas sagged, the construction was supported at the back by a strong pole, so there was no danger that the set would collapse—and looked at the seated Andrea. The movements and facial expression of her character made it clear that he was emerging from deep contemplation; apparently it took the scientist in exile some time to realize what the woman at the table was talking about. Andrea finished singing, and for a while only bells were heard. Then Barbora, the scientist, began to sing.

> I'm not sure I'd be able to help him.
> On the island we sensed these things.
> When after a night of discussion
> the pink light of the sun
> rose above the sea and
> fell on the pages of our works,
> we believed that we were right;
> when the cry of the seagull mingled
> with the wording of laws,
> we knew them to be
> irrefutable. But today
> it all seems to me so unsure;
> I feel that chains of flawless proofs
> are tearing like threadbare cloth . . .

Barbora's voice was quieter still than Andrea's; it was so quiet that her song mingled with the distant sounds of the city, just as the hum of the streets blended in with the music of Chuh-yuh's nighttime sonata. In Barbora's song, too, I could hear lingering tones of an old pain, yet these were more muted than in Andrea's voice, as though relief at the end of a bad period in the scientist's life coupled with extreme fatigue overshadowed all other feelings. Although the scientist could look back on moments of happiness on some island, which was perhaps his homeland, the shadows in his voice and that of his wife indicated that the happy times by the sea had not lasted long and had been ended by a disaster of some kind. The tiredness that echoed in Barbora's voice was also reflected in the movements of her hands. It was remarkable how the timbre of her voice and the subtlety of her movements created a powerful illusion of the figure she was representing, her imperfect costume notwithstanding; the young woman was miraculously gone, and in her place was a tired man who had lost everything, although he felt some kind of happiness in the fact that the fight was over. The woman stood up, went over to the man, who was still standing at the window, and laid her head on his shoulder.

"It hurts me when you speak like that," said the woman, as sung by Andrea.

Time always dissolves fixed shapes
and lets words slowly lose their meaning.
But even dried-up sentences, in which scraps of ancient sense
flutter feebly over isolated words,
like decaying flags flapping
on the towers of a silent, abandoned city,
still bear testimony
to vanished splendor and glory.
As we wander in them, the emotion and reverence
of the victor may be ours.

While his wife sang, the scientist looked at the floor and shook his head, yet he did not interrupt her. She went on:

You say that the glorious laws fell silent
when the song of seabirds stopped sounding
in their words—but do you not hear
when you pronounce the old words
the cries of gulls and cormorants that
sound along with them? Do you not hear

the murmur of surf as it
mingles with their sound? Happy island sounds
will return over and over
with the old words . . .

The scientist looked up. Barbora sang his quiet reply: "Ghosts. All just ghosts . . ."

Chapter 40
Medusa in the Bedroom

The man and the woman paused for a moment, their silence filled by monotonous music. Andrea stepped away from Barbora, walked to the edge of the terrace and gazed in silence over the heads of the audience, toward where the black silhouettes of the trees marked the end of the garden. Apparently her character was looking at the fourth wall of the room, which was invisible to me. I wondered where her gaze was resting; I imagined her looking at the dark, cracked painting of some landscape, in which it was almost impossible to make out the outlines of the objects depicted. Then the wife turned back to the husband. What I heard now in her voice was not respect and kindness, but impatience and anger.

> Have you really forgotten what you were,
> what you've never ceased to be,
> although now you spend your days at the window,
> watching the front of the building opposite
> or the play of the wind in the treetops?
> Have you forgotten
> that you founded a new science
> of relations between urban spaces
> and the seabed; that you were once director
> of the institute of urbanoceanology

and president of the island's university,
whom students loved without measure?

I appreciated the librettist's skill in apprising the audience of the scientist's past through his wife's reproaches.

Have you forgotten those beautiful days
when you lectured in the largest hall,
which was always full?
How you stood before the glass wall that sparkled
with the white waves of the morning sea?
Even the ruler came to your lectures,
sat modestly among the students,
and wrote down your thoughts
in a silence broken only by your voice
and the murmur of the sea beyond the open window.

As soon as the woman mentioned the island, the character of the music changed; for the first time the opera began to produce recognizable motifs, while its monotony transformed into calm tones of seaside happiness; it was as though suddenly a three-dimensional form appeared in the chaotic jumble of stains on the optical wordplay, and pictures of life on terraces overlooking the sea emerged from the mechanical music. The woman continued with her kindly reproaches.

Have you forgotten that your *City and Ocean*
has been translated into thirty-two languages?
Do you think that it's all just a dream?
For us, your book shone bright as a beacon
at a time when the island had fallen
into obscurantism, after the closing of
the Institute of Urbanoceanological Studies,
when your former assistants were writing
books that refuted your work,
claiming brazenly
that there was no relation between the city

and the seabed. I remember
how we copied your book
in secret, and the lucky ones who owned it
in those uncertain days
hid it in the depths of their bookcases.

While the lyre and the bells remained in the key of the sea and island happiness, the flute started a new, dark motif. For a while the two layers intertwined. The husband listened to his wife's words with his head bowed. Then he walked slowly to the table and sat down on a chair. Now Barbora sang:

You exaggerate. I admit that the book
contains a few good ideas, but I wrote it
in haste, as nothing but a teaching aid
for my students. Much in it is unfinished;
theories that at first
promise much and start off
like a chariot course at a circus
end as a soggy, boggy path
that loses itself in a field.
One would need to go back to the book
and rethink it from start to finish.
Maybe one day someone will.

The wife stood behind the chair, placed her left hand on her husband's shoulder and began to stroke his hair with her right. Guessing what she wished to tell him, again he shook his head; it seemed to me that this was his most characteristic gesture. "Never again, not I," Barbora sang,

I lack the strength to go back
to the printed word and the whiteness of paper,
among letters in which,
like broken tools
under a thin covering of snow
in the yard of an abandoned farm,
sit fragments of thought that

I can no longer mend. Never again!
I lack the courage to examine anew
all those difficult questions. But then,
maybe a few months would have been enough
for me to give the theory a coherent shape and
a mathematical expression, linking it forever
by chains of symmetrical equations
to the works of Newton and Einstein
in a single, glowing grid.
If only there had been no putsch on the island,
and after that no terrible
civil war . . . Yes, I believe
I could have done it . . . I remember,
after the heavy fighting on campus, when
we friends and students from the institute
retreated to the hills, how at every camp
I wrote down my calculations
in a notebook. I still believe
that I was close then
to the definitive form of a great equation
giving precise expression to the relation
between urban interiors and life on the seabed.

Gradually the lyre and the bells joined the melody of the flute, which was obviously evoking the period of civil war on the island. There was no furioso, eroico, or patetico; the music expressed only formless, dreamlike movements into which old battles were transformed during their slow descent to the world of memory. I didn't know what to think about the bizarre subject the scientist was engaged with. I would make up my mind once I'd heard more about it, I told myself. Apparently the woman knew something about matters of urbanoceanology, as she asked the man:

Would it really be possible
to calculate which creatures of the sea
are related to things of our world,
and to reveal the mystery of their marine origin?

It seemed that memories of the research to which he had once directed all his energies had roused the scientist from his indifference. Barbora sang:

> We could make it more possible still.
> In moments of despair we could
> call the luminescent blue medusa.
> It would drift about the gloomy room,
> past the wallpaper and the closets,
> like the ultimate comfort,
> which nothing could threaten anymore . . .

The woman joined in dreamily. As Andrea sang, I saw her hands shaking. (Was this her own excitement or the unrest of her character?)

> I imagine it floating
> about the room, its glowing image
> appearing in, then vanishing from
> the oval mirrors
> on the closet doors.
> There would be no need for alcohol,
> no need to dream
> dreams of island terraces . . .

Andrea and Barbora were silent for a moment. The light notes I heard now were presumably telling of the supple dance of the luminescent creature of the sea in the nighttime room. I had the impression that I was distinguishing the movements of the medusa, represented by the ongoing melody of the flute, from the movements of its reflection in the glass, represented by notes on the lyre that would join the flute's melody and then break off. The lyre always sounded briefly and twice, after which it was silent for exactly the same length of time, so producing the idea of a luminescent medusa floating through the dark room, its reflection appearing twice in close succession as it passed two narrow, oval mirrors that were screwed onto the two doors of a dark, varnished wardrobe of the late Art Nouveau period. (In addition,

I couldn't shake the feeling that the bells were expressing the pattern of the wallpaper that covered the bedroom walls, although I had no real evidence for this.) It was strange indeed how the attitude of the music had changed. Having at first refused to submit even to the simple repetition of a motif, it didn't seem to mind that it was now the instrument of such descriptiveness. Yet I didn't experience this inconsistency as something that would violate the unity of the music in any way, perhaps because this unity was so far removed from the context of our own world that there was nothing there to violate.

Chapter 41
The Life of a Guerilla

At the end of the melody describing the dance of the medusa, the woman turned to the urbanoceanologist and said in a civil tone:

> The young scientist I spoke with
> defended in his work the thesis
> that there initially existed
> things and spaces of the city, which,
> at a certain stage in their development,
> began to act on the formation
> of the seabed. In his work
> he writes, for instance, that bookcases
> in rooms with windows to a garden
> are likely to affect the form of
> undersea coral reefs.

It was plain that the woman was trying to pull her husband out of the indifference he now lived in and lead him back to an interest in his work as a scientist. But the woman also knew that it was necessary to proceed with extreme caution, as she wished at the same time to shield him from bad memories connected with his past work. The man said, as sung by Barbora:

> We talked about that often,
> at the university and later in the hills.

Mario, too, inclined to
the theory of the urban origin
of undersea forms.
I remember his quarrels
with Rufio, who championed the opposing
idea that urban things came
from the seabed.

Apparently fearful that the commentary would again get onto too personal a plane, the woman quickly asked:

Which of those two theories
do you think is the right one?

The scientist thought, then replied:

The truth is probably somewhere in the middle.
When the city originated and the seabed was formed,
apparently the influence was reciprocal,
making the sea a dream of cities and the city
a dream of the ocean.
That undersea coral reefs probably would not
have originated without bookcases covered in dust,
from which now a wrinkled hand
but rarely pulls a volume,
is difficult to deny; and those who
still refuse to concede
that the form and movement of the ray were influenced
by drapes fluttering in a current of air in an empty room
on a summer afternoon, by now constitute
a bizarre sect that no one in the world of science
takes seriously. But on the other hand
it is undoubtedly true
that many metal boxes for tea
developed out of the shells of marine mollusks;
they even preserved transitional forms, too,
in rooms and on the seabed—
shells with their upper bowl half-transfigured
into a lid with indistinct outlines

of a map of Ceylon or the Indian subcontinent
beginning to form on their surface.
And serious scientists
have actually never doubted
the submarine origin of the table lamp;
even the pseudoscience that today rules on the island,
which declares shell-boxes to be fake,
prefers to keep silent on the subject.

A fat man dressed in a costume of a black, rustling material was leaving, and for a moment he obscured my view of the stage. I looked around and discovered that only about a quarter of the audience from the beginning remained. Neither the music nor the plot of the opera had greatly engaged the interest of the guests, so they were sneaking away to the illuminated tables on the other side of the villa, where plenty of food and drink remained. Andrea sang to empty garden chairs:

Oh yes, in your book you described beautifully,
in unforgettable lines
that no one will ever erase from the history of science,
how at the bottom of the sea
medusae, siphonophores and sea anemones
slowly turned into lamps,
and how their light grew stronger; how they
first emerged on slimy coastal rocks
and timidly approached
human dwellings.
What force was it
that lit the light within them
and drove them out onto dry land?
Was it suffering or
an unknown submarine joy?

"I don't know," sang Barbora.

On the island we were able
to quantify the manifestations of this force, yet

none of us ever fully understood it.
It never went out, even on land;
here we saw that a thing could pine
for its marine home;
things would like to return
to the seabed, but
by now they are kept from it
by too many walls.
Toward evening, table lamps
call to the distant sea;
the sea hears their voices
and sends them a solitary wave
that advances across the landscape,
but usually it cannot surmount
all the staircases and cold hallways
that get in its way; it tires
and turns into foam, which,
with a quiet fizz, soaks into
the gaps between floor tiles;
it is sucked up by thirsty carpets
and the fringes of drapes shuffling across the parquet
in the nighttime breeze.

Not for long, however, was the scientist able to keep his mind off happy and painful images of the island; again and again they came to him, forcing him to return to his memories.

Mario and Rufio first argued over their theories
on the terrace of the institute, overlooking the sea,
over bedewed glasses containing colorful cocktails.
But in the hills everything changed,
and their scientific disputes
became infected with hate.
I remember the two of them arguing
at night by the fire. It was the time
when none of us knew
whether we were still fighting or just
wandering the woods like confused animals,

sensing the coast,
which might have saved us . . .

The woman interrupted him.

You told me that the tension
between those two stemmed
not just from scientific dispute,
but from the love of both for Leonora . . .

Although the woman had tried to protect the man from his memories, plainly she, too, was now living in the island stories her husband was telling; she, too, was lost in a historical landscape filled with glinting sea and warriors' fires, unable to find her way out. By now the man was fully immersed in his memories of the civil war.

When Leonora died at the White Ravine,
I hoped that Mario and Rufio would reconcile.
But the hatred between them grew.
Then we were separated.
I thought they had fallen
when the scattered remnants of guerilla forces
tried in small groups
to break through the blockade and get to the coast.
They hunted us in the woods like animals.
Mario and Rufio were among the few who
survived the march to the sea,
and some time later both surfaced
at universities on the continent.

"Did they reconcile then at least?" asked the woman.

Barbora sang as the scientist:

I have heard that their hatred burns still
in lecture halls
and at conferences.
I don't wish to know about it.

I don't wish to think of them as angry teachers,
hating each other because of a woman
who is long dead.
These are faded images.
I hold them both in my memory
as the brightest students at the island's Academy,
and as brave and merry guerilla commanders
from the war's beginning. The rest of it
is just a cruel joke of fate
that we can forget about,
just a dream that has no effect
and whose images will soon perish.

Although I was now used to the strangeness of the music, the libretto was giving me more trouble; I was struggling to accept the fact that two entirely different planes—an easily understood plane of human emotion (pain over the demise of the freedom of the island's culture, for instance) on the one hand and the totally absurd ideas of the scientist in exile, presented as fruits of deep research in the heyday of science on the island, on the other—were linked so strongly and self-evidently. It bothered me that I was unable to grasp the meaning of this connection. I didn't even have the impression that the motifs of urbanoceanology were symbolic and needed deciphering. Why had the librettist not written either a story about the lives of university researchers at a time of civil war or a surrealistic text about imaginary relations between the city and marine life? What strange aesthetics had led him to mix the two?

At the same time, however, I felt that the incomprehensibility of this union was a sign that the opera was somehow connected with the disappearance of Jonáš's daughter, even though it had been composed when Viola was a small child. It seemed to me that should I succeed in finding Viola, this oddity would be explained at a stroke, along with all the other mysteries. Who could the librettist be? Was it perhaps Iui Num, who like Chuh-yuh had been a member of the White Triangle? If that was so, then it was possible that the stage designer was Vuh-gah Oo. How did it all tie up, for God's sake? I felt as though I was trying to complete a hopeless jigsaw puzzle in which each piece presented a completely new, unclassifiable shape. Why would these three men create a work that was still more bizarre than their work as individuals? Which faces and names were hidden behind pseudonyms comprising jumbles of sound that forced those trying to pronounce them to engage in grotesque and degrading gymnastics that woke muscles in the face and neck the speaker didn't even know he had? There was a fair possibility that the opera contained a clue leading to Viola—but where should I look for it? Should I concentrate on the music or the story? Was the mysterious key concealed in an image or a word? After the performance, should I conduct another detailed inspection of the set? Feeling resigned, I submerged myself again in the story of the urbanoceanologist and his wife.

Chapter 42
Pure Light

Now Andrea sang:

> It must have been so sad
> to debate questions of science
> by a campfire in the hills, while down below
> the university buildings were burning . . .

The man answered thoughtfully:

> Yes, although the early days in the hills
> were a time of cold radiance,
> during which unexpected, precious ideas,
> more remarkable than all
> thoughts we had had on the coast
> in happier days,
> were born easily,
> like crystals from a supersaturated solution.
> As though the burning university
> seen between the dark trunks of trees
> were a lamp that brought a new light.
> We felt no sorrow
> for the books and manuscripts
> that below us were turning into smoke.

The scientist began to pace the room restlessly. It seemed he had reached a peak that stood high above the surface of reconciliation and indifference, which in recent years had come slowly to cover the landscape of the past.

Still I don't really understand it.
It was as though new ideas glistened
in bare ground exposed
by flames of despair
that burned all vegetation.
Sometimes I wondered if
lack of sleep and constant stress
caused physiological change,
waking retracted centers in the brain;
chambers locked in anticipation
of a distant future
were opened.
It was strange how lightly
The women accepted the new light, and how easily
they moved in it. Leonora and Laura
had been dazzling down on campus,
but in the hills, suddenly we heard
the most remarkable ideas from their mouths.
We felt that we were unable to look toward
the furnace where their ideas took shape.
So out of an excess of light were born
admiration, love and jealousy;
the suffering of men engendered hate
and finally malice,
which then sailed on ships to the continent
to proliferate like a disgusting mold in schools,
in hate-filled notes in scientific papers,
in insincere smiles
at meetings in conference rooms,
in pitiful disputes about the primacy of ideas that,
out on the island terraces,
we had tossed about joyfully like balls,
in the happy days of the legitimate government,

when it occurred to no one
that they should belong to any of us.

The woman got up from the table, walked over to her husband and embraced him.

Think no more about the island.
Outside the heat has relented.
Let us take a walk along the river
or sit for a while
in a garden restaurant . . .

The man was still absorbed in his memories, however, and he seemed not to have heard the woman's words. Gently he extricated himself from her embrace.

The bad images keep coming back,
no matter where I look;
they come out of walls and tangles of branches.
In the street, the faces of strangers
change into faces from long ago,
as though it were not already twenty years
since from the deck of a fishing boat
I last beheld the island's hills as they
dissolved in the haze of a hot midday.

The urbanoceanologist paced the room in a state of ever greater restlessness. His wife leaned against the table and looked at him with sad eyes.

When at night I turn off the light and close my eyes,
always I see the same scene.
It is the eve of the Battle of White Gorge and
Mario is attacking Rufio, yelling at him
for not distributing fairly
the only supplies of food
we have left.
Then they wrestle in the dry pine needles,

in silence, beating fists into faces,
until we pull them apart.
At this moment government soldiers
were closer than we thought.
They attacked at dawn.
Just six of us, just six
out of forty, succeeded in
fleeing to the hills.
Leonora was hit in the chest
by one of the very first shots,
even before she was able to
grab the submachine gun that
was lying next to her. I carried
the wounded Laura to the rocks.
She was raving about a cold light
on the cold granite of university corridors;
in the evening she fell silent and died.
I think at that time she was the only one in the hills
who saw how things were. She understood
that questions of origin, as discussed
at dozens of scientific institutions
and in hundreds of publications,
were absurd. She whispered to me then:
"There is no sense in asking about the beginning,
about the primacy of city or sea.
There is no beginning:
The shapes of city and sea pass through and into
each other in endless change,
each never very far from the other, so that
after a while we cease
to perceive the difference between them.
The wave that ripples drapes and
colored flags in the park is the wave
that leads the gyrating dance of anemones
on an undersea rock;
the tremor that stirs algae
awakens in the leaves of an open book
lying on the top of a round table,

let us say in a garden restaurant
on the shore of the Fürstensee,
whose surface reflects
snowcapped Alpine peaks."
For years I took her words for raving,
but today it seems to me
I discovered from her a truth
that in my book
I was unable to find.
Her half-intelligible whisper
rendered all research pointless.
It does not matter that *The City and the Ocean*
has been translated into thirty-two languages,
just as it does not matter that
during the putsch soldiers smashed precious instruments
for the measuring of relics of submarine life
in our domestic utensils.
What was communicated by Laura's muttering
could perhaps only be captured
in a book without text,
printed in invisible ink,
in which groups of letters
would surface only from time to time,
like bare trees in the fog in the distance,
before they disappeared again . . .

Throughout his monologue the urbanoceanologist continued to pace the room while his wife watched him with resignation from the table. When Barbora sang about the book with the blank pages where letters came and went, straight away I remembered the appearing/disappearing symbol that had taken me to Jonáš's villa and whose mystery had been solved by such a prosaic chemical explanation. Immediately afterward, the beginning of the motif of the Orange Book sounded again, in the melody of the bells; again I heard the familiar series of three rising tones, and again, instead of closing out the shape that was sounding in my head, they shattered into a maelstrom of sound I couldn't grasp.

For Laura, rooms and undersea caves merged;
she said she no longer knew
if she had spent her life in busy cities or on the ocean floor,
or if the faces she knew . . .

Those were the last words that Barbora sang. Without having given any indication that the end was near, the music and the singing had stopped in an instant. The girls on the stage froze—Barbora by the bookcase, which she happened to have reached as she paced the room, Andrea at the table. Barbora's eyebrows were still pulled together, her face held in an expression of returning awe at the thought of an ancient mystery. When the music stopped, Andrea's face, which was fixed on Barbora, was set in an expression of sorrow, admiration and regret. The sudden end of the opera in the garden had produced a puzzled silence. This was followed by woeful applause from the five pairs of hands that remained in the audience. Barbora and Andrea walked to the edge of the terrace, made a little bow, then ran into the house; the musicians loaded their instruments into their cases and offered no thanks. Now it occurred to me why the opera had ended so suddenly, indeed in mid-sentence: The artists had adhered so religiously to the score in the form in which it was discovered that Barbora and Andrea had stopped singing and the musicians had stopped playing at the very place where the last surviving page of the ruined exercise book ended its record of the words and music.

As I departed between two rows of empty seats, it crossed my mind that I might be wrong. I knew of Chuh-yuh's ideas and the love of all the Trianglists for the sounds of silence and emptiness, and now I told myself that the opera never had gone on from here; Chuh-yuh himself had torn the exercise book in half, so breaking off the opera deliberately, maybe because he had wanted the sudden severance to produce in the minds of his audience a maelstrom of forming and decomposing sounds and images—musical phantoms, which, it seemed, he loved more than music itself. And truly I couldn't help but hear in my mind many different imaginary continuations of Chuh-yuh's work, which broke over and perished in one another like waves of the sea. But then I went back to the illuminated part of the garden in front of the house, where the masquers were getting themselves in better mood and the hum of conversation drowned out the inaudible music.

Chapter 43
After the Performance

Again I walked among groups of masquers, drank wine and listened to the jumbles of words that bore down on me from all sides. I heard what I was expecting to hear.

An uncertain woman's voice: "Well, that was interesting."

A candid woman's voice: "I don't understand much about this modern music."

An irritated woman's voice, attached for some reason to the idea of a tough, skinny body: "You kept falling asleep, you're an embarrassment."

A smug man's voice: "Don't pretend you enjoyed it. Besides, no one knew who I was in this costume."

A sheepish woman's voice: "Did you understand it?"

A self-confident man's voice: "Sure, it was a political satire."

By now I was beginning to feel pretty drunk. I was swaying a little, and the words I was hearing were coming free of their meanings and flowing into the maelstrom. In the midst of all this, I suddenly heard a man's voice that differed from all the other voices; immediately I forgot all the other sounds and words in the garden, even though the voice was so far away that I couldn't make out anything of what it was saying. All that reached me was the melody of the sentences, yet I knew immediately that the melody had something to do with the music that had just played itself out on the other side of the house, and with the mystery of the double trident; I knew that the voice came from the world in which Viola had disappeared. Having emerged briefly from the hum, the voice sank back under its surface; for a long time I pushed my way through the masquers in quest of the mouth it had come from. I reached a part of the garden where I was dazzled by the glare of the floodlights, in which the black silhouettes of guests darted hither and thither. At one point I thought I had lost the voice for good, but then it popped up again, just centimeters from my ear; I heard it say: "Maybe we made a mistake; maybe the book really should have remained closed . . ." I had the feeling that the sorrow in these words was flooding the whole garden.

Although I'd never heard the voice before, I was in no doubt about whose it was. I looked in the direction I thought the words were coming from. But at that very moment a group of masquers flooded past me in the direction of a table Bernet's staff had carried onto the front terrace. This table was covered with glittering blocks of ice on which lay eels, mussels and cuttlefish with tentacles spread. I swayed among the masquers, muttering under my breath, "Vuhulum Chuh-yuh has come to listen to his work! Vuhulum Chuh-yuh has come to listen to his work!" And I knew that the voice was speaking of the Orange Book—the book whose pages everyone filled with their own dreams. As I walked among the masks and lights, I was worried that I had lost the composer's voice forever. Fortunately a short time later I heard Chuh-yuh again. Apparently he was responding to an objection: "No, truly I don't regret it. Yet I can't help thinking that it would be better for you if you'd never found out about any of this."

Then I heard the voice that answered his—a voice that dug into my brain like a long, sharp thorn. A girl's voice, it was quiet, willful, saddened and a little rough. It said: "But you know how I felt before—like I was living in a dream. How could I regret the fact that we have repeated the Tannhäuser party after nineteen years. Now anything can happen . . ."

Immediately I was sure that this was the voice of Viola Jonášová. I plunged through the masquers toward where I thought Viola's and Chuh-yuh's voices had come from, but obviously I was wrong about their whereabouts, as now I heard the girl's voice behind my back. "Everything's fine, don't worry. It was how it should be. Those twenty-four hours I spent with Alexander were enough for me. Now I feel that I'd lived only for them . . ." As I turned, I staggered and almost fell. As I went in search of Viola's voice, a great wave of hum washed over me, and Viola and Chuh-yuh were lost to it. I continued to wander chaotically among the masquers, and again I was dazzled by the lights. I looked at eyes through the holes in face masks adorned with stars and clouds, telling myself that these might be the eyes of Viola. All around me was a whirl of phantomlike lights on costumes—neon, streetlamps, the colored lights of mini-casinos. What was the Tannhäuser party Viola had spoken of? Who in heaven's name was Alexander? What should she or should she not regret? Would my quest continue forevermore to amass mystery after mystery? I began to call Viola's name into the face masks that emerged in front of me; through oval cutouts I saw looks of astonishment; people started to dodge me, to float away from me into the darkness. Evidently it hadn't been a good idea to shout Viola's name; probably I'd scared Viola and Chuh-yuh away, because I didn't hear their voices again.

As I searched for Viola and Chuh-yuh, I kept finding in front of me a hand bearing a tray with a single glass of champagne. There were several waiters going about the garden offering drinks to guests; it was strange that this one had taken a fancy to me, but by now I was too tired to give it much thought. Several times I pushed the hand away, but in the end I took the glass from the tray so as to be rid of the troublesome bearer. Realizing the pointlessness of continuing to look for Viola and Chuh-yuh, I gave up running from mask to mask, leaned against a wall of the house and sipped my champagne.

The alcohol, the swirling fabrics, the flashing lights, the laughter and the hum of voices had made me feel dizzy. To refresh myself a little, I circled the house again, going further across the lawn and reaching more distant parts of the garden that were entirely in darkness. From the bushes that lined the garden, I heard the groans of masquers who had turned off all their bulbs and were indulging in games of love. I asked myself how partners had been chosen from among the veiled guests. Feeling ever drowsier, I decided to go home. As I was heading back toward the illuminated villa, I noticed a pointed roof standing tall in the silhouette made by the bushes; presumably this belonged to a pavilion of some sort, and I heard muffled sounds of an argument coming from it. When I was closer to it, I distinguished three voices, two belonging to women, the other to a man.

One of the figures moved, and by the light of a distant lamp I saw the glint of sleek black hair and, briefly, a pale face. I recognized Barbora, still wearing the suit in which she had appeared in the opera. The other girl was Andrea, still in the costume of the urbanoceanologist's wife. The face of the man was hidden in shadow, but I was pretty sure he was Bernet. For a moment, curiosity overcame my desire for sleep. I crept to the pavilion, sat down on the grass and leaned back against a tree.

Chapter 44
Argument in the Pavilion

The words I heard came from one of the girls: ". . . .ou can't mean that seriously!" Maybe it was Barbora: I heard reproach and sorrow in the voice.

Out of the dark came a tired voice that had to be Bernet's. "I'm deadly serious. Maybe I'll return to the treasure when I've settled my affairs, but for the moment . . ."

"Your affairs?" the second of the girls interjected scornfully. "What expressions you're starting to use!"

"You got to know us on the quest for the treasure," said Barbora, so softly that I barely understood her, "and we stayed with you because we wanted to travel with you. Till this point you've been the leader of the expedition. What do you want to be now? What else can you be for us? Have you thought about that, too?"

Before Bernet could answer, Andrea cut in angrily. "Do what you want, but be aware that we're not able to live with a businessman."

"But I am a businessman—don't you understand?" said Bernet. I heard tiredness and suppressed rage in his voice. "I buy and sell stocks and shares, I'm not a poet or an adventurer. I'm sorry if you imagined me to be someone else."

"You don't even believe that yourself," said Barbora. I had the impression of patience in her voice, as though Bernet were a small child. "You know that it's never mattered to us that the papers write about you as a businessman and a parvenu; we've always known that it's not true. You know, too, that we saw you for who you were almost instantly; we understood the amazing, gentle game you've been playing since you were a child—you didn't even have to tell us about yourself. We admired you, and we admired the way you responded to strokes of fate. You've always been such a good player, so why are you now spoiling everything in such a foolish way? I don't know which deity plays this game with you, but I believe that the style of your play has always made him happy and that he, too, has taken pleasure in the game and rewarded you for it . . ."

"The two of you imagine God as a tennis player," muttered Bernet. "I doubt that he's like that."

"Do you think that imagining him as a protector of property and business makes you less superficial than us?" said Barbora. "What gives you the right to think such a thing? Remember the game you've been playing since childhood. Remember that deity's first move, when it handed you the slip of paper with the message about the treasure. You reacted splendidly to that; we're proud of you for it, and it seems that the deity appreciated your reaction at the time. You played splendidly, too, when out of mischief he placed you in the world of finance, to see what you would do."

"And also when he led you into our path," said Andrea, whose anger had abated a little, probably under the influence of Barbora's calmness. "Now he's presented you with this move, and he's watching how you behave. I'd say he was even tenser about it than we are. Don't you see that it's a test? Why are you suddenly playing like someone in the lower leagues? Why all of a sudden are you betraying your great game and turning it into a matter of profit and loss? Why are you dragging the question of property into the game? We're terribly disappointed with you . . ."

I leaned against the tree listening to words that gushed forth and vanished into the darkness, as though this were the beginning of a dream, as though at any moment every word that came from the pavilion would transform and be grouped in the sentences of an Oriental tale filled with genies and golden palaces set in magical gardens. When first I heard the sounds of an argument, as I was approaching the pavilion, I was still under the influence of other conversations I'd heard that evening, and I told myself that the girls were probably blaming Bernet for his recent business failures. Now that I was beginning to understand what the dispute between the girls and their boyfriend was really about, I almost had to laugh at how mistaken I'd been and also at the strangeness of the conversation I was witnessing. The truth of the matter was, the girls were exasperated because of Bernet's greater concern for his property than for a childhood dream he had lived with all his life, and which now they shared with him; they couldn't forgive Bernet for being more interested in staving off bankruptcy than in a game which, their strange theology told them, he had been playing with some lord of fate.

I was listening to voices that echoed in the darkness like some absurd radio drama, tense in my anticipation of what would come next. A strange drama indeed, I thought: Women chiding their lover for his unwillingness to go bankrupt. It occurred to me that this was one of the oddest things I'd encountered so far in my search for Viola. Was the scolding of Bernet for his wish to take care of practicalities just whimsy on the part of inexperienced young girls, or were Barbora and Andrea actually wiser than Bernet and able to foresee a great defeat which would spring from the very salvation Bernet was now striving so desperately to bring about? I wasn't able to answer such a question, and I doubted that any unequivocal answer to it existed; it seemed to me that there were threads of impatience and imprudence in the girls' behavior, as well as a subtle understanding of the nature of things, which perhaps they had learned in the world of music.

"I do understand it, really I do. I understand absolutely all of it. I understand your situation, I understand what you want from me, I understand what the deity expects of me." Still there was a mixture of fatigue and rage in Bernet's voice. I had the impression he was angry at the girls because he felt they were right; but at the same time he was surely terribly worried that he would lose the world that in recent years had emerged from the fog that surrounded him; that he would return to the void he had fallen into in his childhood, which he would now probably never be able to get used to.

"Why don't you two try to understand me a little? Why don't you try to understand how I've lost the ability to play and the appetite for the game . . ." Bernet's anger was still on the rise. "Yes, maybe everything you say to me is true; but I'm not capable of living in a burning house among ghosts from my childhood. I'm in terrible need of rest, and I need to hold on to at least a few things from my world."

"Now is no time for you to rest," said Barbora mildly. "If you rest, you'll fall asleep and wake up a completely different man. You'll lose us, and you'll lose everything that's truly important. You have to stick it out in the burning house a little longer. Don't worry, we'll be here with you."

Andrea wasn't as patient as her friend. "Think about what you're doing. You're longing for the kind of life we've always laughed at together. You may as well marry, start a family, sponsor a soccer club and go to musicals!" she exploded.

"Hang on, Andrea," said Barbora, in an effort to calm her. "You're simplifying things . . ."

It was difficult to tell what Bernet was most irritated by, Barbora's insistent moderateness, Andrea's rage, or the nascent scorn of both girls. He must have felt desperate, as though pinned against a wall; on the one side were all those business partners who had been waiting years for a moment of weakness in him, on the other two angry girls. It was hardly surprising that he wanted some peace and to make it up with everyone; but at this moment, no one was willing to accept a settlement.

"You have no right to ridicule people who do all those things. I know quite a few who go to musicals—good people, whom I respect. I wouldn't mind going to the odd musical myself."

"If that's how you see things, then apparently we really do have nothing to say to each other," said Andrea. It seemed to me that her anger was the fruit of despair at the prospect of losing the person with whom she and Barbora had embarked on a magical quest for treasure, and whom she admired enormously.

"You may be right, maybe they really are great people, but that's not your path," said Barbora.

"At the moment, my path is any path that will lead me out of the trap. I can't pick and choose, and I can't worry about the elegance of my gestures. I'm glad that you enjoyed the game with the deity, but when the playing field is flooded, all games must stop for a while."

All this time Bernet's face was in darkness. I tried to imagine his current expression, but I couldn't unite the various faces that came at me out of the dark. Whereas the voices of the girls contained a mix of battiness and wisdom, I heard a whole choir of voices in Bernet's words—it was as though I was listening to a person who had lived in many lands and whose voice retained tones of all the languages he had spoken in his life. I heard distinctly the voice of the withdrawn, dreamy child the architect had told me about, and I heard the voice of the man who had learned to make decisions easily and spontaneously precisely because he was dreamy and irresolute by nature. He was indifferent to the situations he found himself in because they had nothing in common with the world of his dreams, so there was no need for him to spend much time with them; I imagined Bernet walking across the surface of situations as lightly as an elf. I also heard in his voice tones that surely originated in a business environment and which were still imbued with irony, and tones he owed to his conversations with Barbora and Andrea. It seemed to me that over time all these voices had accepted one another and come to partake of some kind of harmony.

But now I heard in Bernet's voice a tone of unrest, uncertainty, and fear that was seemingly quite fresh. This tone hadn't yet grown into the tangle of other voices, and it actually disrupted their previous unity. I remembered what the architect had told me: The anxious tone almost certainly had its origin in events that unfolded after the appearance in Bernet's life of the porcelain figurine—events that had caused the incipient crumbling of the world he had settled in these last few years and was now used to. Maybe the girls were being unfair to Bernet; maybe he wasn't anxious about losing his property. It might be the case that in recent years all his worlds had grown together and he was now looking on in horror as the disintegration of one world meant the collapse of all the others: of his childhood dream, of his fantastical love, of dreaming, of hedonism, and of numerical magic.

As I was thinking about Bernet, for a while I stopped following the conversation. When I focused back in on it, the talk was of money and ingratitude. ". . . .nd another reason I need money is so I can take care of you," Bernet was reminding the girls, although he surely knew how they would react to these words.

"We don't need you to take care of us!" Andrea shouted. And Barbora said, "What is needed now, is for us to look after you for a while."

Although Barbora never raised her voice and Andrea's words were forever like the start of a delayed scream, there was a gentle strength deep within both voices. The quality of this strength was so elusive that I doubt I would have picked up on it had I not just encountered it in refined form in their singing. Definitely it had something in common with music. I had the feeling that it was a kind of deep, silent spring, out of which the music issued, and which was perhaps identical with the passage of time itself. It occurred to me that this might be the silent spring for which the mysterious Chuh-yuh had searched in his youth on the border between the realms of sound and silence. In the voices of the girls, this power was almost imperceptible, as it was diluted by the many layers of consciousness through which it passed before speech was produced; even so, it contained so much calm and unity that it would surely be capable of bringing harmony and conciliation to a space that was now in ruins—not, perhaps, by unifying the fragments, but by casting a pure, unexpected light on their edges. I understood that in the girls' world, which was fed by the wellspring of music, no ruin existed; that was why they were so exasperated by Bernet's doubt and fear. Maybe Bernet knew that the girls could save him, although he resisted their help like a stubborn child.

"Just leave it for now," he now said gruffly. From the sounds I heard, I guessed that Barbora was stroking him, Andrea was thumping him and Bernet was trying to shake the two of them off.

I was feeling drowsier and drowsier. A few times I fell into a momentary doze, waking whenever my forehead touched my knee. At one point the voices in the pavilion became a monotonous song, probably Chinese, and I heard a Chinese stringed instrument. A Chinese man appeared in front of the pavilion. He was holding a pole to which was attached a lantern that illuminated his thin face and long, wispy beard. Then the melody became a conversation again, the Chinese man disappeared and the lantern became the lamplight from the back entrance of Bernet's mansion. The topic of conversation was unchanged.

"I won't let myself be destroyed because of you," Bernet said.

"Okay, do as you see fit. We've decided that if you won't come with us, we'll look for the treasure alone," said Barbora.

"We made a start on it as soon as we realized that there was nothing doing with you," Andrea weighed in. Again the voices joined in song for a while. The Chinese man wandered close by and the garden began to transform into a paddy field.

Andrea's words jerked me out of sleep. ". . . .e put a sleeping pill in his wine. Once he's asleep, we'll tell Zachary to carry him into the house. In the morning, when he comes round, we'll question him thoroughly. I'm confident he knows the way to the treasure, or at least an important part of the way."

"You'll question him? You're not going to torture him, I hope," said Bernet ironically. By now he was probably extremely tired of all that was going on around him.

"If we torture anyone, it'll be you. As for him, we'll keep him here until he tells us what he knows. We know that no one will think to look for him here."

"What are you playing at, for God's sake? Such childish games!"

"They used to say that you, too, were childish, and you never minded," said Barbora calmly. "If you hadn't been, you would never have gotten so close to the treasure. At least the two of us have remained childish."

"You're not, I hope, intending to repeat the wise words of your experienced friends—that life isn't like an adventure story for children," added Andrea.

Bernet was no longer listening to the girls. "All you're doing is giving me one more thing to worry about," he said angrily. "Do you even know where he is now? I suggest you go to bed before you do something foolish. I'll tell Zachary to look around for him. If he's sleeping somewhere in the garden, Zachary will find somewhere to put him. When he wakes up, make sure you let him go home without any clowning about."

Bernet ran across the lawn to the house. What had Barbora and Andrea been talking about? By now the drowsiness had paralyzed my thoughts almost completely. But the question was so simple that an answer immediately presented itself to me, even though I was tottering on the verge of sleep. Of course the girls had been talking about me. I remembered the insistent hand that had kept offering me a chalice of champagne. If the girls were able to pour sleep-inducing powder into wine as in some adventure movie, I supposed them to be capable of anything. Although I should have been afraid, the feeling that poured into all corners of my consciousness was bliss, stemming from the realization that there was nothing I could do about it now, that there was nothing to consider and no decision to be made. Everything was so simple: I would doze off and sleep under the trees, or someone would find me and lead or carry me off somewhere.

Throughout the time I'd been listening to the conversation, my fingers had gripped the stem of the glass from which I had drunk the sleep-inducing champagne. This grip didn't loosen even while I was snoozing, but now I felt a high wave of sleep take hold of my body and gradually disempower my limbs. I gave in to the bliss as the wave washed all the cramps and tensions out of me. At last the glass fell from my hand; just before I slumped into the grass, I heard the sound of glass shattering on stone.

Before I could sink into a deep sleep, however, I was woken by women's voices. I opened my eyes to see leaning over me two silhouettes bathed in a cold aura from the lamp on Bernet's villa. I closed my eyes again. So the sound of breaking glass had alerted Barbora and Andrea to the spy listening in the dark. I was still smiling beatifically, and I found it great that the girls would now have to look after me. It seemed, however, that they were at a loss as to what to do with me. Maybe they no longer thought their plan of coaxing the whereabouts of the treasure out of me so excellent.

"We ought to take him into the house," said Barbora uncertainly.

"What if he puts up a fight? He's still not asleep," Andrea objected.

"He's almost asleep," said Barbora at last. "Come on, let's try and lift him."

I felt the hands of the girls under each of my arms, and I felt them struggle to lift me. I tried to help, but my legs kept giving way. Once I was more or less standing, each girl put one of my arms around her shoulders. Then we stumbled to the house.

After that I kept falling asleep and waking up again. In my short moments of wakefulness I saw the pale light of the house lamp on the lawn and, in the house, a hallway with many doors. Then I looked on as four small hands laid me down on a soft white carpet, pulled my black clothing over my head, leaving me in only my underwear and a T-shirt, and dragged me to a huge bed. I also saw several Chinese men, a unicorn and a melancholic harpy sitting on a perch in a golden cage; these creatures, however, probably belonged in the world of sleep.

Chapter 45
White Room

I was woken from my dream—in which I was wandering the empty streets of an enormous city unknown to me—by some loud bangs. With my eyes closed, I dug myself out of the bedclothes, in which as I slept I had become more and more tangled, and which now resembled a great spider's web. Although the blankets were thin and light, there were several layers of them; I noticed that some of the fabrics were no bigger than a scarf, while others apparently stretched off into the distance. Once I had succeeded in freeing at least the top half of my body from this soft trap, I prized my eyelids apart and tried to remember where I was, and how I'd come to be here. I lay on a great bed in a large, light room; the light came from outside, and it was subdued and softened by a white curtain that reached from ceiling to floor and covered one entire side of the room. Shadows of branches lay across the illuminated curtain like a gray drawing on white paper. Beyond the curtain, I surmised, was the glass wall that gave onto the garden.

I saw to the right of me how the pale covers gathered into folds and then spread out again. Out of one of the folds, first tousled black hair, then a girl's face appeared; I knew this girl from somewhere. A moment later the covers to the left of me began to move, and in a gap between the fabrics fair hair appeared, followed by a second familiar face. Finally two slim figures in white nightshirts crawled out of the rumpled and tangled fabrics and into the daylight. The three of us sat up in the bed and stared at one another in amazement. Outside the room, meanwhile, the pounding on the door and the shaking of its handle continued.

A voice came from beyond the door. "Open up. It's almost noon, I've brought you some breakfast." The voice was Bernet's, and in it was a tone of conciliation. All that had happened to me during the night was slowly coming back to me: the costumes, the opera, the conversation between Chuh-yuh and Viola, the argument in the pavilion, the sleep-inducing powder in my champagne, how Barbora and Andrea had dragged me into the house and put me to bed. Although no one had mixed sleep-inducing powder into the girls' wine, maybe they had drunk so much alcohol that now they were having trouble remembering who I was and what I was doing in their room.

The pounding on the door stopped suddenly. Still each of us looked into the surprised faces of the others; none of us had yet spoken. All I could hear was the flapping of the curtain in the draft that was probably coming from a gap in the glass wall. I supposed that Bernet was standing behind the door waiting for the girls to make themselves heard. As the silence remained unbroken, he said: "I'll leave your breakfast here." Then I heard retreating footsteps.

I had been looking about the room, which was bathed in a soft light. The walls were painted white, and they were bare; there wasn't a single picture on them. Also white were all the covers on the bed we were now sitting on. I had never before seen such an enormous bed, I realized. It stood on a high stage that was reached by mounting some steps, and which took up almost half the room. The rest of the room was covered in thick white carpet. On this carpet stood three slender metal chairs, a small table made of metal and glass and a tall white wardrobe—this was the only furniture in the room. I saw a heap of crumpled clothing on the floor: my fancy dress and the costumes the girls had worn in the opera.

By now the girls had probably remembered who I was and were figuring out how to behave toward me. In the light of day and with a hangover, last night's decision to imprison me in the house and question me on what I knew about the treasure probably seemed absurd and silly to them, and they were feeling embarrassed. As I looked at the confused faces under the tousled hair, I felt sorry for them and wanted to help them, so I said: "I believe you wanted to hear something from me about treasure. Unfortunately you've come to the wrong place—I know nothing about treasure, nor am I looking for it. I'm sorry, but I can't help you."

"How come you're not looking for treasure?" said Andrea dumbfounded. "You're trying to solve the mystery of the baobab, aren't you?"

"The mystery of the baobab? I've no idea what you mean by that," I said, getting the uncomfortable feeling that yet another unsolved mystery was about to be added to all the others.

"We call the symbol composed of two tridents, a transverse line and an ellipse 'the baobab,'" Barbora explained. "Maybe you've given it a different name. Do you wish to deny your interest in it?"

"Oh, I see—you mean the double trident. No, I've no reason to deny that I'm trying to figure out what it means. Why didn't you ask me straight out yesterday evening at the party? Then there would have been no need to put me to sleep. Although I must say I'm grateful to you for sparing me the chore of finding a cab. And it's a long time since I last slept so well. Anyway, why do you call the double trident 'the baobab'?"

"We've been wondering what it means, too. We've come to the conclusion that it's probably a schematic of a tree," explained Barbora. "The part above the horizontal line represents a trunk and branches, the lower part shows the roots, and the ellipse is the treasure that is hidden in those roots."

"The ellipse at the bottom represents treasure? That hadn't occurred to me. But you're right, the symbol could easily represent a tree with treasure hidden in its roots. What exactly reminds you of a baobab?"

"Nothing, really. We'd just seen a nature program on TV about baobabs, and we liked the word, so we decided to call the symbol 'the baobab.'"

"You're right that 'baobab' is prettier than 'double trident.' Maybe I'll start calling it that, too. But honestly, I'm not looking for treasure and I don't know of any. I'm looking for a girl who went missing two years ago . . . But how do you know that I'm interested in the baobab? And how did you find out that I was at the party?"

"The architect who told you about Bernet and lent you the costume had a fit of conscience this morning about having betrayed his friend, and before he left for the airport he stopped off here and told him all about you. Bernet told us, and we recognized you easily by the factory-at-night costume."

"But didn't the architect tell Bernet that I wasn't looking for any treasure?"

"The architect told Bernet that you'd told him a pretty confused story," Andrea admitted. "But we were convinced you'd made it all up because you wanted to hide the fact of what you were really looking for."

"Well, I'm not looking for any phantom treasure. I'm looking for Viola Jonášová, and believe me, I'm taking an interest in the symbol only because of her."

"Why do you say 'phantom' treasure? Are you claiming that it doesn't exist?" The girls were getting annoyed with me.

"That's not what I said. Maybe the whole matter of the treasure really is nonsense, just a childish fantasy; but it's also possible that there's treasure buried somewhere, and that somehow it's even connected with Viola's disappearance."

"Have you found any clues that might lead us to the treasure?" the girls asked eagerly in unison.

"In my search for Viola I've come across lots of clues, but they're all so ambiguous that I don't know where to start with them, and I can't decide which are true and which are false, which are important and which are insignificant. It does seem to me, in fact, that some of the clues could indicate that Viola went off in search of treasure . . . Do you know what? I could really do with some coffee. Will there be some on the tray on the other side of the door? Bernet went away, I think."

At once and without a word Barbora pulled her legs free of the covers and darted across the bed on all fours; she had mastered the technique of this, probably due to the fact that the girls spent most of their life in this large, elastic bed, which was practically impossible to walk across. She jumped off it and across the soft carpet, which came up to her ankles. Quietly she turned the key of the double doors, opened one of them and peered out into the hallway. Apparently there was no one there. From the floor she snatched up an alpaca tray with the breakfast on it and locked the door. A moment later she was back in the bed, pouring out the coffee. Noticing four cups on the tray, I deduced two things that amused me: First, Bernet knew that I was in the room; second, he was hoping the girls were no longer angry with him and would invite him to join our breakfast. As well as coffee, the tray contained fresh rolls, several kinds of cheese and a lot of fruit.

"Have you found any maps or encrypted messages?" asked Andrea, and Barbora said, "We must seem really childish to you . . ."

I smiled. "All I've found is a schematic of a pump, whose use I don't know. As for your childishness, there's no need to explain anything: I heard the defense of childishness you made in the pavilion yesterday evening."

"So you have to admit we were right," said Barbora. "Bernet forgets how his childishness has rewarded him. We know that the architect told you about the statuette with the coded message. Apart from Bernet, no one would take so much time and trouble over that."

"But that statuette led your friend to the score of the opera, not the treasure," I said.

"In our view there's some connection between the opera and the treasure," said Andrea. "We're sure that it contains a hidden message about the whereabouts of the treasure, it's just that we haven't been able to find it yet. Like a coward, Bernet is backing out of the search just as we're approaching the goal."

"Why do you think that the disappearance of the girl you're looking for has something to do with the treasure?" asked Barbora.

"Because the tangle of clues keeps returning to the same motifs: something going on underground, conspiracy, notes in a mysterious book, fateful events long ago . . . With clues like that, it's quite easy to compose a story about treasure, don't you think?" But I didn't want to get the girls' hopes up only to disappoint them, so I added: "It's true, of course, that you could compose other nice stories out of them too—"

"Could all those stories—" The interruption was from Barbora, and Andrea finished the question: "—be part of a single convoluted story?"

"That, too, is possible. The individual clues lead in various directions, although I often get the feeling that eventually all of them meet somewhere on the horizon. Sometimes I feel that I'm close to the story of stories, that I'm listening to it; but it's like listening to someone in the next room telling a long story of which you can't understand a single word. To me, the story is like a magical tale of the Orient, but that's probably because I know just fragments of it and these fragments are so unconnected that only magic could put them together."

"It's the same with us," whispered Barbora. "All we know about the treasure is given by a few symbols lost in the void. We, too, have filled this void with the dreams, anxieties and fantasies of childhood, which have reawakened in us after many years."

"Maybe you'll forgive me for suggesting that all this might in the end be explained by something pretty banal. That's why I'm afraid to find answers to all the mysteries I've encountered in my search for Viola, even though there's nothing I desire more. But don't be sad—I have the feeling, too, that everything in any way connected with the double trident is so ambiguous and uncertain that the most fantastical conjecture of all could easily turn out to be true. I wouldn't be at all surprised if you found your pirate treasure and I found Viola on the shore of a subterranean lake that was the home of a prehistoric monster. Maybe that's where our paths will meet. I think it would be a pity if you stopped looking for the treasure. How about I tell you everything I know about the double trident? Perhaps there will be something in it that'll help in your search for the treasure. And then you can tell me how you came across the symbol."

"Yes, yes, that's a great idea!" cried the girls.

"Maybe we could look for the treasure together, now that Bernet has deserted the expedition," Andrea suggested.

"The three of us could look for Viola as well, if you wished," added Barbora.

"No, I'm sorry, but I'm not going to look for the treasure with you. It belongs to Bernet, who's been searching for it since he was a child, and to you, because you've stood by him while others have mocked him. Besides, I believe I'll be able to find Viola only if I look for her alone. The clues I've managed to uncover so far would have appeared only to someone working alone, and I think it'll continue to be this way in the future, too. If I find a clue that could lead to the treasure, I'll be sure to let you know. And there's one more thing—I think that you should make your peace with Bernet."

Chapter 46
Discussion About Lights

Although the girls were frowning, I continued. "I think you've been too hard on him. I agree that he's not playing his game too well at the moment. But I don't believe that his partner the deity is as impatient as you; I don't think he despises him for his weakness. I'd say that he knows there are times when it's necessary to rest, times when it's necessary to lose, and times when it's necessary to behave foolishly and tritely. Right now Bernet has been seized by a great fear; he feels like he's drowning and that whatever he tries to lay his hands on slides from his grip. I believe he'll come back to the world he lived in with you. Whoever has found a slit and peered into another space has trouble inhabiting the world where everyone else lives—although touchingly, Bernet is trying desperately to do just that at the moment. Maybe he hates his past and is disgusted by the whole story of the treasure that has been interwoven with his life since childhood, but even such moments of disgust are necessary . . ."

The girls were silent and thoughtful. The drapes rippled behind them. Then Andrea said. "So you truly believe that Bernet isn't about to become a tedious ass?"

"Indeed I do. But I also believe that he won't become one only if you stay with him. I'd like to ask you not to abandon him."

"We owe Bernet a great deal, and that's why we're so angry with him now," said Andrea. "If we're hard on him, it's because we want to save him. We've trusted him ever since we fell in love with him. In the beginning, the amazing, gentle relationship that grew between us, which for anyone else would have been a source of longstanding misery and pain, made us terribly afraid, as we didn't know what to do about it, but we trusted Bernet to find a solution that would make all of us happy. And he did, as naturally and easily as an angel waving its wing. That's why we always believed that as soon as he discovered a few new pieces for the jigsaw he's been playing with since childhood, he'd find the treasure with the same ease."

"And maybe that's already happened," added Barbora. "Maybe all the signs we need are hidden in the opera. And Bernet, instead of looking for them, attends only to his stupid property."

The girls fell silent. I, too, was silent, as I looked at their thoughtful faces and their slender bodies half-submerged in drifts of bedclothes, across which lay the light of noon, subdued by the white curtain. Although I could understand their anger, I would be sorry if they parted from Bernet. Theirs was a remarkable grouping; I was entertained and touched by the union of the girls' impracticality and impulsiveness with Bernet's introversion and ignorance of the world. Almost everyone, including me, would have predicted that a threesome in possession of such qualities, living in a relationship totally morally unacceptable for most of society, would end very soon in a shelter for the homeless. Bernet, Barbora and Andrea, however, lived perfectly naturally in unheard-of luxury; the confusion and helplessness of these three big children had been no impediment to Bernet's becoming one of the most successful men in a world he didn't and had never even tried to understand, nor to the girls' shielding their talent from the tiniest banality that could betray or contaminate their beautiful voices.

Yet I still insisted on the objections to Bernet's way of life I'd explained yesterday to the architect; I remained convinced that a clean game could not be associated with money. The girls didn't realize this; according to them, up to the moment of crisis everything was fine with Bernet, and they were persuaded that money was only an unimportant, inessential result of Bernet's game—a mere shadow behind the lights on the screen. I didn't want to talk them out of this. Perhaps it was a happy mistake, and the girls' admiration had inspired Bernet gradually to become what in their eyes he had been all along—an ethereal elf who needed no money; and I also believed that this admiration would give him the strength to conquer the panic that had recently seized him and was dragging him down.

The union of these three people seemed to me so happy that I didn't exclude the possibility of their actually finding the treasure. I wondered if their search would indeed summon up some treasure from the bowels of the earth, a mysterious dungeon, or the roots of the baobab, even if the way they were now taking was just a tangle of errors, and the double trident, the porcelain statuette, and the stories from Bernet's childhood had nothing at all to do with treasure.

"Why are you looking for the girl, anyway?" asked Barbora, breaking the silence.

"Are you in love with her?" Andrea weighed in.

I laughed. "No. I know Viola only from photographs, a portrait painting and the one time I heard her voice. I'm looking for her because I promised her father I would. Or perhaps because I'm curious and I'd like to solve the puzzle fate has presented me with, which is probably a similar kind of riddle to the one Bernet has been trying to crack his whole life."

Then it occurred to me that what Andrea had just said was not so ridiculous. I had to admit that my obsession in my search for Viola over the past few days did have a little something in common with love. Had it been otherwise, I would hardly have occupied myself for so long with someone I had never met and about whom I knew almost nothing; I would hardly have chosen to play a comic role I wasn't at all prepared for and which was a cross between Philip Marlowe and Heinrich von Ofterdingen; curiosity wouldn't have sufficed for that, or a fondness for detective stories and puzzle-solving, or even sympathy for an old, sick man.

So I said to the girls: "You're right, actually. I am a little in love with Viola, even though I don't know her at all. From the beginning I've been extremely drawn to this creature that runs away and leaves only an ambiguous trail. Sometimes it seems to me that she's just an empty, black spot with a vortex whirling ceaselessly around her—a vortex of words, images, strange faces and fates, outdoor and indoor spaces, stories, thoughts, tones, and above all lights white and colored and lights of day and night. A fascination such as this is maybe a form of love, although before you asked me about it, it hadn't occurred to me."

"What will remain of that enchantment once you find Viola, do you think?" said Andrea.

"I don't know, I haven't thought about it. In my heart of hearts, I don't really believe that I will find her. For me, she's a shrouded black figure in the middle of a swarm of lights, and I can't imagine that these lights will ever move aside so that I can look her in the face."

"If you don't find Viola, at least you'll be able to console yourself with the memory of the pretty fireworks you've seen on your journey," said Barbora with a smile.

"I don't believe in such consolation. The lights that flash and circle around the invisible Viola are will-o'-the-wisps, I suspect, and I feel quite afraid when I imagine where they could lead me. They are cold lights; they bring a strange joy, yes, but it's a cold fever that freezes in the blood, a barren ecstasy that is closed in with its own bliss and which nothing can grow from. Darkness would be more inviting than those lights."

"Still it seems to us that those forlorn lights attract you."

"Yes, they attract me like a drug—I can't help myself. I worry that one day I might live only among them, in a land of distant glimmer; that because of the magnificent lights on the horizon I might completely forget the faces of those close to me and forget about useful, obliging things. Sometimes it seems to me that through my search for Viola everyone else will be lost to me, and that my quest will end with my being left totally alone."

"That's odd, because we'd say that the opposite were true. It doesn't seem to us that you had such a great social life before, but since you've been looking for Viola you've surely met many new people and learned about their lives and their worlds," said Barbora.

"That's true, although from the beginning all these encounters have been attended by the ghost of Viola, which infects everything with unreality and has the power to transform all faces into phantoms. When I look back on those encounters, the faces of the people I've spoken with merge with the images in their stories and characters I invent as I try to reconstruct what happened to Viola . . ."

"Are we phantoms for you, too?" asked Andrea, a little flirtatiously.

I looked at the girls and smiled. At that moment there was nothing at all unreal about them; oddly, they were protected from phantomhood by the fantasticality of their natures—such a mixture of foolishness, naivety, and wisdom could only be real, as it was inconceivable that anyone's imagination could create it. But I couldn't be sure that tomorrow their faces wouldn't transform in my memory into pale masks floating in the darkness among other masks. I didn't mention this to the girls; I didn't have the feeling that I mattered to them enough for it to bother them if I really did see them as phantoms.

Instead of giving an answer, I said, "Night lights must mean something to you, too, as you made them the theme of your masquerade."

"We like night lights, and we don't see any reason for you to be afraid of them; lights are pure and innocent," Barbora instructed me. "I'd say that a person who lives with them can learn in their world a selfless attentiveness and a respect for what is beyond our world and what cannot be exploited in any way, and such a lesson can be pretty good for a relationship with the things and faces that are close to you. We chose night lights as the theme of this year's party because it seems to us that what resides in night lights is somehow related to something that for both of us has echoed at the bottom of music since our childhoods—something that most people who claim to like music hardly ever hear. We came to realize this fully only once we got to know the opera from Popelová Street. It seemed to us that it was the only music that knew of the source of tones, and that its composer had suffered through cold, monotonous music in order to force it to give up its oldest, quietest and most wonderful sound."

Andrea watched Barbora admiringly: She was proud of how

her friend was able, on behalf of both of them, to put words to the feelings they shared. Barbora hadn't convinced me, however, and my worry that my pursuit of Viola could lead me into a cold world from which I would never manage to escape, persisted. The girls didn't know the danger of excessive purity yet—probably they were too young to know, just as they were too young to be able to indulge Bernet's fatigue and his fear.

Chapter 47
Book Found in Amalfi

Again we were silent for some time. Then the girls asked me to tell them the story of my search for Viola.

I had just begun—"Ten days ago, as I was climbing across a dump . . ."—when Andrea interrupted me. "Wait. You must make yourself comfortable, so that you tell your story well and leave nothing out."

The girls embarked on their journey across the bed, on hands and knees, working their way through the heaps of bedclothes, gathering the pillows and cushions that were scattered all about, returning to me with their catch, building the pillows into a kind of pyramid. So I sunk down into this and began to tell the girls my story, from the moment when I stepped on the point of the double trident at the dump. The girls buried themselves in bedclothes, held hands and listened to me with rapt attention.

"It's almost as pretty as the search for the treasure," Andrea sighed, when two hours later I ended my story at the moment in the garden when I'd seen the heads of the two girls bowed over me. "Too bad you don't want us to help you."

"There's only one way you can help me now: by telling me everything you know that may have a connection with the double trident. Yesterday in the pavilion you reminded Bernet that you had gotten to know him through the search for the treasure. How am I to understand that? Did you meet him in an underground passage, in a graveyard at night, or on some exotic island?"

The girls laughed. "It wasn't quite like that, unfortunately."

"We met Bernet in a café," said Barbora.

"Because of a draft," added Andrea. "It was last May. The waiter had opened a window to let some fresh air into the place . . ."

I extricated myself from the nest of pillows and left it to the girls. After a few small modifications, which we made together, the two of them fit into it comfortably. Now it was my turn to lie there and listen.

"Suddenly a draft came in," Andrea continued, "and checks, napkins, and loose pairs of newspaper pages sailed slowly over our heads and up toward the café's high ceiling, where they circled for a while like a flock of white birds before coming down in slow spirals onto the heads of the customers, the tables and the floor. Some of the customers stood up and tried to catch them while they were still in the air. A sheet of paper landed on our table. Barbora picked it up, showed it to me and said in surprise: 'Look, it's Santa Rosalia!'"

"What's Santa Rosalia? So what was on the sheet of paper? And how did it take you to Bernet?"

"Wait a moment, first things first," said Andrea with a smile. "First of all: On the sheet of paper was a drawing of the symbol you know well."

"The baobab?"

"Right, the baobab, although we didn't call it that then. Secondly: Santa Rosalia is the name of a novel and also the capital city of a fictional country in South America where the novel is set."

"And thirdly," Barbora cut in, "when the papers landed on the floor and the tables, all the customers started to pick them up, examine them, offer them around and exchange them. We waved the sheet that had landed on our table and called, 'Santa Rosalia! Santa Rosalia!' But apparently these words meant nothing to anyone. We walked from table to table, showing the drawing to the other customers, and eventually it was claimed by two men sitting at a small table by the window: Bernet and the architect. As we returned the sheet to Bernet, he asked us why we'd called out 'Santa Rosalia!' and we told him about the novel where we'd seen the symbol. That's how we got to know each other, and that's how it happened that we've been searching together for the treasure from the pirate ship ever since."

I listened on with bated breath.

"We found the novel in a cheap guest house in Amalfi, over summer vacation, when we were traveling about Italy," Barbora went on. "It was lying in a drawer of the nightstand, probably left there by the guest who'd stayed in the room before us. It was a torn, greasy paperback, written in French, published by a house in Dijon in 1986, and its author's name was given as Honoré de Verne, which even at first glance was obviously a pseudonym. Later, Bernet tried to find out something about the author on the internet, but apart from a reference to this one book, he found nothing. Also he called the publishing house, to be told that the author had published no other book and didn't wish for his real name to be disclosed to anyone."

"Did Bernet read the book as well?"

"Yes, we brought it back with us."

"So what's the connection between this French novel and the double trident?"

"You criticize us for our impatience, but you're even more impatient than we are," said Andrea with a smile. "We're getting to that, if you're prepared to wait. So anyway, we found a torn paperback in a drawer in our room at the guest house. We'd read the books we'd brought with us on the trip, and we didn't have enough money left to buy new ones, so we were glad of something to read. The next morning we went to a beach on the edge of town, and we took the book with us. I started reading it first. As soon as I opened it, I saw that its frontispiece was a map of a city. There was no detail on the map—it showed only main streets. And these made the shape of the symbol that haunts you and Bernet and, ever since we met Bernet, has haunted us, too."

"Did the novel's story have any connection with what you or I are looking for?"

"It's difficult to say," said Barbora. "I don't think so. But since we started looking for the treasure, it seems to us that absolutely everything is somehow connected with it, and that everything is full of signs and hints about it. But I don't suppose we need to explain that to you, as you surely know what I'm talking about. It's true that when the score of *Medusae of the Past* was discovered, we were surprised by the similarities in the two works. Unlike the opera, the novel is played out in real time and on a real continent, South America, albeit in a fictitious country, but its theme is similar to that of the opera: The story of the novel, too, unfolded in the aftermath of violent political upheaval, and its heroes, too, were connected with the old regime and involved in guerilla warfare against the new government."

"Will you tell me the story of the novel?"

"We'll try, although we're not very good at telling stories," said Barbora.

Andrea picked up on the hint immediately. "Too bad Bernet's not here," she said. "Bernet is a beautiful storyteller."

"Isn't this a good opportunity to make peace?" I asked, to help them out.

For a moment or two the girls rolled about in the bed, not knowing what to do.

"Go to him," I said. "I suppose he's waiting for you. I'd like to hear his telling of the story of Santa Rosalia."

Both girls ran from the room. I lay in bed, watching the play of the shadows on the rippling, sunlit curtain. About half an hour later, the door opened slightly and a hand emerged from the gap to lay my bag and clothes on the carpet; then Barbora's head appeared.

"Please come to the pool. Bernet will be waiting for you there," she said before disappearing. I put on my pants, slung the bag over my shoulder and left the room.

At the poolside, a man in a light linen slacks, sneakers, and a sailing shirt was sitting in a wicker chair under a broad parasol. In the meantime Barbora and Andrea had changed into swimsuits, and now they were diving and racing about the pool; they waved to me from the water as I arrived. Bernet stood up and shook my hand. His delicate features were more suited to a poet than a financier. He had fair hair and pale skin; I could imagine it wasn't good for him to stay too long in the sun. He motioned me to sit down in a chair under a second parasol. Then he poured me a golden drink from a cut-glass carafe that was sparkling on the round garden table next to a bedewed water jug and some documents weighed down by an ashtray.

"I'm very sorry to have caused you such inconvenience," said Bernet.

"I'm not aware of any inconvenience, so there's no need to apologize," I assured him. "But I'd be grateful if you'd tell me about *Santa Rosalia*. Barbora and Andrea promised me that you would. It's important to me: I have a suspicion that there is a connection between the novel and the disappearance of the woman I'm looking for."

"I know," said Bernet. "The architect told me about the missing woman yesterday morning, and a few minutes ago Barbora and Andrea gave me a few more details of your story. Naturally I'll be happy to explain the plot of the novel to you; it would be great if it could somehow help you. But first I should draw you a map of Santa Rosalia."

From the table Bernet took a sheet a paper, turned it over and carefully drew something on it with a ballpoint pen. Then he pushed the page to my side of the table.

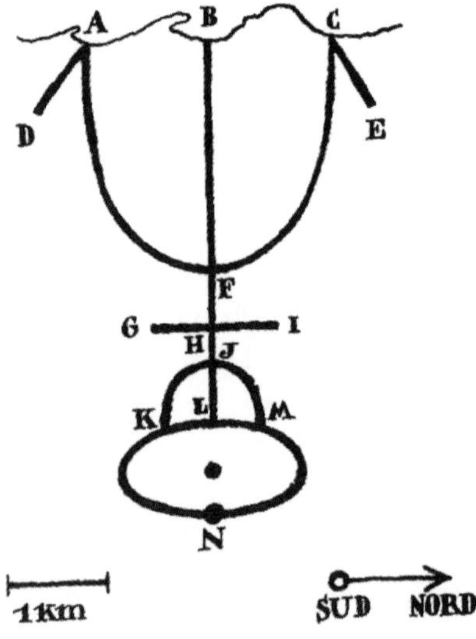

"This was the frontispiece in the book?" I asked, and Bernet nodded. We both took a drink. Bernet settled in his chair, looked beyond the slender yew trees in his garden toward the mist-shrouded city, and began the story.

Chapter 48
Santa Rosalia

"The novel opens with the protagonist leaning against the rail of a ship that is sailing into Santa Rosalia, the capital city of a republic in South America. The hero's name is Pierre, he's thirty-two years old, and he's a bank clerk in Paris. Following his recent divorce, he has decided to take a long vacation and travel the world. The ship whose deck he is standing on has sailed from a neighboring country, where Pierre spent two tranquil weeks on promenades and in beach bars. Pierre knows very little about the county whose capital city he is now sailing into. He has heard that there was a military coup there some years ago, but at that time there were political upheavals in all the countries in the region. What is said about the country's regime doesn't encourage him to respect its government, but from what he's heard, it isn't so much worse than in other countries. Originally this country was not on his itinerary—by all accounts, there are no exceptional monuments, beauties of nature, or sandy beaches there—but as its capital city lies on his route, he has said to himself that he'll stop off here for three or four days. The ship docks in the harbor, which is here . . ." Bernet aimed his pen at a point on the map marked with the letter B.

"Pierre decided in Paris he would take very little luggage with him, buying everything he needed on his travels, so he walks away from the harbor with just a light travel bag over his shoulder. He proceeds slowly down a busy boulevard, reading its name on a marble sign—August 2nd, probably the date of a legendary uprising or victorious battle; but Pierre is not interested in the significance of the date and has no intention of looking into it. The boulevard is lined on both sides with tall palms. It is early afternoon, and the sun is still high above the sea. There is something dreamlike in the way the street runs off into the distance without the slightest hesitation, without a single concession to the terrain or older buildings; it is as though the boulevard emerged on the plain all at once as if by a magic that was still at work on it. At the point where all lines converge, he sees the facade of a large building, whose detail is blurred in the haze of distance. Its central part is covered by a cluster of things that in reality are obviously far apart but together create a whimsy of perspective; Pierre doesn't try to separate these, although it occurs to him that the strange white gleam that surrounds them is probably the spray of a fountain."

Bernet first brought down the tip of his pen on a point that was perhaps a centimeter below the letter B—plainly this was a place on August 2nd Boulevard, along which Pierre was now walking. Then the pen moved slowly down the line, as though following the direction of Pierre's gaze, passing points F, H, J and L, crossing the oval and stopping at point N.

"Pierre has been walking for a quarter an hour or so when he reaches the magnificent entrance to a hotel, its awning lined with poles on which the flags of every state imaginable hang limply. He goes inside and allows himself to be taken to the fourth floor and a room with a high ceiling and gleaming pseudo-Rococo furniture. After the maid has left, he leans against the wrought-iron decorative rail on the narrow balcony, watching the activity in the street through the tops of the palms. Then he lies down on the cold cover of the wide bed and looks at the pattern of the curtains, projected by the daylight onto the white wall. Then, having slept for about an hour, he goes out to explore the unknown city."

Andrea and Barbora swam over, rested arms covered with glistening drops of water on the edge of the pool, and listened to Bernet's story.

"So, with his hands in his pockets, Pierre walks past the

storefronts of goldsmiths, wine merchants, travel agents and banks; he passes many restaurants, at one point pausing to look into an aquarium and watch the slow movement of lobster antennae. At this time of day, customers sit at tables on the sidewalk, drinking colorful cocktails. He is struck by the fact that the line of buildings is continuous, unbroken at any point by the mouth of a side street. But one arcade after another opens up; peeping inside, Pierre sees that the luxury of the main boulevard has spilled over into these, and that the storefronts are aglow with bright bulbs and reflectors. He tries to see daylight at the end of these passages, but sooner or later his gaze is always blocked by a bend."

With a gesture Bernet asked the girls if they wanted a drink; each shook her head, so he poured only into our glasses.

"As Pierre proceeds along the street, he sees ever fewer people; apparently the life of the city is attracted by the sea, and this wave of attraction doesn't reach very far from the shoreline." Bernet showed which section of the main boulevard he was now talking about, bringing the tip of his pen down at a point about three-quarters of the way from B to F. "Also he sees many fewer stores around him. Now he passes the locked doors of palaces—behind their windows he sees the faces of janitors in livery—and exclusive-looking clubs, which have surely retreated deliberately to a quieter section of the main boulevard. At last he reaches a point where streets open up from both sides; these streets are only a little narrower than August 2nd Boulevard."

I put my finger on point F and Bernet nodded.

"The buildings of all four corners are beveled, turning the intersection into a circus. In the center of the circus, Poseidon's hippocamp-drawn chariot emerges from a fountain. In these parts, few cars pass through the streets; in the quiet that reigns here, Pierre hears the slap of water against stone as the jet from Triton's conch hits the backs of the sea horses.

"The large building right at the end of the boulevard is now a little nearer, so that Pierre can make out the huge, regular white portico attached to its facade, but still this mansion seems to him extremely far away. Beyond the circus, there are four more opulent buildings on both sides of the street, after which August

2nd Boulevard changes character completely, now comprising two rows of villas set back from the sidewalk by deep gardens; above the tops of the palms appear pointed roofs with metal weathervanes and upper floors with their wooden shutters open. But instead of heading toward these villas, Pierre turns into a street that opens up to his right. He reads on an overhead marble sign that this street is named after a General Molina."

To show Bernet that I was listening closely, I put my finger on point F and then moved it toward point A. Again Bernet gave a satisfied nod.

"At first he continues to see the kind of clubs and bars he encountered on the last stretch of August 2nd Boulevard, but these soon give way to buildings with gray, peeling walls that may once have been luxury villas but are now either empty or home to migrants from poor parts of the city, who have transformed dilapidated mansions into vertical slums; on balconies Pierre sees laundry fluttering on lines tied between chipped Neo-Baroque columns or pensive caryatids; through courtyard entries he sees that atria have been turned into vegetable plots. As he gets further away from the intersection, the buildings become ever more run-down and derelict; now the roots of shrubs growing on ledges are caught in cracks in the walls. As there is a slight bend in the street, Pierre can't see what's further along, but he senses the progress of decay in the stretch that is invisible to him. It occurs to him that if he were to continue along the street to where it reaches the shoreline, he would see nothing but ruins overgrown with thistles.

"He stops. He feels like he's looking at a scene in an unintelligible drama. He wonders what could have happened in these parts of the city. First of all, it seems, the original residents of Molina Boulevard left their homes for some reason; then, once the street had become a quiet zone of dilapidation, abandoned apartments were settled by people from poor quarters. At the same time, bars and enterprises in need of a reason to disappear from the main boulevard, and the public eye, spilled over into this street, although they were intimidated by the hordes of dark buildings and their unpredictable, nameless occupiers and so advanced no more than a few meters into the street. All this is conjecture, however. Pierre returns to the circus which contains Poseidon's fountain, thinking of how he'll leave the city before he can make sense of the scene that briefly opened up to him, which will stick in his memory always as an incomprehensible image—and this thought stirs up a strange bliss in him.

"He continues in an easterly direction, past gardens enclosed in high railings. He sees, between the trunks of palms and a spreading tree whose name he doesn't know, a terrace with an abandoned rocking chair between slender columns; in a chink in the leaves, he sees part of a white staircase. The occasional car drives past, but in this part of the city he doesn't see a single pedestrian. He stops at a small square on which railings enclose thick tropical vegetation. At the center of this enclosure is a bronze statue of a young man with wavy hair and sideburns; he is sitting on some kind of boulder and staring dreamily along the main street toward the sea, meanwhile preparing to write with a quill on a sheet of paper that his left hand is pressing uncomfortably and absurdly to his knee. At this point August 2nd Boulevard is crossed by a perpendicular street that is lined with gardens and villas; apparently this street ends abruptly in bushes on both sides."

Bernet indicated point H, where Pierre was standing, and then points G and I.

"Pierre continues on his way. Soon the scene changes again. He reaches another crossroads, which, like all the others, opens up into a circus. At the center of this one is a tall obelisk of smooth marble, which probably celebrates some long-ago victory, as its bottom is encircled by a bronze relief on which flags and different types of weapons are depicted. At this place the gardens end."

Although Bernet didn't refer here to the map, it was clear that he was speaking of the point marked with the letter J.

"Now August 2nd Boulevard branches off into three streets. All the buildings here look like headquarters of important authorities. These streets, too, are empty of people, except for the uniformed soldiers guarding the entrances. Pierre opts to take the street on the left . . ." Bernet ran the tip of the pen from J to M. "He is confirmed in his surmise that the buildings house ministries and government offices. Although the soldiers look at the lone pedestrian with suspicion, no one stops him. The street leads him into a large circus." The hand in which Bernet held the pen circled several times over the ellipse. "At the center of the circus is a fountain with a tall, shaking column of water, now colored by the pink light of the setting sun, as is the pale facade of the presidential palace." He brought down the tip of the pen, first on a point at the center of the ellipse, then on point N.

"He walks across the empty circus, casting a long shadow across the paving. He stops in front of the ornamental gate that leads to the palace gardens. Beyond the bars, soldiers stand motionless in the darkening garden, their faces devoid of expression, white tassels on their hats, white lines on their uniforms and submachine guns in their white-gloved hands. Pierre turns to look down the main boulevard toward the sea and the setting sun. Then he heads back to the hotel, feeling glad not to have neglected his tour of the city, as sometimes happens on his travels, so that tomorrow or the day after he will be able to leave with a clear conscience the city and country that he'll forever remember only for the palms on its promenade, its run-down palaces, its dusky gardens, and the pink, fizzing columns of its fountains."

In the course of Bernet's telling the girls had climbed out of the pool, sat down on the white tiles and begun to listen to the story, which they knew from their reading on a beach in the Bay of Salerno.

"The gardens of the villa quarter are ever darker, more fragrant and quieter; the only sound coming from them is the occasional shrill call of a bird. This reminds Pierre of his summer home in the French countryside; he loses himself in his memories and walks for a long time deep in thought. Before he knows it, he's back in the busy part of August 2nd Boulevard. The long shadows of the palms crawl toward him across the sidewalk, which is awash with pink light. This light is reflected from car hoods, bothering his eyes. After a while the sun descends into the tops of the palms and becomes a swarm of flashing lights. The garden restaurants are now full; above their tables, white balls light up and shine against a backdrop of the pink-and-purple-striped sky, causing the contents of plates—the red carapaces of lobsters, the silver skin of fish, and beds of crushed ice in which gray oysters lie—to gleam. Pierre takes a seat on the terrace of a restaurant not far from his hotel and asks the waiter to recommend a good local wine; he sips this as he watches the play of the fading light on facades and in the tops of the palms. The night comes down in what feels like an instant. Now the glow of the white balls floating above the restaurant tables, the dazzling lights of the main boulevard's storefronts, and the colored neon of its facades are supplemented by the streetlamps that stand in front of the palms. The thought that he needs to know no more about this country he'll be leaving tomorrow or the next day than its lights soft and dazzling, white and colored, again stirs in Pierre a feeling that is close to happiness."

It struck me that in spite of the palms, oysters and Spanish names, I didn't have the feeling that what I was hearing was set in an exotic country. It seemed to me that the main hero of Bernet's story was heat—a heat that melted thoughts, memories, and aims and restored to consciousness an older, slower time they had once shared, plunging everything into a life of whispers, waves, and murmurs. This kind of heat had lain for several days in the streets of my city, and it struck me that it had affected the way I'd encountered things in my search for Viola and also which things had appeared, opened and closed to me. If Jonáš had approached me in November, my search would probably have unfolded in a very different way, and quite possibly it would have ended before it properly started. I knew that the reasons that convinced me to set out on Viola's trail included the blissful idea that the search would take place in a world of hot walls and unpeopled summer streets, in an intense heat that released fantastical images in things. Possibly the heat was a yet more powerful drug, a more ingenious trap and a more dangerous lotus than the lights I had argued about with Andrea and Barbora.

Chapter 49
Shots on the Promenade

"In the sounds of evening Pierre distinguishes amid the many human voices the clinking of glasses and silverware, the cracking of crab shells in the jaws of pliers, the distant hooting of ships, and the music of several orchestras, before all these merge into a single peaceful stream. Then out of the blue there are several sharp, loud bangs. It takes a while before Pierre realizes that these were bursts from automatic weapons and they came from close by. The customers on the terrace crawl under the food-laden tables, ladies scream, wine flows over tablecloths. The ripping of these shots into the hum of the promenade and the silence that follows them, produces a strange torpor in Pierre. Suddenly he feels like a member of the audience in a concert hall, waiting to learn what is next on the program.

"He remains seated at his table. In front of the mouth of a nearby arcade, he sees a man lying on the sidewalk, flat on his belly, his arms outstretched, a slowly growing red pool at his side. Next to the body stand two masked figures holding lightweight machine guns with collapsible stocks; the next moment both figures disappear into the arcade. Then Pierre hears the sound of cars approaching and braking, the stamping of feet in heavy boots, barked commands. An ambulance pulls up at the curb, quietly, with its siren switched off; it has appeared so quickly that it could have been waiting a short way off. Paramedics load the motionless body; the ambulance drives away and the sound of its engine dies out. A young woman is standing in front of a gallery, looking at the pictures for sale; Pierre realizes she has been standing in this spot since the attack, differentiating her behavior from that of all other people in the street. She didn't run or protect herself in any way; she just stood where she was, her face turned toward the mouth of the arcade. And Pierre is suddenly absolutely sure that the young woman knew in advance what was about to happen on the sidewalk and watched everything with the expert eye of an assessor; Pierre is reminded of a judge at the World Figure Skating Championships. The woman finally steps away from the gallery window and slowly enters the arcade.

"Once the ambulance has driven away and the soldiers have disappeared, the customers on the terrace—most of them foreigners like Pierre—crawl out from under their tables, look about in confusion, look at each other. A waiter, followed by two busboys, comes out onto the terrace from the restaurant. The customers fall over one another to ask about what happened, but the waiter just smiles and repeats over and over that there is nothing the matter and no cause for anxiety; the restaurant will pay for any wine that has been spilled. The busboys change the tablecloths. And it really does seem that the waiter is telling the truth and nothing has happened; now there is not even a trace of the stain on the sidewalk. It all happened so quickly that the customers are no longer sure what they actually saw and heard, so they think it best that they return to their plates of lobster and swordfish and their bottles of wine. They take up their silverware, and soon the clinking resumes and the wave of conversation rises; the orchestras strike up again. Pierre orders another bottle of wine and immerses himself in the hum that is again flowing over the main boulevard.

"On his way to the hotel he passes lighted storefronts; although it is almost midnight, most of the stores are still open. When he reaches the arcade into which the assassins and the soldiers disappeared, he takes a look inside. He sees a long corridor lined with the radiant windows of goldsmiths' and boutiques, which look the same as the storefronts on the street; there is nothing to suggest that danger lurks in the depths of the arcade. He is strangely attracted by what is invisible beyond the bend in the corridor, and he steps inside in order to find out what is there. At first, all he sees are more storefronts and more bends. He penetrates deeper into the arcade, which changes character gradually. He passes a series of small Chinese and Thai restaurants crammed together; these give way to bars and taprooms with the flashing colored lights of slot machines. The arcade narrows and there is ever less light in it.

"Suddenly Pierre has the feeling that he's walking along an ordinary city street that has a bridge running over it at second-floor level. Then the ceiling really does come to an end; the arcade stops denying that in this stretch it is actually a narrow, winding street; now it feels free to wind busily, until at last it emerges in a street that is almost as wide as August 2nd Boulevard. But this street is like an image of the main street in a nightmare or a vision of catastrophe. There are no lit streetlamps or shining storefronts, and no passing cars; Pierre doesn't even see any pedestrians; the only sign of life in the street is a band of men hanging about on the sidewalk opposite, in front of an illuminated bar. On the other side of the street is a long line of old, derelict mansions that look as though they are leaning against one another for support, fearful that they might collapse at any moment.

"Pierre realizes that the arcade leads south from August 2nd Boulevard, so that now he should be on Molina Boulevard, already quite close to the sea; he looks up at the walls of the buildings and does indeed see a faded sign with remnants of the general's name. It is as he predicted when he looked into this street at the point where it joins August 2nd Boulevard: The buildings in this part of the street are still more dilapidated than those in the eastern part. He heads west, passing several more taprooms and several alleys that probably turn into arcades, too. He has almost reached August 2nd Boulevard when he sees, beyond a bend in the road, the dark sea merging with the night sky. He goes over to a small harbor, where, bobbing about on the stinking surface, there are fishing boats patched with rust; tilting wooden shacks line the shore, and there is a stench of decay."

Bernet stabbed at point A with the tip of his pen. "To his right he sees the lights of ocean liners and the glow of the city's main boulevard. Passing dark warehouses with locked gates and then administrative and customs buildings, he returns along the quiet waterfront to the large harbor where he first entered the city. After that, August 2nd Boulevard opens its light-filled mouth, and minutes later Pierre is at the entrance of his hotel."

Now Bernet was following Pierre's course on the map. First he slowly moved the tip of the pen from point A to point B, then he moved it a short way down the B-F line.

"Please wait a moment," I said to Bernet. "I'd like to be clear in my mind of the route Pierre takes." I picked up the map of the city and drew on it five points which I labeled with small letters.

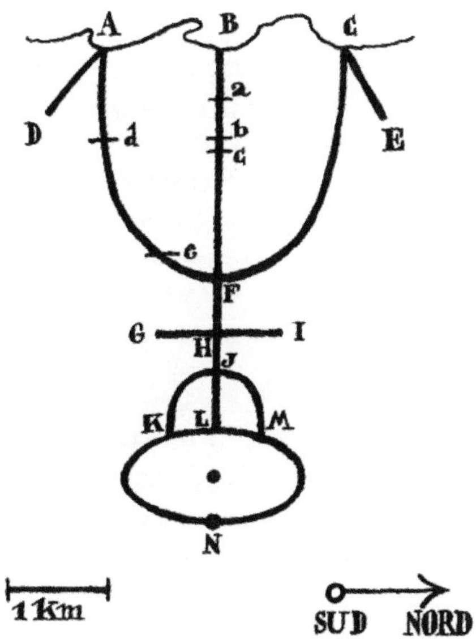

At the bottom of the page, I wrote a key, as follows:

a – Pierre's hotel
b – mouth of arcade; site of assassination
c – restaurant where P was sitting
d – mouth of arcade in Molina St.
e – place P reached when he first entered Molina St.

Once more I ran the pen along the course of Pierre's wanderings in Santa Rosalia, from the moment of his arrival at the port. Having finished this, I wrote the pattern of this path on the edge of the page: BaFeFHJMNLJHFcbdABa. Then, with a feeling of accomplishment, I laid down the pen and asked Bernet to go on with the story.

"Behind the reception desk in the hotel lobby, Pierre sees a small, nimble, bald-headed man in a brown and red uniform, who reminds him of an Italian comedy actor. Although he told himself that afternoon that he didn't want to know anything about this city, as he would be here only for a couple of days, now his curiosity gets the better of him, and he asks the receptionist about the shooting on the main boulevard, the dilapidated mansions on Molina Boulevard and the arcade that joins the two streets. But he learns nothing from the man, who just smiles as the waiter did before him, talks of the capital's most beautiful sights and gesticulates broadly from behind the desk. Pierre repeats his questions and the receptionist forces some tourist brochures on him. When Pierre realizes that he isn't going to get any answers, he leaves the receptionist in peace, goes to his room, throws the brochures in the trash without switching on the light and lies down on the bed. Again he looks at the pattern of the curtains on the wall; now it is joined by the shadow of a palm leaf, projected onto it by the streetlamps, putting him in mind of a tuna in a fisherman's net. He listens to the jumble of sounds coming from the street through the open balcony door, wondering if he'll hear any more gunshots, but the loudest noise is the screech of the bird he heard earlier in the garden quarter. Soon he falls asleep . . . Fancy a swim?" Suddenly Bernet had turned to me.

I shook my head. Although I was tempted by the sparkling water of the pool, I was attracted more by the story of this city that had grown so unexpectedly out of the double trident.

"The next day Pierre wakes up early and breakfasts alone on the hotel terrace in the cool of early morning. He hears the rattle of shutters being pulled up by storekeepers and the sound of water spraying from hoses, flushing litter from the sidewalk; he smells the stench of fish and rotten vegetables. The coolness, the sounds of early morning and the smells evoke a sense of happiness in him. He is glad that he decided to travel, and he is looking forward to the unknown places that still await him. The assassination, the run-down boulevard named for a General Molina and the sorrowful harbor with the fishing boats seem to him now like figments of a dream. He learns from the waiter that the large white ship berthed at the port will sail tomorrow for a neighboring country, and he decides to buy a ticket as soon as he finishes his breakfast. The waiter tells him that the office of the shipping company is on August 2nd Boulevard, about fifteen minutes' walk to the east from the hotel. Pierre sets off toward the office, but as he is passing the mouth of the nearest arcade, he is drawn toward it by the indifferent, ironic breath that blows from its depths.

"He stands irresolute at this entrance. Suddenly he is afraid; a voice is whispering to him, 'If you step into the arcade, it won't be so easy to turn back.' But the greater Pierre's apprehension, the greater his attraction to the arcade. So after a moment's hesitation, he plunges into its quiet coolness. As with the arcade he walked through in the night, in this one, too, the storefronts with luxury goods soon give way to cheap restaurants and bars with slot machines, a variety of mysterious stores with no goods on show, and gloomy cafés with large windows that reflect the lights outside. Pierre wonders if this arcade, too, will transform into a winding alley, but before he is able to find out, he spots the bald head of the hotel receptionist through the window of one of the cafés. The receptionist has noticed him, too; he is waving to him cheerfully, as though they were good friends, and indicating an empty chair at his table.

"Pierre steps inside and sits down. The receptionist, who is now in civilian dress, explains to Pierre that his shift has just ended and he is returning through the arcade to Molina Boulevard, where he lives; it is his custom to stop at this café on his way home for a coffee and a cognac. Pierre senses that the receptionist will be more communicative in the café than he was in the hotel lobby, where he was within view of other staff. Indeed, Pierre has the feeling that the man is waiting for him to ask something. Unable to make up his mind whether or not to do this, for a long time Pierre sits in silence. He realizes that the first question and the first answer might take him to a place it would be difficult to escape from."

"How could he know that?" I interrupted. "A mysterious flash of inspiration? Or does he dread every place that is unknown to him?"

"On the contrary, Pierre likes the thresholds of new places. More than anything, he loves landing piers in ports, airport lounges, and hotel receptions," Bernet explained. "He has the sense that strange places are friendly to him, maybe because he himself belongs in no particular place. There is nothing mysterious about his fear; it isn't the product of some kind of clairvoyance. All the things he encountered yesterday—the shining storefronts, the inaccessible presidential palace, the arcade that becomes a dark alley, the crumbling, overgrown mansions of Molina Boulevard—are letters that comprise some kind of text; letters of an alphabet he doesn't know but is slowly learning. Slowly he is beginning to sense the meaning of the whole text of the city. Pierre has never been afraid to enter dangerous neighborhoods that the guidebooks warn tourists away from—yet in the city he finds himself in now, he does feel afraid. Although he understands its text only vaguely, he is aware of tones in it that could destroy his soul, even though they would represent no danger to most people. But at the same time, he feels a terrible yearning to make sense of the city and its life . . .

"For as long as Pierre is silent, the receptionist leaves him be; he just sits there and smiles. Pierre has the feeling that the man knows exactly which difficulties he is addressing in his heart, and that he knows how this hesitation will resolve itself. Soon Pierre can resist no longer and he asks the receptionist about the shooting, the arcades, and the derelict Molina Boulevard. Immediately the receptionist begins to speak of the city, accompanying his exposition with gestures livelier than those of yesterday at the hotel when he sidestepped Pierre's questions because of the prying eyes of other staff. Before long, Pierre has the feeling that the study of the city's public and private life is a hobby for the receptionist; apparently it gives him such pleasure to talk of the city that he is happy to forgo the bed that awaits him after his long shift."

Chapter 50
A City Transformed

"First of all, the receptionist declares that whoever wishes to understand the city must understand its history. One hundred and twenty years ago, he begins, this settlement comprised only a fishing village, where today Molina Boulevard touches the shore. As trade expanded, the village grew chaotically and spread across the plain—the receptionist expresses the swelling of the original village by spreading his hands and curling his fingers. He speaks of alleys with crooked shacks, and of how these woeful homes were soon overgrown with dry grass and joined by more and more of the same in an unending jigsaw, so that the streets pushed out onto the pampas. Like sleepwalkers, the streets progressed step by step across the plain, sometimes keeping stolidly to the course of the old village lanes they connected with, sometimes languidly dodging rocks, sometimes—again without reason, as though subject to a sudden fit—turning away from the original course.

"Obviously the receptionist identifies his own body with the body of the city: He continues to mime the origination and growth of Santa Rosalia. Sometimes Pierre has to move out of the way as his arms fly through the air in demonstration of the various ways the evolving city penetrated the pampas. The growth of an impenetrable maze of alleys lined with low buildings that covered approximately the same area as the city of today, took only a few decades. After some time, the wooden houses were replaced with buildings of brick and stone, but the city's basic outline continued to express the lethargic crawl across the pampas, the frantic forays into space and the baseless, neurotic changes of direction of its early days. The winding streets still avoided the rocks and the swamps; the former were dynamited, the latter dried out years ago. When deposits of copper were found in the hills, the government of the time had a new port built and the entire city modernized.

"While the receptionist tells the story of Santa Rosalia, Pierre looks through the glass front of the café in the arcade, which in this part is only dimly lit. Many of its overhead lights are broken and apparently no one can be bothered to repair them. He studies the people who walk through the arcade from both ends—uneasy promenading tourists who have come too far in and are wondering whether to turn back; characters from Molina Boulevard, each with a different frown on his or her face; people who may be heading for August 2nd Boulevard on their way to work or because they are about to commit an assassination. He wonders how he should classify the receptionist; judging by his speech and gesticulation, he is probably a deft, restless individual who moves easily between two worlds, knows the secrets of each, and is at home in both and also in neither.

"The country frequently underwent changes of military government. The junta that came to power when the receptionist's grandfather was in the first grade of elementary school decided to launch a large-scale redevelopment of Santa Rosalia on the Parisian model. The generals consulted for two hours before taking a blunt pencil to a map of the city—which in those days resembled a network of cracks on an old wall—and plotting a bombastic vision of three boulevards combining three large harbors, a quarter of luxury villas, an administrative district and a presidential palace. The original plan was never realized; the current outline of the city is a truncated version of it. The streets A-D, C-E, G-H and H-I are the stumps of what were planned as boulevards that would meet in two monumental squares."

I looked at the page with the map and imagined all the short lines Bernet had spoken of in their full, planned length. This gave me something that resembled a pterodactyl stretching its long neck and opening up its membranous wings.

"The receptionist is in the habit of representing in gestures all the forces involved in the life of the city: When he speaks of the plans of the generals, he doesn't neglect to show the outline of the city by means of his body—the upper half of his body is puffed out as far as it will go, and both his arms are thrust diagonally upward.

"Anyway, the generals summoned Miguel García, the country's most famous architect, and handed him the map of city with their scribbling on it. Immediately García issued a warning: There was a danger of tension from the collision of two worlds in close proximity. He advised that the city should undergo gradual change, where the new streets would connect with existing corridors and allow themselves to be formed by power centers that had emerged in the course of the city's evolution.

"'The new network of streets should reflect the dreams of the old town,' García told the generals quietly. His vocabulary wasn't one that the generals readily understood; they smiled benevolently and said that if the city had dreams, these were dreams of chaos and dilapidation from which it needed to wake up as soon as possible. García answered still more quietly that the city dreamed of dilapidation and of splendid new boulevards and squares, and that it would be worthwhile letting it sleep a little longer and listening to the mumbling of its dreams. The generals reacted to this with a brief explanation that they weren't accustomed to losing time in debate with oversensitive civilians; then they handed him the scribbled-on map and dismissed him. Before even the first stretch of the main boulevard was finished, this junta of generals was overthrown by conspiring colonels. After that, one military government followed another; all rulers adopted the reconstruction plans, all kept García on as chief architect, and none allowed any change to be made to the original plans.

"So García did as the soldiers told him and built new boulevards that cut through the jumble of streets. Feeling troubled and anxious, he redrew the crude lines made in the architect's plans by the generals; with sadness he watched the demolition of old houses and the building of new streets. He worried about what would happen when the old town began to recover from its severe injuries; in his mind's eye he saw a dog in hiding, licking its wounds, gathering its hate. He knew that the new boulevards would form new dark corners; he imagined how places where the sap of the city had run, for good or ill, for generations would suddenly be sealed airtight, and here all the juices of city life would accumulate, spoil and transform into poisons hitherto unknown that would eventually penetrate their surroundings. 'If linearity and symmetry should be tomorrow's order,' he muttered as he drew, 'just imagine what will end up beyond its borders! How many gentle unities, imperceptible harmonies and unstable equilibria will suddenly give way to chaos? All the things that will become enemies of order, and the massive darkness order will have to cope with at any given time, even though it will be ignorant of strategy for such a struggle! Will it have any chance at all of victory?' García didn't hold out much hope for it. He attempted at least to take advantage of the precious few opportunities granted him by the reconstruction plans; for instance, he tried to relieve the tension between the two worlds by turning the lanes near the new streets into arcades, hoping that the life of the main boulevards would spill into them in waves that would create smooth transitions, meeting points and places of conciliation. Still his work filled him with dread: He was afraid that it would result in a place that was far more terrible than the murkiest parts of the current city. He felt as though he were designing Hell.

"García's worst forebodings were realized. Once the reconstruction was complete, the city really did break into two worlds—the remnants of the old town, which became known as the Labyrinth, and the new streets, which the generals termed the Axis. With the birth of wide, light streets, the life of the old town withdrew into a darkness that the view from the Axis couldn't penetrate. Its concealment spawned anxious rumors and a dark mythology of dens and traps; and it seems that the myths and nightmares born in the Axis had a retroactive influence on the life of the Labyrinth, by feeding its imagination and gathering strength in the dark corners of its body. The forces of the Labyrinth soon took on a new rhythm; they pulsated; in certain periods they withdrew, collected themselves and matured in silence; in other periods the mature poisons of the Labyrinth spurted into the body of the Axis through all its pores and paralyzed them; a period of peace and quiet, filled with foreboding in which people saw projections of their worst nightmares, caused greater anxiety to the inhabitants of the Axis than direct assaults mounted from the Labyrinth.

"At first the nervous border with the Labyrinth was formed by the two arc-shaped boulevards, the one named for General Molina to the south and the one named for March 20th to the north. Even in times of calm, when passing the mouths of outer lanes and arcades that led to the Labyrinth, people who lived on these streets tended to quicken their pace, imagining that they heard sighs of slumbering evil from their depths. At that time, August 2nd Boulevard was still relatively well protected from the evils of the Labyrinth, and the arcades that connected it with the other two boulevards were peaceful.

"Pierre interrupts the receptionist's story to ask him what he actually means by the evils of the Labyrinth. Should he imagine criminal gangs, mafiosi, terrorists, insurgent groups, dubious sects, organizations of a suppressed opposition, supporters of past governments, family or ethnic clans, gangs of youths, groups engaged in illegal trade and smuggling? The receptionist opens his arms as wide as they will go—Pierre should imagine all this and much else besides. Whereupon Pierre asks him if he believes that everything these groups did falls into the stark category of evil. Are, for instance, anti-government acts of insurgent evil? Pierre doesn't know details of the situation in the country, of course, but such unequivocal condemnation seems to him unjustified. Moreover, the receptionist doesn't give the impression of a loyal citizen who thinks it necessary in every last case to obey those military officers who happened to come out on top in the last putsch.

"The receptionist smiles and explains that it is impossible to strictly separate the activities of individual groupings at large in the Labyrinth. Some enter the Labyrinth with pure dreams of a struggle against a tyrannical government, others with the intention of using it as a springboard for the mounting of raids on the main boulevards' *bureaux de change* and jeweler's stores, but it is essential to the life of the Labyrinth that all streams come together in a single vortex that draws everything in. This means that the revolutionary takes on traits of the smuggler, the robber of the freedom fighter. The receptionist has used the word 'evil' when speaking of the Labyrinth because this word has been adopted by the inhabitants of the Labyrinth as a challenge to the Axis, which came up with it in the first place. The receptionist doesn't wish to deny them a word they themselves have chosen; talk of the evils of the Labyrinth doesn't mean that among the criminality and vice no devoted friendships, tender love stories, kindnesses, noble sacrifices, acts of generosity or nobility have developed.

"In the Labyrinth, then, only those who allow themselves to be borne on the current that flows through this place, are successful. On the one hand, this has made government propaganda easier—it is easy to label opponents of the regime 'bandits,' as there is some truth in this description; on the other, though, it is difficult to fight something that defies stable categories to such a degree. The ambiguity of life in the Labyrinth corresponds, too, with the equivocal attitude of Axis inhabitants toward the dark outside world that surrounds them. Not that they would attempt to sort out the good sides from the bad, the acceptable from the unacceptable. The receptionist says now that when he spoke of the anxiety they felt at the mouths of side streets and arcades, his description was missing something. The people of the new town do indeed feel anxious at these places, but almost always this anxiety is laced with hope and desire. The mouths of the arcades give them the creeps but also attract them; pedestrians quicken their pace as they pass the arcades, not only for fear of bandits but because they must resist the desire to enter them and vanish into them forever. 'I suppose you understand that,' says the receptionist with a conspiratorial smile, and again Pierre asks himself what kind of man this is.

"The time came when Molina Boulevard and March 20th Boulevard could no longer withstand the onslaught of forces from the Labyrinth and gave up the fight. Gradually the people who lived there moved to August 2nd Boulevard, and the houses and mansions they left empty were infiltrated by figures from the Labyrinth, some garish, others gray and shadowlike. The Axis gave up the fight at this line; it drew back and fortified its position on the city's longest boulevard. Soon the Labyrinth swallowed up Molina Boulevard and March 20th Boulevard and transformed them according to its taste. Thus originated the strange world that had so surprised Pierre—a world of broad, empty boulevards, mansions with shabby facades, rampant vegetation on balconies. The battle lines drew closer to the main boulevard; the unsettled life of the Labyrinth penetrated ever further into the arcades that led onto August 2nd Boulevard. Soon the dark surf reached the business zones that García had located in the arcades, and the businesses retreated in terror, toward the mouths of the arcades, where they were within reach of light from the main street. Even so, people today are mistrustful of these businesses; it is rumored that their true owners are leaders of gangs or insurgent groups from the Labyrinth, and that the stores are the eyes through which the Labyrinth brazenly watches the main boulevard and monitors what goes on there.

"It transpired that García's idea of balancing the tension between zones of the city by means of arcades was not a happy one. Instead of relieving tension, the arcades became channels through which the wild energy of the Labyrinth flowed onto the main street. When the mouths of arcades became dangerous places, it was proposed that the arcades should be dammed. The counterargument to this, probably a good one, was that the sealing-off of the Labyrinth would mean the expiration of the last remnants of its connection with the Axis, and that a separate, invisible old town might become a terrifying monster with unpredictable behavior. These voices were joined by others whose motives weren't so pure. On the side of power there have always been many people with a special interest in ensuring that the airholes between the Axis and the Labyrinth remain open. The two worlds aren't always hostile to each other—there came a time when various types of cooperation were forged; the less visible these were, the more effective they seemed to be.

"Although the world of power is apparently seamless, what gives the impression of unity is in fact a fragile balance that is forever being disturbed and reconstituted based on the struggle of many forces. And all these battling forces seek help in the Labyrinth. One advantage of such links is that whoever turns to the Labyrinth with a request for help needn't worry about the appearance of legality. On the other hand, if he wishes to succeed in his dealings with the Labyrinth and navigate its power centers, he must know his way around its complex, unwritten, ever-changing protocol. Knowledge of the Labyrinth's logic (if there is any such thing) is less important than knowledge of its choreography; anyone who enters the old town in search of allies should have a feel for the rhythms of the Labyrinth and an ability to react to them subtly, otherwise there is a danger that he will never return. This is how lively relations are maintained between the Labyrinth and August 2nd Boulevard, and also between the Labyrinth and the residential quarter, and even the presidential palace. Those within the circle of power turn to the gangs and rebel groups of the Labyrinth for help with various disputes, often reciprocating by making it possible for the children of their helpers to leave the Labyrinth and by keeping a protective eye on them as they make their way in society.

"In this way, families that remain deeply rooted in the Labyrinth have their suckers on the territory of the Axis. And when people from the Labyrinth—thanks to their erstwhile clients and present-day protectors—have gained a foothold, they maintain their bonds with where they came from; such links form a capillary network by which moods and dreams of the Labyrinth flow ceaselessly, along with the quiet hum of the old town, to the center of power. Decisions coming from the presidential palace have often expressed the desires and concerns of the Labyrinth; the receptionist explains that many apparently incomprehensible orders and laws are grasped easily when we concentrate on the ceaseless flow of forces between the Labyrinth and the Axis. There is a joke in the city that the true seat of government is the Labyrinth; no one knows the extent to which this is a confirmation of the reality.

"There is also a movement in the opposite direction, explains the receptionist, whose arms are aching from his unceasing depiction of the power flow in Santa Rosalia. Those who lose their battles at the center of power and are threatened by reprisals, disappear into the Labyrinth, where they are practically uncapturable. Once there, some resign themselves to their fate, lie on the crumbling terraces and allow themselves to be pervaded by the lassitude that at certain periods spreads through the Labyrinth like an infection; others, though, make effective use of the currents that flow from the Labyrinth to the center, so achieving from their grim hovels aims that they failed to realize in ministerial office.

"When the excesses become too obvious or enduring and the people of the Axis begin to grumble, punitive expeditions are sent into the Labyrinth. Typically these accomplish nothing; it is never clear whether their failure is due to the fact many commanders come from the Labyrinth and friends and relatives have been warned in advance, or because these commanders have received verbal orders from on high not to be overzealous and so damage good relations between the authorities and the chaos of the old town.

"So the powers of the city are in constant circulation, says the receptionist. People from the Labyrinth make it to the great boulevards, to the residential and government quarters and eventually to the presidential palace; on the other hand, people can slip into the Labyrinth and vanish there. So it happens that a man who in his youth was a member of a dreaded gang meets on the staircase of a luxury house on the main boulevard or in the corridor of a ministerial palace a member of the government who was once a client of his, has just been disgraced and is about to head in the opposite direction, on a journey that will end in the Labyrinth in some dark hole. It can also happen that a ministerial official is promoted to a new post only to discover that his boss is a man who once, in the middle of a dark arcade, pounced on the former minister with a dagger in his hand."

Chapter 51
Beatriz

Andrea and Barbora carried lounge chairs over to where we were sitting. Their eyes closed, they lay exposed to the rays of the sun and continued to listen to Bernet's story. The water in the pool sloshed quietly.

"As the receptionist speaks about the city, the gestures that show the swirling of its forces every now and then become waves, as he greets some figure on the other side of the glass. Sometimes a passer-by draws attention to himself by tapping on the window. Pierre wonders whether the receptionist knows everyone who lives in the Axis as well as every inhabitant of the Labyrinth. The pedestrians beyond the glass wave, too, and some come into the café, sit down at their table for a while and exchange a few words with the receptionist about matters that Pierre doesn't understand. As the receptionist is telling of the failed military expeditions into the Labyrinth, a slim woman appears on the other side of the window; she has come from Molina Boulevard and is deep in thought. The receptionist taps on the glass and the woman turns her head in his direction. Instantly Pierre recognizes the face as the one that was studying the window display of the gallery during yesterday's attack.

"The woman comes into the café and sits down at their table. The receptionist introduces his friend as Beatriz. She and the receptionist speak of people who are evidently common friends or relatives. During this conversation, Pierre studies her face:

It is stern but eager, and paler than is usual in these parts. He can't make up his mind whether the arcs of her eyebrows, which almost touch, and her pursed lips express a habit of contemplation or a morbid obsession with some fixed idea. It occurs to him that he hasn't seen another such face on the main boulevard. He notices, too, that the woman's eyes occasionally move away from the receptionist's face, wander about the room and then come back again; this reminds him of the way a soldier of the advanced guard inspects the danger represented by the edge of a wood on the hillside opposite. This vigilance, he tells himself, must have originated during a stay in the unsettled old town, and it is now written into the woman's features in a script that tells of the anxiety, weariness and sorrow of the Labyrinth. After a while, though, he realizes that something glows behind this script—an older text conveying something of a long-ago world of luxury and pride. He remembers what the receptionist told him of the journey made by some of the city's inhabitants from one place to the other; he has the feeling that the woman has passed through many of the city's territories, and that all of them have left traces in her face.

"Although it seems that the receptionist is fully occupied by the conversation and the demands of his gesticulation, apparently he has managed to monitor Pierre's keen interest in Beatriz, by which he seems to be rather amused. Deftly the receptionist draws Pierre into the conversation. When Pierre and Beatriz move on from the landmarks of the city to a shared fondness for literature, the receptionist announces that he must be going and then makes himself scarce. Pierre wonders if his activities include that of matchmaker, or whether his walking about the arcades has developed in him an amused fondness for bringing together different worlds and then watching what becomes of these connections.

"Pierre and Beatriz talk about art and literature, and about the city and its history. Beatriz speaks only of famous buildings, and she tells him about writers and painters who have lived in the city, and their works; not once does she touch on any of the subjects the receptionist has just told him about in such detail. Pierre learns nothing from her about the development of the city, or the succession of military governments, or the subtle power games and forces that circulate around different parts of the city. They arrange another meeting. That day Pierre doesn't go to the travel agent's, so he doesn't buy a ticket for the ship and he doesn't get on that ship. Although he and Beatriz meet every day, he doesn't let on that he saw her on the main boulevard on the day of the assassination. Several times he postpones his departure. Gradually Beatriz begins to trust him. She introduces him to her friends, who seem to Pierre to be well-mannered, well-educated young men. She meets them in cafés located in the middle of arcades, on the border between the two worlds. If on his first day in Santa Rosalia he hadn't witnessed an assassination in which Beatriz was apparently involved, he would have taken them for a group of local intellectuals. Yet he is in no doubt that this is one of the insurgent groups that dwell in the Labyrinth. Their glances, moments of silence, and sentences interrupted halfway take on new significance. The gallantry the men display toward Beatriz is mixed with military respect, deference to a superior; it is clear to Pierre that Beatriz is commander of the group. He never asks about anything, and neither Beatriz nor her friends speak to him about their affairs, even though they know that Pierre has figured out what they do. They have been playing this game for a month when Pierre realizes that he is unable to leave Beatriz."

Zachary hurried up to the table and handed Bernet a letter that evidently had just arrived by fax. Bernet looked at the letter and frowned; it seemingly brought bad news from the stock exchange, or maybe even from the prosecutor's office. For a moment I had the impression that he was hesitating over what to do, but then he laid the document on the table and weighed it down with the ashtray. Although yesterday he had decided to defend his property, now it was difficult for him to tear himself away from his story for it, no matter that the letter obviously demanded an urgent reply: Zachary continued to fidget in agitation next to the wicker armchair, leaving dissatisfied only once it was plain to him that Bernet truly had no intention of dealing with the message at that moment. As he walked away, several times he turned to check whether Bernet had changed his mind.

"Several times Pierre visits Beatriz in her vast, almost empty apartment in one of the derelict mansions of Molina Boulevard," Bernet went on. "The apartment comprises a series of large rooms that have hardly any furniture in them. The high, cream-colored doors between these rooms are open at all times. It is here that one quiet afternoon Beatriz decides to tell him her entire life story. Her words don't come to Pierre as much of a surprise; in fact, he learns only details of a picture he has long ago painted for himself. He discovers that her father had been secretary of state in a previous government, and that he lost his life when soldiers attacked the presidential palace. Like many others, Beatriz, who was a college student at that time, disappeared into the Labyrinth, where she gathered her peers, mostly former schoolmates, around her and formed one of the city's many guerilla groups that operated from the Labyrinth; all the men took it for granted that she would be their commander.

"When Beatriz has finished her story, Pierre feels that he should tell her something important, so he tells her of his love for her. He isn't sure if love is the right word for the agonizing bond that won't allow him to distance himself from her (sometimes he has the impression that his fascination is with the enticing spaces of the Labyrinth that have seeped into Beatriz's face and gestures), but he considers it pointless to talk about his doubts. Then they make love on the scuffed couch, their breath mingling with the muted sounds of cars that reach them from August 2nd Boulevard and the rustling of peeling wallpaper in the breeze that now and then rushes through the series of empty, sunlit rooms. Pierre quits the hotel and moves into Beatriz's apartment. As he is leaving, the receptionist bows to him from behind the desk with a respectful, wry smile on his face.

"Pierre transfers all his Paris savings to a local bank; he leaves everything behind and gradually stops thinking about returning to Europe. He can no longer imagine life without Beatriz. At first he wonders whether he is bound to the woman, the great mysterious animal of the city, the constant whisper of adventure roused from a long-forgotten child's dream, or those quiet, sunlit hours in Beatriz's apartment on Molina Boulevard—but then he lets these deliberations alone; it is too hot, and even if he were able to resolve the matter, it would change nothing in his life. Another reason he doesn't think about these things is his happiness, even though in Europe such happiness would terrify him and seem to him sicker and more destructive than a junky's enjoyment of his drugs.

"He doesn't want to think about what binds Beatriz to him, but once, when he is lying on the couch, alone in the apartment, watching specks of dust swirling in slanting columns of light, it occurs to him that his girlfriend desperately needs to be close to a foreigner, someone unconnected with the hopeless enterprise to which she has devoted her whole adult life; someone who is not imbued with forces of any of the spaces of Santa Rosalia and represents the blissful possibility of escape, a dream of a different city and a different world. On days when Beatriz is not involved in an operation, they spend long hours in her apartment, lying on the couch in an embrace, not speaking, listening to the sounds of silence that always prevail on Molina Boulevard. Pierre feels himself becoming an inhabitant of the Labyrinth, and he worries that Beatriz will leave him and find herself another foreigner. But in fact she could never give him up: She feels good with him because he doesn't force her into any role, never judges her actions and asks no questions, and she has grown accustomed to his tight-lipped presence that speaks to her in well-known voices of silence in empty rooms, meanwhile flooding her with tenderness and kindness."

How strange, I thought, that the talk was again of sounds of silence. I thought of Chuh-yuh's nighttime sonata. Was this just a coincidence? But I didn't dwell on this thought; I could feel that the summer heat was affecting me in a similar way to the heat of the tropics working on the hero of the French novel; the tension between the discontinuous fragments disappeared because the heat fused them together, creating a structure that was bizarre but solid.

Chapter 52
Opalescent Angel

"Pierre never participates directly in the activities of the group. When Beatriz is away, he waits anxiously in the empty apartment, and he always heaves a sigh of relief when he hears her footfalls on the stairs. Sometimes it happens that Beatriz is brought in wounded, and then he tends her back to health. When meetings of the group are held in the apartment, he sits in silence on a couch in a corner of the room and listens. Soon he realizes that all the arguments conducted here are parts of a single dispute. This dispute is over the extent to which it is necessary to engage with the play of forces between the Labyrinth and the other parts of the city that has been established over several decades. This is the play that the receptionist described to Pierre so exactly on only his second day in the city. Beatriz stubbornly refuses any form of engagement. For her, to give up the struggle and submit to the flow of forces and their strange, regular gyrations in different spaces of the city would be the most desperate defeat imaginable.

"But such an attitude condemns the group to full dependence on its own feeble strength, which is why Beatriz's friends turn against it in ever greater numbers. Arguments become fiercer, for the first time people quit the group, and in the quiet house on Molina Boulevard shouts and banging doors are heard. A faction emerges that is ever more vocal in its insistence that the group's activities are paralyzed by its refusal to tarnish its ideals by some kind of impure alliance—for the simple reason that in the Labyrinth there is no chance of encountering forces that are entirely pure. After several months of arguments, this faction breaks away. Others leave for different reasons: By now they are so tired that even the slight activity in which the forlorn, shrinking group now engages is too demanding for them; at meetings they become quieter, until they sit there as silent as Pierre (indeed, some of them even join him on the couch); one day they fail to appear, and after that they never come again. Pierre often thinks of them; he wonders if they have settled in the Labyrinth in some closed place or have plunged into the stream, so disdained by Beatriz, that flows through the city, letting it bear them away to illuminated streets. There is one more reason why some men leave the group: When they joined it, they were in love with Beatriz—as their love fades away, so, too, do they."

"I'd have thought that some of the group's members hated and despised Pierre from the very beginning," I said. "He comes from elsewhere, he doesn't risk his life as they do, yet he wins the favor of the woman that probably all of them are in love with, some more than others."

"Not at all—everyone likes Pierre," said Andrea without opening her eyes.

"Andrea's right," said Bernet. "Surprisingly, all these urban guerillas really do like Pierre. For each of them, the greatest worry, albeit an unspoken one, is the prospect of Beatriz favoring someone else from the group, as that would change completely a balance of power where up till now everyone in the group has been equal under Beatriz's leadership. They know that the group wouldn't survive such a change; the men would part with feelings of bitterness and resentment that would take a long time to die. They like Pierre because he has rid them of such a worry; the fact that Beatriz has started to live with a foreigner who has nothing in common with their work, has brought them all relief, although none of them would admit this.

"Some years later, another reason is added to why men leave the group: The regime that in the early days was very tough, gradually becomes more moderate. As a result of this, the activities of all urban guerilla groups peter out. With feelings of relief and regret, the conspirators take this development on board; Beatriz, though, refuses to accept that the old game has ended without any side having won, rather like chess players devoting ever less attention and time to their game and finally getting up from the board with some pieces still standing. The expansion of the Labyrinth comes to an end, the pressure system changes and the forces begin to flow in the opposite direction. The border between the Labyrinth and the Axis slowly begins to blur; the calm life of the Axis penetrates ever deeper into the arcades, as is apparent from the stores and restaurants, until in the end its surf washes up on General Molina Boulevard and March 20th Boulevard and the stream of luxury and lights spills, too, into the streets off the circus with the Poseidon fountain, proceeding from house to house until it almost reaches the place where Pierre lives with Beatriz. Having got used to the banging of workmen's hammers breaking down old plaster, one evening they look from the windows of their apartment toward a bend in the road and see a palm tree in colorful neon over the entrance of a newly-opened bar.

"So the operations of the group abate gradually for many reasons. In the end, only two or three devoted members remain. On their occasional meetings at Beatriz and Pierre's apartment, Beatriz continues to pretend that they are conspiring, convincing herself that they are discussing plans that will be implemented as soon as the group recovers from its temporary faintness. Pierre sees from his couch, however, that they visit only because they want to meet up once in a while with Beatriz, whom they used to love, and perhaps also with him, and he understands, too, that the talk is no longer of plans but of ideas and dreams. And as no one apart from Beatriz counts on these dreams ever becoming reality, the topics of conversation become ever more illusory. Seeing that the conversation has glided over into the realm of fantasy, after years of silence Pierre begins to participate, developing colorful visions that deliver the visitors to pleasant dreams; Beatriz listens to these with a solemn expression."

From their lounger chairs, the girls continued to listen with such rapt attention, it was as though they had never read the book. Although they didn't dare to interrupt Bernet, now that he had paused for a drink of water, they called over to him: "Don't forget the opalescent angel!"

"Don't be so impatient. I was just getting to that," said Bernet, as he put down his glass. I was impressed by the amiable patience he showed in his dealings with the girls, and also by the tenderness and admiration that flickered in Barbora and Andrea's every word, even when they were angry with Bernet; and I realized that the relationship of these three people—this love affair between a rich man and two young women that everyone condemned in outrage, of which I, too, might have thought badly before I met them—was perhaps the most wonderful thing I had encountered in my search for Viola.

"At that time, one of the visitors arrives with a tale of an underground corridor, which he overheard in some café. The city's drainage system was built somewhat chaotically before the great reconstruction, and no plans of it existed. So it happened that workmen developing the Axis came across a sewer connecting the Labyrinth with the site of the presidential palace, which was then under construction. The entrance to the sewer was in one of the Labyrinth's many cellars. One of the men involved in the building work drew on a map of the city the exact place where the sewer could be entered. He hid this map in a lamp that was actually a hollow figurine of an angel made of opalescent glass. The winged figure was unscrewed from the base, which contained a socket for the bulb and had an electrical cord running from its bottom. Similar figurines of angels and saints are often found on family altars in the provinces and in poorer parts of the city. The folded map is said to be hidden in the space between the socket and the stand casing.

"Years earlier, the workman died in an on-site accident, and the lamp and its map were lost. Since that time it has been wandering about the Labyrinth in the form of a legend. Such reports are mentioned in the apartment on Molina Boulevard quite often. But this tale more than most bears marks of urban legend or daydream, and not even the man who has come with it believes it. Beatriz hears it out with the same solemnity she demonstrates in listening to all such legends. Although it doesn't cross his mind that this story could be true, Pierre likes the idea of a shining angel with a sketch of an underground corridor hidden inside, so he helps Beatriz as she immediately begins to develop fantastical plans for an attack on the presidential palace.

"Visits become rarer, and Beatriz and Pierre spend most of their time in the quiet rooms alone. Beatriz sinks ever deeper into her dreams, perfecting this to a kind of art: At first her dreams are the bland, translucent and unstable matter of daydreams, but she succeeds in solidifying them and filling them with color to such a degree that they are almost equals of the colored substance from which real perceptions are cut (especially if in their life the world of perceptions has long been limited to the whirling of dust in columns of light, the monotonous pattern of wallpaper faded by the sun and the channels in the corduroy covering of the couch); she succeeds, too, in drawing them out ever further, so that a single continuous dream can now last a whole day. In every story she dreams, at a certain moment a shining angel figurine appears and the entrance to a dark sewer is opened.

"Pierre knows little about her theater of dreams, although he appears in almost every performance, often in the role of future enlightened ruler of the country. The inaction that governs their life, suits Pierre. For years now, he has wished for only one thing: to be with Beatriz, even though he has never known if their union is a sickness, a vice, or the greatest good fortune ever to have come his way. Now, at last, he has Beatriz to himself, and he no longer has to wait nervously in the empty apartment for her to return from the group's operations. The anti-government struggle never really mattered to him, not even at the time when he was new in the country; to him, the ruling government wasn't much worse than the government in whose name the group was acting. He took an interest in the rebellion against the authorities as he would have enjoyed a wild local dance in which he was moved by Beatriz's gestures."

"What do the two of them live on all this time? Pierre's savings from Paris?" I asked.

"They live modestly, and the Labyrinth isn't expensive, and in this way Pierre's savings hold out for fifteen years. After this, former members of the group, now long-time residents of August 2nd Boulevard employed in government offices, pass through the arcades to the well-known house, bringing food and money for them. Beatriz accepts all this as a loan to be returned once the government falls and she can return to her family's villa in the residential quarter. She leaves the apartment ever less. Pierre does the shopping, making long expeditions deep into the Labyrinth, getting to know all its hiding places better than most people who were born there. Often he sits at a table in front of a taproom and empties one glass after another, or on the pier in the old harbor, where he watches the waves for a long time. On other evenings, he passes through the arcades to August 2nd Boulevard and walks about among its lights, studying the windows of bookstores, finding books that were banned even by the government in which Beatriz's father served; when he returns to Beatriz, he never tells her of this. One of his wanders takes him to a particularly remote part of the Labyrinth, where he gets lost in narrow streets whose houses have survived from the city's early days. He looks into the window of a thrift store and there, among the junk, he sees . . ."

"The opalescent angel," I said.

"That's right, the opalescent angel, with an electrical cord wrapped around its base. Of course, it's highly improbable that the plan of the sewer is hidden in the lamp—but Pierre senses that if the wall that divides reality from dream is ruptured once, it won't mend easily. It seems to him that the dream is about to seep into reality through this crack he has just happened upon. For a long time he stands irresolute in front of the store, wondering whether to walk away and try to forget that he has seen the angel, or to take the angel to Beatriz. With foreboding he imagines all the things that the opalescent angel may set in motion; but then it strikes him that in this city he has always gained by shaking the hand of fate. He doesn't know whether his compliant acceptance of fate's call is a manifestation of courage or cowardice, nor does he particularly care; but he does know that it has rewarded him with a life that he would trade for no other, even though his old friends in Europe would think it a desperate one. So he decides to accept fate's offer this time, too: He buys the lamp and takes it home. As Beatriz unscrews it, her hands are shaking. Neither she nor Pierre are in any way surprised to find in the base a carefully folded piece of paper bearing the plan of a sewer system that leads to the cellars of the presidential palace.

"Immediately Beatriz sends messages to the few friends who still visit them: At last the time has come for the operation they have spoken of for so many years. Some of them excuse themselves on grounds of poor health, others tell her straight out that for all these years they have considered the plan to attack the palace a foolish dream. Beatriz tells them all that they are traitors. Their refusal only hardens her resolve, and she prepares to break into the palace herself. It doesn't cross her mind that Pierre might go with her: Even after twenty years, he is still a foreigner who has nothing to do with her struggle against the government. Pierre tries to talk her around. For the first time, he tells her of the books in the windows of the stores on August 2nd Boulevard, but she doesn't listen to him. So Pierre simply tells her that he is going with her.

"One evening they load a carryall with guns and flashlights and set out. In the cellar of the house marked on the map, they open a dusty hatch and descend a metal ladder into the cold depths. For a long time they wade through stinking water, the beams of their flashlights wandering the damp walls. On the spot marked on the map as the point of ascent into the presidential palace, they see a rusty ladder sticking out of a metal shaft; this ladder climbs to another hatch. They climb up the shaft and reach a wheel that is attached to a rusted-in screw. Pierre hopes that the wheel will refuse to budge and they will have to turn back, and this whole crazy adventure will end, but after a while he feels the wheel beginning to turn. They crawl through the circular hole to find themselves in what appears to be a lumber room. Pierre hopes that the door out of this room will be locked, but Beatriz reaches for the handle and they find themselves in a dark, quiet corridor with many high doors along both sides. They switch off their flashlights and take the guns out of the carryall . . .

"At this point the book ends. The author doesn't tell his readers whether Pierre and Beatriz manage to assassinate the country's ruler, whether Beatriz realizes the foolishness of her dream and suggests that they turn back, whether they are arrested or shot by palace guards . . ."

Chapter 53
Conversation by the Pool

For a while none of us spoke. Through narrowed eyes I watched the glittering light on the waves of the pool and I listened to their splashing. At last I said, "It seems to me we've all seen something of our own affairs in that story. To tell the truth, I don't know what to think about it. Maybe it does contain a clue for us, but it may also be one of the false clues that lead us off the trail."

"Perhaps it contains a clue for some, while leading others off the trail," Andrea pointed out.

"The book speaks explicitly neither of hidden treasure nor a missing girl," said Bernet, "although it seems to me that there's an echo of Viola's disappearance in the theme of the woman who goes to the dark parts of the city and refuses to return . . ."

". . . .hile an echo of your search for treasure can be heard in the motif of Beatriz's long-time dream about an angel figurine hidden somewhere in the city," I added.

"Hold on," said Andrea. "Something's not right here. I accept the connection between the angel and the treasure, but how can the novel contain an echo of Viola's disappearance when the book was published in '86? As far as I know, an echo isn't usually produced before the sound it repeats. How old would Viola have been then?"

"Eleven," I said, "But that doesn't disturb me much. In my search for Viola I keep coming across things like this. This case seems to do strange things with time; it's as if the recent past had the ability to influence the distant past. The owner of the music store, too, told me that he had the feeling that Chuh-yuh and Viola were meeting for the first time but at the same time that they knew each other already. And I had the strong impression that there were all sorts of echoes of Viola's disappearance in the story of Dionysius of Gaza, who lived in the sixth century."

"Does this story in which all four of us, so it seems, play some kind of role, contain a time machine as well as pirates' treasure and an underground monster?" said Barbora.

"I wouldn't be against that," laughed Bernet. "But I don't think it will be necessary. Above all, the connection between the plot of the novel and the case of Viola, about which we actually know nothing for definite, is so weak that it's probably just a coincidence, so there's no need to look for a time machine. And if there really is some similarity between the stories of Viola and Beatriz, it may simply have arisen because Viola read the book somewhere and consciously or subconsciously imitated it."

"Or the author and Viola departed from a common source, but while the author developed it in fiction, Viola did so in real life," suggested Andrea.

"Or the novel and Viola's story are just two voices in a long line of echoes that may reach back to the sixth century or even deeper into the past," said Barbora.

"And which will continue into the future, and the centuries to come . . ." said Bernet.

"The lines may at some point have branched off into several lines, and these may have passed through various lands before meeting up again," Andrea added.

"Yes, maybe the points of agreement among the case of Viola Jonášová, the case of the pirates' treasure, and the plot of the French novel are simply the result of the accidental crossing of three lines that have long lived independent lives; maybe each of them comes from a different place on Earth and is heading in a different direction . . ." I pondered.

"And the baobab is the thing that moves along all lines and connects them," added Barbora.

"That's enough," said Bernet. "Such theories aren't bad, but they don't help us much. It would serve us better to consider what the novel can really tell us about our own concern."

"Okay, let's give it a try," I said. "Your concern, if I'm not mistaken, is the search for treasure from a pirates' ship. Although I can't find in the plot of the novel any definite message about where you should look or whom you should seek out, I'd say that the episode with the opalescent angel tells you something about how to go about your search—namely that the truest clue may appear at first glance to be the most fantastical. And that is a pretty positive message; you've succeeded in being faithful to a single childhood experience that probably no one else would have taken seriously."

"But the meaning of the story may also act as a warning that such fantastical clues lead us to disaster," sighed Bernet. "Don't forget that the novel's end is open; it allows for various possibilities, but it doesn't seem to me that a happy ending is among them."

"What are you talking about? That's not true!" said Barbora angrily. "The novel really does end happily. It's great that Beatriz gets into the presidential palace. What happens afterwards, that's just secondary and unimportant."

Bernet was probably about to answer that for Beatriz and Pierre, whether the palace guards were about to shoot them was hardly secondary and unimportant. I was afraid that the girls would again start to argue with Bernet about his principles, so I hurried to ask Bernet what he thought the story had to tell me.

"As far as I know, your concern is the search for a missing girl," Bernet said. "I don't see any definite clue in the novel's plot either, but maybe Pierre's story is telling you that a person can be lost to the world for reasons that are difficult to detect because even the lost person doesn't understand properly what they are—meaning that it's not a good idea to look for logic in something where there may be no logic at all."

"If that's the book's message, it's not a very cheering one," I said. "So far the search for Viola has foundered on the lack of clues rather than the impossibility of finding connections among them. If it were to turn out now that the connections I've tried to discover were not only unclear but non-existent, my case would look pretty bad. It would be as though I'd been trying to decipher symbols on a wall that weren't in fact letters but just random scratches . . ."

"Don't take it like that," Barbora said to me. "I don't think you should worry too much about whether or not the clues you've encountered belong in a group that is bound together by some kind of logic—a melody, a rhythm or harmony that can lead you."

"I think I know what you mean," I said wearily. "But my trouble isn't that I've heard in the clues no melody that might lead me, but that there are so many of these melodies, each completely different from all the others, each leading me in a different direction . . ."

Neither the girls nor Bernet had any answer to this. A silence fell over us again. Then Bernet said: "I'd happily help you in your search, but Barbora and Andrea told me that they offered you help and you refused it. I won't try to persuade you, because I think that you're right: You probably have to search on your own, as do I, Andrea and Barbora . . ."

"So you'll keep looking for the treasure, then?" said Andrea in delight.

"I really don't know yet," Bernet said quietly. "I can't decide. I seem to be making a mess of everything at the moment—I've lost my way to the treasure, I'm not managing to hang on to my assets . . . As to the assets, I don't even know if I've still got any—the news Zachary just brought is bad. The worst thing of all would be if I were to lose you two."

"Don't worry, we'll stay with you," said Andrea.

"We'll be more patient," said Barbora.

"And we won't be so strict with you," Andrea added. "You'll see, things'll be just as they used to be. I'm sure we'll find Captain Boustrophedon's treasure together."

The girls got up from their lounger chairs and each took one of Bernet's hands. I could see that the three of them wanted to be alone now, so I, too, stood up. As I prepared to say goodbye I told them, "I won't forget to let you know if I find anything that may relate to the treasure."

Bernet and the girls accompanied me across the lawn to the gate, which swung open soundlessly at our approach; once I was on the sidewalk, it closed behind me with a barely audible click. I turned to see Bernet and the girls standing on the lawn beyond the bars, waving to me. I waved too. The girls ran back to the pool, but Bernet stood at the gate a while longer. We smiled at each other, but neither of us spoke. I wondered what fate had in store for this kindly immoralist, this impractical self-made man. Would he find his treasure, and would he manage to save his fortune? I didn't hold out much hope for him in either case. Now that Bernet had hesitated once on his dizzying trapeze, it seemed to me barely possible that he should rediscover his former lightness.

I wondered, too, if his girls would stay with him. I had the impression that were they to leave him, Bernet would lose the desire to look for the treasure and save his assets. Maybe he would gradually close in on himself and again become the silent, dreamy child the architect used to know; maybe he would live in a cubbyhole somewhere, and his millionaire's life in his white villa would come to seem like a dream to him. Although the girls had claimed that they would never leave him, and they believed this themselves, I had the feeling that an ordinary life with boring, everyday worries would be too severe a test for them. It was also perfectly possible that only one of them would stay with him; I wondered if it would be quick-tempered Andrea or understanding Barbora. Bernet still stood in silence on the other side of the gate; perhaps he was thinking of my future just as I was thinking of his. We each gave the other a last smile and a last wave and then went our separate ways, Bernet back to the villa and his girls, I down the hill to the streetcar terminus.

Chapter 54
At the Institute

Which trail should I follow now? I asked myself as I walked. All trails had gone cold, I realized. I'd followed every trail I had and none of them had led me anywhere. Had I really reached the end of my search for Viola Jonášová? All the evidence suggested that I had. I felt sad. Would these fragments of an unknown story keep coming back to me till the end of my life, dressed in dreams? I went over all the clues I'd come across and asked myself if any of them still had anything to tell me. Apparently just one course of action remained to me: I would try and find out more about Dionysius of Gaza. Perhaps I would find the kind of clue I was looking for in his writings or in some detail of his life that the porter hadn't mentioned. Though at first glance there was little chance of an ancient philosopher solving the case of a missing girl, on the other hand Dionysius's life and work provided the trail that went back the furthest, and as such they might contain the roots of all other trails.

I remembered a taciturn man with a thick, drooping mustache whose book on the ethics of Plato had been published by my recent employer. Wirth was a recognized expert in Greek philosophy, especially Neoplatonism. He was sure to be able to tell me something about Dionysius and could probably show me the kind of philosophical writings I was looking for. Close to the kiosk and the bench where the architect had told me the story of Bernet, I found a telephone booth. In the Yellow Pages I looked up the address of the institute where Wirth worked. By now it was late in the afternoon, so I decided to put my visit off until tomorrow.

The next day I slept late, and I didn't set out for Wirth's institute until after lunch. It was housed in a spacious two-story square building with a pitched red roof; it was shaded by chestnut trees. Originally, I supposed, this was a farm that had been outflanked and swallowed up the advancing city, which now, several decades on, was trying to rid it of its rural character. But its wide driveway retained the smell exhaled by country houses on hot summer days, and I glimpsed a yard—with a water pump painted green standing between two chestnut trees—that put me in mind of a village square. The institute took up the whole second floor of the building. The offices were approached through a gallery leading to a square courtyard which you could walk all the way around. I reached the gallery via some rickety wooden stairs and walked past a series of doors, most of which were open because of the heat; the offices beyond the doors were narrow and dark. It was very quiet here; all I heard—from somewhere across the yard—was the hum of computer printers, a pleasing, hypnotic sound of the early afternoon of a summer's day in a village.

I saw a heavyset figure that practically filled a kind of apse at the end of the room formed by books and papers stacked on the floor either side of the desk. This was Wirth, without a doubt. From the back he looked pitiful, as though a great evil hand had used his body to plug a gap in the paper mass and he was waiting helplessly for someone to pull him out. I knocked on the open door, and Wirth turned to me. Seeing him in this environment, it occurred to me that his thickset, almost neckless figure had been formed by many years spent bent before his wobbly columns of books and papers. The overfilled shelves leaned at dangerous angles and appeared about to collapse. His face wore its usual somber expression, although he raised his eyebrows—which were as thick as his mustache—in surprise at seeing me there. He gestured wordlessly at an empty chair. I sat with my back to the door. The room was so small that our knees touched. Through the open window above the desk, I could see part of the facade of the apartment building across the way. What remained of the country smell was now lost in the smell of printed paper; the illusion of an afternoon in the country had vanished. I explained to Wirth that I had come to see him because I wanted to know more about Dionysius of Gaza.

"Dionysius of Gaza? Who would that be?" said Wirth, his brow puckered.

Could it be that he'd never heard of him? I was confused. "I mean the Neoplatonist philosopher who went to Persia with Damascius and Simplicius after the Academy was closed."

For a moment he looked at me as a visitor to the zoo looks at a wolverine in a cage.

"No such person existed," he stated baldly, before going on to add: "Unless I haven't gotten to hear of the very recent discovery of a manuscript—which I very much doubt."

"But Dionysius's works were published in the nineteenth century . . ." I began to object.

"Interesting," he said, continuing to scrutinize me. "Can you tell me where you read about this Dionysius?"

I was about to tell Wirth that I'd learned about Dionysius from a porter at a company that produced office machines when I realized that he wouldn't take this as a convincing argument in support of Dionysius's existence. How could I explain to him that as the porter was telling me about Dionysius I'd seen his figure and gestures and heard his voice so clearly that it hadn't crossed my mind for a second that he wasn't real? Why would the porter make up such a complicated story? Or was he himself the victim of a hoax? Wirth briefly enjoyed my embarrassment before turning wordlessly to his computer. It took him a moment or two to dig out his keyboard from among the heaps of paper. He connected to the net and punched in the words DIONYSIUS OF GAZA. Both of us stared at the screen in silence. Seconds later the reply appeared: NO MATCH FOUND.

Wirth then employed all possible search engines in an attempt to turn up any of the following in conjunction with Gaza: Dionysius, Dionysios, Dionys, Denis. All kinds of things were offered, but there was no Dionysius of Gaza anywhere on the net. Wirth turned back to me with his eyebrows raised in amusement; it was as though he wanted to say to me: "That's that, then. Anything else I can do for you?" I didn't know what to think. I asked him to type in "Archibald Archer" and see what he could find. There were a number of references and links to various Archers, none of whom had the first name Archibald and none of whom was an archaeologist or an explorer. Furthermore, the inventor of the typewriter was not called Archer.

As I looked at the illuminated screen and through the window at the wall of the old house, suddenly I understood. I remembered how the porter had lured me into his lodge and how important it had been for him that I listen to his story. I remembered his lament about his sick eyes, his unusual hospitality and the bottle of expensive wine. Now I had the sense that I saw his whole life clearly: After he was forbidden to do his work, the only joy that remained in his life of solitude was the reading of history books; and this gave him such pleasure that after the changes he didn't even try to find work in his field; but when his eyes became so sick that he was no longer able to read, just a single amusement was left to him—as he sat there in the porter's lodge, he thought up stories about the things that surrounded him. He invested these stories with his knowledge of history and philosophy and what he remembered from the adventure stories he had read in his childhood. In this way, his view of the big symbol on the wall had inspired the tale of a neurotic Greek philosopher and an English adventurer. By now I was convinced that if I were to ask him about his fountain pen, the old lamp on his desk or the yellow forklift truck that was parked just beyond the window of the porter's lodge, he would be able to tell me a story of the same length about that.

I didn't suspect him of simply wishing to trick me. Perhaps he didn't know how to write his stories down, or maybe he lacked the strength to do it; maybe his characters and storylines began to fade as soon as he picked up his pen, or his vision problem was so severe that it prevented him from writing as well as reading. And maybe he would have been sorry if the faces he had created and were probably more alive to him than those of real people, should disappear altogether. All this explained why he had wanted to share the lives of his characters with someone else. When I turned up at the porter's lodge and showed an interest in an object he'd spun into a long story, and when he saw how keen I was to listen, perhaps he couldn't resist the temptation to tell me in detail about Dionysius's long journey from Gaza and the magnificent adventures of Archibald Archer that he had dreamed up in his solitary nights in the porter's lodge, as he gazed at the company's emblem. Now I realized, too, that his delight in storytelling was allied with a bad conscience for deceiving me; now I understood that the expensive wine he treated me to was meant as apology and compensation. I wasn't angry at him; on the contrary, I was grateful to him for his story, even though it didn't have anything to do with Viola's disappearance, and I was glad to have provided an audience for it. Besides, Dionysius of Gaza was a worthy addition to the whirl of characters that had emerged from the darkness in Viola's train.

Not wanting to tell Wirth the stories of my search for Viola, I explained to him that I was looking for the meaning of a certain symbol, which was how I'd encountered the story of Dionysius; plainly I had failed to grasp that it was a fiction. Then I got up to go. Wirth asked which symbol this was; I leaned down to the desk, fished out a pencil from a gap between two piles of books, and on one of the sheets of paper that lay there, I made a quick sketch of the double trident. Wirth picked up the sheet and studied it for a long time, all the time frowning and tugging at his mustache . . . And it was clear to me that he wasn't seeing it for the first time. It always began like this; I knew that here in this tight little office another line of inquiry was opening up in this complex case. To which distant landscape, to which recent or ancient past would it lead me? I sat back down and waited for Wirth to speak.

"Strange," he muttered. "I've seen this very symbol before. Arnošt showed it to me last fall. Arnošt is doing his national service here."

"National service?"

"Instead of doing military service, he's here with us. He looks after the computers and the institute's web pages. He'd just returned from vacation at the time, I remember. He came to me, drew that very thing on a piece of paper and asked me if it was a letter that belonged to an ancient script."

"Does it?"

"Of course it doesn't."

"Could I speak with Arnošt?"

"His is the fifth door on the left."

Wirth was still looking at the symbol, perplexed. Perhaps he was wondering if he had missed something and there really was a philosopher he knew nothing about called Dionysius of Gaza who had managed to escape the attentions of encyclopedias and the internet. Then he muttered something unintelligible, laid the sheet with the symbol on one of the piles of paper, by which it would surely soon be absorbed and never seen again, and went back to his books.

Chapter 55
Bay at Folegandros

The fifth door was closed. I knocked and it was opened by a young man with short hair and glasses with square, black frames. There was even less room in his office than in Wirth's, as on both sides of it were shelves filled with computers with dark screens. The mere mention of Wirth and the double trident captured Arnošt's attention, and he invited me in. Obviously he was glad of the opportunity to speak with someone about the trident. He gave up his chair and sat down opposite me. As the door remained open, I could see Arnošt's silhouette against a glowing rectangle otherwise filled with chestnut leaves glistening in the sun, the light awakening the rows of computer screens to a life of dreams.

"I came across the symbol last summer," he said, beginning his story without further ado. "It's not a time I like to look back on. In those days I met up often with a group of young Americans who were living over here, and I fell in love with a girl from California. I saw with complete clarity that Pamela was an arrogant snob who was forever ridiculing and humiliating me in front of the others, but as sometimes happens, this realization did nothing to change how badly I wanted her. I got to know her late last April, and by the beginning of August things had gone so far that I knew I had to get away at all costs, at least for a while. As I thought about where to go, I felt a longing for the south; maybe the heat and light of the southern sun would burn thoughts of Pamela out of my head. So I bought an air ticket to Athens. As soon as I landed, I headed for Piraeus and got on the first ferry to the islands. After that I hopped from island to island without any particular plan."

"And did you stop thinking about Pamela?"

Arnošt sighed. "No, and it was naive of me to imagine that I would. I lay on the shore thinking about her. What I wanted most was to come back and see her again, but fortunately that wasn't possible: the ticket I had didn't allow the changing of the date of the return flight."

So far I had no idea of the path that would lead Arnošt to the double trident, but for some reason I had the feeling that it was on his mind as much as it was on mine; it seemed to me, too, that he was telling me his story in such detail and conveying such intimate feelings because he was expecting me to be similarly communicative in return.

"After I'd spent a few days on Naxos," Arnošt continued, "I took a boat that sailed across the Cyclades to the island of Milos. I wasn't expecting it to stop en route, so I was surprised when halfway through the journey it turned toward a small island. I stood at the rail of the bow as a sleepy, white harbor under scorched yellow-and-orange rocks came into view. I was enchanted by the serenity of the scene, and it occurred to me that here was a place where I might at last forget the evil Pamela. So I threw on my backpack and went ashore.

"I had no idea where I was. The name of the island had been announced over the boat's PA, but it's rarely possible to make out what is said through the rasping speakers on Greek boats. So there on the pier I asked an old woman in a black dress where I was. I learned that the island's name was Folegandros, that the dusty road that led out of the harbor and disappeared in the saddle between two hills went to Chora, where most of the island's inhabitants lived, and that apart from Chora, there were two other villages. I checked in at a nearby campsite and spent my days on Folegandros either at the harbor, drinking coffee and watching the yachts bobbing on the waves, climbing the winding, narrow paths on the steep slopes that overlooked the sea, or wandering the alleys of Chora, which had been built on the edge of a precipice as a defense against pirates. There was even a local legend that told of treasure from a pirate ship that was hidden somewhere on the island."

The mention of pirates and treasure reminded me of Bernet. Then it came to me: The mysterious 'Fol' on Bernet's scrap of paper—that might be Folegandros! Not least as the Cyclades once belonged to Venice, if I wasn't mistaken. Near this little-known island, Captain Boustrophedon, Nero, or whatever his real name was, might have wrecked his ship, the Santa Clara; he and his treasure might have spent several centuries at the bottom of the sea there.

"Even on Folegandros, I didn't manage not to think about Pamela . . . I enjoyed going to a small beach on the west side of the island, where I'd lie around for hours in the flickering shade of the tamarisks that grew out of the sand. In the evenings I'd sit in a taverna that overlooked the beach. Before long I made friends with Kostas, its proprietor. We drank wine or Greek beer until it was dark and I made my way back to my tent down the narrow path worn into the cliff. Once, when we were drinking late into the night and talking about legends and mysteries connected with the island, Kostas suddenly became solemn and enigmatic. He would let me in on something tourists didn't have the faintest inkling about, he said. He described the way to a deserted stony beach on the northwest of the island. He told me to take a snorkel and swim from the most distant tip of the rock on the right-hand side of the bay to a small rock in the shape of a ram's head that stuck out of the sea; here I should change course by fifteen degrees to the right and swim on for another thirty meters. I pressed Kostas to tell me what I was supposed to find there, but he just smiled, continued to look enigmatic and said more than once that I would never forget what I was about to see.

"So early the next morning I set off to find the beach Kostas had told me about. I was expecting to find a wrecked boat of some sort under the sea; I wasn't happy to be giving up my wallow under the tamarisks for this, but I knew that Kostas would be angry if I spurned the mystery he'd offered to me in friendship. After two hours on the road that ran along the ridge of this long island, I turned onto a dirt road and then descended a steep slope to a small bay containing a white pebble beach. I came across a few kids who had spent the night here; some of them were lethargically emerging from their sleeping bags, while others were looking for what shade there was under the wet rock. I undressed, pulled on my goggles, put my snorkel in my mouth and went into the sea, which was yet to warm up. I swam to the rock in the shape of a ram's head. Spots of light flickered about on the pebbly seabed, which remained clearly visible, although it was drawing further away. Beyond the ram's head, less light was reflected from the pebbles, and the seabed became submerged in gloom. Reaching the place Kostas had spoken of, I saw beneath me some kind of mound. Probably an underwater rock, I thought. I took a deep breath and dived; as I got closer to the mound, to my amazement I saw that it was a statue of a naked woman.

"The woman was lying on an ottoman, leaning on one elbow and holding a book in her free hand. She wasn't reading, though: Her forefinger was placed between half-closed pages and she was looking ahead with a smile that seemed to me ironic. It gave me a strange feeling to look into the stone woman's face; I imagined that she had just broken off her reading and looked up from the book to see what the disturbance was. The whole statue was composed of light-colored pebbles—the same as were on the beach and seabed. It seemed to have formed spontaneously; it was as though the woman had risen from the seabed, maybe as a result of some special seismic activity. The impression that she was a natural form was strengthened by the fact that the entire statue was covered in seaweed, which grew on the seabed all around her; each weed swayed to the same slow rhythm. I don't know if it was only the surface of the statue that was made from pebbles, or the whole of it. I tried to peel a few of the pebbles off to see what was under the top layer, but I couldn't: Apparently the pebbles were held together by a strong glue.

"I surfaced many times in order to get my breath before returning to the statue. I approached the pebble woman from all sides. I ran my hands along the smooth stones and wiped the seaweed from them. I'd noticed on the beach that among the white and pale-gray pebbles was the odd one of a different color. The unknown sculptor had used some of these different colors to highlight certain points on the statue. The woman's irises were green stones, and the spine of the book she held in her hand was composed of orange pebbles with an inlaid figure made of small dark green stones . . ."

Arnošt paused for a moment. I looked at the bright aquarium of the computer and tried to imagine the statue at the bottom of the sea. I didn't need to ask Arnošt what the figure looked like, nor was I in any doubt that the volume in the pebble woman's hand was the Orange Book.

"That very afternoon, I went to Kostas and questioned him on the underwater statue, but I didn't find out much from him. He told me he'd discovered it by chance when diving two years earlier. Even then, it had been covered in seaweed; it might have been there for decades or even centuries. I could tell that he was as fascinated by the statue as I was, and that it weighed on him just as it did on me. He admitted to me that he'd never returned to it and had even stopped going to the pebble bay. I realized that I myself didn't want to see this woman of the sea a second time. But I was grateful to him for telling me about her, and our shared secret brought us closer still. That evening we drank more than usual. We spoke of the statue, the mysterious symbol, pirates and treasure in a cave, and for the first time I told him of my love for the awful Pamela. As I fell asleep in my tent, many images came together in my mind: the mysterious symbol, the idea of inanimate things changing into a woman's body, memories of Pam, jealousy of those who knew her, which had followed me even to a Greek island, memories of last year's temporary job at a waste-paper collection point—and all this spawned a vivid dream. In the dream, I was transformed into someone else—a person who had adventures at a collection point at night, where the letters over the entrance changed into unknown characters and packages of waste paper changed into women . . ."

"That's surely the greatest island mystery of all!" I exclaimed. "Just imagine—I read a story with the same plot as your dream!"

"That's not so great a mystery," said Arnošt awkwardly. "Because I wrote it."

"You're Jiří Zajíc? I thought your name was Arnošt."

"That's right, my real name is Arnošt. I'm not called Zajíc either. I wrote the story on the boat that took me back to Piraeus. When I got home I even translated it into English and gave it to Pamela to read, although I knew how that would turn out. Pam pulled the story to pieces; she took it to the café and read from it to the others, appending an ironic comment of her own to every sentence. Everyone was afraid of Pamela, so I just sat there looking at the servile faces that chuckled each time she cracked a joke at my expense, thinking I would die of shame. As you can see, I got what I deserved.

"I wanted to know if the story really was as bad as all that, so I sent it to a literary magazine. But after Pamela's performance at the café, I didn't have the self-confidence to submit it under my own name, so I invented a pseudonym—the first name that occurred to me. Some time later, the magazine published the story, and I told myself that perhaps it wasn't the mess that Pamela said it was after all."

Chapter 56
Fire at the Community Hall

"Still Pamela couldn't decide if she was going to write poems, novels, screenplays or theater plays. Every week she threw herself into something new, and she would waste no time in expounding all kinds of theories about it at the café. But she was never able to finish one thing before she started on another, for which she came up with different theories. Pamela was simply awful; I knew that my love for her was a dreadful sickness, and I hated myself for not being able or even wanting to find a cure for it. I can't tell you how glad I am to have all that behind me . . . At that time, Pamela was getting interested in theater, and she took to reading to us extracts from a play she was writing. I didn't know what to make of these: To me, they were an assortment of the kind of boring conversations you might overhear in any train compartment, and I think that all of us at the café felt the same way, although no one was bold enough to say so in front of Pamela. So everyone nodded as Pamela expounded the muddled theories by which the stage reproductions of banal conversations would somehow provide the audience with a catharsis more authentic than that of a Greek tragedy. I was so cowardly or so much in love that I nodded, too. The theme of the play was a day in the life of a young junkie called Kevin, who lived in Los Angeles. The entire play was no more than a series of incredibly banal conversations between Kevin and his friends, his mother, his mother and his ex-lover. Wary of entrusting her masterpiece to a stranger, Pamela decided to direct it herself, and she proceeded to divide up the roles among her friends at the café.

"One day Pamela came to the café all aglow. It turned out that the previous evening she'd been at the cinema, where she'd hit upon a new theory concerning the staging of her own drama. She claimed that modern drama should be inspired by the film technique that played with images on different scales. When we asked what she was intending, Pamela wasted no time in telling us: there would be a scene in her play in which Kevin spoke with his mother, who was visiting his lair. At a certain point there would be a break in the conversation, which Pam said would be charged with meaning. Kevin would light a cigarette that would then fall from his shaking hand to the floor, which was scattered with greasy, scrunched-up paper and a copy of *Hustler* magazine Kevin had found in the trash. Here was where the new scene that Pamela was so immensely proud of came in. The curtain would come down so that a two-meter-long model of a smoldering cigarette, scrunched-up, greasy paper on the same scale and a huge, dog-eared page from *Hustler* could be placed on the stage. This giant still life was to remain in view for about half a minute, after which the curtain would fall again and the three giant props would be spirited away. When the curtain came back up, Kevin and his mother would be standing on stage and the cigarette and magazine, now in real size, would still be on the floor. The silence would go on a little longer before the conversation between mother and son resumed.

"Everyone at the café nodded awkwardly. We were hoping that Pamela would reconsider, and of course there was a good chance that the next day she would have forgotten these revolutionary ideas of hers and come up with something a little less foolish. But Pam had fallen in love with her theory, and she clung to it. A few days later, we met at the studio of one of her admirers, in order to make a giant cardboard cigarette and a two-meter-high, scrunched-up hotdog wrapper. Today I'm actually grateful to Pamela for this bizarre idea of hers: It was my work on the giant props and the unshakeable feeling that I was a total idiot to be doing it that at last cured me of my love.

"I was pretty surprised one day when Pam informed me that

she might use my short story in her play. She'd had this great idea: The play would begin before Kevin woke up and the opening scene would recount a dream he'd had. This was where the dramatization of my story came in. She spoke with me as though she took it for granted that this would be a great honor for me. After that, she told me that she didn't have any actors and I could play a character from the dream. I wondered why she didn't write the dream passage herself instead of using what in her opinion was a bad short story. Then it dawned on me that Pamela was incapable of thinking up anything but banal dialogue and nonsensical stage theory. Although by this point my love for Pam was on the way out—thanks to the giant cigarette—I told her that she could do what she liked with my story, and I even promised that I would act in her play if she wanted me to.

"In the course of rehearsals my recovery progressed in leaps and bounds. But as my love for Pam faded, I felt ever more embarrassed about appearing in her stupid play. Still, I knew that it was too late for her to find a replacement for me, so I told myself that I'd have to suffer through the play; anyway, it was obvious that it wouldn't be performed more than once. Someone had arranged the hiring of a community hall on the outskirts of the city, and it was here that Pamela's drama was due to premiere. It would be in English, of course.

"Pamela asked me to design a poster for the production. I drew a scene from Kevin's dream of the beginning: The entrance to the waste-paper collection point, with the nighttime sign above it. Although Pam had this posted on many a wall, when the night came, the community hall was half-empty. The show started. I was playing the character from my dream on Folegandros, and I was looking forward to getting it over with. The light from the stage spilled onto the front rows, and as I stood there, I looked at the faces of those sitting in the audience. Then I saw something that caused me to freeze and stop performing for a moment: Looking at me from the third row was the face of the woman I'd seen on the seabed. But it wasn't made of pebbles, and there was no seaweed streaming from it; it was a real live face, and it was following the performance closely. At that moment, my mind produced a vision that keeps coming back to me; a vision that I still haven't managed to banish: The woman of stone rises from her underwater ottoman, emerges on the shore and the white pebbles transform into skin . . ."

I took the photograph of Viola from my wallet and handed it to Arnošt. "Is this her?"

I wasn't surprised to see his dumbfounded nod.

"Did you look for her during the intermission or at the end of the performance?" I asked.

"Unfortunately I wasn't able to, because the show came to a premature end—even before the intermission, and in great confusion. During the making of the scenery for Pam, when we suggested that the smoldering end of the giant cigarette should be made of orange cellophane with a light bulb behind it, Pamela took offense. This was a social drama, not a play for children, she explained angrily, so of course the end of the cigarette must really smolder. When the scene with the giant stub came—a scene Pam was really proud of—the *Hustler* page was ignited by the smoldering cigarette, and the rest of the scenery went up. Fortunately there were enough fire extinguishers in the hall, so we soon succeeded in putting out the fire.

"I remember the silence when it was all over. I stood on the sopping-wet stage with a fire extinguisher in my hand, hearing the water dripping from the stage onto the floorboards of the empty hall. The audience had fled, and people were standing about outside. I rushed out and looked among them for the girl from Folegandros, but I didn't find her. Then I went home.

"Nor did I see Pam again. I learned the next day that after I left, the community hall's janitor had stormed onto the stage and started to yell at her. Pam had yelled back in English, even though he couldn't understand her. In a terrible rage, she had announced that creative freedom was violated here. So she packed her things and went back to California. At the café the day after she left, I couldn't help noticing that everyone was in a good mood. I think we were all a little embarrassed at having allowed ourselves to be terrorized for so long."

"And you never saw the underwater woman again?"

"No. Neither in pebble form nor in real, live form."

Now Arnošt was looking at me eagerly. He was waiting for

me to tell him where I'd gotten the photograph of the girl whose statue he'd seen at the bottom of the sea, and also where I'd encountered the symbol that was on the statue's book. Although I felt sorry for him, it had been a long day and I was too tired to talk about Viola and the trident. So I thanked him for his story and hurriedly said goodbye to him. I had reached the courtyard when something occurred to me; I ran back up the stairs and poked my head into Arnošt's office. I could see hope in his eyes that I was about to tell him something after all, but all I did was ask a question: "In the dream scene, was the hieroglyphic sign from above the gate to the collection point part of the scenery?"

Arnošt nodded.

"And were the letters of the sign made of wood, about a meter high and painted green?"

"That's right. They were blue in my dream, but Pamela liked green, so she insisted that the sign should be in green."

I asked him if he knew what had become of those letters.

"A friend of Pamela's took them. He lived in one of a group of old houses which were demolished not long ago, I think. So I've no idea where the letters could be now. They probably ended up at the incinerator."

Again I thanked Arnošt and made myself scarce so as not to have to explain anything to him. I felt I'd cheated him by failing to tell my story in return, and I determined to come back later and tell him what I knew about the trident and Viola. Although I knew at last who had made the green trident at the dump that had drawn me into Viola's story, and what it had been used for, the knowledge didn't take me any further. Now I really was absolutely clueless, I told myself. Then I had an idea: If the whole story of Dionysius and Archibald Archer had been made up by the porter, how had the company that employed him come by its logo? I decided to pay the porter another visit.

Chapter 57
Café on the Corner

The building of the company where the author of Dionysius of Gaza worked was within easy walking distance. I crossed a prefabricated housing estate that looked practically abandoned, the only indications of human habitation items of laundry hanging motionless on balconies and the occasional sound of a television from the depths of a room. I passed frosted glass doors with wire woven through them, each the same as the last. The only movement in the dazed stillness of the hot afternoon was provided by the silent play of perspective, which wove long, straight lines into ever new and different shapes. In a gap between the last of the housing blocks, a sparse little wood appeared. Beyond this I reached the well-known dirt track, which at first wound around the impossibly long factory wall, which was beige and had large red letters printed across it. The letters opened up to me as they floated past and disappeared, but I couldn't hold them in my memory long enough to create words out of them. After ten minutes the building with the double trident emerged.

The porter-cum-historian came hurrying out of his lodge as I was still approaching the gate. Having overtaken his master, the dog stuck his nose through the bars and whined with delight. The porter, on the other hand, looked contrite. Obviously he knew why I had come back; he had guessed that I'd checked out his story and discovered that Dionysius hadn't been born in sixth-century Gaza, but many years later in his lodge.

"Are you very angry at me?" he asked. "I keep wondering if I did you an injustice by telling you my fictions. I even considered finding you and telling you the truth, but I know so little about you . . . You looked as though you were looking for something important. My silly talk might have confused you and led you off track. I don't know why I did it."

By now he was looking even unhappier.

I smiled at him. "Don't worry about it. You couldn't resist the temptation, that's all. No lasting damage. You're right to assume I'm looking for something important, but you didn't lead me off track, because I wasn't on the right track in the first place—and I don't think I'll ever find it. I'm actually grateful to you for your stories—I'll never forget Dionysius and Archibald Archer. I didn't come here to scold you; I wanted to ask for the true story of the company logo. It's the last clue I have left."

"It was our designer who thought up the logo. Come with me into the lodge and we can give him a call."

The porter was glad of the chance to remedy what he had caused by his indulgence as a storyteller. He dialed an internal line, asked his colleague to take special care with me and then handed me the receiver. I asked the designer whether he had thought up the symbol or had seen it somewhere.

"I have to confess that the idea wasn't mine," said the voice in the telephone. "Six months ago, I was given the task of devising a new company logo, and somehow I left the job until the last minute. I started thinking about the symbol only on the evening before I was due to submit my design. I made various sketches, none of which pleased me. Then my attention was caught by the computer screen, specifically the moving screensaver pattern that had just appeared on it. It was a luminous ribbon that kept changing shape. At one moment it formed a figure that I rather liked . . ."

The designer had told me all I needed to know. It was perfectly clear: The double trident was on the company's wall because the designer had copied it from the screensaver created by the graphic artist of my acquaintance, who had seen it in the portrait of Viola, which had been painted by an artist who had discovered it on Viola's body . . . My very last clue had led me in an arc back to what I knew already. It was a barren branch that grew back into the trunk that had sprouted it. The designer went on to tell me that when in the following days he had been asked about the meaning of the symbol, he had invented one on the spot: The merging and diverging lines indicated communication, while the oval symbolized the product that originated on the basis of this communication. By this time, I was barely listening to him; I used his first pause for breath in order to thank him and say goodbye.

After I hung up I must have looked crestfallen, because the expression of unhappiness returned to the face of the porter, who still believed himself to be the cause of all my misery. He said he still had a few bottles of good wine in the cellar and he'd like to treat me to the best of them. I replied that I'd happily come back to the lodge one evening, when he and his dog were alone in the building; we could open a bottle and I'd enjoy listening to some more of the stories he'd thought up in working hours; I was particularly keen to hear another Archer adventure and also looking forward to learning details of the friendship between Mildred Archer and Oscar Wilde.

"It'll be good to see you," said the porter. "I'll have the wine ready. Perhaps it will interest you to hear what Archibald discovered in a pharaoh's tomb in Egypt. And I can quote to you from the letters Wilde wrote to Mildred."

I returned to the road without sidewalks, a path for trucks that produced high swirls of suffocating white dust. I thought about the porter and Dionysius. In the flock of real and fictional characters that flitted around the missing Viola, the philosopher was in good company, a true cousin of the guerrilleros, urban-oceanologists, painters in invisible paint and composers of inaudible music. It seemed to me that the faces of all these characters mirrored the features of the others, and I couldn't help thinking that Viola's face was somewhere at the dark, invisible center of this mirroring; that all the characters I'd encountered in some way mirrored Viola's face, too; that each of the stories revealed to me was somehow similar to the story Viola was involved in and contained a code that held the key. Sometimes it seemed to me that I was within reach of the outline of Viola's story, that the faces of its heroes were emerging from the fog and I was beginning to make out their words—but then the same thing always happened: These impressions dissolved.

Other factory walls crawled by. Beyond the last of these, the first apartment buildings appeared. Now I was back in the empty streets, where small stones sparkled in the asphalt of the roadway. I thought of how much I liked the phantoms of light and sun, and I realized how sorry I would be when they departed with the end of summer. At the point where two streets intersected, there was a nameless, wide-open space that hadn't been granted the status of a circus. Even so, it had adopted a circus's atmosphere and secrets; it calmed movements, curved them into a ring and steeped them in vanity, theatricality, self-indulgence and dreams. On a sloping corner stood a café with a number of round tables in front of narrow windows. I entered the café's dark interior, bought an iced coffee and took a seat at one of the tables on the sidewalk. As I sipped the coffee, I looked at the street, which rose in a gentle incline. I studied the Art Nouveau facades on the other side of the crossroads, whose reliefs of insipid water nymphs rested among gas outlets like faces of evil robots in a science-fiction movie.

Again I began to think of Viola, how her features spread across the faces I'd encountered, and how her unknown story engendered many other stories. And it seemed to me that the chain of similarities and connections to which I'd been unable to find the key, was now longer still, and that it now included inanimate objects, too. Was not the strange pump she'd commissioned a hermetic portrait of Viola? Or was it a portrait of the monster Viola was fighting? To me, the emptiness of the hot, deserted streets was the emptiness left by Viola's departure, although this emptiness also contained a strange presence: a premonition that was now stronger, now weaker, but never disappeared completely, a hunch that beyond a street corner or behind lace curtains was someone who had met Viola and knew of her secret, who had wandered the underground labyrinth with her. Maybe Viola herself was there. Who was to say that she wasn't just beyond that high wooden fence, or in that yard approached through a shady passage? Perhaps she was walking the long, empty corridors of an administrative building, at the end of her working day.

Again I recalled the sad voice in Bernet's garden, as the masks were swimming about me and the lights swirling. This would remain forever my only encounter with Viola. Perhaps it was just as well that I hadn't found her: Her childlike figure would forever be interwoven with stories of pirates, underwater statues and underground monsters, conspirators, treasure, and secret brotherhoods. As these stories were incomplete, over time they would continue to develop and convolute, and their convolution would be watchful for any opportunity, any encounter with a person unknown, any snatch of conversation overheard in the streetcar, any machine of unknown purpose, any broken-off piece of something at a dump. The convolution would then take possession of all these fragments and draw them into itself for use in its ongoing furcation. After that, I left off thinking and just looked at the facades as the shadows of roofs and goblin-like chimneys climbed across them, at the gentle movement of the leaves of trees, and at a vehicle that was now driving down the street towards the circus, its bodywork gleaming in the sun like a great diamond.

Part Two
Room by the Track

Chapter 1
Gleam of a Piano

When the vehicle reached the circus, I saw that it was a white van. As it turned past the café, it slowed—and I saw painted on its side an enormous blue kingfisher with a fish in its bill. I jumped up, slipped a banknote under my glass of half-finished coffee and chased after the van, which was heading down a long, straight street. I ran along the road, waving my arms, hoping that the driver would see me in his rearview mirror.

I saw that the shape of the van was no longer getting smaller; with any luck the driver had seen me and was waiting. Although I was struggling for breath, I was laughing out loud as I ran. Of course, when all else fails, there's still the *deus ex machina*, in this case in the shape of a taxi driver. When I reached the van, the man leaned out of the window to reveal a round face shiny with sweat.

"What do you need me to move for you, chief?" he said.

I ran around the van and got into the front seat, to make sure he didn't drive away.

"Two years ago you went to the Nereus Company to pick up a special pump with many tubes," I said, once I'd slammed the door. "You had with you a man with a gray beard and a young girl with very short hair. Can you remember where you dropped them?"

The taxi driver pursed his thick lips. "Maybe I do, maybe

I don't," he said. "I don't give out information on my fares. If there's nothing you need me to move, please get out."

I reached into my pocket for my billfold, drew out a one-thousand-crown bill and held it up for the driver's inspection.

"As far as I know, there's no law against your telling me where a fare wanted to be dropped," I said.

The driver was no longer frowning, and the tone of his next words was much friendlier. "You're probably right. I don't think it's against the law. I remember that pump well, because I've never seen another like it. And I also remember exactly where we unloaded it."

"Can you take me there?"

The taxi driver stepped on the gas, and I slipped the banknote into the breast pocket of his shirt. Having taken an exit from a new roundabout I didn't know, we drove along a road lined alternately with sparse deciduous woodland, carpets of yellowing grass and industrial buildings enclosed in high barbed-wire fences. Now and then a village flashed past that appeared to be strewn across a field. We didn't speak, and after a while the driver switched on a country music tape. Over our heads, bridges, concrete overpasses, and blue signposts with large white lettering flew past. Shortly after we arced back toward the city, the driver took us into a street that was little more than a few dilapidated apartment buildings along each side of a roadway. He stopped in front of one of these and pointed at its main door without saying anything.

I got out and took a brief look around. This was the last street in the city. Beyond the wall of the most distant house was some kind of warehouse; beyond that a field stretched to a low horizon. A railway line passed beside the warehouse and was lost behind the buildings. I went into the apartment building; it was dark and surprisingly chilly. A stone staircase rose to the upper floors, its handrail formed of cast-iron flowers with the same designs oft repeated. The protective green paint of the walls had been decorated over the years with thousands of white scratches. It was so gloomy on the ground floor that I had to switch on the light in order to read the names on the mailboxes; none of them meant anything to me.

From above I heard a girl's voice, the slamming of a door, the stamp of approaching footsteps. A little girl appeared in the crook of the stairs. I asked her if Viola Jonášová lived here. The girl stopped and a faint ray of light fell on her from above. She looked at me with suspicion, shook her head and made as if to pass me.

"She's a young lady with short, fair hair," I persisted.

The girl hesitated before saying: "She lives at Mr. Navrátil's." Then she disappeared into the street.

The apartments had heavy composite doors. I walked from one to the next, reading the nameplates, which were set in ornamental brass frames. On the fifth, highest floor one of the frames held a piece of paper slipped in carelessly which bore the name "NAVRÁTIL" in large letters. I put my finger to the wobbly bell and in a state of great apprehension waited for the door to open.

For a long time all was silent beyond the door. Then came the sound of light footsteps and the brief appearance at the peephole of an eye. Again nothing happened for a long time; whoever was standing beyond the door probably couldn't decide whether or not to open up. I was reaching for the bell again when I heard the chain rattle as the door opened a crack.

The sad fragrance of a stranger's apartment caught in my nostrils. Wearing the same corduroy pants and gray T-shirt as in the portrait, there in the doorway stood Viola Jonášová.

Suddenly confused, I racked my brains for something to say. Viola looked at me in mild amazement, then announced: "Mr. Navrátil isn't at home."

"It's you I've come to see," I stammered out at last.

Viola backed into the apartment and reduced the crack between the door and its frame still further.

"Who are you? Did my father send you?" She was poised to slam the door shut.

"Please don't run away. For now it's not important who I am, and I haven't been sent by your father. Well, actually I have . . . but then not exactly. It's all terribly complicated. Please don't close the door. Listen to what I have to say. I promise not to tell anyone where you live, if that's what you want. Not even your father . . ."

Viola stood there frowning at me, moving the door slowly backwards and forwards in its frame. I suppose she was more impressed by my desperate expression than by what I'd said. At last she took two steps back into the dark hallway and pulled the door toward her. I was being invited in.

She led me into a spacious room with furniture that gleamed in the sunlight admitted by three windows. The widest of these spanned the entire arc of a bay that deepened the room at the back. All the windows were run through with parallel and intersecting wire, and dark columns were visible in them. When I got closer to the windows, I saw a high embankment with rails mounted on ties. I was taken aback by how dangerously close the railroad was to the building. It occurred to me that if a train were to stop here, it might even be possible to reach out and shake hands with a passenger standing at a window of the train. The outlines of the windows interwoven with wire were reflected on the surface of a piano that stood at the center of the room as though on an expanse of dark water. On this piano lay several sheets of manuscript paper; I saw that someone had scribbled bundles of notes into the lines in pencil. The soft, pleasing light was absorbed by the reddish carpet and the upholstery of the couch and armchairs. The entire width of the bay was filled with a heavy desk; whoever worked here probably felt like a signalman, I said to myself. On the top of the desk lay a book in an orange cloth binding. At first, it looked as though a large, exotic emerald-green insect were resting motionless on it, but when I got closer I saw that this was the double trident symbol painted or printed on the orange cloth.

Chapter 2
An Old Promise

Viola pointed in silence at the deep, soft couch, which I sunk into. She remained standing by the piano, one hand gripping the lid of the keyboard, just as moments earlier it had gripped the door, as though ready in case of need to unloose on me a demon that lived inside the piano.

"Is Navrátil Vuhulum Chuh-yuh?" I said.

She replied to my question with another. "What do you want from me?"

"I've been looking for you for a long time. Well, actually it's only eight days, but it feels as though I started my search years ago . . . What's more, I feel that because of you, I've traveled the world, even though in reality I've just been running back and forth around the outskirts of the city. In the beginning, I really did promise your father that I'd try to find you, because I was sorry for him. But later I forgot about him entirely."

I saw that Viola wanted to ask me something, and I anticipated her question before she could put it.

"I really can't tell you why I've been traveling the city in search of you. Indeed, I'd be glad if someone could tell me. At first I thought it was out of sympathy for your father, but after that I told myself that perhaps it was because I longed to solve a mystery—but I don't think that's the reason either: It doesn't explain why I've been looking for you in particular and why I wish to know the secret of a particular symbol that I might have been indifferent to. After all, there are many more interesting mysteries than the disappearance of a young woman and the meaning of a symbol. This morning the lovers of Bernet the millionaire gave me what they think is the real reason: According to them, I'm in love with you. Maybe they're right, although that idea had never occurred to me. Perhaps I'll come to understand at least partially why I set out to find you—but only later, after several months or years."

Viola stood at the piano with her head down, saying nothing. Unwittingly her restless fingers touched the keys, producing a dissonant chord that hung long in the silence of the room.

"From the moment I set out to find you, I've become enmeshed in so many stories," I continued. "I've learned about pirates, monsters living in underground lakes, prophets of strange sects, inventors of the typewriter, mysterious books, evil women who change into piles of waste paper, underwater statues, beautiful South American women terrorists, and men learned in bizarre sciences. I'd begun to believe that you didn't exist. I knew so much less about you than about all those strange characters who were supposed to guide me to you, and all the while I had the sense that all of them were leading me off track, tempting me into their labyrinth and their secret gardens. You seemed to me more unreal and more fantastical that all those Gnostic philosophers dreamed up by the night porter and the heroes of the surrealistic opera.

"I spoke with people who knew you—your father, Dominik, and Julie. But instead of bringing some kind of reality to the other stories, they were infected by their fantasticality. And that wasn't all—those who told me the stories became as dreamlike as their characters, as unreal as you. I believe that you know a story that will bring all these stories together into a single cloth. I don't know if you'll want to tell it to me. I do know that in any case I'll live with all the characters I've seen and heard of in the past few days for a long time, maybe my whole life; and I'll live with you, too, because you're forever associated with them, a part of their families; you live in the same land as they do. And I'll always be grateful to you for this company I'd never have kept if it weren't for you."

For the first time Viola smiled. She closed the piano lid with a scarcely audible click. Then she sat down on the revolving stool in front of it and said gently: "Don't worry, I think I understand what you're telling me. Something similar happened to me, and I was just as unprepared for the things that occurred as you were. I, too, witnessed how a story grew and grew like frost flowers on glass, and I didn't know what to do about it either. But unlike you, I discovered that this story was also about me. Without knowing anything about it, I'd been playing a leading role in it since I was born. That's why past and present are so oddly interwoven in the story. Today I can't say whether or not it was good that I heard it. But once I had, it became impossible for me to live as before. I can't go back . . . Everything's changed. All objects have taken on meanings different from before. It's hard for me, and sometimes I don't know how to go on. I could do with speaking about it to someone. The thing is, I'm not allowed to speak with anyone about what happened. It's an old promise that I can't break. Maybe the promise itself is foolish and absurd, but that makes it all the more necessary; precisely because it is impossible to justify, there's no way to invalidate it. We have to be true to it . . ."

Viola's face dropped into her hands for a moment. When she looked up again, it still had the distinct features of a rebellious child that had so impressed me in the portrait but her near-despair had released a kind of terrible fatigue whose origin I couldn't place. It occurred to me that her face looked rather like that of a child who had run away from home, wandered about lost for several days, then sunk into a bed of moss in a state of total exhaustion. I got up and stroked her hair and face ever so lightly. Viola didn't move at all; it was as though she were unaware of my touch. I stood in front of her awkwardly before returning to the couch.

After a while, she raised her head again and spoke. "The story I heard, and in which I'm one of the characters, may truly be the story all your stories have grown from. I'd so much like to tell it to you, it would be a relief to me, too . . . but regrettably, I can't. As I say, it's because of a promise made long ago. Maybe the promise wasn't meant to be taken seriously, but it's twenty years old and those years have made it weightier . . . That's why I couldn't tell anyone—not even Julie—anything; that's why I must have seemed so mysterious and unreal to everyone, although I really didn't mean to . . ."

Again Viola fell silent. She lifted the lid of the piano, fingered a few notes in ascending order, closed it.

"I hurt her," she said, as though she were speaking to herself. "I'm so sorry about that. I think about her often . . . But at that time there was a task that had to be performed, and I couldn't allow anything to delay me . . ."

"And has the task been performed now?" I asked.

"Yes, now it's done," said Viola.

"You haven't even said anything to the person you live with?"

"That's different, of course. Navrátil—you're right, he is indeed Vuhulum Chuh-yuh—was part of the story from the very beginning, even before I entered it by being born. I had nothing to hide from him."

"If you feel sorry for the people you've caused pain, why don't you put things right at least a little by visiting the one you hurt the most and who is still waiting for you?"

"You mean Jonáš?" I heard a sudden chill in Viola's voice. "No, when I was speaking of people I've wronged, I wasn't thinking of my father. I never want to see him again."

Now Viola was silent for a long time. I watched the whirling dance of dust particles in a stream of sunlight over the carpet; it seemed to bring absolution for injustices old and new. I imagined that the dancing light reminded me of something from my childhood, but then I realized that I was seeing something from Bernet's story of the day before: The room I was sitting in was quiet and sunlit just like the one on Molina Boulevard in the imaginary country.

It looked as though Viola would tell me nothing more. I had no taste for disrupting the tranquillity of the room by insisting, pleading or reproaching. I had a sense that the re-appearance of

Viola Jonášová among these silent, shining objects was a pretty good end to the series of events that had begun to unfold at the dump the moment the point of the double trident had pierced the skin of my foot, and that there was no need for anything more.

I stood up and spoke. "An hour ago I was prepared to accept that the story which emerged over the past two weeks would forever remain a collection of unclassifiable fragments. In my view, even in this form it has a certain truth and logic, and I rather like it as it is . . . Maybe it's no bad thing that nothing more will happen to it. God knows what would become of it if its blanks were filled in! In any case, I'd like to thank you for everything."

I crossed the carpet towards the door, Viola my silent escort. I was in the hallway and about to turn the door handle when she laid a hand on mine and said softly, "Please wait a while. Let's go back in. We need to give this more thought."

She led me by the hand back into the room, where obediently I resumed my place on the couch. For a few moments Viola paced the carpet amid the dancing dust. She was so slender that I had the feeling I was watching a luminous ghost.

After that, she curled up in an armchair opposite the couch. Still she didn't talk, and at one point I thought she was crying. When she raised her head, I saw that her eyes were not red, however; perhaps Viola was incapable of tears.

"Don't be angry with me," she said. "It's possible that I long to tell you my story even more than you long to hear it . . . Maybe if I were to tell it all to you—someone who has become part of the story, whom the story has drawn in and ensnared—it wouldn't mean the breaking of the promise after all; perhaps it must remain hidden only from those who have no part in it."

"You talk of it as though it were some kind of treacherous octopus."

"It *is* dangerous, and it's best to be wary of it. But for you, it's too late for caution. The story is thirty years old, and in that time it has learned to live its own life, regardless of the wishes of the characters that appear in it. It has grown many projections that have headed off in every direction; a few of these tentacles have touched you, wrapped themselves around you and drawn you in. By now, you're in the stomach of the octopus along with the rest of us." It was clear that Viola was using these images in order to justify something to herself. "Wishing to conceal something from you would probably be as absurd as trying to warn a rabbit about a python when it was already in that python's belly . . ."

I could see that Viola still hadn't made up her mind, and I waited anxiously. She was holding herself ever tighter. Then at last she drew herself up in her armchair, looked me in the eye and said with determination: "If you have the patience for it, I'll tell you my story. If this really does cause me to break the promise, I hope the others will forgive me for it. It's a story not of heroism but of losing one's way, and despair, and of encounters and miracles."

A moment later she added: "Besides, the ban applied mainly to the Orange Book, and there's no longer any chance of your reading that . . ."

I looked towards the book that lay on the desk. It saddened me to have the mysterious work within reach, yet be forbidden from knowing its content. Having caught my eye and probably guessed what I was thinking, Viola said with a smile: "You misunderstand me. I won't stop you from looking at the book for as long as you like. All I said was that you won't be able to read it."

She stood up, fetched the book from the desk and handed it to me. I ran my hand over the orange binding, a little disappointed that this was ordinary buckram rather than leather or parchment. Then I opened it. I saw two blank pages. At whichever place I opened the book, I saw only white, blank paper. I went back to the beginning and turned page after page, but in the whole book I didn't find a single word, even a single letter. I returned the book to Viola, who put it back on the desk. I recalled the words about the book with the disappearing letters, as sung by Barbora in Bernet's garden. As I settled back into the couch, I asked nothing more; I knew that the book without words could only be explained by the whole story, which Viola had decided to tell me. I was ready to listen to this for several days, should it take that long.

Chapter 3
A Brooklyn Diner

Apparently Viola was considering how to begin.

"I think it all began in the United States," I said, in an attempt to help.

"That's one of the story's beginnings," she replied, nodding. "OK, then, let's start in New York."

She pulled her bare feet up on to the chair cushion; then she hugged her knees and rested her chin on them.

"It seems you know that I was there on vacation two years ago. I stayed in a small hotel on Ninety-Second Street. I spent the first week just walking about Manhattan and visiting all the places my travel guide recommended. On the eighth day, I decided it was time to look at other parts of the city, so I took the subway and got out somewhere in Brooklyn, without a clear idea of where I was. I walked for several long blocks, where the houses were all of unstuccoed brick. Then I crossed the asphalt surface of a seemingly endless parking lot containing hundreds of cars, before eventually coming to a maze of concrete overpasses and underpasses which I struggled to find a way through. When at last I escaped this concrete labyrinth, for that day I was ready to abandon my project of exploring new parts of the city. I was looking forward to sitting in a café on MacDougal Street in Greenwich Village which had already become a favorite of mine and where I usually ended my daily travels. I was glad to spot an overground railroad station. Right next to this was a small diner; I was terribly thirsty, so I went in. I was intending to drink my soda at the counter and then head straight for the overground . . ."

And everything turned out quite differently, I thought, remembering myself two weeks ago, when I'd wanted to take a shortcut across a dump.

"I found myself in a small room where maybe five dark-skinned men were sitting. There was quiet Caribbean music coming from somewhere; this blended with talk in Spanish. A train had just entered the overground station, and I heard the gentle rattle of its windows . . ."

Viola smiled and fell silent. At that very moment, a train was approaching along the tracks in front of the building, and the windows of our room, too, began to quake; they rattled loudly until the sound was drowned out by the growing din of the train cars; greenish, yellowish streaks darted in through the window like a shoal of fish fleeing a predator. As the rumbling of the train died down, there was a final, soft tapping of glass.

At last Viola was able to continue. "Anyway, I was so thirsty that I decided to drink my soda straight down. Only a few sips remained when to my surprise I heard a voice address me in English. Putting down my unfinished drink, I turned to the shortish man standing next to me. He had thick gray hair and was wearing a checked flannel shirt. I'd noticed him on entering the café, when he'd been sitting alone and looking pensively out the window; his bony, heavily lined face had put me in mind of an American farmer. In a calm, soft, slightly husky voice he apologized for disturbing me. He had a strong accent, which at first I assumed was Hispanic. Then he asked me if I was Viola Jonášová.

"I nodded in amazement. The stranger told me his name was Švarc. He'd guessed who I was because of my remarkable resemblance to my mother, whom he'd once known well. In the middle of a sentence, he switched from English to Czech. I asked him to tell me about my mother, explaining that I knew hardly anything about her—my father never spoke of her, because they hadn't parted on good terms, and I'd never met any of her friends. It seemed to me that he was hesitant. Before listening to my mother's story, I should be sure that I really wanted to hear it, he said. It might cause many things in my life to change, and he didn't know that he had the right to change my life. By the tone of his voice and the expression on his face, I understood that this was a warning I should take seriously; he was afraid of something that I, too, should be afraid of. Suddenly I grasped that there really was a danger that my generally happy life would unravel in this small Puerto Rican diner, and that I would find myself in another, unknown world, where perhaps I'd have to remain forever. But at the same time, I felt the attraction of this vague, terrifying thing waiting for me at the edges of his half-open lips. I wanted him to tell me everything, I said. Švarc nodded and put up no further resistance. He'd had to warn me, he said, though of course I had the right to know my mother's story. We sat down at a table by the window and the man from Brooklyn embarked on the story.

"That day we sat in the diner for many hours. Late that night I returned to Manhattan over the Brooklyn Bridge, whose lights were reflected in the dark surface of the East River. On each of the next few days we met at the Puerto Rican diner by the overground railroad station—indeed, we met there every afternoon until I had to return home. All that time, my new Brooklyn friend told me old stories about events with my mother at their center; all of these stories were completely new to me. Švarc was right: I flew home to a different city and a different home. What's more, a story that had slept for many years and been roused from dreams only by the occasional cry of a witness, now awoke and resumed its energetic course. Refreshed by sleep, it was like a snake on the hunt for new food.

"The story I heard in the Brooklyn diner began in the mid-sixties, when a group of young people, most of them around twenty, met often in bars and cafés. All of them were starting out as writers, painters, or composers. They had long, impassioned debates about art. One evening they realized that their constant quarreling notwithstanding, their most important values were very similar. That's when they had the idea of forming an artists' group.

"Although this was hardly a great time to form a group, the young people hankered after the atmosphere of discovery and friendship of the beginning of the century, which they had read about in books. When voiced late at night in the gray atmosphere of the cafés, their ideas seemed to them more beautiful and valuable than the same thoughts spoken in a living room or a university corridor. They imagined a meeting of their artists' group as a coming together of adventurers, the local bar in which they met as a last outpost of Amazonian civilization. Here—before they immersed themselves once again in the rainforest—they would tell of their experiences on their solitary ways, the remarkable plants they had seen and the dangerous animals they had wrestled.

"In those days, Švarc told me, the young people had the impression that the objects in every space they entered shed their old names, so that the old order associated with these names crumbled, and at any given moment a primeval forest opened up to them, and they heard its seductive hum. None of them knew their way about the formless forest that so seduced them by its hum, and no one knew how to behave within it so as not to get lost; no one knew its poisons or was able to read its signals, and no one suspected that as well as adventure, they could expect long, uneventful weeks of emptiness and boredom, which would have to be overcome. But they believed that for their journey they needed nothing more than determination and devotion to their secret; if they could hold on to these, soon they would find wonderful treasures in the forest.

"The group was given a name—Labyrinthos—on the evening it was established in a smoky bar on the edge of the city. Its members were especially proud of its lofty-sounding Greek ending. They espoused surrealism, although they knew very little about it; they used this term to describe the search for a secret, to which they intended to devote themselves. They clung to pre-war translations of *Illuminations*, *Nadja*, and *Les Chants de Maldoror* as though they were valuable relics. When they looked at these works years later, they realized they had made no attempt to understand the sentences they had read in them; they had been excited by them mainly because they had invested the words with unfinished thoughts and nascent images of their own.

"My father was a member of the group. Several years older than the other members, from the beginning he was their acknowledged leader. In debates they tended to wait for him to express his opinion."

"Jakub Jonáš the head of a group of surrealists!" I said in amazement. "That's the most fantastical thing I've come across in the entire double trident story!"

"It's perfectly true," said Viola. "I can show you a prose poem my father wrote in the Labyrinthos period. Švarc gave it to me in Brooklyn."

Again Viola jumped up from her armchair. She bent down to the lowest drawer of the desk and rummaged about in it for a while before removing a twice-folded sheet of yellowed paper and passing it to me. I opened the page out carefully, wary that it could disintegrate in my hands. At the center of its irregular, barely legible typewritten lines was a dark cross of empty space. I read:

When what had threatened darkly since the days of the drunken uprising, although historians have no notion of it, finally came to pass in golden and silver realms, and when the dripstones of a cave on Antiparos recalled the great fire of Nineveh and the pink and blue umbrellas of flower sellers pierced the early-morning waterfront, after some time it was possible to see, through the holes in these ingenious ladies' instruments, the slimy rock of the southernmost tip of Tierra del Fuego, to which sentimental scaly monsters had carried La Coste Castle, having picked it up one night using a complex hoist made from black lace garters. At that time, on some days the walls of the castle were of green velvet that smelled of the precious sweat of the armpits of prodigal daughters, while on other days the shadows of Justina and Julietta, at last holding hands that in accordance with the third axiom of marine algebra (which, unfortunately, is almost completely forgotten everywhere but in the depths of the Mariana Trench) had become vulture's talons, wandered between walls of icy pale-pink brick in which curious visitors, who from time to time strayed into these parts from rainy Albion or snowy Norway, might, after a moment of thorough investigation, discover gutted frozen chickens wrapped in plastic. Feel no shame, my dear, that their sawn-off heads with their woefully open little beaks appear in your dreams in the lower left field of the crest of the white prince, whose arrival has been announced by newsboys on street corners every evening for a whole century, and who is probably just a wooden mannequin from the locked department-store warehouse, if not some kind of complex mechanism in the manner of a dentist's chair. This is a good sign for the forthcoming couturiers' season, and sometimes also a bad one, but ultimately, who can distinguish the soft, delightful music of our vices from the rustling of flowers as yet unreal but whose fragrances overflow, slowly corroding taciturn stations?

While I was reading, the frail paper fell into two pieces. I put these together and handed them back to Viola.

"It's not exactly original, of course," I said, "and it's very forced. But it would be unjust to ridicule writing such as this. God knows what might have grown out of it if circumstances had been different. The hoist made of ladies' garters, for instance, is quite an amusing idea, even though Jonáš probably didn't intend it to be funny. And I rather like, too, the image of a castle built not of brick but of plastic bags for packaging frozen chickens. I can't imagine that Jonáš took this from a book; most likely he had bought a frozen chicken in a supermarket and been struck by the strange hardness of the body in the plastic; something that was a normal, everyday experience for other people seemed to him odd and interesting. Had he remained true to such experiences, had he sought them out, refined them and tried to make connections between them, perhaps in time he would have managed to free their expression from overwrought imagery and cliché. Anyway, unoriginal images, too, may be born of the deepest and truest experience, and who knows what Jonáš was going through at that time . . ."

"My Brooklyn friend said something similar. In his view, one reason why Jonáš's poems were epigonic was that he was the most educated and best informed member of the group. It's true that Jonáš very much wanted to be a leader, and sometimes this desire manifested itself in a way that was pretty intolerable, but Švarc didn't hold him in contempt; he believed that Jonáš's high-handedness at that time was only a distorted expression of the right feeling, and that even the most radical imagination needed discipline and hated arbitrariness. As told to me by Švarc in Brooklyn, in those days Jonáš was able to see more than the other members, and they saw this even in his forced imagery. That's why he kept his authority in the group for a long time; occasional attempts at revolt tended to consolidate rather than endanger his position. Like Jonáš, Švarc was a founding member of the group—they'd set it up when he was starting out as a student of sculpture at the Academy—so he was able to watch Jonáš from the very beginning."

I looked at Viola questioningly. "Wait a moment. Didn't Vuh-gah Oo emigrate in the mid-eighties? And wasn't he a sculptor?"

"That's right. The man I got to know in Brooklyn was indeed Vuh-gah Oo. But at the time I'm speaking of, he didn't yet call himself that—and by the time we met in New York, he'd almost forgotten the name he'd had in the days of the White Triangle."

"And the other members of the White Triangle?"

"Chuh-yuh, too, was present at the founding meeting of Labyrinthos; at that time he didn't use his pseudonym, either. Iui Num came along later—we'll get to him soon."

Chapter 4
Labyrinthos

"What did Chuh-yuh do in the group of surrealists? Compose surrealist music? I didn't know that any such thing existed . . ."

"It seems that Chuh-yuh really did claim at the time that his compositions were surrealist. In the Labyrinthos period, he composed an album of music that he called *Cable Radio in the House of Usher.* It was intended for a small orchestra. There was no chance that an orchestra would actually play Chuh-yuh's music, of course, and he didn't have enough musician friends to form a musical ensemble. So to meetings of the group he took nothing but his scores written in pencil. No other member of Labyrinthos was able to read these, so Navrátil would just tell them about the individual compositions and sing them some of the motifs. Each composition of the *Usher* album began with a direct quotation from a pop hit of the time, after which notes would appear in the melody that didn't belong, small variations that gradually roused a different, dark melody that grew through the body of the original motif like gangrene or a parasite, transforming the melody so that it was ever more monstrous and terrible. At the end of the composition the original melody was still just about recognizable, but it had been made into a monster. According to Švarc, each composition developed like the film in which a scientist gradually changes into a hideous great fly whose body has only distant echoes of his original human form. Although no one else in the group understood music, on the basis of Chuh-yuh's descriptions the other members concluded that his work was sufficiently unconventional and subversive to merit his membership in Labyrinthos. Jonáš, too, praised Chuh-yuh, probably because he was active in a field that was marginal to the group's interests, and in which Jonáš couldn't compete with him."

"Have you ever heard any of Chuh-yuh's compositions from that time?"

"No. The only musical ensemble that ever played them was the imaginary orchestra in Chuh-yuh's head. Nor will anyone ever hear them, because their notations were lost long ago . . ."

"Has Chuh-yuh never tried to reconstruct any of them?"

"I suggested he should. Chuh-yuh said it would be impossible even if he wanted to, as all he could remember of his compositions was the odd snatch of melody. Above all, though, Chuh-yuh had no desire to renew his old works. He said that he liked to return to the ruins of compositions as they remained in his head, but that he liked them as they were now; it was like walking through a large mansion, some parts of which had collapsed completely, while the walls of others were overgrown with murmuring bushes and clumps of confused melody . . . He told me that at one period in his life he'd composed a number of pieces of music for mental instruments—violins, flutes, drums—and for the song of an imaginary bird. These pieces were intended for the concert hall of the mind and for a single listener . . ."

At this point Viola again fell silent. I imagined an aria sung by a non-existent bird. I closed my eyes and it appeared before me, its body covered with white feathers, its wings fringed with gold, its tail long. Then the bird went quiet and vanished, and again I had to think of Viola's father; I realized that Jonáš as the leader of a surrealist group was the thing I had most trouble seeing.

"I can't imagine your father among young surrealists," I said to Viola. "When I try, I keep getting this strange collage, with an immobile colossus surrounded by thin, rubber figures that in the midst of debate keep jumping off the table, going on talking as they swing to and fro before sitting down again."

"A golem among snake-men and snake-women," said Viola, smiling. "But Vuh-gah Oo, who as a sculptor knew the human body well, told me that the shape of the body has a far more formative effect on the spirit than people think, and that Jonáš's body later changed in almost the same way as his soul. I'm told that in the days of Labyrinthos, he was tall and sturdy, but there was no sign of the ponderous, aggressive power that would later threaten to roll over all objects and people in his path. His body was well matched with the movements of the rubber figures—Jonáš jumped up just as often as the others, and his hulking form must have made an impressive sight. In the Brooklyn diner, Oo showed me—to the great amusement of the Puerto Rican customers—how Jonáš would stand up from the table, raise his eyes to the ceiling or maybe the heavens above and spread his arms; apparently like Maldoror, he was offering his forehead to the lightning . . ."

I would never have guessed that Jonáš's mammoth body had such a dramatic past and such venerable relations.

"Later, it seemed to Oo that my father hadn't become fat but that a power which he began to serve and partake of had flowed into his body. This power worked on him for so long that it formed his body into a monument to itself . . . And surprisingly, in the creation of this new body it used the features it had used earlier in making Jonáš a brother, or at least a cousin, of Maldoror."

A sound in the distance blended in with Viola's last words. Viola fell silent when the train was still quite far away; I had the impression that her story was approaching an old wound that still wasn't altogether healed, and that she wished to postpone the moment when she would have to speak of it. So for a while we listened to the whisper strengthen to a brief roar before fading. As Viola resumed her story, her words fell softly into the whisper made by the retreating train.

"Some time in '67, Jonáš brought Valerie, my mother, into the group. She was only seventeen at that time. No one knows where they met, but from this time on, Valerie regularly took part in the meetings with Jonáš. She was the only one in the group who didn't write, paint or compose music, and when debates and arguments were in progress she was always silent. The others took her as someone who belonged with Jonáš; they liked her silent presence, and they missed her when she didn't show up at a meeting, which was rarely, as Jonáš attended almost every meeting and Valerie was always with him."

Viola spoke of her father as "Jonáš," while she used the Christian name of the mother she didn't remember, as though they were friends.

"At the end of the sixties, something changed in the life of the group. It was as though all of a sudden, amid all the unoriginal and forced imagery a weak light was born, and this light slowly grew in intensity. A new language took shape in the typewritten texts and on the painted canvases. The members of the group watched its discovery and growth with fascination; they cared painstakingly for this child born so unexpectedly, and that filled them with happiness. Oo said that although the new language assumed a different manifestation in the work of each Labyrinthos member, it was possible to find in all of them remarkably similar features, especially a kind of deliberate poverty that favored simplistic images in constellations of a few isolated words or lines that floated in a void. The strict, compelling sound of the new language as heard by some members of the group led to their abandoning their literary efforts and turning to the serious study of philosophy or mathematics; they shut themselves up in libraries and learned languages dead and alive so that they could read otherwise unavailable books in the original . . .

"Jonáš remained the leader of the group, although his writings were scarcely touched by the new language. It was obvious that his work was becoming an anachronism, a relic from the prehistory of the group that still evoked sentimental feelings, but to which no one wanted to return. Probably Jonáš heard the new language just as the others did, but he was unable to learn it. His misfortune was his education; he wasn't able to forget everything he'd read; he wasn't able to quit the house he'd lived in with his beloved poets. And so he ridiculed the new writings and images and accused their authors and artists of Traditionalism and Neoclassicism. At every meeting he brought forth Dalí's quote that is was necessary to hate simplicity in all its forms . . . Those he was addressing argued with him, but they did this out of consideration for him, respect for what he'd once meant to them, nostalgia for the early days of the group and, increasingly, compassion. Now no one attacked his leadership, as had happened occasionally before, and Jonáš realized the reason for this with bitterness: It was because no one took him seriously."

As Viola paused, I listened for an approaching train, but there was absolute silence.

"Jonáš took his degree in French and Literary Theory," she went on. "When he graduated from the Faculty of Arts in the mid sixties, his dissertation on the esthetics of Baudelaire caused quite a stir. Straight after school he became a stagehand, something that wasn't as common then as ten years later, and he expressed his contempt for the official scholars of literature and the work of the institutions. But in '68 they offered him an assistant professor's post in the Department of Literature, and he accepted. At that time he commented jokingly at meetings that he would now be able to spread subversive ideas among the students. By then many members of the group knew that serious work was more important and also more subversive than the spreading of smart ideas, but no one said this to Jonáš; indeed they congratulated him on his new post.

"When in 1970 the university purges began, the members of Labyrinthos were convinced that Jonáš would be dismissed by the commission or that he would choose to leave his post. But to the surprise of the others he stayed on, explaining to them that it was necessary that someone reminded young people of books that had been pulped and of names that were now banned or unmentioned. Still the members of the group kept silent. They didn't wish to judge him, although by now they knew that his poems—which a few years earlier they'd greatly admired—were bad. On the other hand, they were more than ever aware of what they owed Jonáš; the language they were now making such efforts to learn and which Jonáš didn't understand, would never have been born without what Jonáš had taught them about Novalis, Nerval, Rimbaud and Lautréamont; had they never met Jonáš, they would never have discovered the land of imagination and freedom they were no longer able to live without, and from which no power could expel them.

"Valerie didn't criticize Jonáš either, but it was obvious that she was unhappy. Jonáš turned up at meetings of the group ever less frequently, and Valerie often attended alone. Then in '74, someone appeared at the meeting with an official literary magazine that contained an article by Jonáš. In the article, Jonáš praised a new book by a favorite of the regime, in which poems extolling the mythical history of power alternated with mawkish lyric poetry about love and nature. Everyone expected Jonáš to explain his conduct, but he never again attended a meeting of the group. Valerie continued to come, but she never mentioned Jonáš. In front of Valerie the others never talked of what had happened, so as not to upset her. And as no one liked to talk behind Valerie's back, the silence regarding Jonáš was total. Švarc told me that in those days he felt pain rather than hatred or contempt; he was still grateful to Jonáš, and it seemed to him that the others felt likewise.

"At that time Valerie was pregnant. The others saw that she was desperate. Some time later, after Jonáš published an article in which at the behest of the regime he joined the pursuit of a persecuted author, my mother left him. Then I was born. Although my parents didn't divorce, Valerie never saw Jonáš again. Švarc told me that Valerie used to take me to meetings of the group in my pram. Later, the group often met at our apartment.

"Valerie looked on in amazement at the contemporary reality. Although she didn't have a TV or read the newspapers, Švarc spoke of how once they were passing the window of an electrical appliances store where footage of some conference was appearing on a TV screen; he'd wanted to move on quickly, but Valerie had stopped in a state of wonder, in which fascination and squeamishness came together. She looked at the faces on the screen as though the TV was an aquarium containing life forms from a strange undersea world. Švarc said that my mother seemed to feel compassion for these creatures. Perhaps she felt something similar for Jonáš; perhaps it seemed to her that he'd been struck by some mysterious disease and she was monitoring his transformation anxiously as people watch the signs of a deadly illness appear on the body of a loved one. Maybe she thought that he needed her help and blamed herself for her inability to live with him any longer, but apart from compassion, the manifestations of Jonáš's illness aroused in her aversion and horror, and these Valerie could not overcome.

"Švarc said that at that time he talked about Jonáš's behavior with many people who knew him. Each of them gave a different explanation of Jonáš's desertion. After hearing the various theories his inquiries provoked, Švarc had to concede that he didn't understand the cause of the change in Jonáš any better than he had at the beginning. Some referred to Jonáš's craving for leadership and power, which had been in evidence since the beginnings of Labyrinthos and was the most unpleasant aspect of Jonáš's personality. Others argued that having realized how bad his poems were, Jonáš was overcome by a sense of self-hatred, and his crossover to the side of the powerful was a humiliation forced on himself as a punishment.

"At that time, Labyrinthos quietly broke up. From then on, Valerie met only with Navrátil and Švarc, and they rarely talked about art. The others faded from view. By then, some of them spent every spare moment writing poems or fiction and regarded debates about literature as a waste of time; for some, the flame of the new language had gone out, although they looked back on it as they quietly survived in official institutions; others went off to boiler houses and trailers, where they studied Kant and Husserl, learned Greek and Sanskrit, translated Plotinus and wrote studies on space and time; the remainder left because they were tired or suddenly forgot what it was they were actually looking for in the world of the imagination. Valerie, Chuh-yuh, and Oo were together almost every day, at our apartment. Chuh-yuh and Oo would bring food, and when my mother had to visit the authorities or the doctor's office, they would look after me."

Chapter 5
Four Friends

"At that sad time, something happened that nobody was expecting, a miracle that for many years only three people knew about . . . One fall afternoon Valerie asked Chuh-yuh and Oo if she could read a few short pieces of her writing to them. From the very first sentence, both were entranced; they listened astonished to language saturated in the fantastical imagery of the early days of Labyrinthos as well as the sober magical objectivity of the later period. Although by the time we met, Oo could no longer remember a single word of Valerie's prose, all those years later he recalled how the waves of her language rose in silence and emptiness, how the tip of each wave formed itself into unexpected images of light, and how when these images began to dissolve they mingled with a new, approaching wave, which itself then transformed into new images . . .

"After that, Valerie wrote whenever she had the time. It seemed to Navrátil and Švarc that her language was ever more translucent; that each of her words was like a lantern shining a light unsullied by the times or by Valerie's own despair. Not a single fragment, not a single sentence of these writings has survived . . . Maybe Valerie herself destroyed them when she was blissfully intoxicated by the idea of the mortality of the text; maybe my father burned them when after my mother's death he acquired her entire estate . . .

"Then Pascal Brison appeared. Pascal was six years younger

than Navrátil and Švarc and a year younger than Valerie. His father, the owner of a small factory somewhere in France, had sent him over here to oversee the introduction of their products under license at a local factory. Pascal was a recent graduate in chemistry. At the university, he'd been one of the best students, but also one of the biggest troublemakers. Every month there had been an offense against discipline to contend with—insolent conduct toward a teacher, a brawl or a drunken disturbance at the dorm—and had it not been for his excellent results, he would have been expelled from the school before the end of his second semester. Pascal was able to drink through the night and go straight from the bar to the examination hall; several classmates tried to imitate him, and all came to grief. He was also a good skier and a keen diver. Every winter he went to the Alps, and he spent every summer vacation in the Caribbean, leaving the lab, study room, and bar behind for two months on baking-hot beaches and under water. In his students years he fell in love three or four times, bombarding each of the girls with letters, gifts, and flowers so that in each of them a sense of astonishment and flattery soon turned to love as intense as the love he was offering them. But Pascal's love never lasted through summer vacation; on his return from the Caribbean, the girl who'd been longing to see him for the past two months found that he'd lost all interest in her.

"At the university, it was assumed that he would devote himself to theoretical research and either sell the family business or hire a manager to run the factory. Although his parents were proud of him, they were afraid of what would happen with the business, which had been in the family's hands for 150 years. So far, in the brief periods between his return from the islands and his departure for the dorm, Pascal had always found time for the factory, proposing to his father certain improvements in its operation and mentioning to him several discoveries he would like to have patented and which might generate the kind of profit none of the previous owners of the factory could have dreamed of.

"Pascal's father was a little confused by this. He was glad that

Pascal continued to be interested in the family business, but at the same time the innovations his son introduced aroused in him such feelings of anxiety and nausea that he preferred not to question him about them in any detail. He didn't want to change the decades-old methods of production; he was altogether correct in his assumption that the company's customers—who bought the same soaps and shampoos as their parents and grandparents had bought, in the same packaging—were attracted by the fact that nothing ever changed. Pascal's father was happy with how the company lived at the center of a small circle and how the products that flowed out of the factory did so slowly and calmly, into the drugstores of the town and the surrounding villages, and from there to the homes of the neighborhood, returning to the factory a stream of money that was similarly slow and shallow. This tranquil flow that involved the company in the life of the region and protected it from world forces, was to him tantamount to happiness. When he thought of the discoveries that Pascal spoke of, he consoled himself by remembering that he himself had had plans aplenty at the time he'd taken over the factory from his own father; but then the old, peaceful rhythm had proved more powerful than his dreams. He hoped that it would be the same with his son and that he, too, would be engulfed by the sleepy flow of products and money, like every owner of the factory before him.

"Pascal delayed the moment when he would have to decide between the factory and a scientific institute. He realized that he lacked the patience of a true researcher, but at the same time he was dismayed by the idea of a peaceful life spent running a small-town factory that had produced the same soap since the times of Louis Philippe. For him, the slow circular current of production and trade in which his father had bathed blissfully his whole life was a stagnant, diseased river. In addition to this, something had happened in his senior year at university that made him even more uncertain and was driving him to despair. He had come into possession of a volume of Hölderlin's poems. Until then Pascal had had no particular interest in literature. He'd started to read the Hölderlin collection only because he'd seen that it contained a poem about the Alps, which he loved . . . Having read the poem on the Alps, Pascal read others. He read of Greece, of islands, of the Indus, of Swabia and Gascony, of slumbering Titans, of gods that departed and might one day return, of genii flying over Asian mountain ranges with silver streams rushing from their heights, of homelessness, kindly land, a mighty sea, and shining ether.

"And he felt that the whole world and his whole life had changed. Now it seemed that he'd been wrong to study chemistry, that he'd done so because he'd misinterpreted a voice that had long spoken faintly but resonantly inside him. Suddenly Pascal saw his whole life up to that point in a new light; it seemed to him that in his study of chemistry, subconsciously he'd been looking for something that had now presented itself to him in its true form. For him the reading of Hölderlin's poems was a convoluted and restless process in which the words attracted and repelled each other, acted on each other and were transformed by this action and so gave off unexpected effects, and combined in various constellations that then came apart; and it seemed to him that now, at last, he understood his interest in chemistry: Chemical processes had always attracted him only because they were a remote, veiled image of the process of poetry; because they reflected it in code. At night he read books by many other authors, most of whom disappointed him, although he did discover a few poets and novelists that again gave him a sense of miraculous chemistry. When school was over and his father asked him to introduce production under license in a foreign country, he was glad. By being away, he was able to postpone the decision about his future occupation; Pascal Brison hoped that half a year—the anticipated length of his stay—would be long enough for him to think everything through and to make up his mind.

"Brison's many talents included an unusual gift for languages, so that within three months he spoke Czech so well that hardly anyone thought him a foreigner—just as many years later he was considered a Greek after a few months on Naxos. One day in a bar, he overheard Švarc and Navrátil discussing a passage from Lautréamont that he happened to have read the previous night, and he approached them. And it turned out that the authors whom Chuh-yuh and Oo had loved since the days of Labyrinthos were the same as those with whom Pascal Brison had learned the basics of the chemistry of the imagination.

"After that, the three of them met often. As soon as Chuh-yuh and Oo entered the café, they would look around to see if Pascal was sitting in a corner, and if he was and looked up from his book and waved to them, they were glad. Such an experience was unusual for Chuh-yuh and Oo—in those days, the gravitational force of Valerie and her world was so strong that they were unable to be friends or even associate with anyone else. Pascal was the first person in a long time they could call their friend. And so the time came when they took him to Valerie. From then on, they would meet up as a foursome."

"Dominik told me about a nephew of Brison's he'd met in France," I said. "So are you telling me that Pascal Brison is Iui Num? If so, we now have the complete White Triangle."

"That's right. Later, when Navrátil began to call himself Chuh-yuh and Švarc took on the name Vuh-gah Oo, Pascal Brison became Iui Num."

The heat of the day had subsided. A wind wafted in through the window, ruffling the sheets on the piano, one of which descended to the carpet in a slow circular movement. The invisible sun reflected red on the metal structures that towered over the railroad. Darkness was gathering over the plains in the distance.

Chapter 6
The Disappearing Book

"One day, when the four of them were sitting at Valerie's and Švarc was talking about his new sculptures, Pascal recalled a discovery of his that he'd wanted to put into practice in the family business. This concerned the paints that took on various colors and then became transparent depending on circumstances and length of exposure. Pascal proposed to Švarc that he use these on his sculptures. But at that time Švarc had other interests: His mind was on three-dimensional shapes that were produced by crumpling up two-dimensional drawings, and the idea of a sculpture on which colors would appear and disappear didn't tempt him. That's why Brison's magic colors made their breakthrough in visual art only many years later, when Dominik began to use them in his paintings.

"Valerie, though, was extremely interested in what Pascal was saying. She realized immediately that there was a connection between Brison's discovery and something which her writing had long been struggling to give shape to. Had it not been for this unexpected connection, perhaps she wouldn't have been aware of this reluctant birth or paid much attention to images found at various places in her prose that nevertheless depicted the same obsession. Only now did she realize that motifs of the transformation and extinction of letters appeared in her prose again and again; in one place, the motif was of a book manuscript in which letters slowly changed into incomprehensible hieroglyphs before the author's eyes—at first the author fought against the letter disease, every day rewriting the characters as the original letters, but then he gave this up and looked on resigned as a new, incomprehensible text was born; in another, it was the image of a long poem that someone found etched on the frozen surface of a lake, which thawed before this person could return to it in order to write it down . . . Valerie had no idea of the meaning of these images, which emerged insistently in a variety of connections, and she told herself that Pascal's discovery might help her find out where they actually came from and what they wanted to communicate to her. At the same time, ideas began to form in her mind of texts that wouldn't only discuss her dreams but actually make them happen.

"Valerie asked Pascal about his paints, and he described all their properties to her in detail. He was very glad that Valerie wanted to use his discovery for her new work. At the time he got to know Chuh-yuh and Oo, Pascal himself was trying to write; he even read a few of his poems to his friends when they met at the café. But after he met Valerie and heard her read her prose, he put aside writing for a long time. He would turn back to it only after Valerie's death, after which his writing would always only be a memorial to Valerie . . . But now we're getting ahead of ourselves. So Pascal prepared for Valerie several sets of paints and the corresponding hard activators. Valerie used the hard activators just to make the paint visible while she was writing; she left the exposition of the text to the soft activators, hence to chance, that is to circumstances that couldn't be determined in advance. Dominik used the same technique when painting his pictures.

"At first she wrote poems in which certain images appeared when the sun was shining and others when it was raining or snowing. The sense of these poems was rooted in the poignant impermanence of letters that were unable to withstand the elements and so were dependent on the weather; the poems touched on the passage of the simplest present time and drew from it the soft power of birth and extinction . . . After that, she wrote several works of prose in which she used a variety of paints for alternative developments of plot—the heroes came together or missed each other, died or were restored to health depending on the weather at the time of reading. Her three friends liked the way her sentences spilled over into a time other than the one assigned to them, they admired how they were fitted to rhythms that weren't the rhythms of the line and the page, and they enjoyed waiting for the moment when a letter was revealed . . . But for Valerie, such texts were just exercises and games, just an experimental encounter of two different times—the time of the reading and the time of the story—by which she examined their behavior and mutual relations; they were no more than preparation for the full task, whose outline began to emerge as she wrote her meteorological prose."

"Have you ever seen one of these changing texts?"

"No. None of this group of texts have survived either. Maybe Valerie herself destroyed them, once her idea of the disappearing book had reached full maturity."

"The disappearing book?" It seemed we were getting to the heart of Viola's story.

"Oo told me about a meeting of the four of them at Valerie's apartment in December '77. He recalled that the first snow had fallen that morning. It was then that Valerie spoke for the first time of a book that was perfectly legible until one day its text simply disappeared into the paper, forever. Oo thought that the final impulse in Valerie's decision to write a book that would become nothing but blank pages was given by the view from her window of things disappearing under the snow. For a long time the three friends tried to talk Valerie out of her plan; they couldn't come to terms with the idea of a work that provided in advance for its self-imposed destruction. They admired Valerie's prose; the thought that her new work was condemned to such a short life before it was even born was insufferable to them. But the idea of a disappearing book was source of particular delight to Valerie. At that time she regulated her life around making it happen, and she took little notice of the objections and entreaties of her friends.

"Probably Valerie herself didn't much understand her obsession with the disappearing book. As she tried hard to grasp the sense of her strange endeavors, the four of them would often discuss her intentions until late at night. In the beginning, one of them conjectured aloud that the pre-programmed destruction of text should release the meanings of its words from the material that bound them to a reality that wasn't worth much, to a time it was best to have as little as possible to do with. But Valerie shook her head at this surmise: That certainly wasn't the case. She felt that her desire to write a book that would soon destroy itself had not grown out of a hostility to reality—she said that the greatest defeat of all would be if those images which control was attempting to contrive out of facts, bodies and landscapes were to declare themselves as real. What she saw as being at the bottom of her desire to create a disappearing book was the wish to plant the life of the text in a soil in which words were at their most fragile and mortal, their most dependent on chance, their least resistant to the currents, eddies and branches of time; this was a soil in which words inhabited space with the same humility as things, and she would draw on its gentle force even at the price of a short life.

"It seemed to her that meaning could be born and preserved only in a living, breathing world of tangible objects and living things, when everything has a beginning and an end; and that the work must submit to its rhythms and pass through all phases of time, which Valerie perceived as the chambers of a wonderful palace. Whoever came to the palace of time, she said, must stay a while in the chamber of anticipation, the chamber of birth, the chambers of the present, withering and decay, the gloomy chamber of memory, which had heavy curtains at its windows, and the dark chamber of forgetting and decomposition, which was in the palace cellars. This last chamber was at the same time one of metamorphosis and new birth, in which the enduring breath of defunct shapes worked quietly at the creation of new shapes.

"Valerie claimed a work can truly live only if no section of this journey is omitted—it must pass through every chamber of the palace of time. By now Valerie had moved away from all books, even those she had formerly loved. Until recently there had been volumes she took off her shelves and opened daily, but now she let them be. She was bothered by the pride they showed in trying to step out of time; she claimed that they paid too high a price for their dubious victory over time. She said that thoughts of the future persistence of a work in unchanged form destroyed the work at the time of its origination, as they prevented its birth from connecting to the gentle force of passing time which was the only thing capable of imparting real sense to the work, and being nourished by it.

"When Valerie talked of the end of the book, she was actually thinking of its beginning and what was before that; of a space of swirling, shapeless forces that preceded the work, breathed life into it and invested in it a mysterious message—a sense of magic that after the work had perished would circulate and create new bodies for itself while going through ever new transformations. Valerie believed that the beneficial effects of the swirling space were killed by the idea that a work's shape was immutable and enduring. Perhaps this very fascination with this space was at the heart of Valerie's longing for a disappearing book . . ."

At this point I couldn't stop myself from interrupting Viola to ask about something that had been on my mind for a while.

"What you're describing are complicated and perhaps ingenious theories," I said. "But I'm afraid there's one simple question they don't answer: To destroy the work, why are some strange paints needed? Wouldn't it suffice to write the book in the normal way and then burn it?"

"Apparently Oo voiced that objection to Valerie. But she wasn't at all attracted by the idea of burning the book, saying that it was essential to her plan that the book be preserved as an object and its pages somehow continue to exist after it had perished, even though no one would be able to read them. Then Oo raised a further objection: Would it not be possible to write the book with an ink pen and then black out the text on a typewriter? But this idea didn't please Valerie either. She said that the blacked-out pages would give rise to the idea that something was missing and produce the impression of loss, thus focusing attention on the past form and perhaps even leading to attempts to restore it. What Valerie wanted at the end was a white surface that would reveal that nothing was missing—that the text was where it ought to be, living in the phase of return to formlessness and new metamorphosis, a phase which was as justifiable and valuable as the phase of the finished form . . .

"In brief, that's the theory of the disappearing book that Valerie arrived at after talking about it with her friends for many hours. But Oo and Chuh-yuh told me that they never took such ideas very seriously. Needing an explanation for her strange longing, Valerie created a system of quite acceptable, harmonized ideas, but this didn't mean that these necessarily had much in common with the roots of that longing. From what Oo told me, maybe she took a dark delight in decline and extinction which needed no explanation. Chuh-yuh believed that Valerie had an inkling that she didn't have long to live and she wanted to humble death by turning its usual game on its head, playing out a parodic drama of her own for the world in which her work would live on. I've given Valerie's decision to destroy her work a lot of thought; to me, too, it seems that it grew out of a premonition of imminent death. But I don't agree with Chuh-yuh that it was an attempt to make something more mortal than she was—I believe that the destruction of the work was intended as a challenge in the face of death; Valerie wanted to show that she wasn't afraid of extinction, so she would surrender to it something extremely important to her . . ."

"Could it be that Valerie believed in her theories on the life of a changing work more than her friends realized, and that when she felt the nearness of death, she told herself that an anonymous future in endless transformations was not only richer and more adventurous but also more certain than a future associated with the preservation of a fixed shape?"

Viola shrugged. "I think the main reason Valerie decided to destroy her book will forever remain a mystery. But from the beginning there was a secondary reason about which there was never any argument. The destruction of her own work was an act of black comedy by which Valerie was responding to the voice of the times. Although she didn't want to listen to it, it kept reaching her ears, if only through jackets of books in the storefront windows she passed, the headlines of newspapers the vegetable merchant wrapped her purchases in, the hit song from a radio on the other side of a wall, and the faces of passers-by, whose features had taken on the toxic grayness of the times. Valerie said to herself: As they ban and destroy books, as they try so hard to make text disappear, why not give them what they want, a book with blank pages from which the text has vanished, never to reappear? She realized that they would be powerless against such a text: They would never be able to destroy, erase or censor a text that had disappeared, although it would forever tremble in the air, spilling over onto pages of other books, seeping between the lines of novels published through official channels . . .

"Later it occurred to Švarc that the voice of the times influenced her act in another way, too. My mother never spoke with contempt of people who devoted all their energies to the collecting of meaningless property; she said that they were resisting evil by the confused fulfillment of a dream of home-building, the source of which was pure and which one day would be cleansed anew. On the other hand, the destruction of what was most precious to her may have been an unconscious gesture responding to the orgy of acquisition and accumulation characteristic of the times."

Chapter 7
Venus and Tannhäuser

"Having thought everything out, Valerie turned to Pascal and asked him to prepare an ink that would be visible for one month and then vanish forever; none of the hard or soft activators would be able to restore it. When Pascal asked Valerie when she would need the ink, she told him that she would work on the novel for a year and only after that write it up in the disappearing ink. So Pascal agreed to bring the ink to her in a year's time."

I interrupted Viola to ask something that had been on my mind for a while. "Were the three of them in love with Valerie?"

Viola took time over answering this. "Oo said nothing about that then, and Chuh-yuh has said nothing about it since, and I haven't put the question directly to either of them. My embarrassment was the least of it—in one sense, the question would have been nonsense, like asking someone which is heavier, a triangle or a rectangle. In the world of Valerie and her friends, the everyday words of our own world acquired new meanings—love as we understand it would be as likely to occur in it as weight in geometry. As I was listening to the stories of Chuh-yuh and Oo, I would often have the feeling that the happenings of which they spoke were captured on overexposed film, in which the colors dissolved in a cold, clear light and the shapes were so sharp that they ceased to resemble each other. Perhaps Oo and Chuh-yuh were in love with Valerie, but in the atmosphere of cold light that spouted from the void, spilling out over everything in their world of that time, their love changed into something else—a feeling for which a new word would need to be invented and out of which grew sheer despair after Valerie's death.

"While my mother was alive, the love dissolved in a light that brought a special happiness and alleviated every desire by its ubiquity. But apparently this quiet happiness was not continuous; there were moments when the light was weaker and the pain and desire returned. Oo and Chuh-yuh each experienced these periods in a different way. Music had always meant so much to Chuh-yuh that at moments of depression he could take refuge in it; Oo, though, was unable to think of sculpture at times of despair. As for Pascal, his was yet another experience. Although he was quick-tempered, he tended to melancholia; his passion long resisted the atmosphere of peace that reigned in Valerie's world—indeed it never submitted to it entirely. He didn't wish to speak of them, but several times Švarc referred to wild scenes, shouting and drunkenness . . ."

The light reflected in the window from the metal constructions had gone out; the room was slowly darkening. Again Viola's last words were drowned out by the noise of an approaching train. This time, the noise stopped suddenly, and there was a sound of squealing brakes. As the illuminated train moved past our room, the continuous strip of light began to flash before becoming a series of squares with rounded corners that eventually came to a halt. The light reached from one end of our room to the other. I saw a passenger pull open the little top window of the compartment in an attempt to see where the train was standing. For a moment he looked into the dark room where Viola and I were sitting; then he slammed the window shut. I knew now that the carriage was too far away for me to touch the hand of a passenger. Soon the train shuddered and began slowly to move. When it was heard no longer, Viola resumed the story.

"Valerie's estimation of how long it would take her to write her novel proved to be exactly right; it really did take her a year to finish it, in December '78. Although her writing gave the impression that its images came into existence one after another, that in each word whole clusters of other words were waiting impatiently to force their way out, and that all Valerie had to do was record them on paper, in fact she worked with difficulty and rewrote each sentence many times. The birth of her novel was still more painstaking than the origination of her earlier prose work; she polished her sentences with such care as if their sacrifice to nothingness would be worthwhile only if nothing was left unfinished in this work that would disappear soon after it was completed."

"But in taking such efforts over the work's fixed shape, wasn't Valerie contradicting herself? Didn't you say that she wanted to surrender the work to an anonymous life of transformation in a shapeless world and that this world must exert an influence from the very moment of its birth?"

"No, Valerie claimed only that at the phase of formation the work should mature from the swirling of nothingness into a fixed shape, and that at the phase of formlessness the fixed shape should dissolve in eddies of transformation; there's no contradiction there. It was precisely this round of formlessness and form that so attracted her."

When Viola saw that I was raising no objection, she went on: "Valerie hesitated over the theme of her book for a long time. Several times she began to write a story before rejecting it—but the rejected novels returned to her work in secondary storylines and insertions and their main heroes reappeared as episodic characters.

"Pascal kept his promise. When Valerie announced that the novel was ready for the final rewrite, he brought her the ink she had requested from him a year earlier. He mixed it according to a formula that originated in this country and had a special history closely associated with Pascal's predisposition for drunkenness."

"Did the formula contain rum?"

"No, it was a little more complicated than that. Only recently Pascal had dreamed of traveling the world for a few years after he finished school, and now the world had shrunk to a narrow strip of city between his rented room, the factory where he worked and the apartment Valerie lived in with me. Often after seeing Valerie, he would end up in one of the bars on his way home, and after that closed he would look out for the shining neon sign of a nightclub. As the times when he was able to pass an exam in organic chemistry after a night of heavy drinking were behind him, he would wake up the next morning with a headache and an unsettled stomach . . .

"Once he sat down in a pub next to a skinny man who was lost in thought. For about an hour they sat next to each other without speaking, drinking one beer after another. On the table in front of Pascal's neighbor was a small round metal box; from time to time the man opened this and took tobacco from it, which he rolled into a cigarette. The box had obviously been handled and knocked about a lot—the picture on its lid was covered with so many scratches that it was impossible to be sure of its theme, although Pascal thought that it showed a rhinoceros hunt. When his neighbor went to the bathroom, he picked it up and took a closer look at it. Now he saw that what he'd taken for a rhinoceros was the edge of a divan curved in an 'S.' On this divan lay a woman in a diaphanous veil; in front of her was a kneeling man in what looked like medieval dress; beyond these figures was a dark lake on whose shore fairies were dancing; at the top of the picture was the arched ceiling of a cave. He considered the picture for a moment and reached the conclusion that it showed Tannhäuser and Venus on the shore of the lake inside the Hörselberg Mountain. On his neighbor's return, it was impossible for Pascal not to ask him what the box had contained before its use as a tobacco tin. His neighbor answered this by beginning to tell the story of his family. At first Pascal regretted having addressed him: He didn't feel in the least like hearing at length about the doings of a family. But before long his attention was engaged, and soon he was following his neighbor's tale with keen interest. It turned out that the biggest problem in the life of this unknown drinker was the same as the one that had driven Pascal from France: Both men were weighed down by their inheritance of the family business.

"But the worries given by the family business to Pascal's new friend were of a different nature to his own. Pascal learned that the drinker's name was Kulhánek, and that in 1905 his family had manufactured a powder for the treatment of eczema once known as 'Kulhánek's Tannhäuser powder' or simply 'Tannhäuser powder.' At the very beginning of the twentieth century, an entrance to a cave had been found in a ravine not far from the city; some children had been playing hide-and-seek in the dense bushes there. Having returned the next day with a lamp, they found themselves in a small vaulted space, where at various heights in the rock there were twelve shallow depressions that formed natural basins; each of these was filled with water in which a bubble occasionally rose to the surface. Although this was no great discovery, on Sunday people from the neighborhood would walk to the entrance of the cave and peek inside with curiosity.

"When Kulhánek's grandfather read in the newspaper about this new cave and its water source, he went to see it straight away. A pharmacist, Kulhánek the grandfather had read various pamphlets on subjects of natural healing and was particularly impressed by Father Kneipp's treatise on hydrotherapy. He took water from all the sources, put it into bottles and then analyzed it. He found that water from the cave was rich in the kind of minerals his books told him had a healing effect on skin complaints. He didn't think twice before buying the land with the cave on it and starting to sell water for the treatment of eczema. Later, he used the mineral water from the cave in the preparation of a powder that was even more effective.

"It was necessary to find an impressive-sounding name for the new product. As Kulhánek the grandfather was a great admirer of Wagner, it didn't take him long to come up with this. The first image to come to his mind in connection with the surface of water in a cave was of the lake inside the mountain of Venus. So he sold his powder in a tin whose lid was decorated with a picture of Venus and Tannhäuser on the shore of an underground lake. Now Pascal had one of these tins in his hand and was studying the figures under the white spiderweb of scratches.

"With money he inherited from his father-in-law's death, Kulhánek the grandfather built a two-story house above the cave. On the facade was a glittering sign composed of gilded Art Nouveau letters that declared the house to be the 'Tannhäuser Villa'; below the sign was a stucco relief of the scene depicted on the tins. Kulhánek the grandfather and his family occupied the upper floor. The lower floor comprised a laboratory and workshop in which three technicians produced the Tannhäuser powder. The cave became a part of the villa's cellars; water was drawn from the cave to the workshop using hand pumps; this wasn't particularly hard work because the sources didn't yield a great deal, so water could be drawn only two or three times a day, each time for just a few minutes. As the technicians pumped and processed the mineral water, their work was continuously accompanied by an aria from Wagner. (It was the job of one of the technicians to work the phonograph by changing the records and adjusting the tension of the spring.) How keen the technicians were on Wagner isn't known, but the constant playing of his music was at the grandfather's command and none of his employees dared protest.

"In the twenties, the son of the founder of the business—the father of Pascal's new friend—made extensive changes to production. At this time the growing city had reached the Tannhäuser villa, which was now just one in a line of villas on a new street. Kulhánek the father had the villa modernized and rid it of its Art Nouveau signs and reliefs. Also he had new tins made, on whose lids the fragile Art Nouveau Minnesänger and the goddess with Mucha-style plaits were replaced by sporty, Art Deco figures that looked rather like tourists relaxing on a beach. Principally, though, he made improvements to the machines on the villa's lower floor. He connected these up by a system of pipes that carried flowing water; in later stages of production a grayish powder was poured into these. He also replaced the hand pump with an electric one. As the water sources yielded so little and the composition of each was slightly different, it was advantageous to draw water from all of the depressions in the rock at one time. For this reason, the pump Kulhánek the father installed in the workshop had twelve tubes of various lengths issuing from its lower part; on the end of these were twelve small pumps, which were submerged in pans in the cave. When the machine was switched on, the water rose from the cave to a cylinder, the main part of which was up in the workshop; the water from all twelve sources was mixed in this cylinder before further processing.

"Above the cylinder, Kulhánek the father placed an aerator that looked like the ceremonial headdress of a Red Indian chief.

This consisted of ninety tubes that narrowed towards their tops and were bent downward. Water flowed from all tubes of the aerator in thin streams, falling with a quiet swishing sound into a circular pan that enclosed the mixing cylinder; from there it continued through tubes to different parts of the machine, which were arranged along the walls of the workshop in such a way that the part of the machine that processed the product in the final stage was right next to the pump; so the underground water ran right around the room on its way to being turned into the powder that spilled out of a narrow opening situated in the center of the final part of the machine into the container prepared for it."

"Did they still play Wagner in the workshop?"

"Not anymore. Although Kulhánek the father didn't want to change the powder's established brand, he'd had to listen to Wagner's music throughout his childhood, and he couldn't stand it. He bought a new gramophone and recordings of foxtrots and waltzes, which provided the sound of the workshop throughout the twenties and thirties. In '48, the business was wound up and the house seized as property of the state, although the family was allowed to continue living in it, and Kulhánek the father even kept his apartment on the upper floor. He kept hoping that he would be permitted to resume production of the Tannhäuser powder, if only in a limited extent. For that reason, he decided that the family should live in the room on the lower floor, which was connected with the cave and in which the machine had remained. His wife sometimes cursed him for this and tried to blackmail him with tears, but Kulhánek the father remained adamant, even though his whole life long he'd tried to avoid conflict. In the end his wife came to terms with the fact that she would have to live with a machine that extended right across the room, although when a family argument was in progress she never forgot to yell that it was like living in Frankenstein's laboratory. At least she succeeded in getting Kulhánek the father to move the pipes that ran along the wall and connected the individual vertical parts of the machine down to the cellar. At first he refused to do this, backing down only when he realized that otherwise there would be no room for any furniture in the apartment."

Chapter 8
Metal Figures

"In '48, Kulhánek the son was six years old. Thanks to his father's naive hope of the restoration of the family business, he spent his childhood in a space that made all his classmates jealous—among seven vertical parts of a machine that stood against the wall like seven mysterious characters. For Kulhánek, these were living beings; he gave each of them a name determined by what their shape reminded him of. So on one short wall of the rectangular room stood the Apache—the pump with the aerator, which reminded him of a Red Indian headdress—and the Flower Girl. The Puppeteer stood against the second short wall; on one of the long walls were the Bird Catcher and the Judge; the Rajah and the pensive Inventor stood opposite the Judge and the Bird Catcher respectively. In the days when the apparatus was still operational, the water from the cave flowed through a pipe from the Apache to the Bird Catcher, the Judge and the Puppeteer, in whose innards it was transformed to a mash that was pushed through a tube to the Rajah, in whose upper part, which Kulhánek saw as a turban, it dried and became a powder; this powder was poured by gravity through an oblique glass tube to the Inventor, where it was cleaned and moved on to the Flower Girl, at whose center was a hole that spewed out the finished powder into a porcelain container. Then the powder was portioned out in tins with a picture of Venus and Tannhäuser on the lid."

"From the Apache to the Puppeteer and from the Puppeteer to the Dancer, you said?"

Instead of answering me, Viola moved to the piano, from whose top she picked up a sheet of manuscript paper. On the back of this, she drew a diagram of Kulhánek's machine.

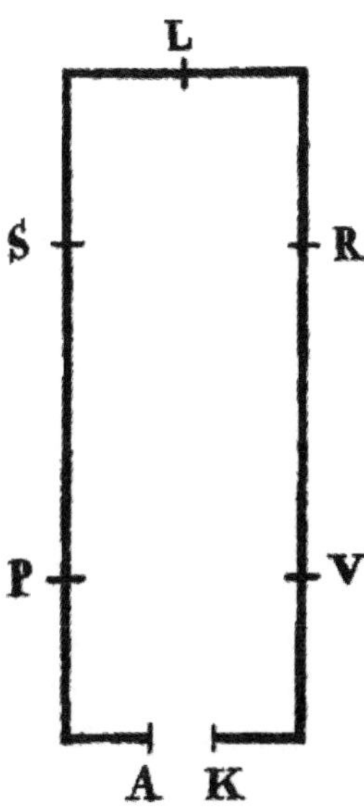

"The mother of Pascal's new friend complained to her husband that the haunted house he was making his son live in would have an effect on his mental health. But even as a child, the younger Kulhánek suspected that it wasn't necessary to take what adults called 'mental health' very seriously, and what's more, he'd never been in the least afraid of the seven metal figures; they were actually his friends, protectors and confidants. His bed was pushed into the gap between the Inventor and the Rajah, so when he awoke in the night he would see at his feet the outline of a dark, slender figure whose top reflected the light of the streetlamp outside, which created the sapphires and rubies set in the turban. The Rajah was awake already because he was about to set out into the jungle to hunt tigers while it was still dark. When Kulhánek raised his head, he saw above him the pensive Inventor, who was currently working on designs for a vehicle that was car, airplane and submarine in one.

"As soon as the lights in the room went out, the figures came to life. Before he fell asleep the child Kulhánek thought up hundreds of stories featuring the metal inhabitants of the apartment. By the time he met Pascal in the bar, he had forgotten most of these, but he told him the few that he remembered. One morning at daybreak, the Bird Catcher heard from his bed a terrified cry from the aviary; on approaching the cage he saw that in the middle of it a naked girl lay dead with a dagger in her heart. The Bird Catcher was charged with the murder and the Judge took a long time patiently unraveling the web of false clues, so proving the guilt of the true perpetrator, the jealous prima ballerina of the local theater. Another story had the Rajah commission the Inventor to design an instrument that would help find precious stones inside the earth, and a year later the Inventor presented him with a golden carillon; in the vicinity of the hiding place of a stone, the instrument would play quiet music whose melody even determined what kind of stone it was. Then there were the adventures all over the world of Apache, who had spent his childhood in the Rocky Mountains, and the Flower Girl, who was born in Montparnasse, beginning when they first met on Madagascar.

"Kulhánek's favorite of all the figures was the Puppeteer. A loner, the Puppeteer stood apart and was the most mysterious of them all. Apparently he cared about nothing but his puppets, but he knew all the city's secrets. Though his puppets appeared to be simple, key-operated figures, they were capable of more than just theater: They cooked and cleaned for the Puppeteer, and when he was sad they played for him on miniature musical instruments; they were able to walk on the roofs and ledges of houses, and to get into any apartment was child's play for them. Although they couldn't speak, in mime they acted out for the Puppeteer what they had seen in the rooms of strangers. It was, in fact, the puppets who stole a document from a drawer that proved the Bird Catcher's innocence in the case of the dead girl in the aviary, so achieving the conviction of the evil ballerina.

"For many years Kulhánek the father hoped that one day he would recommence production of the Tannhäuser powder. At first, he cared for the remaining parts of the machine with tender care; every week he would take them apart and oil them to keep them from rusting. He listened to Radio Free Europe, and it seemed to him that every news story testified to the imminent end of the regime, and he imagined that utterances lost completely in the hum of the jammer were bearers of more hopeful tidings still. Several years passed before Kulhánek the father understood that he would never succeed in reopening the family business. After that, he became less meticulous in his care of the machine. There were ever greater intervals between the days when he cleaned and greased the parts, and in the last years of his life he gave up on its maintenance altogether; he sat at home all day watching the fragments of his machine rust and fall to pieces. He died in the mid sixties, and his wife survived him by only a few months. The youngest Kulhánek was left alone in the apartment with his metal friends, who now looked tired and worn. Kulhánek had lost the ability to think up stories in which they featured, and he'd forgotten many of his old ones. But he remained fond of the Apache, the Bird Catcher, the Judge, the Puppeteer, the Rajah, the Inventor and the Flower Girl, and he couldn't imagine his life without them.

"In 1968 Kulhánek received an offer to recommence production of the Tannhäuser powder under the patronage of some cooperative or other. He sat on the sofa looking at his metal roommates, as if trying to guess from their expressions whether they wanted to return to the work they had performed so long ago, after so long spent in a world of colorful stories and then in idleness. Although the figures weren't able to decide immediately, after a week Kulhánek had the feeling he understood their unspoken answers. What they were telling was: 'We're old and we don't much feel like going to work, and we don't even know if we're capable of it, but we remember your father, who is actually our father too, and out of respect for his dream we're prepared to give it a go.'

"And so Kulhánek began to chase up the missing parts and the many various certificates from the authorities he needed in order to restart production . . . Then came the invasion and the occupation. The cooperative was disbanded. Kulhánek put the new machine parts into the cellar and threw the certificates in the trash. He lived on with his silent roommates, who didn't complain about their fate although their metal faces took on a somber expression. At night when Kulhánek returned from the bar and turned on the light, he never failed to notice how old and dilapidated they'd become, and he told himself that they might not survive him.

"But to his surprise, at the very time he met Pascal there were new hopes that production would restart, even though Kulhánek had long ago given up on such thoughts. Once in the bar he'd begun to tell the unhappy story of the Tannhäuser powder to a drinker he didn't know but who happened to be sitting at a table with him. The drinker remembered the Tannhäuser tins well from his childhood; he'd been plagued by eczema from a young age, and the Tannhäuser powder had been of more help to him than any other cure. One other thing came out of this conversation: The man with the eczema was a high-ranking functionary. He embraced Kulhánek and suggested they proceed on first-name terms. Kulhánek should leave the worrying to him; he'd arrange the license so that Kulhánek would be able to start production of the powder in three months.

"After that, Kulhánek met the man in the bar several more times. These meetings gave him a strange feeling; at first the functionary was so unapproachable that Kulhánek began to wonder if he even recognized him, but once he had five beers inside him the man was again embracing Kulhánek, remembering Tannhäuser and talking of the bright future that awaited the little family factory. Fortunately he was quite a fast drinker, so the unpleasant atmosphere of the beginning never lasted long.

"That's how things were when Kulhánek and Pascal got to know each other. Kulhánek had begun to repair the machines, which by now were in a very bad state. Although his father had left behind some engineering drawings, and, when he realized that he himself wouldn't live to see the workshop back in operation, explained to his son how the whole system worked, in case Kulhánek the son should live to see the fall of the regime, the younger Kulhánek remembered little of this and didn't know much about technical drawing anyway. Pascal was moved by this story, and seeing the extent of Kulhánek's cluelessness in many things, offered to help.

"They went straight from the bar to Kulhánek's home, even though it was after midnight. Pascal inspected the machines and went down to the cave to take samples of the water for chemical analysis. He discovered that the machines really were in a lamentable state. The Flower Girl and the Rajah in particular had become rusted ruins. On Kulhánek's behalf, Pascal arranged for the parts needed to be produced at the factory where he himself worked. In this way the two of them gradually put all parts of the machines in order; then they went down to the cellar for the pipes that would join them back together.

"When the machine was ready for operation, Kulhánek rushed to the bar to notify the functionary, who clapped him on the back and invited him to his office the next day, where he would take a look at the drawings of the machine and the results of the chemical analysis. So first thing the next morning Kulhánek appeared with the rolled-up drawings under his arm at the large, dreary building where his friend from the bar had his office. A secretary had him wait in the hallway for several hours. When at last the door opened and his friend emerged, Kulhánek ran up to him and addressed him by his first name, as he did in the bar, but the functionary quickened his pace and didn't even look at him; within moments he disappeared around a corner in the hallway. Kulhánek ran to that corner to find a long, empty corridor, lined on both sides with dozens of closed doors. He stood there for half an hour, but there was no further movement, not so much as a sound.

"Kulhánek realized that it was pointless to wait there any longer. Like the millionaire in Chaplin's *City Lights*, his friend from the bar was generous and kindly only when he was drunk. In his sober life he felt no need to help anyone, least of all someone who was trying to start up as a private producer. Although he still suffered from eczema and the Tannhäuser powder would probably have helped him, the accusation that his patronage of the powder was an attempt to restore capitalist relations of production would be a far greater unpleasantness to him than a skin complaint.

"Kulhánek wanted to make one final attempt. He would search out the functionary in the bar, wait until he was drunk, and then wheedle out of him the signatures on the documents he needed in order to start production. But the functionary never again appeared in the bar where Kulhánek used to meet him; after the encounter in the hallway of the secretariat, he had probably realized that his drunken friendship with Kulhánek was dangerous for his career, so he changed his bar or taught himself to drink at home. When Pascal saw how devastated Kulhánek was by this last turn of events, he took him out to a bar and they got drunk together. At four in the morning Pascal had an idea as he was standing at the counter: As the machine was now ready for operation, they should perform the Tannhäuser ritual. They should effectuate a single working shift, to which Kulhánek would invite his friends for the ceremonial launch of the machine, for the first and last time. They would all look on as the machine produced a single batch of the Tannhäuser powder for no one; then they would take this out into the garden of the villa and allow it to be scattered by the wind. Kulhánek sighed and said such a ceremony would be a fine thing; the problem was, he didn't have any friends. Pascal told him not to worry about the audience: He would invite Švarc, Navrátil, and Valerie to Kulhánek's apartment.

"So the day of the Tannhäuser ritual arrived, and Kulhánek received five guests: Pascal, Chuh-yuh, Oo, Valerie, and me. Kulhánek had prepared chairs in the center of the room, and each guest took a seat, I on Valerie's knee. The metal figures stood along the walls. Over many years they had become accustomed to independent existence, so that even now that they were again joined by pipes, they produced the impression not of a single machine but a group that had formed in Kulhánek's apartment to perform a shared task. Kulhánek went from one part of the machine to the next and introduced it to the guests: the Apache, the Bird Catcher, the Judge, the Rajah, the Inventor, the Flower Girl. Then he pushed a red button on a small metal box.

"All parts of the machine began to vibrate. Under the feet of the spectators was a deep humming sound like that of a hornet trapped in an overturned cup. As the twelve pumps drew from the cave's sources, they heard the gurgling of water as it rose through the tubes into the room. The vibration of the Apache's mighty body became a rattling shake; the ends of all ninety tubes of his headdress rose and then fell at the same moment; the openings of these produced thin streams of water which fell with a murmur into the round pan that encompassed the pumping unit. After that, they heard the sloshing of water through a narrow metal pipe to the eagerly trembling Bird Catcher. In this part of the machine, which resembled a cage, so giving the young Kulhánek the Bird Catcher's name, something rotated and something swung, there was a muted clanking as though someone were beating a hammer on a table overlaid with felt, and from time to time there was a high ringing sound . . . Everyone watched what was going on in the machine, turning their chairs from one figure to the next. I'm told that I sat in Valerie's lap with my mouth open in delight. Each time the underground water reached the great metal figures, they started to dance; as the water drained out of them, the dance again became a gentle vibration.

"Soon the water was flowing through the tube to the Judge, who swayed when it reached him. From under his metal robe a whirr was heard, accompanied by rustling sounds. From inside the Puppeteer came a ticking at various frequencies and volumes. It was as though there were dozens of watches concealed under his cloak; apparently these sounds were produced by many small cogged wheels. Judging by the gurgling sounds that became audible when the ticking fell silent, what was moving through the pipework that joined the Puppeteer to the Rajah was more mash than liquid. The Rajah gave a hum, which was soon joined by slapping and slurping sounds. All that was heard from the Inventor was a hiss, while the insides of the Flower Girl made a sound like a metal object moving slowly up and down a long grater. When the grater sound suddenly fell silent, at once all the figures stopped their trembling. For about a minute there was silence and nothing moved; all this time the living people were as motionless as the metal figures. Then, with a click, a hole opened up at the center of the Flower Girl, out of which a grayish powder spilled into the container ready to receive it. The Tannhäuser powder had been born again after thirty years.

"The Tannhäuser ritual was first described to me by Vuh-gah Oo in New York. Later, Chuh-yuh told me about it, too. Each of them talked about something quite different. The sculptor's tale was about five metal figures and their mechanical ballet; Chuh-yuh gave a long description of the musical composition of rustles, strokes, whirrs and jingles, giving me the soundtrack to a silent movie. Both Oo and Chuh-yuh were so impressed by the Tannhäuser ritual that both later made use of the mechanical ballet in their work. For Chuh-yuh in particular the mechanical music was a revelation. He talked to me about it in words that resembled Proust's description of the Vinteuil Sonata; even twenty years later he remembered the exact sequence of all the rustling and knocking, so that while he was talking, he was able to paraphrase on the piano certain motifs from the mechanical sonata. What I told you about the sounds of the machines is just the small part of it I can remember from his description."

"How long did the whole performance last?"

"The dance of the machines took two hours. It occurred to Pascal while he was watching it that the properties of the powder would make it a useful ingredient in his disappearing paints. Once the powder had spilled into the container, Pascal suggested Kulhánek make a change in the script; he asked him to leave out the final, garden scene and to give the powder to him for use in his experiments. Kulhánek had no objection to this; in fact he was glad to be able to repay Pascal somehow for all he had done for him. So Pascal prepared a paint with the Tannhäuser powder as an ingredient. Having named this Tannhäuser's Ink, he took it to Valerie for her novel. Tannhäuser's Ink was dark green; after a month it would start to become translucent; after that, it would become invisible and stay like that forever."

Chapter 9
Alexander's Wanderings

"Pascal prepared ribbons impregnated with Tannhäuser's Ink so that Valerie could begin to write her novel on a typewriter. When she was done, she burned the manuscript and all her notes and rejected versions, taking care to ensure that apart from the book written in the Tannhäuser-Kulhánek-Brison ink, not a word of the novel remained. Švarc fixed the pages of the finished novel in an orange cloth binding on whose front he painted in green ink the double trident symbol—Valerie showed him how—that played such an important role in the book's plot. Valerie didn't give the novel a name, saying that it was pointless to name a book that would live only one month. So Pascal, Chuh-yuh and Oo took to calling it the 'Orange Book.' They drew lots for who would read the book first; Švarc was the winner."

By now it was completely dark. The room was lit only by what the windows admitted of the clear night sky. Only with difficulty could I discern the outline of Viola's figure huddled up in a chair. The white and green lights above the track were reflected on the piano and the smooth surface of the closet.

"It was a novel about a man walking through a city. His name is Alexander. His journey begins with an encounter with a girl whom he gets to know in a bar and then takes back to his place. When he gets up in the night for a drink of water, he notices that the canvas bag the girl has thrown over the coat rack in the hall is glowing with a dim, iridescent light. Unable to resist, he takes a look inside. He pulls out a small box made of black wood. Carved into the lid of this is a symbol he has never seen before: a trident crossed by a short horizontal line and stuck into an oval whose upper part is overlaid with an arc in the shape of a lyre . . .

"The light, which is coming out of a crack only half a millimeter wide, changes color, sometimes quickly, sometimes slowly, from purple to blue to green to orange. In the quiet of the night, Alexander hears a hum coming from the box. He presses it to his ear; at first he has the feeling he is listening to the sea; then he imagines he hears the buzz of many distant human voices in which laughter and snatches of melody are mixed. For a long time he tries and fails to identify a continuous melody. Meanwhile he imagines he hears a few meaningless words, such as 'station' and 'cutlery,' but he thinks these may have been inserted into the hum by his own imagination. Then he tries to glimpse something through the crack, but it is too narrow to see through."

"If the double trident were carved into the wood, the bottom of the box would fall off," I objected.

"No, it wouldn't, because at the places where the figure closes, its circumferential lines are broken by narrow bridges."

Still Viola didn't want to turn on a lamp, so she sought out a place on the piano top where the dim green light of the railroad signal was reflected; here, on a piece of paper, she drew the double trident as it was carved into the lid of the little box. I got up to take a look at it.

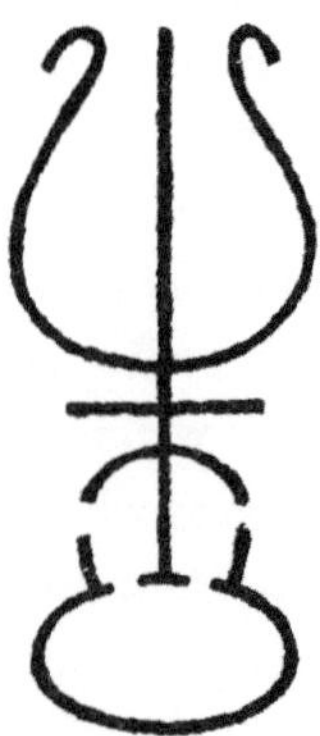

"When he looks at the box, Alexander feels a strange joy he has never known before. The box is locked. After a moment's hesitation, he digs about carefully in the bag—perhaps there is a key in there that fits the box's small lock. But all he comes up with is a crumpled fashion magazine, a handkerchief, a packet of cigarettes with a couple missing, a bunch of large latchkeys, a bag of candies, and a wallet. He goes through the wallet, but it contains nothing but cash and streetcar tickets. All this time he has kept looking toward the door of the room, afraid that the girl will catch him in the act. At last he heads back to bed, stepping quietly across the carpet, stopping in the middle of the room and straining his ears. The girl is still breathing calmly; there is no suggestion that she has been awake. He decides that when morning comes he will confess to the girl that he has been through her bag and ask her to explain the mysterious light. Soon he falls asleep. When he wakes up, he is lying in bed alone; the girl and her bag have gone.

"Alexander can't stop thinking about the mysterious little box. Wherever he goes he asks about it, and before long he begins to meet others who have seen the box, in a variety of circumstances. He comes across clues that lead him to many areas of the city. In the stories of his fellow witnesses he is taken to many distant lands."

"Does Alexander try to ascertain the meaning of the symbol on the box?"

"At certain periods of his quest it seems to Alexander that the symbol contains the entire mystery of the little box, but at others he believes it to be a meaningless ornament that is of no help in his search. One evening, Alexander receives a mysterious guest, who claims that the symbol is actually a diagram of the moat that surrounds the residence of a certain banker in the south of France. He tells Alexander a story about what took place in that garden when he was a child: The banker's young wife was murdered at the place represented in the diagram by the oval at the bottom; the little wooden bridges that break the line of the figure on the box in four places represent footbridges over the moat, and these footbridges played an important role in the search for the killer. The lieutenant of police who went to the banker's residence to track down the killer had to try to do so based on what he discovered about the meetings of the banker's guests on the footbridges and the truthful and false testimonies of these guests concerning these meetings."

"And did he succeed?"

"Valerie didn't like unambiguous solutions, so every attempt to make a plan of the guests' movements, and so shed light on the murder, foundered. But this episode is about a single inconspicuous utterance made by one of the guests in his statement; it is not about tracking down a killer. A long, new episode develops out of this utterance about a hundred pages further on, ending in the polar night on Svalbard. The story of the murder is just one of many episodes. As I said, bits of the novel that Valerie began to write and then rejected were revived as secondary storylines of the Orange Book, their exposition begun in the various places where Alexander is taken in his quest for the mysterious little box. Sometimes storylines intertwine; sometimes they run in parallel, perhaps separated by only a wall, but never crossing; sometimes a storyline is lost suddenly like a creek in the sand, and sometimes it is long gone but then reappears in some faraway place.

"Any of these storylines might show the way to the little glowing box, but it might also be a red herring that leads Alexander away from his target, or a trap that could destroy him. What has long seemed the most promising clue turns out to be a fiction, while something that has seemed altogether incredible takes Alexander within close range of the box and its secret. Several times the box is almost within reach: It glows on the back seat of a Mercedes parked one night in a quiet street on the edge of the city, or Alexander sees its glow through the keyhole of a closed door to which he doesn't have the key—but then the box again escapes to some remote, unknown place, and the search begins anew.

"None of the clues is shown with absolute certainty to be true or false; there is always the possibility that everything is in fact the opposite of how it appears. And as the novel progresses, it is no longer clear whether the object of Alexander's search really is the mysterious box. There are indications that the real aim may be something else entirely—which Alexander doesn't realize, although there are moments when he suspects; we wonder whether this thing will be reached by one of the secondary storylines that appeared to be a false trail, and whether Alexander has held the object in his hand and then put it down, not knowing what to do with it."

Still I wasn't able to tell if Viola had read the Orange Book or knew its contents only from what Oo and Chu-yuh had told her about it. But as no one was waiting for me, and there was plenty of time, I decided I would simply listen, not interrupt Viola with premature questions.

"One of these secondary storylines is of the search for a garden pavilion where a certain map is said to be carved into the wooden walls. On this stretch of his journey, Alexander enters many pavilions, home to many different rotten-wood and coat-of-paint scents; Valerie devoted many pages to these scents. He passes through many gardens and parks and conceals himself on a summer night among the symmetrically trimmed bushes of a palace garden where a party is in progress; on the edge of the city, he clambers over dilapidated fences between overgrown, abandoned gardens; he enters dusty gardens hidden within the confines of tenement buildings.

"Another storyline concerns a machine that Alexander is putting together. He discovers that the broken mechanism he has acquired is a fragment of a large machine. For a time—for reasons that are too convoluted to go into—he believes that he'll be able to find the luminous, humming box once he has succeeded in reconstructing the original machine. No one knows when the machine was dismantled, exactly what it looked like or even what it was used for. Its surviving components have ended up in many different places, some of them alone, while others have been put in other machines. I think Valerie struck on this theme after her encounter with Kulhánek's metal septet.

"Alexander rents a garage, where he sets out the fragments of the machine; then he begins the hunt for the remaining components. He believes that as soon as the machine is assembled, he'll be able to determine from its shape what its function is, and from there its connection with the little box. As he works on reconstructing the machine, Alexander again passes through many spaces, rooms, workshops and depots; he rummages through old junk in storerooms and on dump sites, finding former parts of his machine on the dusty tops of closets in hallways, on shelves and in metal cabinets among pots of paint and old rags; he removes other parts in secret from factory halls at night. He becomes so obsessed with the machine that for a long time he forgets about the little box.

"As he doesn't know what the machine looked like, all he has to guide him are the shapes of the ends on the individual parts. He looks for a part whose end will fit into a joint or a sprocket on the end of one of the branches of the mechanical tree growing in the garage. Slowly the machine grows, but the connections determined only by the shape of a joint or the size of some grooves remain uncertain. At some moments, Alexander believes that the machine he is building is getting close to the original; at others he feels it is getting ever further away. Sometimes he fears that his machine attained the form of the original at an earlier stage of its growth and then moved away from it when, in his impatience, he bolted on to it new, superfluous parts; at these times he begins frantically to strip from the machine everything he has added in the last few months, until he is almost down to the fragment he set up in the garage at the very beginning of his reconstruction work. There are also moments when he thinks that though he will never build the machine in its original form, what he does produce will be still more important and effective."

"Does Alexander succeed in discovering the shape and purpose of the original machine?"

"Maybe with a few more days he would have finished work on the machine and identified its function; maybe he needed only to add a few components, switch a few of them around, loosen what was too tight, tighten what was loose or pull one little lever—and the mechanism would have rattled into life and started to work . . . Maybe then the machine's output would have led him to the little box; maybe he would have realized that the only role of the little box was to bring him to the machine. But Alexander loses interest in assembling his machine, even though he has worked on it for many months, even years . . . Besides, as he is looking for a particular shaft component, he hears a story that entices him onto a different path. And so the Orange Book begins to develop a new storyline . . ."

Chapter 10
Extinction of the Orange Book

"What could have taken him away from his almost-finished machine?" I asked.

"Someone tells him about an apartment where treasure is hidden. This treasure came from a pirate ship that was wrecked off the Greek island of Folegandros . . ."

"That's the treasure Bernet has been searching for all his life!" I exclaimed.

"So it is," said Viola, nodding. "I learned that Bernet was looking for pirates' treasure from Folegandros only recently, from Chuh-yuh, who'd heard the story of the millionaire's obsession from the flautist Bernet hired for the premiere of *Medusae of the Past*."

"Am I mistaken in thinking that the opera was composed by Chuh-yuh?"

"Chuh-yuh did indeed compose the music to *Medusae of the Past*, although the poor flautist is still ignorant of the fact. He's a former schoolmate of Barbora and Andrea, who once told him about how the young Bernet had been taken by his aunt to the apartment of a friend of hers, where he had become bored. There he had read something on a scrap of paper that he believed to be a message about treasure. It seems that as children his aunt and Valerie had been friends, perhaps classmates, so when the aunt came to the city, she went to visit Valerie, with Bernet, who was in her care, in tow. At this time Valerie happened to be planning the Orange Book, and Bernet found her notes on the desk . . ."

"Wait a moment! So that means the little frowning girl on the ottoman was . . ."

"Yes, that was me."

"Why did Valerie put the treasure on Folegandros of all places? Had she ever been there, or had she read about the island somewhere? And what's the connection between all this and the underwater statue?"

"That's too many questions at once. Please don't hurry me—didn't you say that you had plenty of time?" Viola spoke into the darkness in a tone of mild rebuke. "We'll get to all of them in the end. Valerie had never been to Folegandros. She never went abroad. She never saw the sea, even though she longed for it her whole life; apparently, she spoke often of how when I was bigger the two of us would leave this country and go to live somewhere in the south, on the shore of a warm sea, in a landscape where olives and figs grew. She said that she wouldn't mind having to work in a store or as a chambermaid or washer of dishes. In her book, Valerie's longing for the sea and the south was manifest in many places . . . She hadn't even read about Folegandros; she didn't know anything about it. She found it on a map. She was intrigued by its being a small island away from the shipping routes. She studied the thick contour lines, which told her that the coast was composed of steep slopes, and the island's outline, which inspired her to think of secluded rocky bays. So she dreamed up a story in which by a convoluted route a hoard of treasure traveled from the bottom of the sea to a gloomy apartment on the outskirts of a city, and the luster of lost gold, precious stones and pearls was transformed progressively into intangible light.

"So Alexander passed through rooms, gardens, depots, offices, hotels, out-of-service trains, poky little stores, and a great many corridors and passages. Although the main storyline was set in the present, the gray, sorrowful film of the seventies that lay over things like deep-ingrained dirt didn't succeed in obscuring an older, more powerful, indestructible glow in them that was felt in the touch of words; at several stages of Alexander's journey, this glow was concentrated in jewels, night lamps and still reflections . . ."

Viola fell silent. Was this the end of the story, or was she just pausing for thought? When the silence had gone on too long, I asked: "Does Alexander manage to find the little box and to open it?"

Viola moved in the darkness. "Alexander searches for the box for many years. He has many encounters, gets to know many people, things and landscapes, and several times he gets close to the object of his search. But never again does he hold the box in his hands, so he never opens it and never finds out what's inside . . .

"After Oo, Chu-yuh and Num read the Orange Book. And all three of them read it again and again. Several times each was tempted to copy down just one paragraph from it, but he would have considered it shameful to break his promise to Valerie. With apprehension they awaited the moment when the letters would start to fade. That moment came after three weeks. By that time, they were appearing each day at Valerie's apartment possessed by the fear of a man arriving at a hospital where a loved one lies close to death. Then the day came they opened the Orange Book to find that something had happened to it overnight: The letters were more distinct than in previous days, and now they weren't green, but bright purple. Oo and Chuh-yuh looked at Pascal, who nodded and said quietly that the book had now entered the last phase of its existence.

"The four of them stood over the book and watched its demise in silence. Oo and Chuh-yuh remembered that afternoon down to the smallest detail. Both told me of the soft light that came through the window that overlooked the snow-covered park and lay across every object in the room, the smell of thawing snow from the coats on the rack in the hall, the bright, distant sound of the voices of children on sledges, carried on the frosty air. Valerie leafed through the book slowly; in the middle of its pages, new colors—purple, pink, azure, gold—were appearing and the letters were spilling to the sides; it was as though on every page silent fireworks had exploded. Then came the moment when the newborn colors backed away and the letters became green again, and then the green began to fade and the letters were falling into the white of the page like a drowning city, becoming ever less distinct until they vanished altogether (although the odd word or sentence fragment popped up before sinking back beneath the surface of the page). For a few more weeks, lone words and letters continued to emerge, but then the white surface closed over the words forever. Still Oo, Chu-yuh, and Num visited Valerie every day. They would pick the book up and leaf through its white pages with sadness but also a strange delight. They could feel the truth of Valerie's claim that the erased text lived on; although sentences and scenes from the book were dissolving into oblivion, at the same time new plots, shapes and music were welling up.

"The novel about Alexander expired in January of '79. After a year spent writing her novel while having to take care of me and the household, Valerie was exhausted. She didn't want to speak about the book at all. None of the three friends found out whether she was glad about what had happened or she regretted the demise of the book. That February there were heavy frosts. I caught a cold, and Valerie had to take me to the doctor's; she didn't dress warmly enough and came down with pneumonia. When she was taken to the hospital, Chuh-yuh took me to stay with him and took care of me. Valerie's friends visited her several times in the hospital, where she made them promise again that they wouldn't try to restore the text of her novel; now, in fact, she demanded even more of them—none of them should ever so much as mention that there had once existed an Orange Book, so that it would remain their secret forever. On the fourth day she developed a high fever; on the fifth day her friends arrived at the hospital to be told by the doctor that Valerie had died in the night. She was not even thirty years old. I was four. Jonáš took me, and after that I lived with him and forgot about my mother."

Chapter 11
Parting

"Pascal stayed on here, even though every week he received a letter from his father asking him to come home. The posts kept open for him at research institutes had been filled long ago, and he was no longer remembered at the university. Among students, the legend of the genius drinker lived on and acquired an ever more incredible content; for instance, few people doubted that this mysterious figure had been bumped off by an international secret service agency because of some amazing discovery he had made. Pascal knew nothing of any of this, and it's unlikely it would have interested him. After Valerie's death, he took up writing again. And he, Švarc, and Navrátil met up every day, usually in the ramshackle house on Popelová Street, which Švarc was renting for use as a studio.

"Everything they did was an attempt to fill the void left by Valerie's death, her novel's descent into the white of its pages and the extinction of their bright world; it was also a way of remembering her. When Oo and Chuh-yuh tried to remember the first months after Valerie's death, for both of them it was as though its events were lost in a fog. I suppose periods of inactivity alternated with days of feverish action. They could recollect only a few pieces of fiction, sculptures and musical compositions from that time; none of these works was able to tear itself away from the Orange Book, and none of them has survived as anything more than a vague memory. Maybe in those days they came to adhere to Valerie's opinion that a work was something that should live with its author and his or her friends for a few days or weeks before sinking into a world of oblivion and anonymous transformation.

"Oo remembered a work of fiction written by Pascal at that time, the plot of which was linked to that of the Orange Book. In it, Pascal told the story of a solitary rambler who one evening finds himself on the road between two villages. When it comes on to rain, he takes cover in a bus shelter at the edge of a field, where he discovers a box with a double trident on it—the same box that Alexander found in his hallway that night. But now the box has a key in it. The rambler opens the box; inside it, he finds some tiny porcelain figures, which are set in motion by a concealed mechanical device and lit by a bulb in the lid. These figures perform a drama that the rambler watches all night, as the rain beats down on the shelter. Replicas of each character spring up with a click to an oblong window in the center of the lid, like movie subtitles. As morning approaches, the plotline unravels and a catharsis is achieved; but this catharsis generates the beginning of a new plotline. A bus arrives; the rambler closes the box, puts it in his backpack and gets on the bus. On his journey he looks inside the box several times and sees that the drama is still in progress. He looks again when he gets home: still it hasn't finished. From time to time the figures stop moving because the spring that powers the mechanism needs to be rewound. Once this is done, the story continues; it never repeats itself and is always new. The box's finder sometimes watches the play for days and nights on end; at other times he keeps the box closed for several months. But whenever he opens it and winds the spring, the story that unfolds is a new installment in the never-ending serial . . . Maybe this story was intended as the basis of a novel in which Num would describe the life of the rambler in parallel with what was going on in the box, but at that time—in common with his two friends—he lacked the necessary energy and concentration for systematic work."

"What did Chuh-yuh and Oo do at that time?"

"Chuh-yuh composed works called *A Glow in the Hallway*, *A Pavilion in an Overgrown Garden* and *The Bay at Folegandros*.

Nothing remains of the scores of these works either. Oo produced figurines that were supposed to illustrate aspects of Valerie's novel . . ."

"Did these figurines include one of a naked woman and a dragon in the window of a store, by any chance?"

"That's right—Oo told me about that. This was a figure from the Orange Book that bore an encrypted message marking the place where treasure was hidden. But when Oo used the encryption key as described by Valerie in her novel, he wrote down the address of his own studio. God knows what became of the figurine . . ."

"All I know is that at one time it stood on a shelf in the bar of a hotel above Mittenwald in the Bavarian Alps and that now it is owned by Bernet . . ."

"Poor Bernet. By getting himself mixed up in Valerie's story, he changed his whole life . . ."

"I don't think he's ever regretted the fact that his aunt took him to Valerie's apartment. But let's not talk about Bernet; I'd prefer to hear more about Chuh-yuh, Oo and Num."

"Half a year after Valerie's death, they agreed to produce a joint work in her memory. It was obvious the Gesamtkunstwerk in which all three of them would participate could only be an opera. A few weeks later, Num presented the others with the libretto of *Medusae of the Past*. Chuh-yuh set this to music and Oo painted the scenery. It mattered little to them that there was no one in existence who would put the opera on, and that it was highly unlikely that any of them would ever hear it. In various ways Chuh-yuh's music, Num's words and Oo's scenes gave expression to memories of Valerie and the Orange Book."

"What connection did the scenery have with Valerie? Did it show her apartment?"

"No, although on the left-hand panel Oo painted a window with the view from Valerie's room."

"Is what I heard in Bernet's garden really just a fragment of the original?"

"Yes, the opera was much longer, but the book containing the score fell to pieces and most of it was lost. After Oo moved out of the little house where his studio was, no one else moved in. At one time some homeless people slept there—maybe one of them used the score to make a fire."

"Do you know how the opera went on?"

"A woman appeared on the stage. The exiled scientist fell in love with her, but then it turned out that she was an agent of the island's government, sent to the scientist in order to abduct him. The opera then became a kind of thriller in song, featuring motorboat chases across the nighttime sea and wild gun battles . . . During one of their periods of convulsive activity, Navrátil, Švarc, and Brison founded the White Triangle and thought up their bizarre pseudonyms. Although the work of all three was still a dream of Valerie's, rather than the motifs of the Orange Book it now arose out of memories of the transition of Valerie's novel to the realm of the invisible and the strange way that in their last days of life, words lingered on the frontier with silence. Later, there was much talk of the minimalism of the White Triangle; what was actually happening was that Chuh-yuh, Oo, and Num were on the frontier that divided something from nothing, looking for goodness knows what with desperation and sometimes also delight. Maybe they were in search of the seeds of new languages. Perhaps they longed to see Valerie's face in the blank white pages and to hear her voice in the silence that drowned out all tones. It may have been that there was but a single desire—a dream of new, unheard languages in which Valerie would speak to them from a deathly space.

"Oo, Chuh-yuh, and Num never questioned the promise they had made to Valerie—that they would speak with no one of the plot and the history of the Orange Book; that they would make no attempt to record anything from that plot and in any way to keep it in its original form; that they would let the novel fall into oblivion and leave it at the mercy of transformation . . ."

"It seems that they didn't keep that promise. The owner of Tam-Tam told me that there was much talk of the Orange Book in the early eighties."

"Probably the Trianglists did mention the Orange Book by name in the presence of uninitiated persons, but I'm not sure that can be considered a breach of their promise. Don't forget that Valerie herself wanted her work to live on in transformation after it perished. But it lived on, too, in the legends that proliferated around the name 'Orange Book.' By saying the name of Valerie's work in the hearing of others, the Trianglists gave away nothing about it. Quite the contrary, in fact: The title 'Orange Book' gave rise to rumors that made the truth about Valerie's novel even more obscure. One story that did the rounds claimed that it was a book of Chinese divination; I wouldn't be surprised to discover that some Orange Book of Chinese divination really was born out of these rumors. Until my encounter with Oo in Brooklyn, no one had discovered the true content of the Orange Book or who its author was.

"At that time, something happened that surprised all three of them: The lack of words, lines and notes in the works of the Trianglists and their secretive and conspiratorial behavior resulted in the White Triangle, too, becoming entangled in legend, creating an alternative life for it that was far more dramatic, more mysterious and longer than the true one. In actual fact the White Triangle existed for a few months only. And it didn't end well. The elegiac mood produced by pain and memories which erased words, colors, and notes, changed gradually to mannerism and cramp. Toward the end, Num's writing was more theoretical manifesto than prose or poetry, and Chuh-yuh no longer knew how to proceed with silent compositions. Oo's experiments in the perception of things in sculpture had turned his whole world into a gallery of statues; having at first been a source of ecstasy to him, now it was a source of continual boredom.

"Out of this situation, old tensions that had once existed between Oo and Num on account of Valerie forced their way back to the surface. Num started to comment ironically on Oo's work; Oo responded by implying that the reduction of words in Num's work was nothing but an expression of impotence, which Num was attempting to conceal behind complicated theories. The atmosphere at meetings of the White Triangle bothered Chuh-yuh, too. Matters went so far that each of them came to wish that he might never see the other two again. But for a long time all three had the feeling that their meetings were a duty imposed by their common experience, which they couldn't walk out on.

"One day Švarc or maybe Brison made some sarcastic remark, each leapt at the other and they started to fight. When Chuh-yuh tried to pull them apart, Num yelled an offensive name at him. This caused Chuh-yuh's nerves to snap and his fist to strike Num in the face with full force. After that, the fight involved the three of them, and they rolled about the floor of Oo's studio. The fight ended as swiftly as it had begun; they sat on the floor with their heads bowed, breathing heavily. Then Num stood up and went away without a word, and shortly afterwards Chuh-yuh did the same. Seeing Num at the end of the street, Chuh-yuh hesitated for a moment as he considered whether to go after him, but then he went off in the opposite direction. Oo stayed where he was, seated on the floor of his studio. All of them felt terrible, yet in each of them a feeling of happiness was growing at the thought of never again having to see the other two. Three days later Pascal/Num went home and took over the management of the factory from his father. A few months later Oo emigrated to the United States. Chuh-yuh immersed himself in his music more than ever. The works of his new period left experimentation with silence behind and became more classical, although in their notes there remained something of the old, incurable despair; each melody and each bar held an echo of the hospital room where Valerie died and of the last word of her novel as it disappeared into the white of the page."

Chapter 12
Encounter on Naxos

"Chuh-yuh never saw Num or Oo again. He earned money by giving piano lessons. At night he would listen to distant sounds, which transformed in his head to gentle wellsprings or pyrotechnics of notes. Not even after the changes of '89 did he seek a public performance or even publication of his work. I've never learned whether the reason for this was his modesty, doubt about something he had produced, shyness, reluctance to make arrangements, unwillingness to entrust his ideas to interpreters, or loyalty to Valerie's legacy and desire to be her equal in courageous silence. Yet there were moments, too, when he despaired for the music he had consigned to a life of silence in his own mind or on magnetic tapes even he didn't listen to. It was at one of these moments that he came across an article about the White Triangle. Unable to resist, he contacted its author and let himself be persuaded to have at least a couple of his works published."

"What became of the other two?"

"As soon as he got back to France, Pascal Brison burned his formulae for the disappearing paints and documentation on all other discoveries he had wanted to get patents for. He managed the factory, producing the same soap and colognes his ancestor had created 150 years earlier. He never married. Apparently all he desired was to be left in peace, so he adapted to small-town life. He attended church on Sundays and listened to sermons he didn't understand. Two evenings a week, he went to a bar, where he nodded at the conversations of fellow citizens in whom he had no interest. In his bedroom at night he drank wine and read his Lautréamont and his Hölderlin over and over again . . .

"After a few years, the burning anguish became a quiet sorrow. A desire began to grow in him: He would honor Valerie's memory by writing a book that would revive thoughts of their meetings at her apartment. It was obvious to him that he should adhere strictly to Valerie's vision of the endless metamorphosis of shapes, in which every shape—above all the most precious, the one we love best—must pass through a stage of absolute dissolution and oblivion before it can be born from the vortex of emptiness in changed form. Now he realized that the cult of emptiness of the White Triangle period was just one stage—in accordance with the laws of metamorphosis, this stage must be followed by the birth of a new shape out of the nothingness. And it seemed to him that now was the time for a new transformation.

"He knew that his book would reveal neither Valerie's true face nor his own, and he also knew that the apartment with the window overlooking the park wouldn't appear in it. But he sensed that the features of all faces he had encountered at the time of his friendship with Valerie would appear in the faces of the characters in his novel, although he didn't yet know them, and that somewhere in the swirling void the ground plan of Valerie's apartment was transforming into new rooms in unknown lands. He began to wonder what the faces and bodies and the rooms and lands which were about to emerge from a nothingness steeped in ancient images would be like. After years of boredom, reminiscence and daily drinking, he began to anticipate his work with pleasure and so to feel happy again.

"Turning to the deep void inside him, he discovered that without his knowledge, this void had been working on shapes and plots that had lain forgotten for years, conceiving shapes from which were now emerging a stretch of land that looked like a shoreline obscured by fog and the outline of some story or other. Num tried to catch these evanescent shapes, but they always eluded him. Then he remembered how Valerie had spoken of the role played by chance in writing—often a word overheard by accident would evolve and succeed in opening up a scene that had defied expression for many days. He pulled the Larousse dictionary from his bookcase, closed his eyes, opened the book and put his finger down on the page; he opened his eyes on the word 'palmier.' Then he did the same thing a few pages further on; this time his finger lay on the word 'passage.' His third attempt gave him the word 'police.' After that he told himself that it wasn't right that all words should begin with 'P.' He opened the book near the front and by the same process found the words 'ange' and 'architecte.' He decided that this would suffice and pushed the dictionary back into the bookcase.

"What he had were words meaning palm tree, passage or arcade, police, angel, and architect—five words like five stars shining in a nebula of shapeless plots born out of the void. In the proximity of these bright lights, the nebula gradually acquired an outline, and a plot began to form. Under palm trees growing on a boulevard somewhere, police officers were chasing figures that had just disappeared into the mouth of a passage. Pascal wondered who these figures were. Criminals? Revolutionaries? Terrorists? He spotted a shining glass figurine of an angel and saw an architect bent over some kind of plan. As he got closer to it, Pascal saw that this was a plan of a city. In the gloom he struggled to make this out, but then there was a flash of light and he saw a character on the plan that he knew from Valerie's book: The main streets were in the shape of the double trident. Out of these fragmentary images, the plot of a novel began to grow rapidly. The day came when the town received its name: Santa Rosalia. Pascal worked on his Santa Rosalia novel for several months. Obviously the features of Beatriz's face were a reflection of Valerie's, transformed in dreams, and Pierre was Pascal's brother. Pascal published the novel under a pseudonym; after this, he wrote nothing else, it seems.

"At the end of the eighties, the son of his elder sister graduated in chemistry. Straight away Pascal brought the young man into the factory as his deputy, and two years later he handed the company over to him. Then he moved south; in the last few years he'd dreamed of living on one of the Greek islands Hölderlin and Valerie had loved so much, even though neither of them ever went to Greece. He filled a small suitcase with books and left. For a long time he couldn't decide which island he wanted to settle on. Then one day, walking through a maze of narrow streets above the harbor on Naxos, he spotted something on the door of a white house—a notice stating that a room was available for rent in a diaphragm arch over a street. He took the room in the labyrinth of Naxos old town. He often visited the islands nearby—Delos, site of the Apollonian grove, wild Sikinos, sleepy Iraklia. He stayed on Folegandros many times, lying for whole days on the white pebbles of the secluded bay that Valerie had found on the map as a rippling outline; it was here that her book had sent a ship filled with precious stones and pearls to the sea bed. Pascal grew a Greek mustache and sat for many hours in front of a *kafenio*; tourists took photos of him as a typical, picturesque Greek."

"And what of Oo's life in America?"

"Oo gave up making statues and went to work in a real estate office. After work he would sit in the Puerto Rican diner, watching the overground trains, the same images in his mind as in Num's on the terrace of a Naxos *kafenio* and in Chuh-yuh's in this apartment over the tracks, to which he moved after the departure of his friends. Oo, too, longed to visit the islands where several chapters of the Orange Book had been set, at least on vacation, so five summers ago he took a flight to Athens and then traveled by ferry from island to island. One day he was walking through the steep Naxos streets below the Venetian castle when he heard someone calling his name. He looked around to see only a bronzed man with a mustache and curly graying hair, who was sitting in front of a *taverna*. Oo took a moment to realize who this man was.

"Oo and Num were delighted to see each other; the bitterness and hostility each had felt for the other had evaporated long before. Oo spent the night in Num's arch, and the very next day they set off together for Folegandros. In the thirteen years that had passed since he'd read the Orange Book, Oo had visited the island many times in his dreams at night, and he had seen its bays and rocks on the white walls of his Brooklyn diner. Num led Oo to the bay of treasure. As he stood on the hot pebbles looking up at the high, ogre-like rocks, for the first time in an age Oo felt a desire to sculpt. He didn't yet know what this sculpture would look like, but it was clear to him that it would be a memorial to Valerie and her novel. As he had promised Valerie that the content of her novel and everything to do with its origination would remain secret forever, he told Num that he would build a statue on one of the hard-to-reach rocky peaks above the bay.

"Pascal made another suggestion: He would get Oo some scuba gear, give him a few diving lessons, and then he would be able to make his statue on the sea bottom; Num would help Oo as he worked. So Num taught Oo the basics of scuba diving, and before long they set to work. In the waters of the bay, Oo made his last statue, in pebbles. It is a statue of my mother with the Orange Book, slightly open, in her hand. She is smiling. From her gesture, it is not clear whether she is trying to hide the book or preparing to open it wide and offer it for reading. Before Oo went back to New York, he promised Num he would come back to see him next year. But in early spring Pascal had a heart attack and died in the hospital—in a room whose window had a view of nothing but sea and sky . . . This is the story that Vuh-gah Oo told me over six days in the Brooklyn diner. I've added a few details that I learned later from Chuh-yuh."

Chapter 13
Pascal Brison's Diary

"I longed desperately to read the Orange Book. Oo was sad that he wasn't able to help me. He said that I was the only one who had the right to read this text that Valerie had sentenced to invisibility, a life in the mind, extinction in the memories of three people and uncertain transformation. I couldn't imagine that my mother would have objected to his breaking his long-standing promise for me. But the text of the novel couldn't be recovered. In the diner next to the overground railroad, I asked Oo if there really was no hope at all. Couldn't the letters on the pages of the Orange Book be roused even for a short time? Oo said that he'd heard of one chance, but it was so improbable that there was no point in hoping that it would ever materialize.

"And he told me about the evening of the day on which he completed his undersea portrait of my mother. He and Pascal removed their scuba gear, lay on the still-warm pebbles of the rocky cove and watched the darkening surface that concealed the memorial to Valerie, which was now as invisible as the text on the pages of the Orange Book. Oo mentioned to Num his concern that someone might see the statue while diving or snorkeling. Perhaps they should have been more thorough, he said; they could have built their statue in a secluded place and then given it a secret burial deep in the ground. Num didn't share this worry, claiming that true concealment always contained a possibility of discovery, even if an incredibly small one. For instance, we might conceal a letter by filing it away in one of tens of thousands of volumes in a great library, but if some power were to deposit it at the center of the Earth, it wouldn't be hidden in the proper sense—its absence would be closer to non-existence than true concealment. Part of concealment, he said, were the hands groping about nearby and the footsteps that got closer and then further away.

"Oo argued that in such a case, one couldn't talk about Valerie's novel as something concealed, as there was no longer any power on earth that could restore the lost words to its blank pages. Groping hands and footsteps getting closer to the book were just movements and sounds to which the life of the novel was indifferent and by which it was untouched. Num replied that the text of the Orange Book wasn't protected absolutely against regaining its visibility—but the probability that it would again appear to someone was so slight that it was more a dream than a real possibility. Num explained to Oo as they lay on the shore that there was a hard activator for Tannhäuser's Ink that could make the script visible for twenty-four hours, but that this activator was a material that was a mix of many ingredients, and on top of that, it was highly likely that the most important of these ingredients was today impossible to acquire.

"Num said that although the activator mixture was recorded in his diary, which had probably been left with Chuh-yuh, he'd written this diary in one of his most resistant paints; the person who brought its text back to life would need to know Num's old formulae—and Num had burned these on his return to France. For the novel to become visible again, a fantastic coincidence was required. Although he was pretty sure that this would never happen, he was convinced that this tiny hope or threat accounted for the true concealment of Valerie's work and its secret: Without it, the Orange Book would come more and more to resemble a pile of pages on which nothing had been written.

"So Num was the only person who could render the script of the Orange Book visible. Oo believed that he would have been happy to do this for me—nor would Num have hesitated to break his promise for me, he said. But by then, Num's body had lain for three years in a cemetery overlooking the Aegean Sea, and the formulae that might have revived his diary had perished in a fire earlier still. So I accepted the fact that I would never know Valerie's novel, although I would continue to dream of the lives of its characters, picture the rooms and gardens they entered, figure out incidents that Oo wasn't able to recall—so that years later I would no longer be capable of separating my own ideas from what Oo had told me . . ."

"Just as this very afternoon I was sure I would weave the story of your life into various shapes, so that I wouldn't be able to distinguish what I'd discovered in my search from what I'd come to by contemplation and what I'd dreamed up," I said quietly.

"I wanted at least to see the Orange Book, take it in my hands and leaf through its blank pages. I was pretty sure that in was still in Chuh-yuh's possession—I couldn't imagine that he'd have disposed of it. Oo didn't know Chuh-yuh's address. At the time he'd left the country, what he'd wanted above all else was solitude, and he hadn't even said goodbye. Years later he'd written to Chuh-yuh at his old address, but the letter had been returned to him marked 'Addressee unknown.' But Oo did at least tell me Chuh-yuh's real name, so as soon as I got home I called around all the Navrátils in the telephone directory. The problem was, Chuh-yuh didn't have a phone—he still doesn't. All his life he'd loved the murmurs and sounds of the city, and he was able to listen to them for hours on end as though they were pieces of music. He'd always considered the telephone, with its crude ring, as an enemy; he was willing to put up with it only once its sound had been transformed to a faint hum by the intercession of many house walls."

"So how come he lives in an apartment where the trains make such a terrible racket?"

"The sound of trains has never bothered Chuh-yuh. In fact it's one of the sounds he likes best. What he hates about the ring of a telephone isn't its loudness but the way it tears into the fabric of other sounds. The sound of a train getting closer and further away is always soft, as it beds down in and rises from the field of sounds."

Viola paused for a moment. I sensed that she was a little fearful of what was to come next and was considering how much she should tell me.

She resumed slowly. "When I got back from America, for several weeks I was in a state of feverish excitement. I couldn't stop thinking about the events of my mother's life that Oo had told me about. I was haunted by images from her lost book, and reality paled in the presence of memories and visions. More than once I found myself in a part of the city unknown to me, having become lost in my thoughts while in the street. This is a period of my life I don't like to look back on . . . With these thoughts, I closed myself up in my room. From out on the landing I heard my father's shuffling steps and heavy breathing; I didn't know whether to pity him or hate him. I wanted to run out of the room and yell questions at him: Do you remember Labyrinthos? Do you remember Valerie? Several times I almost did this, but then I imagined how he would look at me from under drooping eyelids with dull eyes, and I imagined his whispering voice . . . And then I'd think of how he'd cared for me lovingly all my life and of how as a child I'd worshiped him; so in the end I always lay down on my bed and pressed a pillow to my head so as not to hear the rustling sounds that in recent years had become my father's existence—sounds that were difficult to distinguish from the creaking of old furniture and the whisper of a draft passing through peeling wallpaper.

"Then I would run away again and sit around until the early hours in pubs and wine bars, finding strange friends and lovers whose faces are all mixed up in my memory and whom I would fail to recognize several days later; I went to wild parties in the apartments of strangers, the morning after which I was glad to remember very little of what had gone on. Then one morning I awoke feeling sick; there was a burning sensation low in my abdomen, to the right. I looked at where the pain was coming from and saw tattooed on the skin of my belly the symbol from Valerie's book. I took fright and jumped out of bed. Then images from the dreams of that night slowly came back to me; rather than playing in a continuous reel, these images were like the individual panels of a comic strip: the red neon of the tattoo parlor that I and a group of my nighttime friends had been passing on our way from one bar to the next; someone—me, I suspected—had come up with the idea that we should all get a tattoo; the big man wearing a black leather vest over a bare chest, his head shaved and his nostrils pierced with numerous metal rings, a buzzing needle in his hand, asking me about the design I'd chosen; me picking up the mirror from the table next to me, breathing on it and then drawing something—the double trident—on its steamed-up glass; the man with the needle asking nothing more, just smiling and bringing the tip of the needle toward my body.

"About five weeks after I came back from America, I went to the dentist's. In the waiting room I was flicking through a music magazine when I came across an article on the White Triangle. If I was hoping to find something about Chuh-yuh in it, I was disappointed—the author had only the vaguest information on the Triangle and considered Chuh-yuh, Oo, and Num to be figments of the imagination, born of some 1980s mythology! Even so, I contacted the magazine's office, got the author's address and paid him a visit at his store on the station concourse. Then I had a stroke of luck: In the meantime, Chuh-yuh had been in touch with the owner of the store, who told me the day and the hour of their next meeting . . .

"Although I was glad to have tracked Chuh-yuh down, I was annoyed that he'd spoken with a stranger about matters connected with the Orange Book—matters that were part of its secret by association. At that time, I still took for granted that the promise given by Oo, Chuh-yuh, and Num to Valerie must be kept—I being the only person not covered by Valerie's command. Only later did I begin to understand Chuh-yuh's fear that a past containing Valerie, the White Triangle, Alexander, and all the rooms, gardens, and islands of Valerie's book would disappear like a continent that had fallen into the sea; only later did I begin to understand his feeling that the life Valerie had dreamed for her work—one of anonymity and endless change—wasn't enough. I have ever greater sympathy with his anxious desire to preserve names and original shapes—it's an anxiety I'm coming more and more to share. Every night I lie in my dark room unable to sleep; I fight with my mother, complaining to her that she had no right to sentence her work to nothingness and a ghostly life of echoes in other works. Later Chuh-yuh felt pangs of conscience for having spoken of the White Triangle and allowing his old compositions to be published, and for having lacked Valerie's strength in his inability to watch with indifference the gradual warping of shapes. But by this time I was able to tell him myself that I doubted Valerie's aim was disciplined adherence to fixed rules; I believed that she had accepted that changes wrought by time could justify or even demand a direct breach of the promise.

"Anyway, I turned up at the store at the station on the day of its owner's appointment with Chuh-yuh. Chuh-yuh was startled by his first sight of me—he thought he was looking at Valerie's ghost. Later, he told me that the cause of his confusion was the empty station hall, which seemed to him an even more suitable residence for ghosts than an old castle. The feeling that he was seeing a ghost lasted only a few seconds, however; like Oo, Chuh-yuh soon realized who I was. Once he and the storekeeper had conducted their business, Chuh-yuh and I left together. In front of the station he waved down a cab, and we drove to his apartment. Then at last I had the Orange Book in my hands and was able to leaf through the blank pages that concealed the long, convoluted story of a man wandering about a city. Chuh-yuh presented me with the book, saying that it belonged to me. I took it home and locked it in a desk drawer."

"Chuh-yuh must have been delighted to see Valerie's daughter again, after so many years . . ."

"He was, yes. Since we met it seems nothing can disturb his happiness. For the first time in his life, he no longer feels the need to compose music. Although I'm touched by his joy, I feel embarrassed. I don't deserve the radiant looks he keeps giving me. I can't take any credit for having Valerie's face; I'd lived my life without taking an interest in my mother or trying to find anything out about her life . . .

"That day Chuh-yuh told me a few more stories that Oo had forgotten. And he learned from me about Oo's life in America, Num's French and island periods, the reconciliation of his two friends, the undersea memorial, Num's death, and the fact that

Num's diary supposedly contained the specifications for a material that might rouse the Orange Book from its sleep for one day. I gave Chuh-yuh Švarc's New York telephone number and offered him my cell so that he could say hi to him after all these years. Chuh-yuh called him at once, and although he had no intention of installing a phone in his apartment or getting a cell on account of Oo or anyone else, he bought himself a phone card and now he phones New York regularly from the phone booth on the corner of the street."

Chapter 14
Palace of the Memory

"Chuh-yuh, too, wanted me to be able to read Valerie's novel, but he saw no way of recovering the text. Together we leafed through Num's diary. When I looked at the blank pages of the diary, my feelings were of a completely different order to what I felt on examining the Orange Book, whose pages didn't seem blank to me; rather, it was as though nothing were visible on the paper because the pages were overcrowded with images—I imagined a blackboard on which someone had drawn in white chalk one shape over another for so long that all that remained was a continuous area of white. But the pages of Num's diary were truly deserted; each of them reminded me of the cold metal doors of an impregnable vault. Sadly I thought of how beyond one of these doors, the key to the Orange Book was concealed.

"From the time of our meeting, Chu-yuh and I saw each other every day. When I asked him to tell me about his life after the White Triangle, he said there was nothing to tell: He'd made his living as a piano teacher and spent almost all the remaining time composing music. He'd lived with several women one after another, but at the time we met he'd been alone for several years. I was glad that Chuh-yuh didn't feel that he'd wasted his life, a feeling that was present in Švarc's every word and gesture, and one that probably tormented Pascal Brison in the small French town and on the Greek islands. Unlike Num, Oo, and Valerie, Chuh-yuh had never longed to visit a foreign country. Once he told me that no travels in exotic locations could compare with the adventures he experienced when composing. These adventures were set in the wild and wonderful land of silence, in which clusters of notes would emerge unexpectedly, playing imaginary instruments, some of the notes then dissolving in the vague hum that was like a white mist, others staying around, transforming and inviting other notes in.

"Chuh-yuh also lived in his memories, of course, and he would never forget Valerie and the Orange Book, but his notework took up so much of his time that he didn't have much left for thoughts of the past. Besides, his memories and his music drew increasingly together, so that eventually the border between them disappeared. Images from the past gradually lost their shape and came more and more to resemble swirls of notes, while the memory itself transformed into music.

"About a month after we met, Chuh-yuh called me with some news that had upset him. He'd just read about an exhibition of paintings that by all accounts were painted in disappearing paints. He hadn't recognized the artist's name. Had someone made a similar discovery to Pascal Brison's? Had Pascal's formulae somehow been preserved? I set out for the exhibition at once, and, having seen it, called Dominik and arranged to meet with him. He told me how in a bar in a small French town he'd seen his first picture in disappearing and reappearing paint. He also told me how Num's nephew had discovered a third of Num's documents: Although on his return to France Pascal really had destroyed his formulae, he'd completely forgotten having xeroxed some of them while still at the university.

"The discovery of Pascal's formulae was a possibility I'd ruled out completely, so the news that copies existed of at least some of them caused me to live for several days in a state of joy. But once I had Dominik's copies of Pascal's Xeroxes in my hand, I realized that this miraculous discovery might not mean much. Pascal's nephew had presented Dominik with many phials containing hard activators, and the surviving documentation included details of the composition of many other activating substances, but still these accounted for just a fraction of the original amount; besides, it wasn't at all clear that the activator that would work on Pascal's diary could be found in the samples themselves or the formulae. At first I stole small amounts of different activating substances, which Chuh-yuh and I then heated under Num's diary. In the end we tried them all; none of them produced a reaction from the ink Pascal had written in. All that was left for us to try was to mix all the activators as the surviving formulae described and then test them one by one. This task might take us months or years, and even then we couldn't be sure that the activator we wanted was among the surviving documentation. So within a few days, our joy turned to despair."

"Wouldn't it have been easier to confide in Dominik? I'm sure he would have helped you look . . ."

"As I told you earlier, I was still convinced that the promise Oo, Chuh-yuh, and Num gave Valerie had to be kept. It seemed to me that silence and concealment were parts of my mother's work, and that if I made its history public, I would destroy it in barbaric fashion. Although Oo and Chuh-yuh believed that a brief rebirth of the Orange Book for the sake of Valerie's daughter was in consonance with the spirit of the work, and that they should have no pangs of conscience about it, I could tell that it would bother them if I let a stranger in on the secret."

"But wasn't this just pure jealousy? Didn't they simply want to keep your mother's book to themselves?"

"I don't know. I don't want to unpick their motivations, and I'm not sure even they would be able to do so themselves. But maybe you're right: Sometimes I had the impression of a pretty tight mesh that had grown out of their Valerian cult of devotion, fidelity, and asceticism, along with their selfishness and disinclination to share this precious treasure from their past."

"But did Chuh-yuh have the right to demand your silence? You said yourself that in speaking about the White Triangle and allowing his old compositions to be published, he wasn't exactly guided by his promise; he even named the Orange Book in one of his titles."

"It's not so simple. Above all, it's not clear whether the promise also applied to the White Triangle, which was created only after Valerie's death. As for the Orange Book, who can say if the order of silence also applied to the title it was given by Valerie's friends? It's not its true name, after all. And now—well, I, too, wonder whether it was right to keep the promise; I'm not even sure what the promise actually demanded, what actions were faithful to it and what actions represented a breach. Maybe the eyes Valerie wanted the Orange Book hidden from have changed over the years and the validity of the promise has expired. Who can be certain?

"Perhaps Valerie imagined her work's life in the memory as a busy oriental palace where everything is in constant motion, shapes are in endless transformation, precious cloths billow, fragrances overflow and colored lights flash from room to room. Perhaps she thought that a life of such lavishness would endure in some form or other even after the palace had transformed to a ruin and lost its name, that flowers and shrubs would grow on its ruined walls and its stones would be put into new buildings . . . Immediately after Valerie's death the text of the novel really did lead a happy life of transformation in the memories of three people. But after a time it fell into a dejected languor. Although in those years its warped shape gave rise to a number of works, I believe that it smothered the seeds of several others by its weight and its shadow. Memory can be a sparkling mansion, but it can also be a cold, decaying ruin. Worse still, by her act Valerie had wanted to mock the monster of power, but by silencing her work hadn't she acted unwittingly in its service?

"Only recently did I realize, to my surprise, that Valerie had maybe been too young to know such things. Earlier this would never have occurred to me: I was aware only of the wisdom in her kindly gaze—a wisdom that could make out the dreams of the things she touched. But this wisdom mingled strangely with childishness and foolishness. In many ways, my mother was no more experienced than anyone else; as her gaze brought everything to life, she didn't know anything about the period of dull sleep that is part of where things reside. When she wrote the Orange Book, she was a few years older than I am now, yet I feel myself to be much more experienced than she was, in all sorts of ways. Sometimes I find myself thinking of her as my daughter, and I want to give her advice and protection . . ."

Viola stood up and began to pace the room. I watched her dark silhouette extinguish the green lights above the tracks.

"Fidelity," she said, as though she were speaking to herself. "But fidelity to whom, in fact? Valerie, too, has undergone change in the place she is now—memory. It's only there that she has come of age. For the sake of our image of Valerie as she was then, do we have the right to erase the figure she has become in people's minds? Wouldn't that be like forcing a person to remain a child their whole life?"

She sat down again and curled up in the armchair, so that its shadow merged with hers. The long constellation composed of the glowing green dots above the tracks vanished for a fraction of a second, to be replaced by red ones.

Viola was almost whispering now. "Sometimes I imagine that I can hear my mother's voice, and that it has something urgent to say. It is difficult to hear in the hum of the mind, but there are times when I think I understand it: My mother is calling to me that she was wrong then; that in the twenty years she has inhabited the realm of memory and forgetting, she has learned to know its grayness and its boredom, and that the death of shapes doesn't have to mean the birth of new life. She is telling me that she wants to put her instructions right and remove all obligations to stay silent. If I hadn't heard this voice, I wouldn't be telling you what I'm telling you now . . ."

Again I heard a train, but Viola was oblivious to its approach. I could hear that she was speaking, but above the roar of the carriages I couldn't make out her words. She stopped talking only when the rumbling was directly below the window. Once this had died down, she went on: "It's pointless to think about what Valerie's instructions actually were, though. Anyway, no one'll read the text of the Orange Book, and that's the most important element of the story. These days, no one's interested in tales of Labyrinthos, Jonáš's marriage, and the White Triangle—probably you'll be the last person ever to ask about them. If Chuh-yuh and Oo were to decide tomorrow that the ban was no longer in place and to tell everything they've kept secret all these years, they'd discover that there's no longer anyone who wants to listen."

Chapter 15
Dance of the Larvae

I didn't want us to keep going over the meaning of a very old promise and the extent to which it might be violated. I was afraid that such deliberations might lead Viola to regret her decision to speak and cause her to clam up. I thought it best to reintroduce the painter into the conversation.

"It took Dominik a long time to come to terms with your disappearance," I said.

"Oh, Dominik . . ." There was annoyance in Viola's voice. She straightened up in her chair, as though she were a puppet whose strings had been pulled. "Dominik thought that I was using him, although he couldn't figure out what for. I can well imagine the sort of thing he came up with—he had a pretty big imagination. But I couldn't tell him the truth, could I?"

Viola was on the defensive again. It seemed to me she was continuing an ongoing conversation that she conducted in her mind with people she had met and then hurt.

"I didn't visit Dominik just because of the formulae. Yes, I had a task to perform, but I looked forward to going, too, in the beginning at least." Whose ghost was she justifying herself to? Dominik's or her mother's? "Dominik happened to be going through one of his good periods: For a time, his discovery of Pascal's paints had resolved the conflict within him. But before long things were back to normal . . ."

"What kind of conflict?"

"The conflict between a resigned view, which leaves things as they are, and an obsessive need constantly to decipher things as though they were secretive hieroglyphs. When we were getting to know each other, I liked his calmness; many times I watched him for hours on end as he painted his urban landscapes. I remember how his brush would hover over the empty canvas, getting closer and then further away, looking for the place it would touch; and it seemed to me then that it was not just Dominik's mind that was nearing a great change but his whole body, and that the memory of some barrier or blind wall was breaking up and producing a rhythmic, swirling stream that went right through his body, rousing memories from times long past, feeding on these memories and then retreating to his fingers and flowing to the tip of his brush, where it was transformed into lines and shapes. I believe that Valerie was dreaming of a similar transformation of things when she condemned her book to such a short life . . .

"How strange it was when we embraced and I felt how all those urban landscapes had dissolved in his body and were echoed in his touch! I had the feeling that this touch was bringing back the vibration of torn sheet metal on a building site, the movement of a piece of polythene on paving, the sway of bushes in the wind, the slow, dreamy movement of a train on a distant viaduct . . .

"But then Dominik began to change. I watched his transformation anxiously, without knowing what was happening to him and what strange disease was taking hold of him. I didn't yet know that this was the return of a sickness he'd suffered from all his life, and which had just been in brief remission . . . It took me a while to understand the nature of Dominik's disease and to realize what a vicious circle he was caught up in—his sickness grew out of the best of health and his health was a continuation of the worst crises of his sickness."

"Could you tell me a little more about it?"

"Dominik often spoke of fidelity to things. He knew that a picture—irrespective of whether people called it realistic, abstract or fantastical—could grow only out of such fidelity, and that this demanded patience and calm above all. He told me many times that things can be understood only by those who are able to observe shapes and colors calmly and wait patiently for shapes to dissolve in the great lake of memory and forgetting that resides in the depths of the body, until they connect with other shapes and gestures that have settled there; then new shapes—in which old, previously unacknowledged dreams of things, their secret memories, disturbing kinships and ancient rhythms that have frozen in their structure all rise to the surface—can begin to crystallize in the lake's waters. And I saw that in his good periods he was a master of such alchemy.

"But the stream comprising everything that poured out of all objects became ever stronger; Dominik looked on as inanimate objects produced a lava-like flow of hundreds of melted stories telling of their past and present and hundreds of hitherto unformed worlds that had been closed up inside them; this flood always caused Dominik to fly into a panic. The first images spilled from things that were just opening up as a dramatic, unearned gift; they were misty, incomplete, half-born or half-expired images. Then suddenly their fertile shapelessness became an agonizing, unsolvable puzzle. In horror, Dominik would watch the whirling dance of the numerous beings that never got beyond the larval stage; meanwhile other beings were born which, like the Mexican axolotl, filled all available space. He would look on in disgust as shapeless matter gave birth to more shapeless beings before it was properly born itself; the shapelessness of birth became indistinguishable from the shapelessness of death; dead bodies swelled up, intertwined in stinking orgies, gave birth to more dead bodies . . . To Dominik, it seemed that all these liquid universes pouring out of things were appealing to him to decipher them and give them shape, yet all the time he knew that his entire life would not be long enough to learn about and express even a small fraction of even one of them. And I watched as his calmness and his patience transformed into unbearable restlessness and unquenchable fever."

"And after that?"

"After that, what had to happen in this sorry drama, did happen. Confronted with this restless, anxiety-ridden knowledge and an impatient gaze, things fell back into silence, closed themselves up and drew all images and worlds into themselves. The monstrous dancing stopped, and objects regained their firm outlines; but these outlines were silent and surrounded by emptiness. Dominik fell into deep despair, which some time later gave way to resignation, which gradually gave birth to calm, and in this calm things would speak once again . . ."

"And so began another turn of the devil's wheel . . ."

Viola seemed to be nodding in the darkness. "Pascal's paints raised the hope in Dominik that he might succeed in breaking out of his vicious circle, but they served only to speed up its revolution. I'm surprised that Dominik imagined that such a cheap conjuring trick could stop the devilish wheel of his sickness; it's a wonder to me that he thought chemistry might solve his problem and rid him of his fear of monsters and the agonizing necessity to choose between what should receive a shape and become visible and what should remain shapeless and invisible, and between the questions he would answer and those he would leave forever unanswered. How could he not know that a shape has value only if it emerges from a background of scintillating, shapeless universes that were once rejected due to the birth of one shape and will remain forever unborn?

"Dominik believed that Brison's paints were the cure for his sickness, but I could see that they led only to destruction, as the treatment they offered was illusory. I know I should have helped him, but I had a task to perform and lacked the strength to pursue anything else. At that time, I was scurrying after the text of the Orange Book like a figure in a computer game, and I was prepared to kick any obstacle out of my way. Today, I don't like to look back on the time when the invisible novel roused a frenzied selfishness in me—when I exercised no consideration for others. Even then, there were moments when I stopped running, felt horrified by what I was doing and was overwhelmed by self-disgust. But those moments were brief, and soon I was back on the trail of the Orange Book.

"I told myself that I would put everything right once my task was fulfilled. But my quest for the Orange Book ended almost two years ago, and since that time I've done nothing but rest after the terrible exertions of those months when I was gripped by the fever that seized me in the Brooklyn diner and never left me. Sometimes I think that I'll be tired until the end of my life. And the horror or the sense of nausea at my own behavior which I had no time to deal with at the time when the Orange Book was revived has not gone away. Everything has piled up and stored itself inside me; and now that it's all over, like a badly digested meal, these feelings are letting me know that they're still there. Only now am I experiencing everything to the fullest; every night I wake up after two or three hours' sleep and toss and turn in bed as I inspect all the bleak images in my mind; I fall asleep just as everyone else is waking up. I think about all the same things over and over, and the worst of it is, I feel that I've ruined everything for Valerie: I tell myself that she chose such a peculiar manner of writing because she wanted to create not a book, but a drama that would play out over many years—and at the moment of dénouement I tarnished her work by my selfishness and damaged it by hurting others in its name . . ."

Her words turned into a wail, which was drowned out by an intensifying roar beyond the windows. As I looked out into the darkness, it occurred to me that the red lights of the railroad looked like the lights of a boat; suddenly I felt as though I was on the river, sitting in the cabin of a steamer with its engine turned off and heading indomitably toward a waterfall. Again streaks of light swept through every window; a short, frantic film was projected across all the smooth surfaces in the room. Wanting to distract Viola from her bad thoughts, I asked her if she'd managed to find the right activator for Pascal's diary. She became a little calmer and prepared to go on with the story.

"As I was telling you, in secret I took samples of different activation solutions from Dominik's studio. Actually it's ridiculous to say that I did it in secret; it may have been like that in the beginning, but later Dominik just played along with it. At night, as I was pouring samples of the hard activators into my own phials, I knew that Dominik was only pretending to be asleep and watching me with narrowed eyes . . . Yet he never mentioned anything. He began to view me as an enemy who needed to be watched, but he didn't want to be caught doing it . . . I became a part of the hostile, shapeless world that was hiding its secrets from him and setting him thousands of unsolvable puzzles and thousands of impossible tasks. I believe that he started to hate me then."

I remembered the enmity that had separated Chuh-yuh, Oo, and Num, and which Num had perhaps anticipated in the story of Mario and Rufio in his libretto for *Medusae of the Past.* I felt sad. How strange it was that so much hate had arisen out of Valerie's pure gesture! Had she known how much pain and anger would be born out of the blank pages of the Orange Book, would she still have insisted on her dream of a hidden work? But then I thought of Oo's reconciliation with Num and then Chuh-yuh, and I told myself that the light Viola had spoken of—the light in which the Orange Book had originated—couldn't be extinguished just like that.

Chapter 16
Tannhäuser's Return

"Just as Chuh-yuh and I had given up hope of ever finding the activation solution, a scene in a film we were watching on television triggered something in Chuh-yuh's memory. About ten years earlier he'd been living with a girlfriend. One morning he'd awoken to a quiet mumbling sound; he'd opened his eyes to the sight of his fully-clothed girlfriend standing over Num's diary. She was reading something syllable by syllable, with difficulty. Still half in his dreams, Chuh-yuh got up and went to look over her shoulder. He saw groups of indistinct letters rising out of the diary's pages. By turns these letters darkened and then blended back in with the whiteness of the page, as though a fog were rolling over them, now dispersing, now thickening. Chuh-yuh's girlfriend was in a hurry to leave for work; Chuh-yuh gave her a quick goodbye kiss and she was gone. Now fully awake, Chuh-yuh began to leaf through Pascal's diary, but all he saw in it were white pages with a few last letters quickly disappearing into them.

"Chuh-yuh tried to figure out what had happened to make that morning different from others and so cause the letters of Num's diary to revive just a little. And at last it came to him: His girlfriend had been wearing a perfume so strong that he had been aware of it even in his state of drowsiness. Obviously the perfume had been an ingredient in a soft activator. So he went to a number of perfumeries, in each of which he stated that he wished to buy a gift for his wife and sniffed at all the bottles the sales assistants brought to him. In the third store he visited he found what he was looking for.

"We tried the perfume out at once. The letters really did appear, although they were indistinct and short-lived. Still, we now knew one ingredient of the soft activator, and this might help us. At Dominik's place, I took another look at the formulae and found Pascal's note that an ingredient in one set of soft activators was this particular brand of perfume. So I copied down details of the composition of the corresponding hard activator, which we then mixed with the perfume. Chuh-yuh and I heated the solution up with bated breath. When the first letters began to show themselves distinctly on the pages of Num's diary, we fell into each other's arms."

Viola got up and turned on the lamp that stood on the piano. The reflection of its white shade in the dark window was like a ghostly castle on the horizon.

She sat down again before continuing. "As the letters darkened, we were presented with a report on the private life of Pascal Brison. Num wrote of his love for Valerie, and he wrote about Chuh-yuh and Oo. Both of us felt that we had no right to read his intimate diary, so we flipped through the pages in search of an entry giving details of the composition of an activator for Tannhäuser's Ink, and at last we found one. Half of the mass of the activation solution was composed of various substances that weren't difficult to obtain. But a curiosity of the solution, one that made it different from all other hard activators, was that its other half contained what it was to activate—namely the Tannhäuser powder. So it was a kind of self-activator in which the main ingredient of the disappearing paint was the same as the main ingredient of what it was to make visible. The Tannhäuser Ink would wake itself. At that moment, we understood why Pascal had told Švarc on Folegandros that a fundamental ingredient of the activation solution would probably be impossible to obtain: There was little reason to believe that Kulhánek's machine hadn't been consigned to the scrap heap long ago.

"Our only possible next move was to find out about the state the Tannhäuser production line was in. So we set off for Kulhánek's place in trepidation. Chuh-yuh had no idea whether

Kulhánek still lived in his apartment over the cave. He didn't even know if he was still alive; and if he was, would he remember a man he had seen once, twenty years earlier? After the changes of '89, nothing more had been heard of the Tannhäuser powder, and it was highly probable that the parts of the machine—presuming that they still stood in Kulhánek's apartment—had not stirred since that evening twenty years earlier when Chuh-yuh and I had been in the room in the villa.

"It took Chuh-yuh a long time to find Kulhánek's villa. He rang the bell of the first-floor apartment and a tall, thin man opened up. Obviously he recognized Chuh-yuh at once, and obviously he was very glad to see someone who had taken part in the ritual manufacture of the Tannhäuser powder years earlier. He was taken aback by the sight of me, but he recovered immediately. 'By God, how you've grown!' he said with a smile, as he invited us in. Along the walls of the large, long room stood tall metal things that looked more like statues than parts of a machine. Did an ancient memory of metal beings dancing to a music of squeaks, ticks, and rustles rise to the surface of my mind? Kulhánek asked about the others who had taken part in the Tannhäuser ritual along with us, Pascal in particular. Chuh-yuh told him that Švarc lived in America and Pascal and Valerie were dead. For a while we sat in silence. I looked from one metal figure to another and at Kulhánek's face and hands, and I said to myself how remarkable it was that Kulhánek had come to resemble his machines from all the years he'd lived with them. There was nothing soft about his body; it looked as though his skin covered the same metal parts as were in the machines. With radiance in his eyes, he said: 'It's just wonderful. I'm so glad that you've come. We've thought of you so often.' I had the feeling that the machines along the walls were looking down on us and smiling.

"Kulhánek had never stopped living among the metal figures. After the changes of '89, as in '68 he'd asked them whether they were willing to resume the production of the powder. This time, however, they had told their roommate: 'We're too tired for that now, and we see that you, too, are tired and don't want to begin again. So let's leave things as they are. We're perfectly happy together as we are.' But when Chuh-yuh told him about the Orange Book and the role of the Tannhäuser powder in its story, Kulhánek said, before Chuh-yuh plucked up the courage to ask him, that we should have no fear, of course he would manufacture the amount of powder required.

"It mightn't be that easy, though, he said apologetically: The machines really had worked for the last time on the day Num, Chuh-yuh, Oo, my mother, and I had seen them. Now they were in a pretty woeful state, Kulhánek, in his solitary life, caring for them as little as he cared for himself. He stood up, walked from one machine to the next and tried carefully to move different parts that protruded from them or were easily reached when he put his hand under their sheet-metal coverings. Sometimes no sound came from the machine's insides—maybe the part Kulhánek was holding was no longer connected to anything; at other moments the machine set up a terrible creaking that often contained rattling and ended with a crash—as something inside came loose and fell, to land somewhere in the mechanism's bowels. I noticed how alert Chuh-yuh was to all this. I imagined he was remembering the times when he had scorned musical instruments and listened for days to endless, seamless symphonies of sound; later, he confirmed to me that he'd had the feeling that he was back in a concert hall he'd abandoned long before. Although the sounds coming from inside the machines, testifying to the separation of what was once joined and the coalescence of what was once separate, were anything but encouraging, Kulhánek was still smiling as he completed his tour of inspection. I shouldn't worry, he said: He'd soon have things up and running again."

"Which of the figures did you like best?"

"I liked them all, but most of all, I think, I liked the Apache, with his ceremonial headdress made of tubing. Between the girth of his cylindrical part, which was embedded in the floor, and the circular hole cut into the parquet, there was a narrow slit; I leaned down to this slit and felt the cold, damp air rising from below the ground. I remembered the cave and asked Kulhánek to show it to me. As he hadn't been there for many years, it took him a long time to find the keys on the shelves in the hallway. We went down into the cellar, where Kulhánek unfastened a padlock on a wooden door that looked like the door of an ordinary cellar compartment. In the beam of his flashlight, I saw a tight, vaulted space with many recesses and shadows. Twelve dark pipes stuck out of the cellar's ceiling in different directions, like the roots of a tree. The ends of these pipes were sunk into twelve natural, water-filled trays of different heights.

"First thing the next morning, Chuh-yuh and I turned up at the villa in our work clothes. First of all the three of us brought up from the cellar tubes that connected the machines. Then we took the metal figures apart one after another, cleaned them, searched in the metal mazes inside them for bits that had come unstuck, fastened these back in place, screwed back on what was hanging off and pulled out what had gotten wedged in. Unfortunately it soon became apparent that all twelve pumps and the collection chamber above them had rusted right through.

"Kulhánek had kept Pascal's drawings of the pumping system. I took copies of these to several firms, all of which turned me away. Then Kulhánek remembered a conversation he'd had at the bus stop a few months earlier, with a young woman he'd known by sight, as she and her parents lived in the same street as he did. Before the bus arrived, he'd succeeded in finding out that she was an engineering graduate and worked as an engineer for the Nereus Company, which manufactured pumps to order. He suggested that I seek out this woman, who had seemed to him pleasant and helpful."

Chapter 17
Julie

"So I took myself off to Nereus. As I entered the building, I still didn't know if I would take Kulhánek's advice and make straight for Julie; coming from the lips of a lonely, aging man, an enthusiastic recommendation of the professional capabilities of a young woman didn't sound very convincing, especially as it was based on a single conversation between them as they were waiting for a bus. But then I entered the room where the designers worked and saw just one woman among all the men. As she was seated close to where I stood in the doorway, I saw immediately her smile as she bent over her drawing board and studied the circles, squares and polygons drawn in pencil on tracing paper. I pondered on where I knew such an expression from; then it came to me—I'd seen a similar affectionate smile on the face of a butterfly collector as he was studying his specimens in their glass cabinets.

"I was so surprised and entranced by Julie's care for her geometric shapes that I walked up to her at once, without hesitation. As she worked on the pump, we became friends, and I told her how struck I was by the way she looked at squares, triangles and circles. Julie had laughed and said she'd liked light, smooth objects since she was small, and she liked geometric shapes more than anything because they were the lightest and smoothest of all. Her room was full of silk fabrics, drapes, ribbons and fine fringing; all it took was a slight breeze for everything to flutter and shiver. She couldn't quite understand how some people found geometry a sad, cold realm; for her it was as agreeable as a garden, and triangles, squares and circles were the flowers that grew in it. She even claimed that every geometric figure had its own smell. Once she told me how at the age of eight she had seen, for the first time, a designer using compasses and a ruler to draw shapes that were lighter than the finest fabric and smoother than the smoothest mirror; it was then that she knew what she wanted to be."

"But to be a machine designer a knowledge of geometry isn't enough . . ." I objected.

"Of course it isn't. Julie had to know a lot about the physical and mechanical properties of shapes and take these into consideration, but she imagined them just as thoughts and moods of the structures of the geometric world. She took little interest in what came out of her drawings, and she went down to the Nereus machine shops, where these drawings were used in the manufacture of pumps, only when she had to. She thought of material things as reprobate offspring of geometric drawings, and she was even a little ashamed of them."

"Maybe this was because her love of geometric design concealed a distaste for reality," I speculated.

"A distaste for reality? No, those words are too strong. But it's true that she was a little squeamish about the heavy bodies of machines smeared with oil and grease."

Viola paused for a moment and looked at her reflection in the glass. "By this time, I could no longer bear to be around Dominik. For him I'd become a hieroglyph to decipher at every turn and also an enemy whose every movement needed to be monitored closely. It was different with Julie. Julie approached my secret with a light touch, like her silk fabrics and her compasses and rectangles. That she didn't understand many of the things I did, didn't mean that there was something missing between us—just as the fact that her drawings lacked weight and a third dimension didn't mean there was anything missing in them."

"I can't agree with that," I interrupted. "Julie told me that she often inquired about what the pump was to be used for, and she also confided in me that she thought all the time about machines the pump could be fitted in, and worlds in which such machines might belong."

"That's true, Julie did ask me about the purpose of the pump, and I gave her some kind of answer—but this was just a game, which we enjoyed. I'm sure Julie wasn't longing to solve the mystery of the pump: She was afraid that if she did, our game of ideas and images would be burdened with the drabness of reality. And surely that would have been just as unpleasant to her as the heavy, stinking machines in the Nereus workshops that parasitized on Julie's drawings and even pretended to be the aim of her butterfly-loving life."

What Viola was saying now failed to convince me, however. I suspected that she was explaining Julie's behavior in this way because to do so made things easier for her; her pursuit of the text of the Orange Book left her with little energy to deal with other complicated matters. In the games she played with Julie, there was too powerful a sense of the pain Julie went through as Viola retreated from her into an unknown world to which Julie had no access and the foreboding that her friend would disappear into this world for good. But it was possible, too, that what Viola was saying was true of the time she and Julie were friends, and that their lighthearted games of imagination transformed to sadness and despair only after Viola abandoned her friend.

"Anyway, Julie drew up a detailed diagram based on Num's sketches, and this was then used to manufacture the pump in the Nereus machine shops. In the meantime Kulhánek, Chuh-yuh, and I repaired the rest of the machine. I couldn't tell Julie that the pump she was working on was for use in an underground cave that was fifty meters away from the house where she lived. That's how it happened that I went to Julie's every day smelling of grease and oil—I was coming direct from Kulhánek's."

"That must have been something of a problem for Julie, as she didn't like machines . . ."

"Curiously enough, Julie actually liked the smell of oil mixed with the smell of perfume. Maybe she felt the transformation of greasy, sticky reality into an incorporeal odor as a triumph of lightness over gravity that compared with the transformation of a heavy mechanism into fine lines on tracing paper . . . By the time the pump was ready, I'd gotten to know Julie's parents, and I was worried they might see me as we were unloading the pump a few dozen meters from their house. That's why Chuh-yuh and I first brought it here and stored it in the yard. Only after midnight did we order another taxi and move it to Kulhánek's. That night we didn't go home: Kulhánek supplied us with blankets so we could get a little sleep, and at six in the morning we were already fixing the pump in the opening in the floor.

"By this time, Julie could already sense that I would leave her—and that's why my leave-taking from her was the same as with Dominik. I left Dominik because his questioning, reproachful looks were a source of ever greater irritation to me. It was different with Julie—I felt good when I was with her. Sometimes in her company, I even stopped thinking about the Orange Book. I was tempted to stay with her, forget all the sad stories from the seventies and eighties and let Valerie's book sleep on. But then there were awful moments when I thought what a terrible betrayal it would be if I were to leave the novel about Alexander in the spell of the white pages; and I told myself that I was already erring in devoting myself to something else—in thinking about someone other than Valerie, and it became ever clearer to me that I would have to leave Julie behind. Julie was always smiling, which made it worse for me and increased my need to flee.

"Julie never asked me to stay with her, but on the evening of the day when we installed the new pump, for the first time she was unable to hide her sorrow. When she called me and I took my cell in my oil-stained hand, I was on the same street as she was, several gardens and fences along. Julie was trying to sound calm and cheerful, but suddenly she could take it no longer and started to cry. Although I switched off my phone immediately, the few sobs I'd heard were enough for me, and minutes later I was ringing the doorbell of her parents' villa. Julie didn't ask how I'd managed to get there so quickly.

"I stayed with her that night. I couldn't sleep for wondering whether Chuh-yuh and Kulhánek had succeeded in getting the pump working. I lay in bed with my eyes open, listening to the sounds of the night and trying to make out the sound of the pump among them. Julie didn't sleep much, either: She was glad that I'd come to be with her, but she guessed that this would be the last time we'd see each other. At around 3:00 a.m., at last I thought that I was hearing the gentle drone of Kulhánek's machines. I sat up in bed and listened hard. Then I saw Julie looking at me. She tried to say something, but I snapped at her to be quiet. I'm still sorry I did that."

Chapter 18
Flight

"At daybreak, when Julie had at last fallen asleep, I crept out of the villa. I crossed the garden though trees that rose out of the mist, opened the gate and dashed back to Kulhánek and Chuh-yuh. By the time I entered Kulhánek's apartment, the pump had already done its work, although what was left of the underground water was still being processed by the system. Kulhánek and Chuh-yuh were sitting in silence in front of the Flower Girl, looking intently at the dark opening at her center. I sat down next to them; now the three of us were silent. After a while something happened: A thin trickle of gray powder spilled through the opening and down into the plastic container. After ten minutes this trickle ceased; Kulhánek stood up, carefully poured the powder into a little white box, screwed on its top and handed it to me.

"Back at Chuh-yuh's place, we carefully mixed the Tannhäuser powder into a solution with the other activating ingredients, which we'd prepared already. According to Pascal's diary, we had fifteen hours to wait: The text would begin to wake up at ten o'clock in the evening. Suddenly I was afraid, and I asked Chuh-yuh to be with me at the moment the text began to appear; but Chuh-yuh said he shouldn't read the Orange Book again, so I would have to face the revelation alone—now the book was a matter for just Valerie and me. I remember my dreamlike state as I carefully took the solution home by taxi; and I remember being in my room, preparing the burner, the tripod, the beaker I would heat the solution up in, and the book stand. In the meantime, the phial with the solution remained locked up in a drawer, next to the Orange Book. I tried to read, but I was too restless; I walked back and forth across the room, and eventually I left the apartment and wandered the evening streets.

"When I got home again, the clock in one of the rooms was just striking ten. Having locked the door behind me, I stood in the middle of my room with the phial in one hand and the Orange Book in the other, listening for my father's footfalls on the landing; there was no sound in the villa. Carefully I poured the contents of the phial into the beaker, fixed the opened book into the stand so that its pages were free enough for the steam rising from the activation solution to reach them, and then I lit the burner. For a long time nothing happened, and again I had the desperate fear that all my efforts were in vain. But then the white pages began to give up clusters of letters, and these burgeoned and merged in coherent text.

"Pascal's notes told me that the text should remain in its activated state for twenty-four hours; after that the letters would disappear forever—neither the activator containing the Tannhäuser powder nor anything else on earth would wake them . . . So I wanted to make use of every second of the short life of the letters. All night I read about Alexander's wanderings through the city in search of the shining box, libraries, gleaming display cases, heavy, stuffed armchairs in strangers' apartments he entered, women he met, longed for, made love with and then deserted, philosophers and scientists who sat with him at a window overlooking an untended garden or a concrete yard and expounded their theories, metal parts that came together, regrouped in ever new constructions, then separated and ended up on dusty shelves, and pirates' treasure with pearls, rubies and sapphires that sparkled one evening in a dingy apartment on the city's outskirts. And the many lighted rooms that Alexander passed through came together in my mind, as they did in his, into a shining necklace, which was gradually extinguished in the darkness of forgetting; the ground plan of Alexander's way formed a labyrinth—an intricate line reminiscent of the mysterious symbol, as though it were answering a question whispered by the symbol on the lid of the box, although the answer was as incomprehensible as the question . . .

"And it was as though Valerie's sentences were unrolled by the same wave that carried Alexander from one stranger's room to the next; a wave that sometimes plunged forward into unknown spaces and sometimes lapped quietly and circled on the spot, sometimes divided into many streams and sometimes pulled everything into a single stream, sometimes chased an elusive image and sometimes transformed into impatient expectation of the unforeseen . . .

"As I was reading, several times I heard my father's heavy step out on the landing. He was sure to have noticed how restless I'd been that day, and the sight of my light burning all night must have made him worried about me. He paced about in front of my door, but he didn't dare knock on it: He'd broken himself of the habit of asking me about my secrets; in actual fact, in recent weeks we hadn't spoken at all, but he could probably sense my fear. I reached the end of the novel as day was breaking. For a while after that, I lay on my bed and watched as the trees in the garden emerged from the early-morning mist. Then I turned out the light and began to read the novel again from the beginning: I wanted to revel in Valerie's sentences for as long as I could. When night came around again and I needed to turn the light back on, I'd read the book a third time. After eleven, the letters began to fade and my gaze wandered in confusion among the lines; I was searching for images that I'd be able to keep in my mind . . .

"And then a thought struck me: Valerie didn't have the right to condemn the book to eternal silence, did she? In the moment she finished writing it, it had taken on a life of its own and no longer belonged to anyone. Seized by the desperate desire to save the novel, I felt myself hating my mother and her peculiar decision, which struck me now as whimsy; and I felt anger with myself for not having determined to save the work earlier. I locked the book and its fading letters back in the drawer and ran outside, intending to buy a roll of film for my camera. It was a few minutes after midnight and all the stores were closed. I ran through the empty streets until I spotted between buildings the shining, bright-colored sign of a gas station, which I raced toward. I can remember the startled expression on the sales assistant's face as I rushed in, panting; he must have taken me for a robber and been expecting me to point a gun at him.

"I bought several rolls of film and hurried home with them. On the landing, I encountered my father, who raised a hand to show that he wished to speak with me, but I darted around him and locked myself in my room again. I put the first roll of film into the camera and prepared the flash. But when I opened the Orange Book, I saw that all that remained on its pages were a few scattered words that were about to fade out entirely. I took a couple of shots but then conceded the hopelessness of the task and discarded the camera. So now the text really had died; now nothing would bring it to life again; as Num had written, only now were its words no longer hidden—the book might as well have been in the bowels of the earth or on the surface of a distant star. All that I have left of the Orange Book is this photograph."

Again Viola rummaged about in a desk drawer, searching for the photo. I crossed to the piano and she handed the photo to me. I studied it in the light of the lamp. It showed two pages of an open book; these pages had a few words scattered across them; the words were so pale that I read them only with great effort.

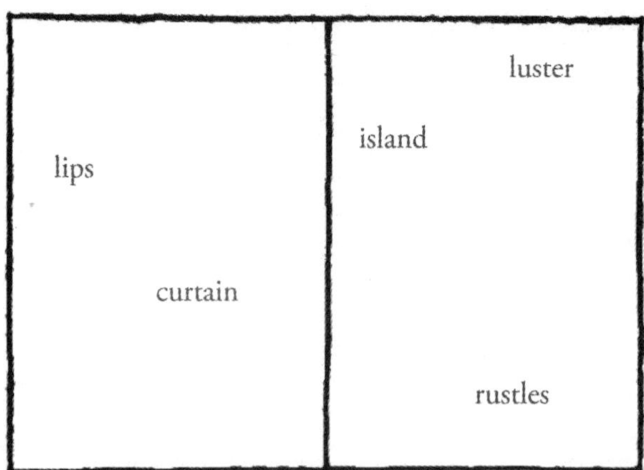

"As I pored over the empty pages, my despair became a bodily pain, as though a spike were moving slowly and continuously through my bowels, backward and forward. I wasn't even able to weep. In my thoughts, I cursed my mother and told myself that I hated her. I yelled at her in anger: What were you thinking? Was that any way to behave? Where did you take the right to tell people what they should and shouldn't do? Beyond the locked door my father paced, and I heard his heavy breathing; from time to time his anxiety was so intense that he tried the handle of the door.

"Toward morning my anger dissipated, leaving only emptiness. By now my father had gone to his room, and the villa was silent again. All I heard was a buzzing in my ears, as though I were listening to one of Chuh-yuh's old compositions that comprised the smallest noise. I realized that I would no longer be able to live with my father, just as twenty-three years earlier my mother had found herself unable to live with him. I packed a few things and took the first morning streetcar to Chuh-yuh's place. Chuh-yuh didn't attempt to talk me out of anything, and he told me that I could stay with him for as long as I liked. So now I live here, making a living doing translations, which I'm paid for in Chuh-yuh's name so that my father can't track me down . . ."

Chapter 19
Apparition by a Garage

So ended the story of the double trident whose point had stabbed me in the foot two weeks earlier.

One thing still wasn't clear to me. "How did you find out about the play at the community hall?"

"I saw a poster that showed the double trident as part of some lettering in hieroglyphics, and I went to the play out of curiosity. I've no idea how the author came by the character."

"As it happens, I know something about that. The play's opening, dream scene, where the mysterious lettering appeared, was written by someone else—a man who'd seen the double trident made of pebbles, as part of the undersea statue off Folegandros."

"The undersea statue," said Viola. "I'd like to go and see that one day . . ."

The hands of the clock on the wall were approaching midnight. We were silent for a long time; I looked from Viola to the dark glass in which our figures were adorned with colorful lights, like jewelry. There was no longer any reason for me to remain in the room by the railroad, so I stood up in anticipation of saying goodbye. I'd asked all I wanted to; there was nothing more I wanted to know about Viola's life, nor did I want to pump her for details of her mother's novel.

I was on the point of leaving when I remembered something. "Did Valerie invent the double trident symbol all by herself, or did she take inspiration from somewhere?"

"That's something I forgot to tell you about. Shortly after she decided to write a novel—in December '77—Valerie had a strange experience. It was Chuh-yuh who told me about it, and it seems that Valerie told this story to him alone. Of the three friends, I think she liked him best and had the closest relationship with him, maybe because he was the calmest and never bothered the others by confiding his feelings in them, as Num sometimes did, and Oo, too, from time to time. Valerie and I were out for a walk in the snow-covered city; as it began to get dark, we were on our way home. Again it came on to snow, and soon the snow was swirling wildly around the streetlamps and in front of the Munching Mouse tavern, whose lit windows we passed. The tavern was on the corner of a blind alley, along each side of which three houses were crowded together. Behind these houses the lane ended at a number of garages with their rusty, corrugated-iron fronts pulled down; beyond the garages was nothing but a snow-covered bank. The one streetlamp in the lane was broken, so the only light that reached it came from two or three windows on the upper floors of the tavern and a window on the side of the building; the gloom around the garages was illuminated only by the just-fallen snow."

Viola sat down, so I resumed my place on the couch.

"Valerie thought she saw something in front of the dark garages. It might have been a snow-covered bush or part of some apparatus or other that someone had brought from one of the garages and was now coated in snow. She hesitated before deciding to take a closer look and turning into the alley—Valerie wouldn't have been able to write what she did if she'd lacked curiosity. We went through the virgin snow to the garages. And there she saw a thing that she couldn't name and didn't understand. Before a pulled-down garage front with indecent graffiti written all over it, a fragile snow figure—symmetrical in shape—had grown out of the ground to a height of about one meter. It was not quite finished: Some power was drawing falling snowflakes to the ends of its arms and holding them there, so that the figure was still growing, as though filling out in accordance with a predetermined plan.

"At first, Valerie believed that the flakes were attaching

themselves to a construction of thin wire, which was invisible in the gloom. She put her hand to one of the snow figure's arms, which fell apart at her touch; it was made of nothing but snowflakes, and it was building slowly but steadily. Where it was broken, the snow figure began immediately to repair itself, growing at the damaged place more quickly than in other places; within moments symmetry had been restored. After about ten minutes, the figure was apparently complete: It was no longer attracting snowflakes or growing or changing in any way. Now the flakes fell peacefully beside it. But at the disruptive touch of Valerie's or my hand, it began immediately to repair itself, new flakes flocking to the damaged spot.

"As Chuh-yuh was telling me about this, it seemed to me that a distant memory of my fingers touching cold, twiglike arms was coming back to me. Apart from my recollection of Kulhánek's machines, it was all that remained in my mind from my life with Valerie; and maybe even these were not genuine memories, but fictions born out of the stories Chuh-yuh and Oo had told me. Anyway, Valerie looked at the snow figure, wondering whether she was witnessing a physical phenomenon unknown to her, or a miracle. I still don't know what it was. We stood in front of the garages for about half an hour, quietly, hearing only muffled voices from the tavern. Then the snow figure began to crumble, and within a few minutes, there was nothing left of it."

"Was the figure in the shape of the double trident?" I asked.

"No, but it was very similar. It looked something like this . . ." Again Viola took a sheet of paper from the top of the piano. The figure she drew on it by the light of the lamp was one I didn't know.

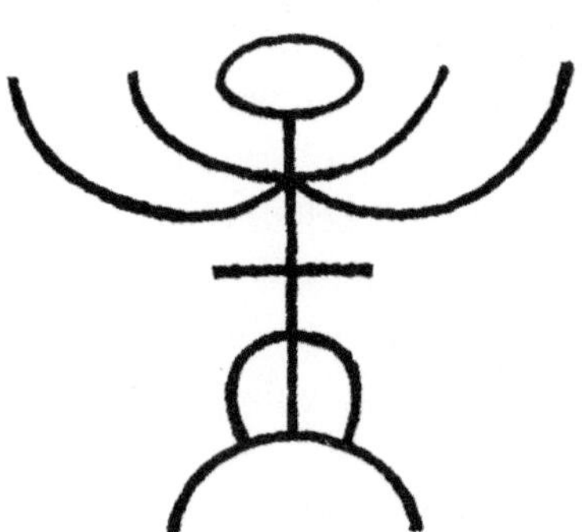

"When we got home, the idea came to Valerie that she could use the mysterious figure as the central motif of her novel, interconnecting it with all other motifs. In the first drafts, Alexander found on the lid of the little box the figure we saw in the snow before the garage fronts. But in the course of her writing Valerie modified the figure several times, until at last she came up with the double trident. Maybe the original figure struck her as too complicated, or perhaps she thought that the novel itself should create the mystery of its central motif, and so it wouldn't be appropriate to use anything already connected with another mystery . . ."

That really was the end of the story of the trident. We stood in silence at the piano, and I studied the figure for a long time. Then I looked up and for the last time saw the pale reflection of the room in the window pane, the lamp shining on the horizon and the thin, bright outlines of our bodies.

"I should go," I said. Viola didn't attempt to detain me.

I had passed the threshold of the apartment when I turned back and said to Viola, who was leaning against the door frame: "I think you should visit your father."

"I'll think about it," she said with a smile. Then she disappeared into the dark hall and closed the door softly. I couldn't find a light switch in the corridor, so I stumbled down the dark stairs. It was midnight and still oppressively hot and humid outside. The streets were empty, and only a few windows in the buildings around were lit. From an open first-floor window I passed, I heard snoring. It took me a long time to get out of this dilapidated quarter and reach a broad boulevard, where the streetcar rails were brightly lit and a taxi with its light on soon emerged from a side street.

When I got home, I opened a bottle of wine and carried it to a seat by the window. My search for the trident and the missing person was over: Clues which had been unconnected just that afternoon had come together and formed a closed chain. Tomorrow I'll at last be able to get on with writing my book, I thought, with no interference from the mysterious trident, and no lost girl. I tried to think through the details of the plot of my novella, but my concentration was poor, as I couldn't stop thinking about the end of Viola's story; again and again I recalled the fragile snow shape by the garage fronts. In the dark sky above the low workshops the snow figure revealed itself to me amid the stars like a charmed constellation, sometimes transforming into the double trident before regaining its own shape. I knew the street Viola had spoken of—for a time I'd been a frequent visitor to the Munching Mouse tavern, although it had closed many years ago. My book can wait a little while longer, I told myself. Tomorrow morning I would go and take a look at the lane that ended in old garages and make some inquiries about a symbol in the snow.

MICHAL AJVAZ was born in 1949 in Prague. He graduated from Charles University in 1973, and during the seventies and eighties he worked as a janitor, a night watchman, and a gas station attendant. He did not publish his first book until 1989. He is currently a researcher in philosophy at Prague's Center for Theoretical Studies. He has published eight works of fiction, an essay on Jacques Derrida, a book on Edmund Husserl, a book-length meditation on Jorge Luis Borges called *The Dreams of Grammars, the Glow of Letters*, and a philosophical study, *Jungle of Light: Meditations on Seeing*. He was awarded the Jaroslav Seifert Prize in 2005 and the Magnesia Litera Prize in 2012.

ANDREW OAKLAND's translations include Radka Denemarková's *Money from Hitler*, Martin Reiner's *No Through Road*, Michal Ajvaz's *The Golden Age* and *Empty Streets* (both available from Dalkey Archive Press) and the autobiography of architect Josef Hoffmann.

MICHAL AJVAZ, *The Golden Age.*
The Other City.
PIERRE ALBERT-BIROT, *Grabinoulor.*
YUZ ALESHKOVSKY, *Kangaroo.*
FELIPE ALFAU, *Chromos.*
Locos.
JOE AMATO, *Samuel Taylor's Last Night.*
IVAN ÂNGELO, *The Celebration.*
The Tower of Glass.
ANTÓNIO LOBO ANTUNES, *Knowledge of Hell.*
The Splendor of Portugal.
ALAIN ARIAS-MISSON, *Theatre of Incest.*
JOHN ASHBERY & JAMES SCHUYLER, *A Nest of Ninnies.*
ROBERT ASHLEY, *Perfect Lives.*
GABRIELA AVIGUR-ROTEM, *Heatwave and Crazy Birds.*
DJUNA BARNES, *Ladies Almanack.*
Ryder.
JOHN BARTH, *Letters.*
Sabbatical.
DONALD BARTHELME, *The King.*
Paradise.
SVETISLAV BASARA, *Chinese Letter.*
MIQUEL BAUÇÀ, *The Siege in the Room.*
RENÉ BELLETTO, *Dying.*
MAREK BIENCZYK, *Transparency.*
ANDREI BITOV, *Pushkin House.*
ANDREJ BLATNIK, *You Do Understand.*
Law of Desire.
LOUIS PAUL BOON, *Chapel Road.*
My Little War.
Summer in Termuren.
ROGER BOYLAN, *Killoyle.*
IGNÁCIO DE LOYOLA BRANDÃO, *Anonymous Celebrity.*
Zero.
BONNIE BREMSER, *Troia: Mexican Memoirs.*
CHRISTINE BROOKE-ROSE, *Amalgamemnon.*
BRIGID BROPHY, *In Transit.*
The Prancing Novelist.
GERALD L. BRUNS, *Modern Poetry and the Idea of Language.*
GABRIELLE BURTON, *Heartbreak Hotel.*
MICHEL BUTOR, *Degrees.*
Mobile.
G. CABRERA INFANTE, *Infante's Inferno.*
Three Trapped Tigers.
JULIETA CAMPOS, *The Fear of Losing Eurydice.*
ANNE CARSON, *Eros the Bittersweet.*
ORLY CASTEL-BLOOM, *Dolly City.*
LOUIS-FERDINAND CÉLINE, *North.*
Conversations with Professor Y.
London Bridge.
MARIE CHAIX, *The Laurels of Lake Constance.*
HUGO CHARTERIS, *The Tide Is Right.*
ERIC CHEVILLARD, *Demolishing Nisard.*
The Author and Me.
MARC CHOLODENKO, *Mordechai Schamz.*
JOSHUA COHEN, *Witz.*
EMILY HOLMES COLEMAN, *The Shutter of Snow.*
ERIC CHEVILLARD, *The Author and Me.*
ROBERT COOVER, *A Night at the Movies.*
STANLEY CRAWFORD, *Log of the S.S. The Mrs Unguentine.*
Some Instructions to My Wife.
RENÉ CREVEL, *Putting My Foot in It.*
RALPH CUSACK, *Cadenza.*
NICHOLAS DELBANCO, *Sherbrookes.*
The Count of Concord.
NIGEL DENNIS, *Cards of Identity.*
PETER DIMOCK, *A Short Rhetoric for Leaving the Family.*
ARIEL DORFMAN, *Konfidenz.*
COLEMAN DOWELL, *Island People.*
Too Much Flesh and Jabez.
ARKADII DRAGOMOSHCHENKO, *Dust.*
RIKKI DUCORNET, *Phosphor in Dreamland.*
The Complete Butcher's Tales.

RIKKI DUCORNET (cont.), *The Jade Cabinet.*
The Fountains of Neptune.

WILLIAM EASTLAKE, *The Bamboo Bed.*
Castle Keep.
Lyric of the Circle Heart.

JEAN ECHENOZ, *Chopin's Move.*

STANLEY ELKIN, *A Bad Man.*
Criers and Kibitzers, Kibitzers and Criers.
The Dick Gibson Show.
The Franchiser.
The Living End.
Mrs. Ted Bliss.

FRANÇOIS EMMANUEL, *Invitation to a Voyage.*

PAUL EMOND, *The Dance of a Sham.*

SALVADOR ESPRIU, *Ariadne in the Grotesque Labyrinth.*

LESLIE A. FIEDLER, *Love and Death in the American Novel.*

JUAN FILLOY, *Op Oloop.*

ANDY FITCH, *Pop Poetics.*

GUSTAVE FLAUBERT, *Bouvard and Pécuchet.*

KASS FLEISHER, *Talking out of School.*

JON FOSSE, *Aliss at the Fire.*
Melancholy.

FORD MADOX FORD, *The March of Literature.*

MAX FRISCH, *I'm Not Stiller.*
Man in the Holocene.

CARLOS FUENTES, *Christopher Unborn.*
Distant Relations.
Terra Nostra.
Where the Air Is Clear.

TAKEHIKO FUKUNAGA, *Flowers of Grass.*

WILLIAM GADDIS, JR., *The Recognitions.*

JANICE GALLOWAY, *Foreign Parts.*
The Trick Is to Keep Breathing.

WILLIAM H. GASS, *Life Sentences.*
The Tunnel.
The World Within the Word.
Willie Masters' Lonesome Wife.

GÉRARD GAVARRY, *Hoppla! 1 2 3.*

ETIENNE GILSON, *The Arts of the Beautiful.*
Forms and Substances in the Arts.

C. S. GISCOMBE, *Giscome Road.*
Here.

DOUGLAS GLOVER, *Bad News of the Heart.*

WITOLD GOMBROWICZ, *A Kind of Testament.*

PAULO EMÍLIO SALES GOMES, *P's Three Women.*

GEORGI GOSPODINOV, *Natural Novel.*

JUAN GOYTISOLO, *Count Julian.*
Juan the Landless.
Makbara.
Marks of Identity.

HENRY GREEN, *Blindness.*
Concluding.
Doting.
Nothing.

JACK GREEN, *Fire the Bastards!*

JIŘÍ GRUŠA, *The Questionnaire.*

MELA HARTWIG, *Am I a Redundant Human Being?*

JOHN HAWKES, *The Passion Artist.*
Whistlejacket.

ELIZABETH HEIGHWAY, ED., *Contemporary Georgian Fiction.*

AIDAN HIGGINS, *Balcony of Europe.*
Blind Man's Bluff.
Bornholm Night-Ferry.
Langrishe, Go Down.
Scenes from a Receding Past.

KEIZO HINO, *Isle of Dreams.*

KAZUSHI HOSAKA, *Plainsong.*

ALDOUS HUXLEY, *Antic Hay.*
Point Counter Point.
Those Barren Leaves.
Time Must Have a Stop.

NAOYUKI II, *The Shadow of a Blue Cat.*

DRAGO JANČAR, *The Tree with No Name.*

MIKHEIL JAVAKHISHVILI, *Kvachi.*

GERT JONKE, *The Distant Sound.*
Homage to Czerny.
The System of Vienna.

JACQUES JOUET, *Mountain R.*
Savage.
Upstaged.
MIEKO KANAI, *The Word Book.*
YORAM KANIUK, *Life on Sandpaper.*
ZURAB KARUMIDZE, *Dagny.*
JOHN KELLY, *From Out of the City.*
HUGH KENNER, *Flaubert, Joyce and Beckett: The Stoic Comedians.*
Joyce's Voices.
DANILO KIŠ, *The Attic.*
The Lute and the Scars.
Psalm 44.
A Tomb for Boris Davidovich.
ANITA KONKKA, *A Fool's Paradise.*
GEORGE KONRÁD, *The City Builder.*
TADEUSZ KONWICKI, *A Minor Apocalypse.*
The Polish Complex.
ANNA KORDZAIA-SAMADASHVILI, *Me, Margarita.*
MENIS KOUMANDAREAS, *Koula.*
ELAINE KRAF, *The Princess of 72nd Street.*
JIM KRUSOE, *Iceland.*
AYSE KULIN, *Farewell: A Mansion in Occupied Istanbul.*
EMILIO LASCANO TEGUI, *On Elegance While Sleeping.*
ERIC LAURRENT, *Do Not Touch.*
VIOLETTE LEDUC, *La Bâtarde.*
EDOUARD LEVÉ, *Autoportrait.*
Newspaper.
Suicide.
Works.
MARIO LEVI, *Istanbul Was a Fairy Tale.*
DEBORAH LEVY, *Billy and Girl.*
JOSÉ LEZAMA LIMA, *Paradiso.*
ROSA LIKSOM, *Dark Paradise.*
OSMAN LINS, *Avalovara.*
The Queen of the Prisons of Greece.
FLORIAN LIPUŠ, *The Errors of Young Tjaž.*
GORDON LISH, *Peru.*
ALF MACLOCHLAINN, *Out of Focus.*
Past Habitual.
The Corpus in the Library.
RON LOEWINSOHN, *Magnetic Field(s).*
YURI LOTMAN, *Non-Memoirs.*
D. KEITH MANO, *Take Five.*
MINA LOY, *Stories and Essays of Mina Loy.*
MICHELINE AHARONIAN MARCOM, *A Brief History of Yes.*
The Mirror in the Well.
BEN MARCUS, *The Age of Wire and String.*
WALLACE MARKFIELD, *Teitlebaum's Window.*
DAVID MARKSON, *Reader's Block.*
Wittgenstein's Mistress.
CAROLE MASO, *AVA.*
HISAKI MATSUURA, *Triangle.*
LADISLAV MATEJKA & KRYSTYNA POMORSKA, EDS., *Readings in Russian Poetics: Formalist & Structuralist Views.*
HARRY MATHEWS, *Cigarettes.*
The Conversions.
The Human Country.
The Journalist.
My Life in CIA.
Singular Pleasures.
The Sinking of the Odradek.
Stadium.
Tlooth.
HISAKI MATSUURA, *Triangle.*
DONAL MCLAUGHLIN, *beheading the virgin mary, and other stories.*
JOSEPH MCELROY, *Night Soul and Other Stories.*
ABDELWAHAB MEDDEB, *Talismano.*
GERHARD MEIER, *Isle of the Dead.*
HERMAN MELVILLE, *The Confidence-Man.*
AMANDA MICHALOPOULOU, *I'd Like.*
STEVEN MILLHAUSER, *The Barnum Museum.*
In the Penny Arcade.
RALPH J. MILLS, JR., *Essays on Poetry.*
MOMUS, *The Book of Jokes.*
CHRISTINE MONTALBETTI, *The Origin of Man.*
Western.

NICHOLAS MOSLEY, *Accident.*
Assassins.
Catastrophe Practice.
A Garden of Trees.
Hopeful Monsters.
Imago Bird.
Inventing God.
Look at the Dark.
Metamorphosis.
Natalie Natalia.
Serpent.

WARREN MOTTE, *Fables of the Novel: French Fiction since 1990.*
Fiction Now: The French Novel in the 21st Century.
Mirror Gazing.
Oulipo: A Primer of Potential Literature.

GERALD MURNANE, *Barley Patch.*
Inland.

YVES NAVARRE, *Our Share of Time.*
Sweet Tooth.

DOROTHY NELSON, *In Night's City.*
Tar and Feathers.

ESHKOL NEVO, *Homesick.*

WILFRIDO D. NOLLEDO, *But for the Lovers.*

BORIS A. NOVAK, *The Master of Insomnia.*

FLANN O'BRIEN, *At Swim-Two-Birds.*
The Best of Myles.
The Dalkey Archive.
The Hard Life.
The Poor Mouth.
The Third Policeman.

CLAUDE OLLIER, *The Mise-en-Scène.*
Wert and the Life Without End.

PATRIK OUŘEDNÍK, *Europeana.*
The Opportune Moment, 1855.

BORIS PAHOR, *Necropolis.*

FERNANDO DEL PASO, *News from the Empire.*
Palinuro of Mexico.

ROBERT PINGET, *The Inquisitory.*
Mahu or The Material.
Trio.

MANUEL PUIG, *Betrayed by Rita Hayworth.*
The Buenos Aires Affair.
Heartbreak Tango.

RAYMOND QUENEAU, *The Last Days.*
Odile.
Pierrot Mon Ami.
Saint Glinglin.

ANN QUIN, *Berg.*
Passages.
Three.
Tripticks.

ISHMAEL REED, *The Free-Lance Pallbearers.*
The Last Days of Louisiana Red.
Ishmael Reed: The Plays.
Juice!
The Terrible Threes.
The Terrible Twos.
Yellow Back Radio Broke-Down.

JASIA REICHARDT, *15 Journeys Warsaw to London.*

JOÃO UBALDO RIBEIRO, *House of the Fortunate Buddhas.*

JEAN RICARDOU, *Place Names.*

RAINER MARIA RILKE, *The Notebooks of Malte Laurids Brigge.*

JULIÁN RÍOS, *The House of Ulysses.*
Larva: A Midsummer Night's Babel.
Poundemonium.

ALAIN ROBBE-GRILLET, *Project for a Revolution in New York.*
A Sentimental Novel.

AUGUSTO ROA BASTOS, *I the Supreme.*

DANIËL ROBBERECHTS, *Arriving in Avignon.*

JEAN ROLIN, *The Explosion of the Radiator Hose.*

OLIVIER ROLIN, *Hotel Crystal.*

ALIX CLEO ROUBAUD, *Alix's Journal.*

JACQUES ROUBAUD, *The Form of a City Changes Faster, Alas, Than the Human Heart.*
The Great Fire of London.
Hortense in Exile.
Hortense Is Abducted.
Mathematics: The Plurality of Worlds of Lewis.
Some Thing Black.

RAYMOND ROUSSEL, *Impressions of Africa.*

VEDRANA RUDAN, *Night.*

PABLO M. RUIZ, *Four Cold Chapters on the Possibility of Literature.*

GERMAN SADULAEV, *The Maya Pill.*

TOMAŽ ŠALAMUN, *Soy Realidad.*

LYDIE SALVAYRE, *The Company of Ghosts.*
The Lecture.
The Power of Flies.

LUIS RAFAEL SÁNCHEZ, *Macho Camacho's Beat.*

SEVERO SARDUY, *Cobra & Maitreya.*

NATHALIE SARRAUTE, *Do You Hear Them?*
Martereau.
The Planetarium.

STIG SÆTERBAKKEN, *Siamese.*
Self-Control.
Through the Night.

ARNO SCHMIDT, *Collected Novellas.*
Collected Stories.
Nobodaddy's Children.
Two Novels.

ASAF SCHURR, *Motti.*

GAIL SCOTT, *My Paris.*

DAMION SEARLS, *What We Were Doing and Where We Were Going.*

JUNE AKERS SEESE, *Is This What Other Women Feel Too?*

BERNARD SHARE, *Inish.*
Transit.

VIKTOR SHKLOVSKY, *Bowstring.*
Literature and Cinematography.
Theory of Prose.
Third Factory.
Zoo, or Letters Not about Love.

PIERRE SINIAC, *The Collaborators.*

KJERSTI A. SKOMSVOLD, *The Faster I Walk, the Smaller I Am.*

JOSEF ŠKVORECKÝ, *The Engineer of Human Souls.*

GILBERT SORRENTINO, *Aberration of Starlight.*
Blue Pastoral.
Crystal Vision.
Imaginative Qualities of Actual Things.
Mulligan Stew. Red the Fiend.
Steelwork.
Under the Shadow.

MARKO SOSIČ, *Ballerina, Ballerina.*

ANDRZEJ STASIUK, *Dukla.*
Fado.

GERTRUDE STEIN, *The Making of Americans.*
A Novel of Thank You.

LARS SVENDSEN, *A Philosophy of Evil.*

PIOTR SZEWC, *Annihilation.*

GONÇALO M. TAVARES, *A Man: Klaus Klump.*
Jerusalem.
Learning to Pray in the Age of Technique.

LUCIAN DAN TEODOROVICI, *Our Circus Presents . . .*

NIKANOR TERATOLOGEN, *Assisted Living.*

STEFAN THEMERSON, *Hobson's Island.*
The Mystery of the Sardine.
Tom Harris.

TAEKO TOMIOKA, *Building Waves.*

JOHN TOOMEY, *Sleepwalker.*

DUMITRU TSEPENEAG, *Hotel Europa.*
The Necessary Marriage.
Pigeon Post.
Vain Art of the Fugue.

ESTHER TUSQUETS, *Stranded.*

DUBRAVKA UGRESIC, *Lend Me Your Character.*
Thank You for Not Reading.

TOR ULVEN, *Replacement.*

MATI UNT, *Brecht at Night.*
Diary of a Blood Donor.
Things in the Night.

ÁLVARO URIBE & OLIVIA SEARS, EDS., *Best of Contemporary Mexican Fiction.*

ELOY URROZ, *Friction.*
The Obstacles.

LUISA VALENZUELA, *Dark Desires and the Others.*
He Who Searches.

PAUL VERHAEGHEN, *Omega Minor.*

BORIS VIAN, *Heartsnatcher.*

LLORENÇ VILLALONGA, *The Dolls' Room.*

TOOMAS VINT, *An Unending Landscape.*

ORNELA VORPSI, *The Country Where No One Ever Dies.*

AUSTRYN WAINHOUSE, *Hedyphagetica.*

CURTIS WHITE, *America's Magic Mountain.*
The Idea of Home.
Memories of My Father Watching TV.
Requiem.

DIANE WILLIAMS,
Excitability: Selected Stories.
Romancer Erector.

DOUGLAS WOOLF, *Wall to Wall.*
Ya! & John-Juan.

JAY WRIGHT, *Polynomials and Pollen.*
The Presentable Art of Reading Absence.

PHILIP WYLIE, *Generation of Vipers.*

MARGUERITE YOUNG, *Angel in the Forest.*
Miss MacIntosh, My Darling.

REYOUNG, *Unbabbling.*

VLADO ŽABOT, *The Succubus.*

ZORAN ŽIVKOVIĆ , *Hidden Camera.*

LOUIS ZUKOFSKY, *Collected Fiction.*

VITOMIL ZUPAN, *Minuet for Guitar.*

SCOTT ZWIREN, *God Head.*

AND MORE . . .